Two Novels
by
Charles McKelvy

The Dunery Press

Write us for a free catalogue:
The Dunery Press
P.O. Box 116
Harbert, MI 49115

The Dunery Press publishes the work of Charles and Natalie McKelvy exclusively.

CLARKE THEATRE (ACT II)
Published in 1997 by The Dunery Press
Copyright 1997 by Charles McKelvy

Cover Illustration by Charles McKelvy

Library of Congress Catalog Card Number: 97-065370
ISBN: 0-944771-20-3

Other Books Published by The Dunery Press

By Charles McKelvy:
TALES FROM THE OTHER SIDE, a collection of two articles and four novellas (1996)
PLAYS WITH FIRE, a collection of one-act plays (1994)
KIDS IN THE WOODS, a story for children (1993)
ODIN THE HOMELESS AND OTHER STORIES, four novellas and a short story (1990)
CHICAGOLAND, four novellas (1988)
The James Clarke novels (in chronological order):
HOLY ORDERS (1989)
JAMES II (1991)
CLARKE STREET, consisting of two novels, THE MAYOR OF SKID ROW and THE AGE OF PEACE, and an essay (1993)
CLARKE THEATRE (ACT I) AND OTHER WORKS, consisting of the novel CLARKE THEATRE (ACT I), a play, and two short stories (1995)

By Natalie McKelvy:
FANNIE & LIZA AND OTHER STORIES, one novel and three novellas (1997)
CROZ & RAY AND OTHER STORIES, six novellas (1996)
EDDIE & MIKE AND OTHER WORKS, five novellas (1995)
DEAD BABIES AND OTHER WORKS, four novellas (1994)
THE GOLDEN BOOK OF CHILD ABUSE AND OTHER WORKS, four novellas (1993)
CREAM TORTES AND OTHER WORKS, four novellas and an epic poem (1992)
MONA AND THE ARABS AND OTHER WORKS, three novellas (1991)
PARTY CHICKS AND OTHER WORKS, three novellas and an epic poem (1990)
MY CALIFORNIA FRIENDS AND OTHER STORIES, four novellas (1988)

For my sister, Missy, who would still be my favorite sister even if I had ten others

Table of Contents

Clarke Theatre (Act II)

"Everybody has his own theatre, in which he is manager, actor, prompter, playwright, sceneshifter, boxkeeper, doorkeeper, all in one and audience into the bargain."

— Augustus William Hare

Chapter One

"Jimmy, it's for you."

Despite the withering heat and humidity, and lack of air conditioning, James Gordon Clarke III was cavorting in a distant field with death's little brother, sleep.

His wife, Joyce Anne Gilmore Clarke, or simply Joyce Clarke, had slept fitfully and had been easily awakened by the telephone the morning of July 4th, 1993.

"Jimmy! Phone call for you! On your phone! Which you forgot to turn off last night!"

Jimmy Clarke heard his first and only wife as through a glass darkly but kept his head buried in his sweat-soaked pillow and his body entwined in a tangle of sheets. A ceiling fan spun uselessly overhead, stirring the tepid air from one side of the tiny bedroom to the other.

Joyce nudged his protruding bare butt with her big toe and hollered, "Jimmy, you have a phone call! Get up!"

Jimmy withdrew from sleep's sweet embrace and faced his frazzled wife.

"Huh? What? Who is it?"

"Some guy from Blue Star Players."

Jimmy sat bolt upright in bed. "Blue Star Players?!? This could be destiny!!"

"At seven o'clock in the morning?"

"Joyce, you don't understand theatre."

"I certainly hope not," Joyce said, staring at the mess her husband had made of their marital bed.

Jimmy bolted out of bed and raced naked to the phone in the broom closet he called his office.

"Hello," he said, trying not to holler, "this is Jim Clarke. How may I help you?"

A man replied in a dry voice: "Jim, you don't know me, but I've heard a lot about you. Especially last night."

"You mean about my play, *No Dice*?"

"Yes. I'm really sorry I couldn't be there to see it, but a number of our people from Blue Star Players were, and I heard from several of them after the show. Jim, the reviews are in — and the critics are all saying you're the new Eugene O'Neill."

"Well, thank you. Thank you very much, uh . . ."

"Oh, I'm sorry. Didn't I introduce myself? No, I guess I didn't. Bad habit of mine. But I'm working on it. Jim, I'm Martin Gregory, and I'm the new president of the board of the Blue Star Players, and I was wondering if we might get together some time for a little chat about a new project we're starting at our theatre."

"How about this afternoon?"

Joyce ran half-clothed from the bedroom and waved frantically at her husband, but Jimmy ignored her.

Hey, the man had just had his first play produced at the Glenn Art Studio in beautiful Glenn, Michigan, and he was ready to move on to Broadway. Or at least down the Blue Star Highway to the Blue Star Players in sunny South Haven.

"This afternoon? You live over by the lake, don't you?"

"We're practically on the lake."

"You live in Havencrest, don't you?" Martin Gregory was referring to the 52 wooded acres on Lake Michigan in which Jimmy and Joyce cohabited with 87 other siteholders.

Although they loathed their timid neighbors, they were able to tolerate them because the simpering suburbanites only occupied their cottages during the summer months. Thus, Jimmy, Joyce, and a handful of others had their own private estate from Labor Day to Memorial Day. Not a bad life if you can get it.

"Yeah, we live in Havencrest," Jimmy said. "In fact, it was the inspiration for *No Dice*. I was walking by a cottage last summer when it was so cold, and I heard these people arguing. See, they don't have a TV — still don't and probably never will — and one thing led to another, and I wrote the play."

"Which by all accounts was brilliant. Which is why I'm so keen to talk to you, Jim, about this new project we're launching at Blue Star Players."

"Please, call me Jimmy."

"I'll do that. Now you were saying we might get together this afternoon. At your place. Which is practically on the lake."

"Yeah. Unless you already have plans. I realize it's the 4th of July and . . ."

"No, Jimmy, I don't think we have any plans. Let me just check with Corva."

Martin Gregory clicked the hold button, and Jimmy slapped his thigh and hollered: "Yes!!"

Joyce tapped him on the shoulder.

Jimmy turned to her and said, "He's got me on hold. You can talk."

"Thank you, master. Jimmy, I don't want anybody coming over here today. I don't want to see a soul for at least three decades after all the crap we've just been through putting up your play."

"It wasn't crap, Joyce. It was great!"

"Great?!? God, you're worse than those stupid women who go out and have one baby after another. No memory for pain. Absolutely none. I swear . . ."

"Hello, Martin," Jimmy said, shushing his wife with his finger, "what's the word from your wife?"

"Corva's not my wife. She's my lover."

"Right. Sorry. So what'd she say — are you free to come over this afternoon. We don't have air-conditioning but we do have a halfway decent ceiling fan or two, and we can always head down to the beach after we talk."

"Corva lives for the beach, so we'll be there at two if that's all right."

"That's fine, Martin."

"Anything we can bring?"

"Just your smiles and your swimsuits," Jimmy said, ignoring Joyce's frantic waves. Jimmy instructed Martin on how to find "the delight in the dunes we call the Dunery" and clicked off.

Joyce paced furiously and then put it in plain English: "Jimmy, we don't have a thing in the refrigerator. What are we going to feed these people?"

"I'll pop out to the store, Joyce. Chill out."

"We're broke, Jimmy. We can barely afford to feed ourselves, let alone . . ."

"Joyce, we're rolling in money after the last two nights. We even have a hundred dollar bill. Do you believe it — one guy actually bought two measly $7 tickets with a hundred dollar bill. We're rolling in money, and we're going to have even more after I sign on as a resident playwright with Blue Star Players."

"Jimmy!!"

"What?"

"How do you know they want you to write plays? Maybe this guy just wants you to paint scenery or something."

"Joyce, you have to learn to be more optimistic. You can't live life with no hope all the time."

"I'm a realist, Jimmy. I was the one who said from the start that Byron Street Books was never going to be commercially successful, and I hate to say it, but I was right."

"It's The Dunery Press. We're calling it The Dunery Press now, Joyce. Byron Street Books was when we lived in Chicago, but we don't live there anymore. We live here in beautiful southwest Michigan where the . . ."

". . . sun never shines in winter, and the summers are so hot even the bugs buy air-conditioners."

"Last summer you said it was too cold."

"That was last summer. This summer is unbearably hot."

"Maybe we should call that Klaus Williams guy who put in the air-conditioning at Burt Babbington's." (Burt Babbington being the lead in Jimmy's play, *No Dice.*)

"How many times do I have to tell you, Jimmy, we can't afford air-conditioning. We can barely afford to . . ."

". . . eat and buy toilet paper. I know. Mea culpa, mea maxima culpa." Jimmy beat his breast with his fist.

"Stop that!"

"No. It's all my fault. Publishing our own books was my idea, and all it's done is sucked money out of us and put us deeply into debt. That stupid children's book alone was . . ."

"KIDS IN THE WOODS was a beautiful book, and we should really be proud we published it."

"You think so, Joyce?"

Joyce sighed. "I know so. It's a wonderful book, and it's brought pleasure to hundreds of kids. And you had a good time going to those schools and libraries reading it — didn't you?"

"Don't get me started on that disaster in Michigan City. Not to mention our brilliant illustrator and his 'color book', and that thing he lives with who can't understand why we didn't make him rich and famous and why . . ."

"All right! All right!! Enough. Go to the store and use the money from the play to buy some goodies for this idiot and his wife."

"She's his lover."

"Whatever. But don't expect me to entertain them, because I've had enough of theatre, Jimmy. And I would think you have too after what you've just been through. God, it took years off your life. I thought you were going to kill that Burt Babbington for being so slow to learn his lines, and the crap you had to put up with from that dreadful Douglas Iglesia and that little doormat who follows him around, not to mention the great and wonderful L. David Hinchcliff and . . ."

"All right, Joyce, you made your point. Enough all ready."

Jimmy padded back to the bedroom, pulled on a swimsuit and headed for the door.

"Where are you going?"

"For a swim before the Havencrest hordes descend on the beach and scare all the dead alewives away."

"What if you get a cramp and drown? You'll leave me a widow and I'll go crazy because I'll never talk to another living soul. Jimmy, you're all I have."

Jimmy turned and looked at the woman he loved with his entire heart and soul. His heart melted and he went and hugged her. She shuddered and wept on his shoulder.

"It's been rough on you, hasn't it?" Jimmy said.

Joyce dried her eyes with the back of her hand and looked up at her husband. Which is precisely what had attracted her to him the first time she met him when he came to her parents' suburban Chicago mansion to cover her sister's suicide for the Municipal News Bureau of Chicago, or Muni News.

"Yes, it has been rough on me. But it's been rougher on you, Jimmy, and I'm worried."

"Worried?" Jimmy said pulling away. "Worried about what?"

"Well, I know you're not going to want to hear this, but you've been putting on weight and . . ."

"I'm not putting on weight."

"When was the last time you stepped on the scale? I notice you avoid it like the plague."

"That stupid thing was never accurate."

"Jimmy, I took it to the doctor's office and tested it against their scale. It's perfectly accurate, and I bet if you went and stepped on it right now, you'd find that you're at least 20 pounds overweight."

Jimmy pushed away from his wife and stomped toward the door. "That's crazy, Joyce," he said, "I might be five or six pounds over, but that's it. I swim; I bike; I . . ."

"You eat your grief, Jimmy. And you've started drinking a lot again. Look at last night. In fact, you're hung over this morning, aren't you? That's why I could barely get you out of bed to talk to that guy, isn't it? You have a hangover."

Jimmy braced himself against the doorframe to keep the room from spinning and exhaled. "Joyce, it was my first play, and we sold out both nights. So naturally I was going to have a few drinks with the cast and director."

"I'd call that more than a few drinks."

"Joyce, I'm going to go swimming, okay?"

"Fine, but I'm going to hate you for the rest of my life if you have a heart attack and leave me a widow."

"I'm not going to leave you a widow."

Joyce turned on him and walked into the cramped kitchen to fix herself some breakfast. "Anything you say," she called over her shoulder.

"What?"

"Go swimming!!"

"Fine. I will."

And he did. A mile out into the bracing blue water of the second greatest Great Lake, and a mile back. Jimmy overtook a school of perch on the way out and spooked a steelhead on the return leg.

If I'm so overweight, he thought, how can I beat the fish at their own game?

Huh, Joyce? Answer me that.

Joyce didn't have to answer, because Jimmy knew.

He knew he was more than five or six pounds overweight. He suspected the awful truth that he was medically obese. But he didn't want to admit it. Not yet.

When then?
When I'm ready to admit it.
When's that going to be, you big goof?
Who're you calling a big goof?
You, you fat drunk.
I am not a fat drunk.
Are too.
Are not.
Are too.
Are not . . .
Jimmy was still muttering to himself as he surged out of the surf
and nearly collided with old Mildred Mackermyer.
"Why if it isn't Eugene O'Neill himself," the old broad said,
adjusting her tattered straw hat for a better look.
"Mrs. Mackermyer. What a pleasant surprise."
"Oh, I love coming down here early when it's so still and so fresh.
It's so spiritual. Don't you think?"
Jimmy nodded at the retired schoolteacher.
The retired schoolteacher patted the playwright's arm and said,
"I wanted to tell you how much Walter and I enjoyed your play the
other night. And so did all the other Havencresters. It's all we've
been talking about ever since. In fact, I sent the girls to see it last
night, and they had such a good time. Did you see them?"
"Uh, yes. Sure. I think they were . . ."
"Oh, they thought it was just lovely. Our Jennifer's interested in
theatre, you know. She's studying coastal land management or some
such thing at some school in Florida – but you probably already
know that if you talked to her last night."
"Actually, Mrs. Mackermyer, I didn't get a chance to talk to her
and, uh . . ."
"Sonya. Jennifer and Sonya. I don't know why everybody has
such a hard time remembering their names. Of course, I used to get
them confused when they were little. Couldn't remember if Jennifer
was older or Sonya. Silly old me. I was their mother, and I couldn't
get their names straight. Not like they were twins or anything. I
mean, they're practically five years apart. Or is it six? You know, I
can't quite remember. But Walter would know. Walter is so good
with dates. He never forgets a date. That's why he taught history,

you know. At Eastern Michigan in Ypsilanti. Walter would have loved to have taught at the University of Michigan — I mean, we live right in Ann Arbor, but he never got along with the chairman of the history department at Michigan.

"We know them, you see, from our church. Well, it's not really a church, you see. We're Unitarian-Universalist, and we really call it our fellowship. You should come some time. We go to a fellowship meeting right here during the summer. Well, it's actually in South Haven, but we always tell people that we're in South Haven when we're here in Havencrest for the summer, because South Haven is only . . ."

"Mrs. Mackermyer?"

"What, dear?"

"Isn't that a great blue heron out there?"

"Where?!?" the old duck quacked, close to orgasm.

"There," Jimmy said, pointing out over the lake.

Mildred Mackermyer shifted her ratty old sundress and squinted. "That's a sandhill crane."

"No, it's a great blue. Look at the way its neck is folded back in flight."

Mildred Mackermyer cupped her hands over her eyes. "I don't see the neck. Where are you looking?"

"At the front of the bird, Mrs. Mackermyer. Look, I've got to get back to the cottage. We've got company coming, and . . ."

"We've got company coming, too. All the way from Kansas. Walter's brother Harry. He's bringing his slides. He's been all over the world, you know, working with agricultural ministers of countries like China and Zaire helping them to increase their agricultural output. We're going to have a program at the Red Barn. I do hope you and your wife Germaine will come."

"Her name is Joyce."

"That's right. Joyce. Silly me. Well, I do hope you'll come, because Harry was the one who patented — now what was it he patented — oh, yes — something to do with hay. That's it. I tell you — don't get old. Your brain just turns into a big bowl of mush. But I know Harry's invention had something to do with hay. Now, I don't mean to suggest that he invented hay itself. Good heavens, no. Harry invented something to do with rolling hay. That's it. A machine that rolls the hay. I'm sure you've seen rolls of hay out in the fields."

"Sure."

"Very good," Mildred Mackermyer said, as if to a bright student.

"Well, Walter's brother Harry is the one who invented that machine that rolls the hay like that, and he says it's revolutionized agriculture around the world. Plus, he's been doing some amazing things with rice. I don't quite understand it all, but he's going to explain it with his slide show at the Red Barn next Saturday. I do hope you'll bring your wife Germaine. We never see her at the beach."

"Her name is Joyce."

"Right. Silly me. It's a wonder I can keep my own name straight half the time. Why do you know, I transposed two figures at the bank the other day and overdrew our checking account by $300."

"Accidents happen, Mrs. Mackermyer. Look, I've got to get up and have breakfast and . . ."

"Oh, don't let me keep you. I'll just talk your ear off all morning if you give me half a chance." Mildred Mackermyer patted Jimmy's arm again. "Well, I'm so glad I ran into you this morning. It was meant to happen, don't you think?"

"Absolutely."

"Karma brought us together."

"Right. And now I'm afraid it's going to have to tear us apart, because my blood sugar's crashing and . . ."

"Oh, you mustn't let your blood sugar get too low, or you'll lose your center."

"I beg your pardon."

Mildred Mackermyer drew an air circle with her fingers and began a long and convoluted explanation of the meaning of life as understood among the moronic moonbeams of Ann Arbor.

Jimmy tapped Mildred Mackermyer's shoulder and said, "I'd love to stay and hear your entire theory, Mrs. Mackermyer, but if I don't eat some breakfast real soon, I'm going to gnaw my arm off."

"Oh, you mustn't do that, dear. Our Jennifer wouldn't approve. She's a vegetarian, you know. Walter calls her a 'dessertatarian' because all that silly girl eats are sweets. Sweets and peanut butter and popcorn. Lands sake, how a young woman can live on such a diet is completely beyond me, but . . ."

"Look, Mrs. Mackermyer – a turkey vulture."

"Where?"

"Over there," Jimmy said, pointing way down the beach.

Mildred Mackermyer tottered off in that general direction, and Jimmy raced back to the Dunery before another doddering old Havencrester could accost him.

Joyce had her head buried in a thick book with tiny print when he tracked sand into the house.

"Jimmy, don't track sand into the house," she said without looking up.

"I'll sweep it up."

"No you won't."

"Yes, I will."

"No, I'll sweep it up, because I'm always the one who sweeps up the sand after you've tracked it into the house."

"You're right. But I'll sweep it up this time."

Joyce sighed and closed her book. "Just take your shower, and I'll get your breakfast."

"Joyce, I can fix my own breakfast."

"By the time you fix it, you're going to pass out. How far did you swim out there?"

Jimmy shrugged. "Half a mile – I don't know."

"Half a mile, my eye. You probably went two miles. At least. And all by yourself on an empty stomach."

"Mildred Mackermyer was down there."

"Oh great. So you start drowning, and that shriveled-up old bat is going to save you. Jimmy . . ."

"All right, Joyce. You made your point. I'm heading for the shower."

"And I'm going to make you a nice healthy breakfast."

"I always eat a healthy breakfast."

"I'd hardly call two bowls of candy a healthy breakfast."

"What do you mean 'candy'? They wouldn't put pictures of all those athletes on the box if wasn't good for you."

"Have you ever looked at the ingredients, Jimmy? The sugar content alone is enough to kill a . . ."

"All right, Joyce. You made your point. I'm heading for the shower."

"You already said that."

"No, I didn't."

"Yes, you did."

"Did not."

"Did too."

Jimmy gestured for time-out and said, "Let's stop arguing, all right?"

"I'm not arguing. You are. You're the one who invited some crazy theatre people over here on the 4th of July and went swimming out into the middle of the lake on an empty stomach."

"You know what your problem is, Joyce?"

Joyce considered her husband. "What?"

Jimmy drew an air circle with his fingers and said, "You've lost your center."

Joyce laughed in spite of herself and sent her husband to the shower.

When he emerged cool, clean and refreshed, she presented him with a bowl of steaming oatmeal topped with the first blueberries of the season.

"Now this is a healthy breakfast," Joyce said.

Jimmy nodded enthusiastically as he chowed it all down. Then he made himself some killer coffee, poured it in his travel mug and blasted out the door to get provisions for the entertainment of theatre magnate Martin Gregory and his lover, Corva.

"Wait," Joyce said, running after him.

"Wait for what?"

"I want you to deposit most of that money in the bank. We need it to live on."

"You mean I can't take the hundred to the race track?"

"There aren't any race tracks around here."

"Well, there're some in Chicago. With this kind of money, I could take a powder and . . ."

"You keep your powder right here, big boy. And put most of that money in the bank."

"Aye aye, skipper!"

Jimmy saluted smartly and puttered off in the blue 1992 Honda Civic hatchback he and Joyce called "Angel Car."

He dutifully dumped a big wad of money in the night deposit at the bank and then took his "patented shortcut" to the supermarket in South Haven.

What's the hurry, Jimmy thought. I'm a produced playwright about to get some fabulous offer from the Blue Star Players, and it's time I kicked back and basked in glory.

He was gloriously basking a short time later when he wended his way past Burt Babbington's log cabin hacienda. Scene of last night's cast party during which director L. David Hinchcliff went skinny dipping in Burt's pool and revealed to one and all that he was spectacularly under-endowed.

Jimmy smiled at the memory, and then he hit the brakes.

There, at the end of Burt's freshly graveled half-mile drive, was a pile of discarded designer food and booze from the party. The fabulously rich Burt Babbington was clearly not one for left-overs, and the extravagantly impoverished playwright Jimmy Clarke was not ashamed to do a little dumpster diving when it suited his purposes.

So he popped Angel Car's hatch, and dove into Burt Babbington's private landfill.

"Joyce is gonna love this," he muttered as he dumpster dove. "I'm gonna save her a ton of money, and . . ."

"Back out of there and hold your hands up where I can see them!"

It was Burt Babbington, and he had a gun. Aimed at Jimmy's backside.

Chapter Two

Jimmy backed out of there and held his hands up where the aging Air Force veteran could see them.

Then he slowly turned and said: "Burt, it's me — Jimmy Clarke."

Burt Babbington squinted. His eyes were still sore from two nights under the stage lights. Not to mention all the designer booze he had swilled at last night's cast party.

"Burt, it's me — Jimmy Clarke. The playwright. *No Dice* — remember?"

Burt lowered his German automatic pistol with the 15-round clip and nodded dimly. "Say, it is you, old sport, isn't it?"

"Yeah," Jimmy said, lowering his hands slightly. "It's me."

Burt looked around suspiciously. "Well, you never know— do you? The kind of creeps they allow to just drive around here. I tell you — there ought to be a law against allowing creeps to just drive around here."

"You sound just like Glenn Kurtin," Jimmy said, referring to the honky golfer Republican Burt had brought to life in the great hall of GAS, aka: the Glenn Art Studio.

"I'm not a bit like that jerk," Burt said, waving his pistol. "Me — I'm just a laid-back New Deal Democrat. Liberal down to the tips of my toes."

"Yeah, right. Uh, Burt, would you mind not waving that gun?"

"It's a pistol, old sport. Not a gun. When I was in basic training in the Air Force, our drill instructor caught this kid calling his rifle his gun. Made him take down his pants and hold his dick in one hand and his rifle in the other. Then he had him repeat a hundred times: 'This is my rifle, this is my gun, this is for shooting, this is for fun.'" Burt chortled dryly at the memory. "We all had a good laugh over that one, I'll tell you."

"I bet you did. Look, I'm sorry to have disturbed you this morning, Burt. I realize it's early and . . ."

"Never too early to call on friends is what I always say." Burt looked at his pistol and grinned sheepishly. "Bought this thing on my last trip to Europe. Had a devil of a time getting it through customs. Had to get the man in charge to sort it all out. I mean they told me at the gun store in Germany there'd be no problem. Packed it in a special case and everything with all this fancy paperwork. Nobody does fancy paperwork like those Krauts." Burt chuckled. "There I go calling them Krauts. I do sound like that Glenn Kurtin guy, don't I?"

"Just a little bit. He'll be in your head for a while, I'm afraid. And by the way, I wanted to tell you again how wonderful you were last night, Burt. I was just blown away by your performance."

"Oh, you're just saying that. I made a royal mess of things Friday night, and I think I just got through by the skin of my teeth last night. Otherwise that crazy Iglesia character would have kicked me to death with those cowboy boots of his. You see the steel toes on those things?"

"Yeah, pretty lethal. Well, look, I realize this looks pretty ridiculous — me going through your garbage and everything this early in the morning — so I'll just put it all back and be on my . . ."

"No. You're welcome to have it. In fact, I tried to unload it all on everybody last night. I guess you and your fair lady had already left by then. It was just that Hinchcliff character and that little slut of his and my stage son and his — well, whatever she is. All naked as jaybirds in my swimming pool. I thought I was going to have to call the police to roust them. I think they were smoking some of that old loco weed. That's what we used to call it in my day — loco weed. There I go again — I swear, you brainwashed me into sounding just like that dreadful Glenn Kurtin character. Just like the North Koreans brainwashed a whole bunch of our guys into being commies. A whole bunch of 'em stayed in North Korea after the armistice, you know."

"Yeah, I remember reading that somewhere. Well, look, Burt, why don't I . . ."

"No, you want to keep that food — it's yours. Heck, I was just going to throw it out. In fact, I did throw it out. Well, I had the caterers throw it out. You know what those people charged me, old sport?"

"A lot I'm sure. But the food was really terrific. Especially the potato salad. I've never had potato salad that good."

"It's the dill. That's what Z.Z. says. You have any of her egg-lemon bread from Chicago?"

"Yeah, it was terrific."

"You bet. But you don't want to eat too much of that stuff. Put on an inner tube real fast." Burt pointed at Jimmy's ample middle. "Speaking of which, I'd go kind of easy on the egg-lemon bread, old sport. You could stand a few sessions out on the old tennis court with my pro. He'd work it right off you in no time flat."

"I'm sure he would. Well, if you don't mind my keeping this stuff, I'd sure appreciate it because . . ."

"You having a little shindig today?"

"Well, this guy from Blue Star Players called this morning and wants to . . ."

"Say, why don't I call the rest of the cast and our learned director, and we'll all pop by your place for a little post-play R&R? I'll fire up the old Mercedes convertible, and Z.Z. and the gang and I will help you finish off my food. What would be a good time?"

Oh, Jimmy thought, is Joyce ever going to kill me. Tear my guts out and . . .

"You're doing it again, old sport," Burt said, waving his German pistol in front of Jimmy's face.

"I beg your pardon."

"You're talking to yourself again. Bad sign. Saw lots of guys in Korea doing that. Shell shock. Went around muttering to themselves about Chicoms. That's what we called 'em, you see. Chicoms—for Chinese Communists. The guys who were there during the fighting said the Chicoms would stage these human wave attacks that made it look like all of humanity was charging at you. They'd blow these little bugles, and on they'd come, yelling and screaming and waving rifles and even bamboo sticks—heck, I guess half of them didn't even have rifles. Just poke you to death if they got close enough. And our guys would fire their machine guns at them until the barrels got red-hot, and those crazy Chicoms would just keep charging at them. I sure hope we never go to war with those people again."

"Yeah, me too. Well, why don't you tell everybody to stop at 2? That's the time I told the guy from Blue Star Players and his . . ."

"Fourteen hundred sharp, old sport. You can count on us all being there. I'd ask if there's anything we can bring, but since you've already gotten everything you need out of my garbage, I guess I'm covered."

"Definitely."

Jimmy gave Burt directions to the Dunery and headed for home with a heavy heart.

Joyce had her head buried in a thick book with tiny print when he schlepped Burt's discarded goodies into the house.

"How much did you spend?" Joyce said without looking up.

"Actually, Joyce, you're gonna love me, because I didn't spend a dime."

Joyce put down her thick book with tiny print and grinned at her resourceful wonderboy of a husband.

"You mean you . . ."

"I put most of the money in the bank like you told me to, and I was driving to the grocery store when I happened to pass by Burt Babbington's hacienda, and I saw all this food and stuff from the party in his dumpster. So I . . ."

". . . dove in his dumpster." Joyce rushed to her husband and kissed him. "That's brilliant! Absolutely brilliant. Now you can put the rest of the money in the bank."

"Well, actually I was kind of hoping to take a little pleasure trip into Chicago. You know—to reward myself for being a successfully produced playwright."

Joyce sighed. How could she deny such a wonderboy? "All right. But then it's going to be bread and water for the next couple of months because . . ."

". . . we're broke. Don't worry, Joyce, this Martin Gregory guy is going to make us rich this afternoon. I can just feel it."

Jimmy took the first load of food and stuff into the kitchen and dashed out to Angel Car for the rest. When he returned to the house, he had composed himself sufficiently to say: "Uh, Joyce, uh, I happened to run into Burt when I was diving in his dumpster and something . . ."

"He was up at this hour?"

"Yeah. Not only up, but he pulled a gun on me. He thought I was . . ."

"He pulled a gun on you?!?"

"A pistol actually, but . . ."

"Jimmy!! That's terrible!! What if it went off – I'd be a
widow – all alone in the woods with a pile of thick books with tiny
print."

"Well, it didn't go off, and, uh, well, Burt sort of invited himself
over this afternoon."

"That cheap old bastard's coming here?!?"

"And Z.Z."

"*Her*, too?!?"

"And he's going to call the cast, and the great and wonderful L.
David Hinchcliff and the Tiffster."

"What?!?"

Jimmy put his hand on his wife's shoulder, and she angrily
brushed it away.

"Joyce, I'm sorry. It's just that Burt kind of took me by surprise,
and I was basically stealing his garbage and . . ."

"Jimmy, I thought I made it clear on the way home last night – no,
this morning – that I had had enough of theatre. You got your play
produced, at great cost to your physical and emotional health and to
my emotional health – and that's it. We went to Burt's wretched
party last night and mingled with those dreadful friends of his, and
now it's time to get on with our lives."

"But, Joyce, my career as a playwright is just beginning. This one
woman at the party last night told me *No Dice* was as good as
anything she's seen at the Goodman or Steppenwolf in Chicago.
Better, she said."

Joyce shook her head. "This is going to be Byron Street Books all
over again."

"It's The Dunery Press. We call it The Dunery Press now, Joyce.
We don't live in Chicago anymore. We live in Michigan in the dunes
which is why . . ."

" . . . we renamed it The Dunery Press. You don't have to lecture
me, Jimmy. You know how I hate to be lectured. It's just what my
father did to me every night at dinner for my entire childhood."

"Sorry."

"Just don't lecture me – all right?"

"All right." Jimmy inhaled, held his breath for five seconds,
exhaled slowly, and said: "So, uh, what do you say about having
these people come over today? I mean, if I'm going to have a career

as a playwright I need to build relationships with the local theatre community, and these people *did* act in my first play for free, and I thought . . ."

"All right. Fine. You're going to have them come over whatever I say, so what difference does it make what I say?"

"Joyce!"

"Jimmy!"

They looked at one another for the longest moment, and then Joyce sighed and said: "Of course you can have them come over, and I'll do my best to be the loyal wife of the playwright. But I'm just warning you — these theatre people give me the creeps."

"Me, too."

"Then why do you want to be a playwright? Why not just write novels that nobody reads and hide out here in the woods?"

Jimmy chewed on that for a second and said, "I guess I still have the fame bug."

Joyce shook her head sadly and went to the kitchen to make preparations for the gala theatre party she didn't want. Jimmy joined her, and they had the Dunery buffed and polished down to the last roofing nail when Martin Gregory and his lover, Corva Coleman, arrived in an ancient green Volvo stationwagon with Eastern Michigan University, University of Michigan, and Grand Valley State University decals on the rear window.

Corva, who was affirmatively African-American, popped out of the car just as old Mr. Potter tottered past.

Yes, the same tottering old fool who had wandered on-stage during the dress rehearsal just as Marlene Small, playing Mary Alice Kurtin, was stomping off-stage yelling at her stage father: "Well, you're dead as far as I'm concerned!"

Prompting the bewildered Mr. Potter to stare into the harsh stage lights and mutter, "I'm not dead. I've had a stroke, but I'm not dead."

Now, at the sight of a living, breathing "colored girl" on the sacred grounds of Havencrest, old Mr. Potter had another stroke. Not a lethal one, mind you, just another nozzle spray of blood into some important sector of his brain. Like the one that controlled the ability to focus on present realities.

"The Mackermyers brought a colored girl here once," old Mr. Potter proclaimed. "They're from Ann Arbor, you know. Damned liberals. Thought they'd integrate Havencrest. Well, let me tell you, there was a firestorm of protest at the next siteholders meeting. They're lucky they're still members – the Mackermyers that is. Of course, I have nothing against the colored myself. As long as they stay on their side of the tracks. That's the way it was in my day, you see. The colored stayed on their side of the tracks. Now, I guess they feel free to live on either side of the tracks. But not in my day. No sir. Colored boy wandered onto our side of the tracks – it meant trouble for him. Yes, sir. Lickety split." Mr. Potter clapped his bony old hands for emphasis and showed his rotting old gums to advantage.

Corva Coleman and Martin Gregory stared dumbstruck at the blithering old fool.

The blithering old fool looked right through them and continued: "In my day, the only colored you saw on the trains were the porters. That's right – the porters. And I've got to say, there were some damn good ones. Really knew how to turn to and earn a fellow's respect. Not like today. No, sir. Nobody earns a fellow's respect anymore. Nobody cares. Whole country's going to hell in a handbasket if you ask me, but then nobody ever asks me anymore. Not even my wife. Doesn't listen to half of what I say. Well, what are you gonna do? Can't complain. Doesn't do you any good. Course, it doesn't cost you anything, and what else is free anymore? That's what I'd like to know."

Martin Gregory and Corva Coleman nodded woodenly and rushed to the little blue house they had had so much trouble finding.

Jimmy and Joyce greeted them at the door, and after introductions and pleasantries, Corva Coleman said, "Who was that dreadful man we just met out in front of your house?"

Joyce peered out the window and smiled. "Oh, that's old Harold Potter. Did he start blithering at you?"

"He actually used the word 'colored'," Corva said. "And 'girl.' Is he like straight out of the Dark Ages or what?"

"The Paleocene epoch actually," Joyce said.

Corva laughed.

Joyce smiled. She liked people who laughed at her jokes. "He probably thought he was really being liberal by using the word 'colored.' He's from Chicago originally. He had some political job for the first Mayor Daley."

"Part of the old plantation politics," Corva said.

"Exactly. Well, how about the cook's tour, and then we'll start in on all the fabulous food Jimmy brought home from the cast party last night."

Martin Gregory, whose middle was every bit as ample as Jimmy's, licked his lips and said, "I'm always ready to chow down."

Corva, who was as trim and fit as Joyce, smiled sadly at her man and said, "You're going to die of a heart attack and leave me a widow. Before we're even married."

"That's what Joyce is always saying to me," Jimmy said.

"You only go around once in life," Martin said, "so you've got to grab all the gusto."

"Right on," Jimmy said. "Speaking of beer commercials, how about a cold one?"

"You're on."

The two men headed for the brewski vault while the two women wandered out to the back deck for a look at the deep woods that lay just beyond.

"So," Jimmy said, handing Martin a cold, green bottle of Frankenmuth Pilsner, "what's this new project you're starting at Blue Star Players? I'm all ears."

Martin Gregory leaned back against the kitchen counter and took an appreciative sip of Michigan's finest. "First, let me congratulate you on your excellent taste in beer."

"Thanks," Jimmy said, clinking bottles with Martin. "Actually, this is compliments of Burt Babbington, the guy who played the lead last night. In fact, I hope you guys don't mind, but I ran into him this morning, and he sort of invited himself and the rest of the cast over today."

"The more the merrier I always say."

"Exactly. Anyway, Burt was the one who bought all this stuff for the party last night, but I told him to be sure and get Frankenmuth. He wanted to get Budweiser, but I assured him that stuff wasn't fit for a mule to drink."

"Or piss."

Jimmy swigged his beer and said, "I think I'd rather drink warm mule piss than cold Budweiser."

"Me too."

The two men savored their suds, and then Jimmy repeated his question.

Martin Gregory set his bottle on the counter, rubbed his hands and said, "Well, I'll come straight to the point. Since they built that gaudy new community auditorium thing down at Lake Michigan College, we've been losing patrons. Long-standing season ticketholders, mind you. They'd rather go down to Benton Harbor and hear Ronnie Milsap and see some splashy Broadway musical touring out of New York than see us do *The Fantastics* for the ten-thousandth time. We can't afford the royalties on the big splashy Broadway musicals, and our stage is too small to put up most of that stuff, so we've been seeing a steady erosion of our patronage base."

Martin Gregory didn't seem like he was going to come to the point any time soon, so Jimmy said, "So what are you going to do about it?"

Martin Gregory blinked at the directness of Jimmy's question. He was basically a free-lance computer repairman, and was unaccustomed to dealing face-to-face with human beings. Which is why he seldom attended board meetings of the Blue Star Players. Despite the fact he had been elected president. But then that's what vice presidents were for, right?

Jimmy waved his hand in front of the mild-mannered computer repairman's face. "So what are you going to do about it, Martin?"

"I beg your pardon."

"The erosion of your patronage base. What are you going to do about it?"

Martin took another pull of Frankenmuth, swallowed slowly, set his bottle down and was about to answer when Burt Babbington and Zoe "Z.Z." Zell arrived in Burt's vintage white Mercedes convertible. Followed almost immediately by Maye Michaels in her rusted-out Ford Escort, Marlene Small on a massive mountain bike, and, miracle of miracles, the great and magnificent Douglas Iglesia complete with Spanish grandee outfit and emotional bat-girl, Constance Myers.

Douglas Iglesia might have waited until the last possible minute to appear on opening night to dazzle his adoring public as Christopher Kurtin, but he was painfully punctual when there was free chow to be chomped.

"What about our fearless leader and Tiffany?" Jimmy said to Burt.

"They weren't in, but I left a message on their machine. They'll turn up, old sport. Don't you worry. Now how about another helping of that terrific potato salad you fished out of my garbage this morning?"

Jimmy was about to make Burt's wish his command when a sobbing Tiffany Ann Starbuck appeared at the door.

Joyce ushered her in at once and said, "Tiffany, what is it? What's the matter?"

All chatter ceased as the great and wonderful L. David Hinchcliff's editorial assistant collapsed on the sofa and sobbed: "David's left me. He's gone off to California and left me. I went down to the lake and was going to drown myself, but I'm too good a swimmer. So I came back and was going to pour gasoline from the lawnmower over myself and burn myself to death in the garage, but while I was looking for matches, I saw the blinking light on the answering machine and thought maybe it was David. Maybe he had changed his mind and was coming back. But it wasn't David. He's not coming back!! He's left me. My life is over. I have nothing to live for without David."

Tiffany put her hands to her face and bawled.

Maye Michaels and Marlene Small encircled the Tiffster with womanly comfort and chorused: "What do you expect? He's a man — they're all shits."

Chapter Three

Maye Michaels and Marlene Small continued plying their womanly comforts until the Tiffster regained her composure. The others breathed a collective sigh of relief and got on with the serious business of partying down on Burt's designer chow and booze.

"So," Jimmy said, cornering Martin Gregory in the kitchen, "you were going to tell me before our little dramatic interruption about your plans to win back those hordes of lost patrons."

"Right," Martin said, eyeing the refrigerator. "How about another 'Frankie'? They go down mighty smooth."

"Right you are."

Jimmy decanted two cold green Frankenmuths, and the twosome retreated to a kitchen corner where Martin finally spelled it all out: "Well, I don't have to tell you that there's a pent-up demand around here for sophisticated theatre. You already know because by all reports, you really packed them in the last two nights."

"Yeah, I'm really happy. In fact, one guy even bought two tickets with a hundred dollar bill."

Joyce passed within earshot and said, "And I made him put it in the bank. And the only reason we packed them in the last two nights is because it's the Fourth of July weekend. And because the Tunas are bored out of their minds. We could have put on a play about mud dabbing, and they would have packed the place."

"Joyce!"

"I'm just stating the obvious, Jimmy."

"Well go state it somewhere else, all right?"

"Fine. You don't want to listen to my views, I'll keep them to myself."

"Joyce!"

"Jimmy!"

"You two been married for a long time?" Martin Gregory said, laughing nervously.

"Too long if you ask me," Joyce said.

"I'll second that," Jimmy said.

"Maybe I should . . ."

"No, you're fine, Martin. I'm just a little overwhelmed by all this theatre business. I'll let you and Jimmy finish your discussion in peace."

"Thanks, Joyce," Jimmy said, tightly.

Joyce smiled tightly in return and trotted off to check on the Tiffster's mental health.

"Don't pay any attention to her," Jimmy said, laughing nervously. "She just hasn't come around to my way of thinking about the theatre yet."

"Sounds like Corva."

"You mean Corva doesn't like theatre?"

"Hates it. I have to drag her to plays, and then she complains the whole time."

"Boy, does that ever sound familiar. Let me guess — Corva's idea of a hot night is sitting on the couch with a thick book with tiny print."

"That's her to a T."

"And Joyce. Corva didn't go to the University of Chicago by any chance?"

"'fraid so. Joyce too?"

"Where else? I swear — you come out of that place, and all you want to do for the rest of your life is curl up on the couch with thick books with tiny print."

"Amen."

"So, you'd like to tap into the Tuna market — get all these rich Chicago people into your theatre. Like we did for *No Dice.*"

"Exactly. Which is why I called you this morning."

Ah, Jimmy thought, the wheels of logic turn.

"I beg your pardon."

"Nothing."

"But you just said something. At least your lips moved."

"Bad habit of mine."

"Shell shock," Burt Babbington said, passing with earshot. "Lot of guys who saw heavy fighting in Korea talked to themselves like that. Course, old Jim here didn't see any heavy fighting in Korea or Vietnam for that matter, but then I guess we kind of put him through some combat situations getting *No Dice* produced. I tell you — that was the first time and the last time for me, old sport. I don't think I have another play in me."

Thank God, Jimmy prayed.

"See, there he goes again. Definite case of shell shock."

Burt Babbington bounced off to bother someone else, and Jimmy said, "So, you were about to tell me why you called me this morning."

"Yes." Martin Gregory sucked the last vital juices out of his Frankie and added, "But first, how about another . . ."

"Your wish is my command, sire."

Jimmy served the president of the Blue Star Players Board of Directors another cold green Frankenmuth and prodded him for details.

Martin sipped his suds, set the bottle on the counter, put on his most deliberate theatrical look and said, "Well, the simple truth of the matter is we need to get more bodies into Blue Star Players, or we're going to go dark. We simply cannot continue to operate with heavy deficits. We have to find a new patronage base, and, well, we were all watching your little experiment with great interest. By the way, Douglas Iglesia was just elected to our board to fill an unexpired term, and, well, he was acting as our scout. And believe me, his reports have been most favorable. Especially this morning. Isn't that right, Douglas?"

Douglas, who was passing within earshot with a burgeoning plate of designer chow, nodded between bites and said, "That's right, boss. We really packed 'em in. Both nights. Of course, it was because of the great art work I did on the posters and programs, and because I helped develop the play. I mean, it was a decent play to start out with, but after all the development work I did on it, it really took on a life force all its own. Isn't that right, my sweet?"

Constance Myers, who was following in the great man's wake, chirped, "That's right, Douglas. Absolutely."

They passed out of earshot, prompting Martin Gregory to say: "So, we've been thinking for some time about developing a second stage program for more sophisticated work. We produced two performances of Sartre's *No Exit* two years ago, and people went nuts. We attracted patrons we had never seen before, and some of them have been begging us for more. And now we're ready to offer

more. In fact, we're going to call it Second Stage at Blue Star
Players."

"Sounds great. I'll come and see *No Exit* any day."

"Actually we want you more as a playwright than a patron.
Although we'd be more than happy to sell you and your lovely wife a
pair of season tickets."

"Better count Joyce out. She's not a . . ."

". . . theatre person. I know. Anyway, we were thinking maybe
you'd care to write a play for Second Stage."

"How about *No Dice?*"

"That'd be fine, except we're looking for something original."

"But *No Dice* is original."

"But it's already been produced. We'd like to premiere one of
your plays. Surely you must have some other ideas for plays."

Jimmy fiddled with his mustache and put his brain on auto-sort
and came up with a lot of cranial clutter.

Martin watched the playwright move his lips without talking and
smiled indulgently. "The creative process at work, eh?"

"I think I've got brain lock," Jimmy said. "I'm afraid the old
noggin's been put through the mill lately, and — wait, it's coming to
me. Yes, here it comes! Hang on!"

Martin hung on to his beer bottle and said, "I'm all ears."

Jimmy closed his eyes the better to visualize and sputtered:
"What I'm seeing is a one-act play set in a barber shop. Yeah, just
like the one I go to in Saint Joe."

"You go all the way to Saint Joe to get your hair cut?"

"Yeah," Jimmy said blinking. "Anything wrong with that?"

"Well, South Haven is full of hair stylists. Why don't you go to a
hair stylist in South Haven?"

"Precisely because I don't want my hair styled. I just want a
good, old-fashioned haircut at a good, old-fashioned barber shop,
and that's just what I get in Saint Joe. They've got a stack of SPORTS
ILLUSTRATEDs, the ballgame on TV, and stuffed fish on the wall.
Even a barber pole out in front."

"Come to think of it, it would make a great set. And I know just
where we could get some old barber chairs," Martin said, visualizing
victory over declining patronage.

"You like the idea?"

"Yes. I see potential. But what would the play be about?"

"Well," Jimmy said, freewheeling, "every time I go in my barber shop, there's always some old guy who looks like he's there for his last haircut. So I'm thinking of calling it – oh – something like – yeah – *The Last Haircut.*"

Martin's eyes widened. "Oh, I like that. Just the title alone would attract patrons. *No Exit,* now *The Last Haircut.* We'd be the most Off-Broadway theatre in Michigan."

"Why not? Anyway, I see a simple set – two barber chairs and all the usual stuff in a barber shop including the stuffed fish on the wall and the pile of SPORTS ILLUSTRATEDs.. And just three characters. A barber, a young customer and an old customer. And the old guy is coming for his last haircut. He doesn't really know it, but he senses it and . . ."

"So this would work on all kinds of levels."

"Yeah, I guess it would."

"Oh, this is brilliant. When can you start writing?"

"Well, probably not until the party is over. I suppose I could kick-start the old brain in a day or two."

"Our next board meeting is Wednesday, August 18. Think you could have a rough draft by then?"

Jimmy didn't want to make it look too easy, so he struck a contemplative pose. "Well, if I go and have an R&R day in Chicago this week to recover from *No Dice* . . ."

"We can't afford to send you to Chicago for the day," Joyce said, passing within earshot.

Funny how she always seemed to be passing within earshot when the subject of spending money was being discussed.

"Joyce, you said I could go."

"Jimmy, we'll talk about it later. All right?"

"But, Joyce, I need to go to Chicago to recover from *No Dice* and freshen my brain so I can start writing a new play for Blue Star Players. Martin just commissioned me to write a play for Blue Star Players and . . ."

"Did you say commissioned?" Joyce bounced over to join the conversation, her fame button all aglow.

"Well, yes, I suppose that's what I'm proposing," Martin Gregory stammered.

Joyce clutched Jimmy's arm in ecstasy. "This is wonderful. Just wonderful."

Jimmy watched the dollar signs dance in his wife's eyes and cleared his throat. "I suppose I should give some thought to— uh, financial arrangements."

"I'm sure we can come to a mutually satisfactory agreement," Martin said, draining the last of his Frankie.

Jimmy immediately got him another and was proposing a toast to a long and happy collaboration when Tiffany Ann Starbuck sidled up next to Jimmy and said, "I've also got a proposition for you, big boy."

"It better be decent," Joyce said, wedging in between them.

"Oh it is," Tiffany said. "Completely. In fact, you'll like it, Joyce, because it means your husband will be making money."

Suddenly, Joyce thought, our financial woes are over.

"Now *she's* moving her lips without talking," Martin said.

"It's from all those PCBs they dumped in the lake," Jimmy said. "Rots the old brain stem and turns you into a babbling idiot. Better to just drink beer."

"Hear, hear," Martin said raising his bottle.

Not to be upstaged, Tiffany cocked her amazing hindquarters and said, "Don't you want to hear what my proposition is?"

"Yes," Jimmy said, thinking for some reason of the real redhead's glistening nether regions. The ones he had seen up close and personal on more than one occasion at the offices of the weakly weekly HAVENCREST HIGHLIGHTS. "I'm all ears."

"Well," Tiffany said, "I was just talking to Maye and Marlene, and they said I should keep the paper going. That I should be the publisher. And you should be the editor, Jimmy. You did such a good job while David and I were up in the Porcupines, I think you should just come and do it every week. I'd like pay you and everything. But the thing is that we have to keep it going. Because this town needs the HIGHLIGHTS. I mean just because David like up and left and took off to California and like totally destroyed my life and gave me no reason to live is no reason the HIGHLIGHTS and I shouldn't go on living. Right?"

The others nodded in amazement.

"I mean I was all ready to torch myself in the garage earlier, but then I played back my answering machine and came here, and thank God I did, because Marlene and Maye really straightened my head out. There's nothing like talking to other women when you've got problems. Women really understand. But then there's nothing like a good, hard man when you're horny. Don't you think, Joyce?"

Joyce shot dagger-death rays in the general direction of Tiffany's glistening nether regions and nodded grimly. As if to say, touch one little hair on his chinny-chin-chin, and I'll bite your fucking kneecaps off, bitch.

"What?" Tiffany said, blinking. "You like moved your lips, Joyce, but nothing came out."

"I don't think you wanted to hear what she was thinking," Jimmy said. "Isn't that right, Joyce?"

Joyce nodded grimly.

Tiffany stepped gingerly away from the seriously married couple and pivoted. "Well, anyway, getting back to the discussion I just had with Marlene and Maye — they said I should rise above it. Not let some stupid man like David like totally ruin my life because he has to go and run off to California and find himself or some stupid thing." Tiffany choked back a sob and added, "I hope there's like this really, really, really big earthquake right after he gets there, and it like swallows him up, only he's still alive, and he's way down in this deep, dark hole in the earth, and then it like slowly closes and crushes him to death. And it'll be on TV so I'll get to watch. And I'll make a tape of it, and play it over and over and . . ."

"Tiffany!" Joyce waved her hand in front of Tiffany's face. "Snap out of it, Tiffany!"

The color drained from Tiffany's face and hair. Blood pooled in her belly and her breathing slowed. Then her eyes fluttered, and the birds sang in her head.

"Sorry," she said, looking around sheepishly. "Just had a little brain fart there. Jeez Louise. I went like totally ballistic, didn't I?"

"It's good for you," Joyce said. "Got to get that stuff out, or it'll kill you."

Tiffany smiled her Pancake Princess smile and shrugged. "Yeah, you're right. Got to get it out, or it'll kill you." Her smile vanished in a twinkling, and she grabbed the air with her hands. "But if I ever get my hands on that son of a bitch, I'll wring his fucking neck! So help me God!"

Marlene Small and Maye Michaels hearkened to the call of female rage and chorused: "Right on, sister!"

Burt Babbington and the zaftig Zoe Z.Z. Zell zeroed in on the kitchen, and Corva crept in after them, followed by Douglas Iglesia and his emotional bat-girl, and the talk turned to war stories about *No Dice*.

But Jimmy happily observed that those dollar signs continued dancing in his wife's eyes until all of Burt's designer chow and booze had been consumed and the last guests — Douglas Iglesia and his emotional bat-girl, naturally — departed in peace.

"So what do you think, Joyce?" Jimmy said, returning from seeing them off.

"I think you can clean up the mess."

"Of course. But that's not what I meant. I meant: what do you think of my getting a commission to write a play for Blue Star Players and helping Tiffany put out the paper?"

"If you ask me — I think Tiffany wants you to put out. And if you ask me, I didn't hear that Gregory Martin character say one word about money."

"It's Martin Gregory, and he said we could reach a mutually satisfactory arrangement on the money front. I'll ask around and see what I should charge."

"Who are you going to ask, Jimmy?"

"I don't know. I'll find somebody. Or a book or something."

Joyce sighed and padded over to the couch and picked up a thick book with tiny print.

Jimmy watched her for a moment and then shuffled into the kitchen where he tackled the leavings of the most dazzling theatre party ever held at Havencrest. When he was finished, he put on his best game face and padded into the living room and cleared his throat.

Joyce put her finger on the passage she was reading and looked up.

"Joyce?"

"What? You've interrupted me right in the middle of Canetti's pithy discussion of the 'Expectation of Command among the Pilgrims at Arafat.'"

"Sorry. My God, if I had any idea you were reading something that scintillating, I never would have interrupted you."

"What do you want?"

"I finished cleaning everything up."

"Good for you."

"Yeah. Well, I was kind of wondering — you know we do have all that money from *No Dice*, and like I said earlier, I could really use some R&R in Chicago. To clear my head so I can start writing *Last Haircut* for Blue Star Players."

Joyce clapped shut Elias Canetti's brilliant CROWDS AND POWER and sighed. Then she smiled so big and so wide. "How can I deny you anything? You're my love blot, and I can't say no to you. Come here, you."

Jimmy caught the glint in his wife's eyes and slipped out of the kitchen apron. "What do you have in mind, Joyce?"

"I'm going to put my womanly scent all over you as a warning to that little slut Tiffany."

Jimmy grinned and said, "Better use lots of scent, Joyce, because I think she's going to need a pretty big warning."

(Lights down, romantic music up, scene ends in marital bliss.)

Chapter Four

Jimmy sat on the Chicago-bound South Shore silverliner and smiled at the dune meadows and forests blurring past his window.

I guess I do have her wrapped around my little finger, he thought, consciously trying not to move his lips. So as not to alarm the other passengers on the blissfully air-conditioned train. Of course, I did have to drive down to Michigan City and take the South Shore when it would have been so much easier to catch Amtrak in Bangor, but by saving money on train fare, I got her to agree to let me eat lunch at the Moon Palace in Chinatown.

Not bad.

Not bad at all.

Jimmy heard some sound escape from his pursed lips and glanced around.

Nobody heard a thing. The other passengers were too busy grooming themselves in public or listening to their bored children ask for the ten-thousandth time: "Are we there yet?"

Jimmy settled as far back in the unyielding orange plastic seat as he could and fished a spiral notebook and Parker fountain pen out of his shirt pocket.

He waited for the muses to alight on his shoulder.

They were busy elsewhere, but a red-tailed hawk took flight as the train sped past its arboreal lair, and a doe and two fawns poked their noses out of the dense Indiana forest skirting the tracks. There were cattails galore and then suddenly a great, surging steel mill. Proof positive that America was still a mighty manufacturer.

Jimmy wept for joy.

Well, almost.

Then he uncapped his fountain pen, opened his notebook and scribbled:

"THE PLACE: Father & Son Barbershop in downtown Hometown, America.

"THE TIME: A lazy summer afternoon in the present.

"THE PLAY: One Act. One hour (approx.) No Intermission."

Jimmy reviewed what he had written and scratched out "one hour" and replaced it with "40 minutes." Then he scratched that out and decided to leave the time blank for now.

No sense in boxing myself in, he thought, moving his lips.

A bored kid across the aisle elbowed his mother, pointed at Jimmy, and demanded: "Mommy, how come that man is talking to himself?"

Mommy slapped the kid's hand down and hissed: "Shut up and mind your own business."

Ah, Jimmy thought, family values at work.

The little boy cried, and Mommy slapped his face. "I told you to shut up, and I meant it. How can we have fun today if you keep asking stupid questions?"

The little boy, who would grow up to become a serial killer of women who looked like Mommy, went deep inside himself and hid.

Jimmy nodded thoughtfully and wondered what his dear old rich mother was doing that day. He had recently received a postcard from her postmarked Edinburgh, Scotland. That's right, he thought, she's off on another one her bus tours of Europe. Good for her.

And good for me for having nothing to do with her anymore.

Jimmy took a deep breath from the diaphragm, and penned the players in order of appearance:

"Kid, 18. Just graduated from Hometown High School. Not sure what he wants to do with the rest of his life, but he is sure he is never going to have a bad hair day. That's why he comes to Pete faithfully every three weeks. Wears latest fashions and cares dearly about how the opposite sex sees him. Rich kid of type-A parents who were never there for him. Bored out of his mind. Parents keep him financially dependent by giving him enough money so he does not have to work.

"Pete the barber, 48. Been a barber his entire adult life. Wanted to go to a Major League try-out after his big year as a high school baseball star, but his father prohibited him, saying: 'No damn kid of mine's gonna be some tobacco-chewing, womanizing lout who plays a kid's game in a silly uniform. If it was good enough for my father to be a barber, and it's good enough for me — then it's good enough for you. Now put away that stupid glove and go to barber school.' Pete did as his father told, but he still knows in his heart he could have made it into the majors. The other chair is empty because Pete's father died some years back, and he had no luck in talking his own son into being a barber. Actually, he didn't have the heart to do it.

"Mr. Bluffington, 67. A regular customer his entire life. Pete is the third member of the family to cut his hair. Retired salesman. Sold refractory bricks to steel mills 'back in the old days when they knew how to make steel in this country.' Took an early retirement at 59 and has been bored out of his mind ever since. Wife nags him constantly, so he looks for any excuse to get out of the house. His tri-weekly haircut is one of the few pleasures left in his life. He goes religiously to the barbershop despite the fact he has liver cancer, and his hair is a lifeless thatch that never grows. He served in the navy during World War II at a naval air station in Maine. Never saw any real action. Has three adult children and eight grandchildren. Or is it seven—he never remembers. Besides, that's the wife's job.

"First sports announcer

"Second sports announcer"

Jimmy saw everything that he had written, and behold it was very good.

He smiled at the beaten little boy across the aisle.

The little boy flashed a quick smile in return before Mommy could catch him.

Jimmy shook his head and thought of all the electric train rides he had shared with his mother from Wynnwood into Philadelphia. For a day of "fun in the city." Just like this little guy across the aisle was supposed to be having with his Mommy, except his Mommy should have had her tubes tied at the age of 13, because she was clearly incapable of nurturing human life.

The little boy across the aisle giggled at the man talking to himself. Mommy clopped him up side the head, and he was quiet for the rest of the 90-minute ride into Chicago.

Jimmy sighed and looked out the window at an eastbound mixed commodities freight train on the Conrail main. Eastbound to New York and possibly Pennsylvania. As in home.

No.

As in place of birth.

Not home.

Home is where the heart is, and the heart is in Havencrest, Michigan. With Joyce. And only Joyce.

Jimmy sighed again and sealed his lips for the remainder of the trip.

Then he set scene one to paper:

(It is a lazy summer afternoon at the Father & Son Barbershop in downtown Hometown, America. There are two chairs, but only one barber. The place is appointed with the usual barbershop bric-a-brac: a price list, mirrors, and the requisite tonsorial equipment, a mounted muskellunge, a girlie calendar from an automotive supply company, a stack of well-thumbed SPORTS ILLUSTRATED and FIELD & STREAM magazines, a few copies of ROLLING STONE to please the younger customers, the morning paper, faded yellow ribbons, peeling "Support the Troops" stickers, three American flags, and a message in a cheap frame that reads: "The time a man spends fishing is not counted against his allotted time on earth." There is a bank of chairs for waiting and a color television tuned to the ballgame. At rise, Pete is finishing the Kid's buzz cut with his usual flourish. The Kid has his nose buried in ROLLING STONE magazine.)

Pete: Well, Kid, that about does it. You look like a million bucks — all green and wrinkled. (Puts down scissors and holds hand mirror for Kid to see his handiwork) What do you think?

Kid: (Looks up from ROLLING STONE and peers into mirror for the longest time. Then he nods.) It's pretty cool.

Pete: Pretty cool?!? Kid, it's a masterpiece. You told me the girls were falling all over you after that last haircut I gave you.

Kid: All right, you're good, Pete. But I don't see Bill Clinton flyin' in here and payin' you 200 bucks for a haircut. Besides, you left a little too much on top.

Pete: Where?

Kid: (Points) There. How many times I have to tell you, man? I want a buzz. Not some hair-do. If I wanted some hair-do, I'd go to that stupid place at the mall.

Pete: Right, Kid. (Puts down mirror and gets buzzer) Here, hold still, and I'll get it. (Works meticulously on Kid's already perfect haircut and then gets mirror) There, how's that?

Kid: (Takes another long look) Better. Well, I gotta blow this popstand. Meetin' some buddies at the beach. Can you like do a

better job of gettin' all that hair outta my neck and ears this time?
Last time it was the worst. I mean there's nothin' worse than bein'
all hot and sweaty at the beach playin' volleyball and havin' all those
little hairs stuck to your neck. You know?

Pete: (Sighs) I hear you, Kid. Hold still.

(Pete is carefully brushing hair off Kid's neck and ears when Mr.
Bluffington shuffles into the shop) Hey, Mr. Bluffington! I was just
about to send out the Mounties for you.

Mr. Bluffington: (Waves brusquely and settles wearily into chair)
It's this dumb downtown parking. It's all bollixed up. Had to circle
three times before I could find a decent parking place. Can't you do
something about it, Pete? Your old man wouldn't have stood for it.

Pete: I'll try, Mr. Bluffington. But you know what they told me
at the last city council meeting.

Mr. Bluffington: Ah, nuts is what I say. It's all these darn law
suits. It's gotten so they're all afraid of their own shadows. Some
kid trips over a crack in the sidewalk and ten thousand lawyers
descend on city hall. You wouldn't have seen that in my day. No sir.
(Picks up SPORTS ILLUSTRATED and idly thumbs it)

Pete: (Holds mirror for Kid to see) There, Kid, how's that? No
hairs on your neck, and you still look like a million bucks.

Kid: (Looks for a long time) Not bad for a rookie, Pete. Stick
with it, and maybe Clinton *will* fly in for a $200 haircut.

Mr. Bluffington: You talking about that no-good, draft-dodger
who cheated on his wife?

Kid: I'm talking about *our* president, Mr. Bluffington.

Mr. Bluffington: You mean *your* president, don't you, Kid?

Kid: (Shrugs and tosses ROLLING STONE on magazine pile) It's
too nice a day to argue politics with you, Mr. Bluffington. Besides,
it's a free country.

Mr. Bluffington: (Tosses magazine aside) That's the problem
with this country these days — too much freedom. You kids have it
too easy. In my day, we had to walk ten miles to school. Now
they've got these gol-darn buses going every which way. Gotten so
you have to stop every three blocks while one of those monsters
discharges another load of fat, lazy kids.

(Pete undrapes Kid, who he gets quickly to his feet and approaches Mr. Bluffington. Then he thinks better of it and turns to Pete.)

Kid: How much do I owe you, Pete?

Pete: How long have you been coming here, Kid?

Mr. Bluffington: Since he was knee-high to a grasshopper. When your grandfather was running the shop, Pete, haircuts were a nickel. What can you get for a nickel in this town now-a-days? The five-and-dime even had to change its name. Now it's owned by some big outfit from Japan. I tell you, Pete, those Japs are taking over this country.

Pete: It's actually a Canadian company, Mr. Bluffington. And they're real nice folks. I met them at the last chamber of commerce meeting, and . . .

Mr. Bluffington: Ah, nuts is what I say. You wouldn't have seen the Canadians buying up good, old-fashioned American businesses in my day. They stayed in Canada where they belonged and made ginger ale and hockey sticks. Nobody makes ginger ale and hockey sticks like those Canucks.

Kid: (Sighs) So how much do I owe you, Pete?

Mr. Bluffington: Can't you read, Kid? Prices are listed right up there. Course they probably don't teach good, old-fashioned readin', writin' and 'rithmatic in the schools anymore. You don't even pray in school anymore. But in my day you did. Believe you me. And you didn't pass until you knew your multiplication tables backwards and forwards. And I mean backwards and forwards.

Kid: So how much do I owe you, Pete?

Pete: Six bucks, Kid.

Kid: (Digs in pocket and hands Pete a five and four quarters) Thanks, Pete. Stick with it — you might have a future in this. See ya later, Mr. Bluffington. (Leaves in a blaze of youthful exuberance)

Jimmy saw everything that he had written, and behold it was very good.

Very good indeed, he thought without moving his lips.

He looked out the window and watched a mountainous landfill lumber past. Actually, Jimmy thought, we're passing the landfill, but it appears to be passing us owing to the laws of train travel, physics, and the general harmony of the spheres. Or something like that.

Jimmy shook his head and smiled at his reflection in the window. He was happy. Very happy. He had written a brilliant opening to what he knew would be his next smash-hit play.

Slated for a world premiere at the celebrated Blue Star Players in lovely South Haven, Michigan.

Never mind that they're know as "Bull Shit & Piss" to the cognoscenti. They have lights and a raked auditorium with a real stage, and a parking lot, and even air-conditioning. At least I think they have air-conditioning. Of course, they have air-conditioning, and heating.

Yeah, I'm sure they do.

But the important thing is they'll produce my play. Get the actors, direct the damn thing, sell the tickets, do the marketing and all the rest of the crap that I had to do myself for *No Dice*. I'll get to sit back and just be the celebrated playwright for a change.

And maybe when I go up to take my bow after the premiere, some idiot like Tiffany Ann Starbuck won't douse the lights on me.

Jimmy inhaled a vast measure of fame vapor and was happy. Totally so.

He capped his Parker fountain pen, closed his spiral notebook, and restored those wondrous items to his shirt pocket.

Then he settled back and enjoyed the rest of the ride into Chicago — all without moving his lips.

He passed happily through the subterranean horror that was Randolph Street Station and popped up the stairs at Randolph and Michigan into a luminous summer day in Chicago.

Jimmy went to a nearby bagel bakery and noshed a fresh batch of walnut, raisin-bran bagels with cream cheese. He washed it down with two cups of killer coffee and then set out on foot to find release from the trauma of producing his first play.

Correction, he thought. Producing, directing, stage managing, marketing, casting, and counseling the cast of my first play.

But he wasn't bitter.

Not in the least.

Rather, he was strangely infected with the drama bug.

Actually wanted to have another go at it.

Just like women who keep having kid after kid despite the fact that each birth is like shitting a basketball.

Proof that humans don't remember pain.
Or else why are there so many of us?
And why do we keep making war on one another? Two big ones in this century alone.

You'd think, Jimmy thought strolling under the "Loop" elevated tracks on Wabash Avenue, that the people who survived the horrors of World War I would have done everything to prevent the greater horrors of World War II. But it was precisely one of those survivors, namely an Austrian corporal named Adolf Hitler, who sent out the invitations to World War II.

Of course, Jimmy thought aloud, he insisted that the war be won in lightning fashion so as to preclude the use of gas — I mean the poor guy *was* gassed in the trenches during World War I, so . . .

"I agree."

"Huh," Jimmy said, looking about.

He had somehow stopped for a light at Madison and a bum had sidled up next to him.

"I agree," the bum said. "You were talking about Hitler. Not very loud, mind you, but I could hear you. I hear things nobody else hears, and let me tell you — Hitler was no fool. Ordered his generals not to use gas when they launched the blitzkrieg against France. Didn't want his troops suffering in the trenches like he did in the first war."

"Right," Jimmy said. He gave the reeking ragamuffin all the change in his pocket and crossed with the light.

Jimmy looked back. The man wasn't following.

He looked ahead and saw other so-called "homeless persons" posted at regular intervals like needy streetlights. All with their hands out. All with stories to tell.

Jimmy made a mental note to write a play about a homeless person.

A homeless woman, he thought. Yeah. A homeless woman who could have been a great photographer except that this shithead stole the negative to her greatest photograph. Tricked her out of it when she was in college. And he went on to make a ton of money on it, and she ended up on the streets, shitting in doorways and panhandling strangers. Like that poor creature up there. And that one over there.

Jimmy nodded happily and spontaneously bounded up the steps to the elevated station at Adams.

Figured maybe he'd hop a northbound Ravenswood and visit the old neighborhood. Forgo Chinatown for lunch at one of the old haunts on Lincoln Avenue.

But then a splashy red sign caught his eye.

The Chicago Transit Authority, or CTA, had finally finished the tunnel linking the Dan Ryan and Howard lines and wanted the world to know about it. Specifically, the CTA wanted Jimmy Clarke to ride its new "HODAN" line to Chinatown.

Jimmy went them one stop farther and got off at 35th Street.

"Great ride," he told the conductor.

The conductor shrugged. One ride on the CTA was the same as 10,000 others to him.

Jimmy bounded up the escalator and stopped short when he hit 35th Street.

There, looming in the near and far distance, was this great concrete eyesore called Comiskey Park. Jimmy looked to the right where the real Comiskey Park had been and saw nothing but a parking lot.

Jimmy staggered to a bench in the park at the north end of the parking lot, pulled out his pen and notebook and auto-wrote the following lament to old Comiskey Park:

Joni Mitchell was right:
They will fool you every
Time.

And
Put a fucking
Parking
  lot
In place of
Those spaces that
Were once dear to
So, so
  many and are
Now lost and

Forgotten
and
Torn down
Completely.

And in its place
Sits a hulking mass
of concrete
Shit
for
Blue-collar assholes
Who
Made a ton of money
Sticking it to one another
(the old-fashioned)
Way —
Up the ass
Without
   a
     condom!

Jimmy closed his notebook, capped his pen, spit in the general
direction of the new ballpark and marched north toward Chinatown.

He knew as he walked past the unassuming bungalows of
Bridgeport that no one would ever publish his poem. But he didn't
care. He had expressed his feelings in print, and he was the better
for it.

And he was the hungrier for it.

Onward to Chinatown, he resolved.

The Moon Palace or bust!

In no time flat, Jimmy Clarke presented himself to a friendly
waitress who took his order for steamed dumplings, rice cakes in
soup, and an ice-cold bottle of Tsing Tao beer brewed and bottled in
the Peoples Republic of China. He ate everything on his plate and
in his bowl, ordered another beer, licked his chopsticks, left a
generous tip and strolled down Wentworth to the Chinatown branch
of the Chicago Public Library where he pulled a guide for
playwrights off the shelf and perused it to the background

accompaniment of an English class for native speakers of Mandarin Chinese.

From what Jimmy could ascertain from the book's conflicting bits of information and great gobs of gas was that he should charge $20 for the first performance of his play and $15 for each subsequent performance.

Sounds good, he thought. If Blue Star Players does six performances of the *Last Haircut* that means I make — hmm — yeah, $95.

Not as much as we made on *No Dice*, but — yeah, actually it is if you factor in all the expenses.

What is it Joyce is always telling me about gross and net and all that good . . .

". . . All that good."

Jimmy looked up and saw that an elderly Chinese gent was parroting his spoken thoughts.

Jimmy blushed and smiled.

The Chinese gent blushed and smiled.

Jimmy sealed his lips and returned the book to its shelf. He spotted a collection of work by his favorite playwright, Eugene O'Neill, and took it to his table.

The elderly Chinese gent judged the book by its cover and said, "Eugene O'Neill."

"Awesome playwright," Jimmy said, cracking open the book.

"Awesome playwright," the man repeated.

Jimmy put his finger to his lips, and the man did likewise.

Then Jimmy dove in for a dose of truly great American theatre and remembered as he read how he had knocked them dead at Penn State playing Ebon Cabot in *Desire Under the Elms*. He had done such a convincing job of being strangled during the third act that the director had nearly stopped the play to see if he was all right.

Damn, I was good.

"Damn good."

Jimmy blushed at the elderly Chinese gent and handed him the book of O'Neill plays. "You want to learn some really good English, sir, read this."

Then he hoofed it back up Wentworth and over Cermak to the Chinatown stop on the CTA's new and exciting HODAN line.

Jimmy took the next available train to Adams, alighted and spent a productive afternoon browsing bookstores and visiting pen counters. He was sorely tempted to buy himself a dazzling new Waterman fountain pen to add to the ones that were gathering dust and taking up valuable space on a shelf under the kitchen counter, but he could feel Joyce's icy fingers on his neck as an unctuous sales creature asked: "Is there anything in particular I can help you with today, sir?"

"No, just looking."

The sales creature nodded curtly at the door and moved down the counter to assist a customer with real net worth.

Jimmy walked off lunch, bought a bag of walnut, raisin-bran bagels and boarded the 5:10 South Shore train for Michigan City. Jimmy listened to the sat-out secretaries loudly tell one another and the world how they had single-handedly kept corporate American afloat for another day. Never mind that their "moronic" bosses were still at work—these gals had put in long, hard days and don't you ever forget it.

Ever.

Jimmy polished off a bagel, gazed out the window for a while and then capped off his gloriously refreshing day with these words:

SOUTH SHORE

South Shore silverliner
Slides
Along the South Side.
Headed south
Then east
For THE CITY,
Which to locals
Is Michigan (City).

As on
The other side.

Of the Lake.

He saw all that he had written, and behold it was very good.

Very good indeed for a produced playwright who was bound for glory.

Chapter Five

Jimmy cleared his throat and said: "So, ah, Tiffany, now that I've helped you put the first HIGHLIGHTS to bed, what about my salary? What are you going to pay me?"

Tiffany turned off the light table and slid up next to the new man in her life. Married or not — didn't make a lick of difference to the former Pancake Princess of Glenn, Michigan. The very woman who had won the contest by giving a judge a white-glove handjob.

Tiffany touched Jimmy's tusch and nodded at the bedroom where Jimmy had first spied her glistening nether regions.

"I've got to get home," Jimmy stammered. "Joyce is expecting me."

"At 11:30 at night? She's in bed already, isn't she? I mean, didn't you like tell me that she goes to bed every night at 10?"

"Yeah, but . . ."

"But nothing, big boy. Your wife's in bed. Having her own sweet dreams. You can have your own sweet dreams right here with me. In my bed. Come on, what do you say?" Tiffany brushed her hand down Jimmy's pants. "No, you don't have to say anything. Your cock's talking for you, and it wants to take a walk to the bedroom where I'll pay you for all your hard work today. And even give you a bonus or two."

Jimmy inhaled and looked for an exit.

Tiffany blocked it. "Come on, Jimmy, be a sport. We've both worked our butts off all day getting this stupid paper out, now let's smoke some reefer and fuck like bunnies. It's what David and I always did, and . . ." Her lip curled at the mention of her abruptly departed lover, and she cried.

Jimmy gave her a tentative pat on the back. "You miss him, don't you?"

Tiffany nodded, clutched Jimmy, and sobbed on his shoulder.

He patted her back and made comforting male noises.

Tiffany cried her eyes dry and looked up at Jimmy with great doe eyes. "Why do all the decent men have to be married?"

Jimmy shrugged.

"I mean, why couldn't I have met you before you married Joyce, and why did I ever think that David was the answer to my prayers? What a shithead. I hope he rots in hell. I really do hope there is a giant earthquake, and it swallows him up and slowly crushes him to death. I really, really, really do."

"He might not get swallowed up by an earthquake, but life will catch up with him. It always does. And if you want revenge, all you have to do is live a good life."

"You think so?"

"I know so. Well, look, I'm really beat, so I think I'm going to head home and . . ."

"We don't have to fuck," Tiffany said, clutching at Jimmy. "We could just give each other blowjobs or something. That wouldn't be like cheating on Joyce or anything."

Jimmy shook his head. "Tiffany, let's call it a night. Okay?"

"How about if we just get naked and jerk each other off. Or just watch each other jerk off. And talk dirty and stuff. That wouldn't be . . ."

"Tiffany!"

"What?"

"Aren't you tired?"

"Yeah, but I'm so fucking horny, and you're right here, and David used to play this song from one of those old '60s groups about how if you 'can't be with the one you love/ love the one you're with,' and you're the one I'm with and . . ."

"Tiffany, I'm going."

"But you can't!"

"But I am." Jimmy gently pushed her aside and made tracks for the door. He turned and said. "And we do need to talk about money. You said you were going to pay me for being editor, and although I really enjoyed putting out the paper today, I'm not doing it for my health. I've got to make some money."

Tiffany angrily threw up her hands. "First you won't fuck me, and now you're hitting me up for money. Get out of here, you asshole!!"

"Tiffany!"

"Leave!! Now!!"

Jimmy exhaled and went straight home.

Joyce rolled over when he clomped into the bedroom and moaned: "What time is it?"

"Close to midnight."

Joyce sat up and said: "Midnight?!? What have you been doing all night?"

"Putting out the paper."

"Putting out for Tiffany is more like it."

"Joyce! That's ridiculous, and you know it."

Joyce sniffed and fully awakened. "If it's ridiculous, then why do you smell like her cheap perfume. I bet that bitch has been rubbing up against you all night. Hasn't she?"

"Joyce!"

"Stop 'Joycing' me and answer me, Jimmy. What's been going on over there at that rag?"

"Nothing's been going on over there at that rag. We put out the paper. That's all. And if I smell like her perfume, it's because we were working in close quarters. You've been there. You've seen what a rabbit warren it is."

"Yeah, and I've also seen the bedroom that's conveniently located next to that pathetic excuse for a layout room. Is that where you took your breaks, Jimmy? Huh? Answer me that?"

Jimmy collapsed on his side of the bed and pulled his shoes and socks off. Then he wriggled out of his shorts, underwear, and climbed under the comforter wearing his t-shirt.

"Jimmy!"

"What?"

"What are you doing?"

"Going to sleep. What's it look like I'm doing, Joyce?"

Joyce poked her husband in the ribs.

"Joyce! I'm trying to go to sleep."

"You can't go to sleep smelling like that. And you're not going to sleep until you tell me exactly what happened."

Jimmy rolled away from his wife and set his breathing for deep sleep. "Joyce," he murmured, "nothing happened. Absolutely nothing. In fact, she called me an 'asshole' because I made sure nothing happened. I think she tried to fire me, but I'll fix it all in the morning. Now go to sleep and . . ." Jimmy went to sleep and immediately began snoring.

Joyce poked him sharply in the ribs. Right where it hurt and tickled at the same time. Right in the spot known and beloved by wives the world over.

Jimmy awakened with a start and hollered: "Joyce!"

Joyce rolled him her way and said: "You're not going to sleep until you tell me exactly what happened with that little over-sexed harpy."

"Joyce, nothing happened with Tiffany. Scout's honor. Cross my heart and hope to die. Now would you go to sleep and let me go to sleep?"

"Not until you give me a detailed explanation."

"Joyce, I've given you a detailed explanation."

"No, you haven't."

"Yes, I have."

"Have not."

"Have too."

"Have not."

"Have too."

Jimmy and Joyce made the mistake of looking one another in the eye. There was just enough moonlight to show the old sparkle, and that was all the oldly-weds needed to initiate some serious nookie. And then they both slept like dogs after a hard day of chasing bunnies.

On the morrow, Jimmy went for a refreshing swim in the lake, ate a hearty breakfast and went to his phone to call Tiffany. He was about to lift the handset when the contraption sounded the alarm for an incoming call.

It was a penitent Tiffany Ann Starbuck.

Chastened by the morning sun and dehorned by a serious session with the cordless, five-speed vibrator L. David Hinchcliff had bought her for when he was away.

"Hi," she said, all sugar and spice and everything nice. "It's me. Tiffany Ann. I'm like really, really, really sorry for the way I acted last night. And I really, really, really didn't mean to like fire you and all, because I like really, really, really need you as editor. Because I can't do all this without you. I mean, you write such good stories, and you're so easy to work with, and, well, like I'm really, really,

really sorry I called you an asshole, because like the last thing in the whole world you are is an asshole."

Tiffany inhaled and added; "So, are you like coming back this afternoon? Because I like need you to cover this ribbon cutting down at the marina at 2 and . . ."

"Tiffany?"

"Yes."

"What about the money?"

Tiffany's throat constricted, but she managed to say, "Yeah, the money. I was going to get to the money. See, like there's a little problem right now with the money. I went and talked to this lawyer first thing this morning – oh, what a hunk, I mean you should have seen his office. He has this like totally awesome green leather chair. He let me sit in it and everything, and he has a Daytimer that matches his chair. And a briefcase. All in the same green leather. I don't think it's from green cows. I sure haven't seen any green cows, but . . ."

"Tiffany."

"What?"

"What about the money?"

"Well, I was going to get to that, you silly. Why do you think I went to see this hunk of a lawyer first thing this morning?"

"So what did he say?"

"He said David left me in a precarious legal and financial situation. But he thinks he can straighten it out."

"So you'll be able to pay me a salary as editor."

"Yeah. But . . ."

"But what?"

"Well, not right away. But soon. Okay?"

"How soon?"

"Why are you so hung up about money? I mean aren't you guys rich or something? Everybody around here knows you like inherited money from your rich family back east."

"What?!?"

"Yeah. You're like from New York or somewhere, aren't you?"

"Pennsylvania."

"Well that's in the east somewhere, isn't it?"

"You could say that. But I don't see how everybody thinks we're rich. We drive a Honda Civic and live in a dump in the dunes."

"But you live in the dunes, and besides, I saw on some TV special that the really, really, really rich don't act like they're rich, and you and Joyce sure don't act like you're rich. In fact, you have a real relaxed attitude toward everything. And that's just what this guy on this show said. He's like from Australia or somewhere so he should know."

Jimmy rubbed his forehead.

"Tiffany?"

"What?"

"Even if I was rich, and believe me – I'm not, I'd still need to make some money for what I do. Simply as a matter of professional pride."

"Sure. I understand."

"So, what are you going to pay when you are able to pay me?"

"Well, David was paying you $25 per column. Right?"

"Yes."

"So, that's what I'll pay you. If you write more than one column or story, like you did yesterday, then you'll make more money. Like yesterday. You'll make $75 when I can pay you because you wrote three stories."

"What about the editorial I wrote?"

"That doesn't really count as a story, because you're like the editor."

"Ah ah. The meat of the matter. Aren't you going to pay me for being editor? Look at all the extra work I did yesterday helping you get the paper out."

"Yeah, but you're not here this morning helping me deliver it. If you were really the editor, you'd be here this morning helping me deliver the paper."

"What about that high school kid David had?"

"He got a better job at McDonald's."

Jimmy sighed and said: "Look, Tiffany, I'd love to help you deliver the papers this morning, but I've got to get cracking on this play I promised the Blue Star Players."

"You mean Bull Shit & Piss?"

"Yeah, but I promised them a play and . . ."

"What's wrong with *No Dice*?"

"They want an original play."

"*No Dice* is an original play. You can't get more original than *No Dice*. And you can't get a better director than David." Tiffany's throat cracked and she cried.

"Tiffany?"

"What?" she sobbed.

"Are you all right?"

"I'm fine. I guess I'll just have to deliver the papers all by myself. Men. My mother was right. They always let you down when you need them the most. Look what happened to her. Every time she had another baby, the guy she was with split. Men. Who needs 'em. Especially now that I found that vibrator David left me. Did you know it has five speeds?"

"So you'll pay me $25 per story?"

"Take it or leave it."

"And you'll pay me $100 for the four stories I wrote yesterday."

"Seventy-five dollars."

"What about the editorial?"

"What about it?"

"It was a story—I expect to be paid for it."

"But you said you practically wrote it in your sleep—it was so easy."

"Yeah, but . . ."

"So I'll pay you $10 for editorials and $25 for regular stories. How's that?"

Jimmy chewed on that for a second and reluctantly agreed. Like I have any fucking choice.

"What?" Tiffany said.

"Nothing."

"No, you were saying something. You were talking to yourself again, weren't you? Gol, you really should see a doctor about that. I mean, sooner or later you're going to end up being like a totally twisted serial killer or something if you don't like get some medication to take care of that."

"Right. Look, if I'm going to cover that exciting ribbon cutting at the marina at 2, I'd better get cracking on my play."

"Crack away, stud puppet, and I'll deliver the papers — all by myself."

"Tiffany, if you really need help, I suppose I could . . ."

"No, you have fun with your little play, and I'll deliver the papers. All by myself."

"Okay. Good. Well, I'll see you after I cover the ribbon cutting."

"Yeah. Bye." Click.

Jimmy wanted to bite the head off the phone. Instead, he cranked up his venerable computer and pounded out the following:

Pete: Well, Mr. Bluffington, it's your turn at bat.

Mr. Bluffington: (Struggles to feet and puts himself in barber chair) Cheapskate didn't give you a tip, did he, Pete?

Pete: You know he never gives me a tip, Mr. Bluffington. He's saving his money for college in the fall.

Mr. Bluffington: Hah! That kid's parents are rich enough to buy and sell this town ten times over, and he can't even give you a measly tip. And did you get a load of that car he drives around in?

Pete: Yeah, it's a real . . .

Mr. Bluffington: Monthly nut on that nazi tank's gotta be more than the GNP of most third world countries. You wouldn't have seen kids driving around in fancy German cars in my day. No sir. We all rode bicycles and delivered GRIT magazine and sold eggs. Heck, most of us worked at the fruit docks all summer for 25 cents a day. And there weren't any coffee breaks and two-hour lunches in those days. No sir. They got a solid 12 hours out of you, and you worked.

Pete: Right, Mr. Bluffington. (Carefully drapes his customer and takes up scissors and comb) So what'll it be today? The usual?

Mr. Bluffington: Of course, the usual. You think I want to look like some Injun on the warpath like that damn kid?

Pete: No, Mr. Bluffington, I'm sure you don't.

(Pete begins fussing over Mr. Bluffington's dried thatch of gray hair without really doing anything. The two stare at the ballgame on television.)

Mr. Bluffington: For cryin' out loud — he had him by a mile. Where do they get these catchers? Pay these bums a small fortune, and they can't even get a guy at second. Heck, I've seen Little

Leaguers with better arms than that. And look at this stupid pitcher. His hair was any longer, he'd have to wear braids.

Pete: Some of them practically do, Mr. Bluffington.

Mr. Bluffington: Well, you wouldn't have seen that in my day. No sir. Can you imagine Babe Ruth or Joe DiMaggio with hair halfway down to their behinds?

Jimmy looked at all he had written, and behold it was very good.

So very good, that he wrote the rest of Scene One in a single sitting, ending with these lines:

Pete: That about does it, Mr. Bluffington. (Exchanges mirror for scissors and holds for Mr. Bluffington to see) There, how's that?

Mr. Bluffington: (Stares for the longest time) Not bad, Pete. Stick with it. You might have a future in it. Now get these darned hairs off my neck.

Pete: Yes, Mr. Bluffington. (Meticulously whisks all the hair off Mr. Bluffington's neck and ears) There, how's that, Mr. Bluffington?

Mr. Bluffington: I think you missed a few, Pete. I can still feel some hairs down my neck. Once you start sweating, you never can get those things. The wife always says I should take a shower when I come home from the barbershop, but she ought to know by now that I only take a shower in the morning when I get up. We pay enough for hot water as it is without me taking two showers in one day.

Pete: I hear you, Mr. Bluffington. (Whisks the back of Mr. Bluffington's neck again) There, how's that? Did I get them all this time?

Mr. Bluffington: (Feels around neck with fingers) I think you did it, Pete. By golly, I think you got 'em all. Well, I expect you'll have another customer in here before long, so I'll just mosey on home and see what the wife wants me to do next. After I get — what was it she wanted me to get again?

Pete: Boneless chicken breasts and the dry-cleaning.

Mr. Bluffington: Ah, right.

Pete: (Removes apron and shakes it out) There you go, Mr. Bluffington.

Mr. Bluffington: Right. (Stands shakily and digs in pants pocket) Six bucks, right, Pete?

Pete: That's right, Mr. Bluffington.

Mr. Bluffington: (Carefully counts out six singles and hands them to Pete. Then digs in pocket again and produces two quarters which he regally hands his barber) There you go, my good man. Don't spend it all in one place.

Pete: I won't, Mr. Bluffington. See you in three weeks?

Mr. Bluffington: (Shuffles to door and turns) Unless you're planning to get hit by lightning or one of those stupid fish drags you into the lake. (Turns and departs)

Pete: (Watches him go and then looks grimly at his 50 cent tip. Goes to cash register and says to mirror:) Cheap old bastard.

(Lights fade, scene ends)

Jimmy nodded.

Jimmy smiled.

Jimmy stayed in the saddle and galloped into Scene Two.

To wit:

(It is another lazy summer afternoon three weeks later at the Father & Son Barbershop in downtown Hometown, America. The television is tuned to the ball game, and Pete is finishing the Kid's buzz cut with his usual flourish. The Kid, of course, has his nose buried in ROLLING STONE magazine.)

Pete: Well, Kid, that about does it. You look like a million bucks — all green and wrinkled. (Puts down scissors and holds hand mirror for Kid to see his handiwork) What do you think?

Kid: (Looks up from ROLLING STONE and peers into mirror for the longest time. Then he nods) It's all right.

Pete: All right?!? Kid, it's my best haircut yet. I was even thinking of taking a picture of you and sending it to one of my trade magazines.

Kid: Dream on, Pete, because I still don't see Bill Clinton flyin' in here and payin' you 200 bucks for a haircut. As usual, you left too much on top. Jeez, how many times do I have to tell you?

Pete: Where on top?

Kid: (Points) There. Man, you goin' blind and deaf on me, Pete, or what? I want a buzz. You dig? Not some hair-do like they give out at the mall. Why don't you hire some young dude to take care of the young customers like me? They got young dudes doin' hair out at the mall. You got that empty chair just sittin' there, Pete.

Why don't you hire a young partner? I mean, it's not like you're getting any younger.

Pete: (Sighs) Right, Kid. (Puts down mirror and gets buzzer) Here, hold still, and I'll get it. (Works meticulously on Kid's already perfect haircut) I think I do a good job on your hair. For an old guy. Hey, I haven't even hit 50 yet, and I bet if my father had let me try out for the majors like I wanted, I could still be out there with Nolan Ryan and those guys. I don't want to take anything away from that third baseman the Cubs have now, but they couldn't have found a more solid man on the hot corner than me. Nothing got by me when I was in high school. Nothing. I was all-state, you know.

Kid: No kidding, Pete. Gee, you've only told me about ten thousand times. But you didn't answer my question.

Pete: (Continues buzzing Kid's hair) What question?

Kid: Why don't you hire a young guy to be your assistant? You'd get a lot more young dudes in here. I mean, it's cool that you finally started putting ROLLING STONE in here, but if you're going to compete with that place at the mall you've got think young, Pete. Hey, you might even hire a babe. You know?

Pete: My wife would kill me if I hired a — you know. Besides, I can't afford to hire somebody else. I'm just barely squeaking by as it is without taking on an employee. There's health insurance, state and federal taxes, not to mention . . .

Kid: What about your kid? He's not doin' diddly. Why don't you make him come in here and help you? At least on Saturdays when it's busy.

Pete: (Turns off buzzer and sighs) I can't, Kid. I just can't.

Kid: Why not? Your old man made you become a barber. According to you, you could have made the majors if you'd gone to that try-out, but he made you go to barber school and become a barber like him.

Pete: Yeah. He said: "No damn kid of mine's gonna be some tobacco-chewing, womanizing lout who plays a kid's game in a silly uniform. If it was good enough for my father to be a barber, and it's good enough for me — then it's good enough for you. Now put away that stupid glove and go to barber school." I can hear him saying that like it was yesterday. (Snaps on buzzer and continues working on Kid's hair)

<u>Kid</u>: So why don't you tell your kid the same thing? I mean face it, Pete — the dude's never gonna make it as a musician. No offense or anything, but there's like one zillion guitar players out there, and your kid ain't exactly . . .

<u>Pete</u>: I want him to have a crack at it. If he fails, well, he fails. But at least he'll have had a crack at it. Which is more than my father gave me. Besides, three generations is enough for this shop. When I retire, I guess that'll be it. This'll be just another boarded-up business on Main Street. (Finishes haircut, gets mirror and holds it for Kid to see) There, how's that?

<u>Kid</u>: (Takes another long look) Better. Well, I'd stick around and rap with you, Pete, but I gotta get out to the community college and register for some classes before it's too late.

<u>Pete</u>: I thought you were going to Michigan State.

<u>Kid</u>: Nah, I changed my mind. I'm gonna stick around here. You know — take a few classes at the community college. I'll probably go to Michigan State my junior year. But I don't know.

<u>Pete</u>: What do your parents say? They both went to Michigan State. I thought they wanted you to . . .

<u>Kid</u>: They don't care if I live or die, Pete. All they care about is getting seats on the 50-yard line for the Michigan game.

<u>Pete</u>: Well, if I were you, Kid, I'd be sure and get a college degree. From what I read in the paper, you can't get a . . .

<u>Kid</u>: I don't see you going out and getting a college degree, Pete. I don't see a lot of people on MTV going out and getting college degrees, and they could buy and sell this stupid town ten times over.

<u>Pete</u>: Right, Kid. Who am I to give you advice?

<u>Kid</u>: Exactly, man. Now just get all these little hairs off of my neck, will ya?

<u>Pete</u>: (Sighs) Sure, kid. Hold still. (Pete carefully brushes hair off Kid's neck and ears) Gee, I wonder where Mr. Bluffington is? He's usually here by now. I'm going to have to send out the Mounties for him.

<u>Kid</u>: Didn't you hear?

<u>Pete</u>: Didn't I hear what?

<u>Kid</u>: The old fart died last week.

<u>Pete</u>: What?!? (Staggers back against mirror) I didn't see anything in the paper about it.

Kid: They didn't put anything in the paper. He blew out his liver from all that booze he drank. Family wanted to keep it all hush-hush.

Pete: But, he was a war veteran. He was . . .

Kid: They didn't want to make a big deal out of it, so they didn't. I'm surprised the guy lasted as long as he did. My old man says his liver was like totally shot, and I remember from biology class that that's the one organ you can't live without. I mean that and your heart, you know. Course, you probably couldn't last long without your lungs either, but you know what I mean.

Pete: But, he . . . I . . . did you go to the funeral?

Kid: Nah. But my parents did. They go to all the funerals in this town. You'd think my old man was the mayor or something. It was just immediate family and a few close friends. You know. But the cool thing was that Mr. Bluffington had requested that he be cremated. They scattered his ashes out on the golf course. I mean that's the ecological thing to do if you ask me. Stupid to take up all that land for cemeteries. You know?

Pete: (In a state of shock) I hear you, Kid. But why didn't anyone call me? I would have gone to . . .

Kid: You were just his barber, Pete. (Shrugs and tosses ROLLING STONE on magazine pile) That's all. Hey, it's no big deal. People die all the time. You know?

Pete: But his wife could have called me. She called me every time he was here and . . .

Kid: Chill out, Pete. You're making a big deal out of nothing. (Pete undrapes Kid, and he hops off the barber chair) What do I owe you, Pete?

Pete: How long have you been coming here, Kid?

Kid: Like Mr. Bluffington always said — since I was knee-high to a grasshopper. But I still don't know what I owe you.

Pete: It's on me this time.

Kid: What?!?

Pete: You heard me — it's on the house. Now get the hell out of here!! I'm closing for the rest of the day.

Kid: Sure, man. But i'm tellin' you, you're gettin' freaked out about nothin', because . . .

Pete: GO!!!!

Kid: All right, man. See you in three weeks unless you split a gut in the meantime. Jeez, Louise!! (Leaves in a blaze of youthful exuberance)

(Pete closes door behind Kid, hangs "closed" sign in window, pulls down window shades, turns off lights and television, and collapses in his barber chair where he finally releases the grief of a lifetime and sobs and sobs and sobs.)

(Lights fade, play ends)

Jimmy sat back and smiled at all that he had created. He knew it was good, and he could just picture opening night at Blue Star Players.

The steady stream of cars filing into the parking lot.

The buzz of excited patrons discussing this daring new work by the hottest playwright to illuminate the American stage since Tennessee Williams.

Then a dazzling performance by the very best actors in the Blue Star Players' stable.

Jimmy scratched his chin.

Yeah, he thought, Douglas Iglesia would do as Pete the barber. He'd do rather nicely. Even though he's a four-star, raving asshole, I'm sure . . .

"Jimmy!"

"What?"

"Keep it down over there — I'm still writing."

"But I just finished my play, Joyce. I was just thinking of who's going to be in the cast at Blue Star Players."

"Well, keep your thoughts to yourself, because I'm still at it."

Jimmy mouthed the immortal words of Horace Rumpole: "She who must be obeyed."

"What?"

"Nothing."

"Don't you nothing me. You just said something about she who must be obeyed, didn't you."

"Well, it's true, isn't it?"

"Jimmy, I'm trying to write."

"You're the one who's keeping the conversation going."

"Am not."

"Are too."

"Am not."

"Are too."

Joyce got up from her computer and stalked into Jimmy's writing booth. She grabbed his ear and said, "If you don't shut up this very second, I'll rip your ear off. Do you hear me?"

Jimmy nodded, and Joyce freed his ear.

Then there was silence in all the house as Joyce returned to her keyboard, and Jimmy took off down to the lake for a long, languid victory swim.

Chapter Six

Tiffany Ann Starbuck got around to paying Jimmy on a fairly regular basis, and the two of them put out a professional product every week.

And Jimmy never again identified the white mayor of South Haven as the black mayor of Covert in a photo caption. He wrote witty editorials about the wonders of the Kal-Haven bike trail between South Haven and Kalamazoo, the cool comfort of South Haven's very own Sherman's Ice Cream, and the need to preserve the Black River as a haven for God's feathered creatures.

Joyce pumped out newsletters for her client in Chicago, and the heat and humidity bore down on them both.

On one particularly oppressive July morning, Jimmy couldn't get his computer to boot up. He was going to print copies of *Last Haircut* to send to Martin Gregory in advance of the fateful August 18th meeting of the board of directors of the celebrated Blue Star Players.

"Shit!" Jimmy cursed.

"Keep it down over there, I'm trying to write," Joyce hissed.

"My computer won't boot up."

"Turn it off and try it again."

Jimmy turned it off and tried again.

Nada.

"Shit!"

"Jimmy, I'm trying to write."

"My computer won't boot up. It's so fucking humid in here, my computer won't boot up."

"Well, mine did. Maybe you should cover yours at night like I do. Now keep it down over there. I'm still — oh shit!"

"What's the matter?"

"My screen just went blank. No, wait — yes — no — shit!"

Jimmy rushed to Joyce's writing booth and watched as weird messages flickered across her monitor. Joyce hit various keys, banged her hard drive, and generally cursed a blue streak.

Jimmy took Joyce's phone and dialed a familiar number.

"Jimmy, what are you doing?"

"Calling information."

"Information? What . . ."

"Yes, do you show a listing in South Haven for a Klaus Williams?"

"Who are you calling?"

Jimmy shushed his wife and nodded grimly when the operator told him there was no listing for a Klaus Williams in South Haven. "How about Williams Heating and Air Conditioning. Could you try that?"

The operator did and hit the jackpot.

Jimmy took the number and dialed it before Joyce could utter another protest.

The crabby Slovak who had air-conditioned Burt Babbington's palace for the cast party answered on the 15th ring, muttering around a cigarette: "Williams Heating and Air Conditioning. Klaus speaking."

"Mr. Williams, this is Jimmy Clarke. I'm the playwright you met over at Burt Babbington's when you were . . ."

"I remember you. You were the one I was telling about how I seen that musical in Vienna after we got out of Czechoslovakia after them communists took over the country. You wrote a musical or somethin' too, didn't you?"

"It was just a play, Mr. Williams. No music."

"How can you have a play without music? I can't imagine a play with no singin'. Every play I ever been to had singin'. Course, I ain't been to that many plays. Just that one in Vienna I seen after we left Czechoslovakia when the communists took over. Course, it ain't Czechoslovakia no more. Now it's the Czech Republic and Slovakia, and I tell you them poor Slovak relatives of mine over there ain't got a pot to piss in because them damn Czechs kept all the good stuff for themselves."

"Mr. Williams?"

"What?"

"Uh, the reason I called is — well, I was wondering if you could come over and put in air-conditioning for us. It's so hot and humid here that our . . ."

"Tell me about it. I'm dying here. And all I got is this stupid fan that goes on the fritz about every five minutes." Klaus Williams kicked his stupid fan for emphasis and lighted a fresh filterless

Lucky Strike from the glowing stub in his mouth. "Hottest summer I can remember since I was in the army down in Texas. Now you want to talk about hot — that was hot. Ain't nothin' hotter than Texas in the summer. That's a kind of heat that would make the Devil himself sweat. And we didn't have no air-conditionin' in the barracks. Not even ceilin' fans or nothin'. But we was young and crazy — what did we care? See, I joined the U.S. Army because I was so grateful to America for givin' me my freedom and . . ."

"Mr. Williams?"

"Yeah?"

"Could you come over and put in some air-conditioning for us?"

Joyce stopped banging her hard drive and hissed, "Jimmy, we can't afford air-conditioning."

Jimmy covered the phone and hissed back, "Joyce, if we don't have air-conditioning we're not going to be able to earn a living. Neither of our computers are working because of the heat and humidity." Jimmy uncovered the phone and added, "How about coming over right now?"

"Well," Klaus Williams said, taking a long pull from his Lucky Strike, "I got so much work I don't even know where to start. That bed-and-breakfast on Blue Star Highway is having all kinds of problems with their system, and I got a system right here on my dining room table that I'm working on for a guy in Glenn, and there been five other calls just this mornin'. Not to mention the ones from yesterday. Plus, I been havin' problems with my kid — see, I went through a messy divorce, and the ex filed this suit for custody sayin' I'm some kind of bum, but now she's taken up with this new guy who ain't worth his weight in horse manure, and . . ."

"Mr. Williams?"

"Yeah?"

"Could you come over right now? Please?"

"You're that fella who wrote the musical or somethin', ain't you? Your voice is real familiar."

"That's because I met you at Burt Babbington's. Twice, actually."

"Yeah, your hair was all wet — like you just been swimmin' or something."

"That's because I had gone for a swim in Burt's pool."

"That's right – he had a swimming pool. And a tennis court, and a whole bunch of cars. Say, you wrote a musical or somethin' that they was gonna perform somewhere around here. And that Mr. Babbington guy was gonna be in it. He looks like an actor if you ask me. Maybe you could get me a ticket or somethin'. You bein' the playwright – you ought to be able to get me a ticket."

"I would, but we already performed the play, Mr. Williams. A couple of weeks ago, actually."

"Ah, well, when it's a big hit on Broadway, you be sure and get me a ticket in the front row. Then I'll tell everybody I known you when you weren't such a big shot."

"Right. You could also tell everybody you were the one who put in the air-conditioning system that enabled me to continue writing plays. How's that sound?"

"That sounds pretty good."

"Well, how about coming over and seeing what you can do for us. My wife's Slovakian, and she's been dying to meet you."

"You're wife's a Slovak?"

"Jimmy," Joyce hissed, "don't lie to him."

Jimmy shushed her and smiled into the phone. "That's right, Mr. Williams. Well, part Slovak. Her mother was from Slovakia. Her father was in the U.S. Army, and they met right after the war in Austria."

"Hey, I probably know her mother. What was her name?"

"Why don't you come over, and I'll have Joyce tell you all about her mother. And she's just making some of those little Slovakian pastries . . ."

"She's makin' badabumskis?"

"Yeah. Hot as it it, she's making badabumskis. With fresh peaches and blueberries and . . ."

"You know how long it's been since I had fresh badabumskis?"

"A long time, I bet."

"You bet it's been a long time. Well, I might be busier than a Russian with three bottles of vodka, but I always got time for fresh badabumskis. How you get to your place? Wait, let me get somethin' to write with. I just had a pencil around here a minute ago – ah, there it is. Okay, shoot."

Jimmy shot and got off the phone.

Joyce got right in his face. "What do you mean telling him I'm half Slovakian? And badabumskis — or however you say it? Where did you come up with that? I don't know the first thing about baking badabumskis."

"They have them at that bakery on Blue Star. Or something like it. I think they're Polish actually, but he'll never know. I'll run out and get some before he shows up. Chill out, Joyce. You're going to leave me a young widower if you don't calm down."

"I'm going to leave you a widower!!! Hah!! And where do you get off telling him to come over here and put in air-conditioning? We don't have enough money to afford . . ."

". . . 'groceries, let alone sewer and water. So how are we going to pay for air-conditioning?' I'm going to break through as a playwright, Joyce. Blue Star Players is going to make us rich and famous. Maybe even you'll start writing plays for them, and pretty soon we'll be getting calls from big-time Broadway producers and then . . ."

"Stop!!!"

"Why?"

"Because you're delusional. You're worse than when we started Byron Street Books."

"It's the Dunery Press now, Joyce. We live in Michigan now, Joyce, and . . ."

"I know we live in Michigan, and I know we renamed it the Dunery Press, but I also know it's been a huge crashing failure. We haven't made a single penny on the business that you said was going to make us rich, and now you're starting all over again with this stupid playwriting crap."

Jimmy pulled his wife's metaphysical arrow out of his heart and pressed bravely onward.

"Joyce," he said, "it's the heat and humidity that's affecting you. And all the work for your client. You're suffering from heat exhaustion. Believe me, when this guy comes over and puts in modern air-conditioning just like he did for Burt Babbington, we'll be in fat city. It'll be cool and dry in here, and our computers will boot up with no problem, and we'll crank out all kinds of great plays and . . ."

"Stop it!" Joyce put her hands to her ears and ran to the living room couch. She collapsed in a heap at the far end and shuddered violently. Then she lifted her eyes to the peak of their knotty pine ceiling and muttered, "Why can't we be rich? Why can't the MacArthur Foundation send us a big check for being geniuses?"

"Call your parents, Joyce. They're loaded. Kiss up to them, and they'll . . ."

"What, and tell them I'm a good little girl, and I didn't mean any of those things I told them after my sister torched herself in their garage. That they were normal, well-adjusted, happy, loving parents, and we were really this big, happy, well-adjusted fucking normal family in the suburbs living the American dream."

"Well, you don't have to go that far, but . . ."

"Why don't you call your dear old mother? Talk about loaded. What hostile elder tour is she off on now? Getting her fat old ass hauled around some European ruins while . . ."

"Joyce!!"

"You started it."

Jimmy sighed and headed for the door.

Joyce looked at him and asked, "Where are you going?"

"To the bakery to get some badabumskis, or whatever the hell they're called. I figured I'd have them heating up in the oven when Mr. Williams arrives so he'll think you just baked them."

"Jimmy, we can't afford badabumskis let alone air-conditioning."

"Joyce, we can't afford not to have air-conditioning. Unless you want to go back to writing on a manual typewriter. I don't think our clients would like that, and I sure know it would be a pain in the butt for plays."

Joyce exhaled the entire contents of her lungs into the living room and stared morosely at her exhaust.

Jimmy turned at the door and said, "Are you all right, Joyce?"

Joyce waved him away, saying, "Just go."

Jimmy went, but he carried with him the image of one totally miserable wife.

She'll be happy once we have air-conditioning, he decided as he maneuvered Angel Car out of Havencrest and into the real world. That's it. Yeah. A decent air-conditioning system like the guy put in for old Burt, and we're in fat city.

And Blue Star Players is going to do a bang-up job of producing
Last Haircut, and some scout from New York will be in the
audience, and the thing is going to have legs and . . .

"What did you say, dear?"

Jimmy blinked and saw that old Mildred Mackermyer was
walking along the road next to his car. She had obviously overhead
him talking to himself.

"Nothing, Mrs. Mackermyer," Jimmy said, blushing.

"Oh, you writers! Such eccentrics. Why Walter and I know this
real writer back in Ann Arbor who talks to herself all the time, and I
think . . ."

"Right," Jimmy said, punching the gas pedal.

He was at Ye Olde Swedish Bakery and Sweet Shoppe in no time
flat and asked the corn-fed beauty for a dozen of "those things
there."

"You mean the svenskapikas?"

"Yeah, whatever." They'll pass for badabumskis. Hell, one butter
encrusted piece of white doughy crap is the same in one dirt-bag
country as the other.

"I beg your pardon."

"Uh, I said—give me six peach and six blueberry. Okay?"

"Sure."

The young woman in white clutched at the glistening goodies
behind the counter, and Jimmy dug in his pocket for cash.

As he did so, a little man wearing thick glasses and a dark goatee
tugged at his sleeve.

Jimmy turned and said, "Yes?"

"You're the playwright, aren't you?"

"Yes?"

"The one who was written up in the papers a couple of weeks
ago?"

"Yeah, that was probably me."

"The one who did that play at Glenn Art Studio on July 2 and 3?"

"That's gotta be me, unless you're talking about a parallel
universe."

The little man with thick glasses and a dark goatee laughed
mirthlessly and got right to the point. "Well, I'm Dr. Peter Phillips,
and I'm the Director of Musicology and Youth Empowerment at

Saint Giles by the River Episcopal Church here in South Haven, and
I was wondering if you might not like to write a play for us. I
couldn't help but read in one of the articles on you that you had
spent some time in an Episcopal seminary, and, well, I've been
putting together a youth theatre program at Saint Giles by the River
Episcopal Church here in South Haven, and we we've come up with
a fine little piece of theatre from a woman priest in New York, but
we need something else to round out the program, and after what I
read about you in the paper — and Monica and I did intend to come
to see your little play, but something came up with her
daughter — well, I thought maybe I'd be able to lure you back to the
church by asking you to write a play for us. So what do you think?"
    Fame.
    Fortune.
    Broadway.
    The Great White Way.
    Film deals, interviews on NPR . . .
    "I beg your pardon."
    "Oh, sorry. Bad habit of mine."
    The little man with the thick glasses and dark goatee stared
clinically at Jimmy and said: "You were talking to yourself. You
know, I do a little hypno-therapy on the side. Maybe you'd like to
schedule an appointment with me, and we could work on some of
the underlying reasons for such pathological behavior."
    Jimmy blinked at the little man with glasses and the dark goatee.
Suddenly the bright lights of Broadway weren't shining so brightly.
    "Thanks, but no thanks. I've had enough therapy for one
lifetime."
    "Au contraire, mon frère. Nobody is done with therapy until
therapy is done with her, and it certainly appears that you have some
unresolved issues to explore. And no better medium in which to
explore than the penetrating world of hypno-therapy."
    God, a fucking talking brochure, Jimmy thought.
    "See, there you go again," the little man said, peering at Jimmy.
"You've got so many unresolved conflicts floating around in there
from your troubled childhood that they're manifesting themselves
inappropriately in public. Now, what do you say we make an
appointment for you right now, and . . ."

"I thought you were looking for a play."

"I am. But as a lay minister, I'm also looking to help my fellow person. Especially she or he who still suffers."

Jimmy groaned and plopped his cash on the counter. The fresh young thing took his money and went to make change.

"It's very kind of you, Mr. Peters, but . . ."

"It's Doctor. Doctor Phillips."

"You're a medical doctor?"

"No," he stammered, "a doctor of philosophy. I earned my Ph.D. at the University of Michigan. I wrote my dissertation on 'Comparative Musicology of Mass Cultures as Expressed in Sacred and Secular Modalities.' Perhaps you've read it — it's on file at the South Haven Public Library."

"Sorry, I haven't worked my way back to that shelf yet."

"Well, you should, because you'd discover from reading my rather insightful work that music is the engine that drives all of human affairs. And it has been from earliest recorded history right through to the present, and I see it taking on an even more vital role in our future affairs. Why, just look at the explosion of the so-called 'World Music' scene."

"Yeah, I listen to *Afro-Pop Worldwide* on NPR. Pretty hip stuff they play."

"And that's not the half of it," the little man said, his eyes widening.

The fresh young thing returned with Jimmy's change. Jimmy thanked her for her glistening svenskapikas, pocketed his money, and headed for the door.

"Wait," Dr. Peter Phillips, Ph.D. said.

Jimmy turned. "Wait for what? I'm not interested in therapy. I've had enough for one lifetime."

"We can talk about therapy some other time, but I want you to sign off on writing a one-act play for our Youth Empowerment program at Saint Giles by the River Episcopal Church here in South Haven."

Jimmy took his hand off the door handle. "A one-act play you say?"

"Yes, something that would run about 20 minutes and would complement the piece we have from this woman priest in New York.

She's an African-American lesbian, and her piece is a light-hearted monologue about the trials and tribulations of being an African-American-lesbian-feminist-Episcopal priest in an oppressive patriarchal society dominated by Euro-centric-Caucasian-heterosexual males."

"You mean white dudes like us?"

Dr. Peter Phillips, Ph.D. reddened. He cleared his throat and pressed on: "What we have in mind is something dealing with the history of the church. Maybe . . ."

"How about Thomas Cranmer?"

"Thomas Cranmer? You mean . . ."

"The Archbishop of Canterbury who was burned at the stake in 1556 for being a bad little Protestant boy."

"Did you say Protestant?"

"Yeah, as in the *Protestant* Episcopal Church. At least that's what they called it when I was growing up."

"Well, we don't call it that anymore. The General Convention dropped the 'P' word some time ago. It's obvious that you are seriously 'unchurched.'"

"Right. Well, if you want to get a 'churched' playwright to write something for you, be my guest." Jimmy grabbed the door handle and exited.

Dr. Peter Phillips, Ph.D. scurried after him and intercepted him at Angel Car.

"Sorry, I'm just expressing some of my own agenda. You see, I came to the Anglican Church from the Roman Church, and I've always considered myself a lower-case Catholic, and I still do. As do many others at Saint Giles by the River Episcopal Church here in South Haven. But as the Republicans are fond of saying, we have a big tent, and there's plenty of room for our, uh, lower-case Protestant sisters and brothers."

Jimmy exhaled. "Well, that's a relief. So you want me to write a play about Cranmer or not?"

"Oh, we do. Absolutely."

"Good. Because I've always been interested in him — you know, he was the author of the BOOK OF COMMON PRAYER and the one who got old Henry the Eighth off the hook with Catherine of Aragon, and . . ."

"I am quite aware of who Thomas Cranmer was."

"Good. Well, how about a play about his trial? I saw *A Man for All Seasons* not too long ago and was thinking Cranmer's story would be just as compelling as Thomas More's. I mean if the Catholics make such a big deal out of him for getting his head chopped off for refusing to recognize Henry as supreme head of the church in England, then we Protestants should celebrate the trial and burning at the stake of a true Protestant martyr, Thomas Cranmer. Author of the BOOK OF COMMON PRAYER and what eventually became the 39 articles, a Fellow of Jesus College, Cambridge, and an all-around nice guy."

Dr. Peter Phillips, Ph.D. swallowed hard. He had been working on swallowing hard as part of his own personal hypno-therapy, and it now enabled him to overcome the urge to strangle this impertinent, unchurched, fat lout of a pretentious, Protestant playwright.

"What was that?" Jimmy said.

"I beg your pardon."

"You were just talking to yourself."

"I was not."

"Well, it sure looked like you were."

"Really?"

"I'm afraid so, Doc."

Dr. Peter Phillips, Ph.D. frowned and picked nervously at his dark goatee. "Well, we all have our bad habits, don't we?"

"I guess so, Doc."

"Please don't call me that."

"What?"

"You know."

"You mean 'Doc.'"

"Yes."

"Fine. What should I call you?"

"Doctor Phillips would do rather nicely."

"But you're not a medical doctor. I only call medical doctors doctor. See, my wife Joyce went to the University of Chicago where they have more Ph.D.s per square inch than Iowa has corn per acre, and not one of them insisted on being called doctor. And we're talking about Nobel laureates and stuff like that."

Doctor Peter Phillips, Ph.D. puffed out his sunken chest and and forced a smile onto his face. "You like being difficult, don't you?"

Jimmy shrugged. "Sorry. I've just been through kind of a difficult period."

"I'm telling you — a couple of hypno-therapy sessions with me, and we'll get to the bottom of what's really bothering you. Plumb the depths of your troubled psyche."

I bet that's not all you'd like to plumb, Doc, Jimmy thought.

"What was that?"

"Nothing."

"I'll bet it was nothing," the good philosophical doctor said, licking his lips. "Well, I don't want to keep you any longer."

"Yeah, I've got to get back and heat these up for this air-conditioning guy so he thinks these are homemade badabumskis."

"But those are svenskapikas."

"Ah, one mess of lard-soaked white doughy crap is the same in one dirtbag country as it is in the other. He won't know the difference." Jimmy opened the door and tossed the sack of glistening goodies on the passenger seat. Then he turned and said, "So, you want me to write this play about Cranmer or not?"

Doctor Peter Phillips, Ph.D. tugged at his goatee and nodded. "Yes, I would like to see a play about Cranmer. I assume you'd work in the burning at the stake."

"How could you write a play about Cranmer and not work in his being burned at the stake? The place where he was turned to toast is marked by a bronze cross set in the street in Oxford. We're talking about one of the seminal events of the Reformation here. I mean, he called himself a 'Protestant candle.' You know that?"

Doctor Peter Phillips, Ph.D. yanked on his goatee and shook his head. Something he actually didn't know, but he couldn't admit it orally.

"So don't worry, I'll work in the burning at the stake bit. When do you want this?"

"How would three weeks be? I'm thinking of producing our afternoon of theatre in late September, and if you could get me ten copies of the script in three weeks, that would give me time to cast the play."

"I'm only thinking of having three characters."

"Excellent, because I don't think I could find more than three actors for your play. We have a rather small youth group at the moment, but that's the whole point of this program — to attract more young people to Saint Giles by the River Episcopal Church here in South Haven."

"Right. So you won't really need ten scripts. I mean it's expensive to . . ."

"No, come to think of it, I'll need twenty. Yes, why don't you have twenty printed up."

"Twenty?"

"Yes, twenty. And meanwhile, don't be a stranger at Saint Giles by the River Episcopal Church. We celebrate the Mass, or as you Protestants say — Eucharist, at 9 o'clock every Sunday morning."

"Right. Uh, what about money?"

"Money?"

"Yeah. As the playwright, I'd expect to get paid something. Not a lot mind you, but . . ."

"Oh, I think we could see our way to passing a collection plate for the playwright's pence. Would that suit you?"

Jimmy envisioned a packed church full of appreciatively generous Episcoes and their pals and nodded.

"Good, then I shall be looking forward to reading your play in three weeks." Doctor Peter Phillips, Ph.D. handed Jimmy his card and said, "Just deliver the scripts to the church or to my home. Do you know where Dunewood Acres is?"

"Drive by it all the time."

"We're the last house on Dune Meadow Lane. The one with the green roof and red mailbox."

"I'm sure I won't miss it."

"I'm sure you won't either."

Jimmy got in Angel Car, waved at Doctor Peter Phillips, Ph.D. and backed away from Ye Olde Swedish Bakery and Sweet Shoppe. He was fishing for first gear, when a spry woman with silver hair appeared from nowhere and rapped on the windshield.

"Wait!" she commanded in a trained voice.

Jimmy switched off the ignition, smiled and said, "I'm waiting."

The woman caught her breath, leaned down and said, "You don't know me, but I've read all about you in the paper. Your play *No*

Dice, I mean. At the Glenn Art Studio. Oh, I can't tell you how much I wanted to come and see it, but my ex was just like that dreadful lead in your play, and, well, I've been working on some serious co-dependency issues with my Alanon sponsor, and she didn't think it would be appropriate for me to see a play that dealt so forcefully with alcoholism as a family disease. I mean to tell you, it ravaged my family, and I'm still feeling the effects.

"And if I had gone to see your play, which by all accounts was absolutely marvelous, why I probably would have gone right up on stage and started enabling. It's in my nature, but I'm working on it — a day at a time, thanks to my higher power, whom I chose to call the White Goddess. But do listen to me ramble on. Here you are, trying to get out of the bakery — you've probably got company coming or something, and this crazy old woman appears out of the blue and just starts filling your ear with all of her problems."

Jimmy nodded, thinking he couldn't have said it any better.

"Well," the woman said, extending a bony hand, "I'm being awfully rude, aren't I? Here I am doing my usual ambush routine, and I haven't even introduced myself. I'm Jessica Springer, but call me Jess. All my friends do."

Jimmy took Jessica "call me Jess" Springer's hand and forced a smile. "Nice to meet you. I'm ..."

"Oh I know your name. It was splashed all over the paper. You're the new Eugene O'Neill. Wasn't that what that wonderful Maye Michaels wrote?"

"Something like that."

"Well, she got it right. Let me tell you." Jessica "call me Jess" Springer reclaimed her hand and squatted so she could talk face-to-face with the new Eugene O'Neill. "Anyway, I know you've got places to go and people to see, and don't we all in this crazy, topsy turvy world of ours, but I wanted to tell you that in addition to being a working actress — that's right I've had my Equity card for more than 30 years, and I'm on the road half of my life driving to Chicago or Detroit for commercial calls — half of which I don't get anymore because of the rampant ageism and sexism in this patriarchal society of ours, but we won't go into that — but what I wanted to tell you is that I've been hired part-time by the Glenn Consolidated High School to teach drama.

"They've never had a drama teacher before, you see—just this dreadful woman who'd come in and put on *Oklahoma, Music Man* and all the other war horses every fall. But this year, the principal has asked me to challenge the students. Have them sink their teeth into some contemporary drama with contemporary themes. And I've already picked out some dynamite scenes from this book of scenes for teens by this nifty woman from Oregon—Paula Peters or Petra Paulson or something like that. But I don't have enough for an entire evening, which is where you come in."

A fat Chicago tourist, or Tuna, appeared in a belching black BMW and signaled his desire for Jimmy's parking spot with a touch of his teutonic horn.

Jimmy waved merrily at the rich asshole and smiled so big and so wide at this wonderful Jessica Springer creature. God bless her, for she was the second person to sprinkle fame dust on him in the course of a single visit to Ye Olde Swedish Bakery and Sweet Shoppe.

"I better get going before this jerk has a heart attack," Jimmy said, "but if you want me to write a play or something, then I'm . . ."

"Oh, that would be wonderful. I was hoping you'd say yes. I'd need it in three weeks."

"Three weeks?"

"Yes. And twenty copies of the script. And it should be a one-act. No longer than 30 minutes. Contemporary theme. No music. Definitely no music. A one-act with as few props and scene changes as possible. And no more than four characters— the majority of whom should be females, because if there's one thing I've got plenty of at that high school is girls. Girls, girls, girls."

The Tuna touched his teutonic horn again, and Jimmy waved merrily at him. But Jessica "call me Jess" Springer sprang to her feet and charged at the BMW.

"Can't you see we're having a meeting here?!?" she screamed at the Tuna.

Terrified, the fat, balding Tuna powered up his tinted window and speed-dialed his Mommy on his car phone. He got her answering machine, so he clicked off and speed-dialed his favorite 900 phone sex number and clutched at his little pecker for comfort until the bad lady went away.

Jessica "call me Jess" Springer rubbed her palms in triumph and returned to the playwright's sensible little car. Just like hers, actually, except, of course, her Civic was a year newer, and much, much cleaner.

"Boy," Jimmy said, "you sure shut him up."

"Sweetie, when you've been around theatre as long as I have, you get used to giving good, orderly direction. Plus, Alanon has done wonders for my self-esteem. I'm no longer the doormat I was when I was trapped in that loveless marriage to that raving alcoholic who I enabled to drink like a fish and pretend he had a real career all those years. But the past is history, and the future is a mystery, and all we have is the here and now, and what I'm here now to say is I'm looking forward to getting twenty copies of your script in three weeks. That's not a problem, is it?"

Write two plays in three weeks, plus help the Tiffster get out the weakly weekly, not to mention grocery shopping, and laundry, and doing . . .

"Excuse me."

"Nothing."

"Your lips were moving, but I couldn't hear what you were saying."

Jimmy shrugged. "It's the strain of producing my first play. No, it won't be any problem getting you the play in three weeks. I was thinking of . . . " Jimmy looked around and saw a young woman with a Palisades Nuclear Power Plant emblem on her t-shirt and added, "Of, uh, doing something about a young woman who's just out of college, yeah, and her first job is working for this nuclear power plant in Michigan, yeah, and she's from Pennsylvania, and this is her first Christmas away from home, and she's really lonely and . . ."

"That sounds wonderful! Well, you'd better get back and hit those keys." Jessica "call me Jess" Springer handed Jimmy a card and said, "You can usually reach me at this number, but try me at this one if you can't, or this one if I don't answer at the other two, otherwise try the school office, but they're terrible at giving messages."

"How about if I just bring the scripts over to the principal's office when I'm finished, and you can call me?"

"That would work. As long as you put your phone number on the scripts."

"I always do."

"Well, I don't want to keep you any longer." Jessica "call me Jess" Springer extended her bony hand and added, "It's been such a pleasure talking with you, Clarke."

"Clarke?" Jimmy said, taking her hand in his.

"Yes, that's your name isn't it?"

"My last name actually. My first name's James, but please call me Jimmy."

"Jimmy is a little boy's name. I'll call you Jim."

Jimmy smiled tightly, squeezed the woman's hand and broke free. "Three weeks," he said.

"Three weeks," Jessica "call me Jess" Springer said.

Jimmy fired up Angel Car, shifted into reverse, eased out the clutch and backed away from the bakery. Then he braked abruptly, stuck his head out the window, and called, "What about money? We didn't discuss money."

Jessica "call me Jess" Springer shrugged merrily and said, "Oh, don't worry about money. I have a discretionary budget – we'll see that you're well rewarded for your efforts. Now all you have to do is get home and hit those keys, Jim."

Jimmy nodded at her and backed away from Ye Olde Swedish Bakery and Sweet Shoppe and hit the beautiful Blue Star Highway with the refrain from Joyce's favorite "fame" song looping in his head: "I'm gonna be in the movies, mm hm, they're gonna make a big star outta me, mm hm. Oh, I'm gonna be in the movies, mm hm, they're gonna make a big star outta me . . ."

Chapter Seven

When Jimmy returned to the Dunery, he caught Klaus Williams in the act of captivating his soft-hearted wife by showing her his hernia.

"See," the chain-smoking Slovak said, lifting his shirt, "I got to wear this belt, otherwise the stupid thing just pops out on me. One time, I was all the way under this bed-and-breakfast on the Blue Star when the thing popped out on me. I was puttin' in duct work, see, and I was all the way under — as far away from the hatch as you could get, and my stupid flashlight was goin' on the fritz on account of my stupid kid had used it the night before without tellin' me, so there I was with spiders and God knows what else crawlin' all over me — and you know we got black widows and brown recluses in this part of Michigan — I mean, one bite and I coulda been a goner."

"So what did you do?" Joyce asked, absolutely mesmerized.

"Well," the wizened little air-conditioning man said, "I done the only thing I could think of — I rolled over on my back, and I tucked that stupid hernia in with my fingers. Then I slid outta there on my butt, got in my truck and drove myself over to the hospital."

"What'd they do at the hospital?" Joyce said, barely glancing at her husband.

"They wanted to operate on the spot. Cut me and fix it once and for all, but I told 'em I didn't have no insurance, and that stopped 'em cold. Plus, as long as I wear my belt, I'm fine. But I wasn't wearin' my belt that day, but now I wear it every day."

Jimmy cleared his throat and stepped all the way into the living room.

Klaus Williams lowered his shirt, fired up a fresh Lucky Strike with his Zippo and picked tobacco out of his teeth. He nodded at Jimmy and said, "You got a real nice place back here. I never known that such a nice place existed back here. I mean, I drove by eight million times, and you'd never know such a nice place is back here. I mean, from the way it looks from the highway, it's just some garbage dump or somethin' back here. Not somethin' nice like what you got here."

"Yeah," Jimmy said, "we're real happy with it. So, Mr. Williams, have you been telling Joyce about how you can put in a really wonderful air-conditioning system for us like you did for Burt Babbington?"

Joyce shook her head sharply at her husband and said, "Why don't you go heat those up in the oven, Jimmy?"

"But . . ."

"Just heat them up. I told Mr. Williams the truth, Jimmy. I told him that I'm not half Slovakian, and that I don't make whatever you call those things."

"Badabumskis," Mr. Williams offered.

"Exactly. And that you'd gone to the Swedish bakery to get those Swedish things, and he said that would be just fine with him, so why don't you go heat them up and make some of your killer coffee, and I'll continue talking to Mr. Williams."

"All right. But what about air-conditioning? What kind of system can you do for us?"

Klaus Williams studied the glowing end of his cigarette for clues. Then he sat back on the couch and declared, "Geothermal."

Jimmy and Joyce looked at him as though he were Zeus uttering a godly decree from Mount Olympus.

"Geothermal?" Jimmy and Joyce said.

"Yeah," Mr. Williams said, "I could do a prototype system for you people that would cut your electric bill so low, the power company would think you're runnin' an auxiliary generator or somethin'. Not that some people don't do such things — one of my old army buddies is off the grid. Got himself a place up in northern Wisconsin. Lives completely off the land. Has the solar panels, a woodstove, and grows all his own food, and bags himself a couple of good-sized deer that he dresses down for meat, plus all them rabbits and fish and what have you, and he just basically told the power company and the phone company and the gas company and everybody else to take a flyin' leap off a big cliff. Me, I'd like to go that route someday, but I got so many problems with my ex, and my no-good kid, and this nursing home where my mother was before she passed on — took me for thirty grand, and I've been after them for four years now and haven't seen a cent of it, and . . ."

"Time-out, Mr. Williams," Jimmy said, signaling time-out.

"Jimmy," Joyce said, "go heat those up and make some coffee. I told you, I'd talk to Mr. Williams."

That's just the problem, Jimmy realized. This dirt-bag has poor old Joyce in his thrall, and she's between books and winding up her current newsletter for her client, which means she's ready to take on a poor-soul project, and this character would keep ten Mother Theresa's working overtime, and . . .

"Jimmy, stop talking to yourself and go heat those up and make some coffee."

"I wasn't talking to myself."

"Yes, you were. Now go to the kitchen and cook."

"That's right," Klaus Williams said, relaying to a fresh cigarette from the remains of the last one, "you were talking to yourself at that Babbington guy's log cabin or whatever that place was. That Babbington guy said maybe you should see a shrink or somethin'."

"I've seen all the shrinks I need to see for one lifetime."

"I don't know," Joyce said, looking at her husband with concern and irritation. "Why don't you go to the kitchen and heat those up and make some . . ."

"Killer coffee. Yes, dear."

Jimmy sighed enormously and went to the kitchen where he threw the svenskapikas in the oven and made some of his killer coffee. The kind that puts hair on the chest of blushing maidens.

When he returned to the living room with the goodies ten minutes later, he found his wife ready to follow Mr. Williams in search of the Congo dinosaur.

"Oh, Jimmy, Mr. Williams has been telling me all about this wonderful system he's going to design for us. We're going to be his laboratory, and the genius of the system is that it's going to use groundwater as the heating and cooling medium, and groundwater maintains a constant temperature throughout the year."

Jimmy poured Mr. Williams a cup of his killer coffee and settled in his favorite chair. "That sounds great," he said, "but will we have air-conditioning this summer? Because, our computers wouldn't boot up this morning . . ."

"No problem," Mr. Williams said, sipping the coffee. "You'll never have no more problems with your computers again. Say, what'd you put in this coffee — motor oil or somethin'?"

"Jimmy gets his coffee Fed-Exed all the way from Seattle, don't you?"

"Yes."

"Well, they must put motor oil or somethin' in there with it, because this is the strongest coffee I had since I was in the army."

"If you don't like it, Mr. Williams, I can . . ."

"No, it's fine. It's just stronger than what I'm used to is all." Mr. Williams fingered a warm blueberry svenskapika and rammed it into his mouth. It was down the hatch before Jimmy or Joyce could blink. Then the amazing Mr. Williams took a big gulp of scalding coffee and a long drag from his Lucky Strike, all in one seamless motion. The man had an oral fixation that just didn't quit.

"So, getting back to this wonderful air-conditioning system you're going to design for us, Mr. Williams. Is . . ."

"It's also a heating system, Jimmy," Joyce said, jumping in. We're going to have moist heat in the winter and cool dry air in the summer, and it's all going to run off groundwater. Isn't that right, Mr. Williams?"

"That's right. Your problems will be over. You can sit in here on a hot and miserable day like today and just thumb your noses at all the other poor slobs around here what don't got no air-conditioning, because my system is gonna keep you so cool and dry, you'll wonder why you didn't call me sooner."

"That sounds great, Mr. Williams," Jimmy said. "So when can you start? How about today? No time like the present."

"Yeah, that's what they always said back in my village in Slovakia. Did I tell you about them German soldiers what used to give us candy? They was half-starvin' themselves by the end of the war, but we'd go out there and hold our hands out, and they'd give us candy. Practically the only thing they had to eat, and they'd give us candy out of their rucksacks. Yep. But not them Red Army soldiers what supposedly 'liberated' us after the Germans left.

"Biggest bunch of barbarians you ever seen. I seen one of 'em drinkin' out of a toilet. That's right. He was one of them slanty-eyed ones from Siberia or somewhere, and I guess he never had no toilets where he was from, and when he saw his first one in our village, he got down on his knees and drank out of it like a dog. Me and some of the other kids was hiding and watchin', and one of the kids burst out laughin' — I mean you couldn't help yourself 'cause it was the funniest damn thing you ever seen. But that Russian or whatever he was didn't think it was so funny when he heard my little friend laughin', and he found my friend, and pulled him out and shot him dead. Right there. While the rest of us watched.

"People talk about how bad the Germans were, but they never done nothin' like that in our village. Nothin'. Well, they carted off some Jews at the beginning, but nobody liked them much anyway, and they said they took 'em to some fancy camp somewhere where they sat around and ate caviar from the Red Cross and what have you."

Klaus Williams sighed, stuffed another svenskapika in his mouth, devoured it in a gulp, chugged half a cup of hot coffee, and relayed to another Lucky Strike.

Jimmy raised his eyebrows at Joyce, but it was in vain. The woman was awestruck by the pure pathos that was Mr. Klaus Williams, heating and air-conditioning contractor supreme.

Jimmy sighed and said, "That's quite a story, Mr. Williams, but when do you think you can have our air-conditioning system up and running?"

"Jimmy, Mr. Williams was telling a story."

"Yeah, but you're finished, aren't you, Mr. Williams?"

"I'm never finished with my stories. You see, every time I tell 'em, I remember some new detail. Like what that kid was wearing. The one that Russian or whatever he was shot. He had this shirt one of the German soldiers give him. That nice wool the Germans make. Not rough, but soft. Yeah, a real soft wool. Comfortable and warm. And it was green. The color of the pine trees. I remember that green. And the blood. You never seen so much blood come out of a little kid. Didn't think it was possible, but it was. See, that Russian or whatever he was, shot the kid right in the heart.

"Then he just walked away like all he had done was swat a fly or somethin'. When he was gone, we come out of our hiding places and tried to save our friend. But there was blood pumpin' out of his chest like a geyser. Like one of them things me and the ex seen at Yosemite that time we drove all the way out there to have a nice family vacation for our kid. Course, lot of good it did — she divorced me anyway, and the kid turned out rotten, and . . ."

"Mr. Williams!!"

Mr. Williams and Joyce blinked and looked at Jimmy.

Jimmy inhaled and said: "Mr. Williams, we need air-conditioning! Right now!! Which is why I called you. Because I saw what a great job you did putting in air-conditioning right away for Burt Babbington, I figured you could do the same for us. And it's absolutely essential that we have air-conditioning immediately, because our computers wouldn't boot up this morning, and if our computers don't boot up, then we can't work because we're both writers, and if we don't work, we don't make money, and if we don't make money, we'll starve. So what do you say, Mr. Williams? How about starting on our wonderful geothermal air-conditioning system right now? Since you're already here."

"Well," Klaus Williams said, taking a long pull from his Lucky Strike, "like I told you on the phone — I got so much work I don't even know where to start. That bed-and-breakfast on Blue Star Highway is having all kinds of problems with their system, and I got a system on my dining room table that I'm working on for a guy in Glenn, and I had five other calls before you called. Not to mention the ones from yesterday. Plus, I been havin' problems with my kid — see, I went through a messy divorce, and the ex filed this suit so that . . ."

"Mr. Williams!!"

This time it was Joyce, and she was just as exasperated as her husband.

"Yes?" the wizened air-conditioning man said.

"How about if you at least take a look around and see what it'll take to put in this geothermal system you're talking about? As long as you're here."

Mr. Williams stubbed out his Lucky Strike in the salad bowl Joyce had provided as an ashtray and shrugged. "Yeah, that would be a good idea. As long as I'm here, I might as well take a look around and see what it'll take to put in a geothermal system for you good people."

Jimmy sprang to his feet, took Mr. Williams by the arm and led him on a tour of the tiny Dunery. Naturally, Joyce tagged along and put in her 50 cents worth every chance she got.

At tour's end, Mr. Williams flamed up another Lucky Strike and declared the following: "Well, if I can get this guy Gus to work for me — he's one of them A.A. people you see — well, one week he goes to A.A. and the next he falls off the wagon or whatever they call it and gets himself so stinking drunk he looks like them Russians or whatever they were what liberated my village at the end of the war. Anyway, if he's sober this week, and I'm pretty sure it was last week he was drunk, then I'll get a hold of him, and we'll come out tomorrow, and I'll get him under your house and put in the duct work. Me, I'm getting too old for crawlin' under houses, plus with my hernia — even with the belt, but Gus'll go anywhere. He was in Vietnam, see. One of them tunnel rats what crawled down them holes the Viet Cong dug all over the place, and blew 'em to kingdom come.

"But one thing you don't want to holler when Gus is under your house is: 'fire in the hole.' See, he told me that's what they said when they planted the charges in them tunnels the Viet Cong dug all over God's creation and . . ."

"What's all this going to cost us, Mr. Williams?" Jimmy interrupted.

Mr. Williams eyes twinkled and his mind immediately calculated the cost of that new "previously owned" Chevy panel truck he had seen on the lot of Rudy's Really Good Motors on the Blue Star. "Well, if you could give me a check for three grand now, and another three grand in a month, that ought to do it."

Jimmy was resigning himself to a life without air-conditioning when Joyce cheerily chirped: "I'll write you a check on that credit card account we have."

"What credit card account we have?" Jimmy whispered.

"Don't you remember?"

"All I remember is we crashed all our credit cards."

"Yeah, but right at that time, we got that pre-approved application for Discover. 'Discover new debt.' Remember?"

"Vaguely."

"Well, we can write up to $7,000 in checks against our account, so I'll just write a check for the whole amount. How's that sound, Mr. Williams?"

Sounded great to Mr. Williams, but Jimmy wanted to know how Joyce was going to swing this.

"Don't worry," she said, "I'll just reshuffle the numbers. It'll all work out. You'll see."

With that, she wrote a credit card for $6,000 payable to Klaus Williams and handed it to the wizened air-conditioning man with the glowing eyes and Lucky Strike.

He promised to return on the morrow with the legendary Gus and departed in haste for Rudy's Really Good Motors on Blue Star Highway.

"Well, that solves the air-conditioning problem," Joyce said, waving at Mr. Williams' dust.

"I don't know."

"What do you mean, you don't know? Jimmy, the man is a fellow artist. He's a kindred spirit. A rebel with a cause. He's just like us — a misunderstood genius. I could have listened to him all day."

"I've already heard all his stories at Burt's, Joyce, and believe me, the guy is a broken record. Let's just hope he's as good as his word."

"He came through for Burt, didn't he?"

"Yeah, he sure did. Although he got it all done with seconds to spare as I recall."

"Don't worry, Jimmy. He'll be here first thing tomorrow with his friend Gus, and we'll have air-conditioning within a week. Two at the most."

Jimmy waved his hand in front of Joyce's face.

"What are you doing?" she said, swatting his hand away.

"Checking to see if you're having hot flashes or something."

"I'm too young for menopause."

"You never know. Maybe all the toxins in the lake have caused you to . . ."

"Jimmy!!"

"What, Joyce?"

"Would you knock it off and go for a swim or something?"

"Actually, I'd rather go to the library."

"Why the library?"

"For one thing, it's air-conditioned. For another, I ran into two people at the bakery who basically commissioned me to write original plays for them. And they both want the plays within three weeks."

"What?"

Jimmy told Joyce all about his encounters at Ye Old Swedish Bakery and Sweet Shoppe with Dr. Peter Phillips, Ph.D., and Jessica "call me Jess" Springer.

Then before his wife could negate his positive feelings about his playwriting potential, he sprang off to the delightfully air-conditioned South Haven Public Library where he found sufficient material to write the following introduction to his one-act play about Archbishop Thomas Cranmer:

"Although inspired by the events surrounding the execution in 1556 of the Archbishop of Canterbury, Thomas Cranmer, this play is not bound by them.

"For the record, Cranmer was a Fellow of Jesus College, Cambridge and made Archbishop of Canterbury in 1532. He annulled Henry VIII's marriage to Catherine of Aragon and pronounced a similar judgment on Henry's marriage with Anne Boleyn three years later. Each queen bore but one child . . . Catherine delivered Mary I, and Anne produced Elizabeth I. Henry's third wife, Jane Seymour, bore him his long-awaited male heir — Edward VI.

"After Henry's death, Cranmer was one of the most influential counselors to Edward VI, and advanced the Reformation in England. He was chiefly responsible for the decidedly Protestant versions of the BOOK OF COMMON PRAYER . . ."

Jimmy lifted his Parker fountain pen from the legal pad and nodded.

"Common Prayer," he whispered. "I'll call the play *Common Prayer.*"

He wrote his title on the top of the page and continued thusly:

". . . that appeared in 1549 and 1552. Mary ascended the throne in 1553. One of her first acts as queen was to repeal her half-brother's Protestant legislation, bringing Cranmer into immediate conflict with her. He was excommunicated by the Pope and degraded of his church office before being burned at the stake on March 21, 1556."

Jimmy went on to list his primary sources, and then created the setting and characters for his passion play. To wit:

"THE PLACE: England. The throne room of Mary I, Queen of England; the jail cell of Archbishop Thomas Cranmer in the Tower of London; the site of his execution by burning at the stake.

"THE TIME: 1556, the year of Cranmer's execution.

"THE PLAYERS:

"The Queen, Mary I, Queen of England. Wears red satin robe and a ruby crucifix.

"The Intercessor, The Queen's messenger to the Archbishop. Wears white cowl and a wooden crucifix.

"The Archbishop, Thomas Cranmer, Archbishop of Canterbury. Wears black academic gown and silver crucifix.

"(At rise, the Queen is seated on her throne at stage left. There is a wooden stake at center stage with piles of bound kindling on either side. The Archbishop sits writing at a simple wooden stable at stage right. There is an empty chair opposite him. Spotlights are directed at the Queen, Archbishop and stake. All else is in utter darkness. The Intercessor draws within the Queen's light and bows.)"

Jimmy looked at all he had written and beheld that it was very good. Very good indeed.

Then he proceeded to write the entire passion play in one sitting. In air-conditioned comfort, of course.

And when my computer doesn't boot up tomorrow because of the heat and humidity, I'll come back here and write the happy Christmas play for Jessica "call me Jess" Springer.

And everybody will love what I wrote, and by the end of the year, I'll have three more plays produced and it's not unreasonable to expect that a Broadway scout will be in the audience of at least one of them, and/or a Hollywood producer, and it's just a matter of time before . . .

"Shush!"

Jimmy blushed at the earnest little girl down the table with the stack of thick books with tiny print and an annoyed look on her face.

"Sorry," Jimmy said to the Joyce-in-training.

"How can a person read with you making all that racket?"

"You're right. Sorry."

But Jimmy wasn't sorry. He was glad he had said all he had, because he believed in his heart that he was destined to be a famous playwright.

In a matter of weeks, if not months, and if I play my cards correctly, then . . .

"Shush!"

Jimmy blushed, went home and jumped in the cool, blue lake.

All the while singing softly to himself: "I'm gonna be in the movies, mm hm, they're gonna make a big star outta me, mm hm. Oh, I gonna be in the movies . . ."

Chapter Eight

Miracle of miracles: the weather took a turn for the cool and dry on the morrow, enabling Jimmy and Joyce to happily boot up.

Jimmy keystroked *Common Prayer* into his awaiting hard drive, and then, when Joyce was finished writing for the morning, he printed up hard copies of *The Last Haircut* and *Common Prayer.*

Then, as he was dashing out the door to take the plays to the local speed-o-print, he bumped into Mr. Klaus Williams and the amazing Gus.

Jimmy raised his eyes to the heavens and rejoiced.

"You're talkin' to yourself again," Mr. Williams said, relaying to a fresh Lucky Strike.

"Sorry," Jimmy said.

But he wasn't sorry.

No, he was delighted at how things were turning out on this fresh and pure morning in late July. So full of promise, so full of life, so full of an air-conditioning man who actually came when he said he was going to come.

Well, it was a bit on the sunny side of 11 o'clock, but the guy's here, and he brought . . .

"What's that?"

"Nothing."

"You know," Mr. Williams said, "that Babbington guy was right — you ought to see a shrink about that. You know there were some good ones in Vienna. Or so I heard. Not that I'd ever go to see one of them people myself. Course, my ex goes. Tried to get me to go when we was still hitched up. Said it would have saved our marriage, but the only thing that would have saved our marriage was a good kick in the butt. And I don't mean me. I mean her. But that's not the way you do things here in America.

"But back in the old country, when a woman got out of line, why the husband was perfectly within his rights to give her a good kick in the butt, and no judge in his right mind would ever say there was . . ."

"Mr. Williams?"

"Yeah?"

"Is this the amazing Gus you were telling us about yesterday?"

"Oh yeah. That's Gus." Mr. Williams jerked his thumb at a rotund "Michigan Hillbilly" in a stained Detroit Tigers t-shirt, John Deere ballcap with adjustable strap shown to advantage, torn and leaking blue jeans, fully vented sneakers, and a mouth full of rotten teeth and gums that would have caused an entire dental school to go running into the woods, shrieking: "Run away, run away!!"

"Nice to meet you, Gus," Jimmy said, waving.

Gus grunted and spit something foul into Jimmy's overgrown yard.

Mr. Williams explained, "He ain't on the wagon this week. I thought he would be, but he ain't. It was all I could do to get him out here this morning. Best thing — don't talk to him. I'll just get him under your house — maybe tell him that he's back in Vietnam lookin' for them little Viet Cong — and he'll be happy as a fly on a fresh pile of horse shit."

"Yeah, I bet he will. Look, I've got to go into town and make copies of these plays and . . ."

"That's right. They was gonna perform your play or somethin', and that Babbington guy was gonna be in it, but I remember you sayin' there weren't no songs in your play, which is kind of funny because the only play I ever seen was in Vienna, and it had lots of nice songs in it. I don't know how you can have a play with no singin' in it. Just don't make no sense to me, but then a whole lot of what's goin' on in this crazy world don't make no sense to me. Only thing I know, is they shoulda let Ronald Reagan stay in office. Now there was a man you could trust. And that old cowboy sure told them Russian bastards where to get off. Had 'em shakin' in their boots. That's what we need right now is good old Ronald Reagan back in office where he can tell them no-good . . ."

"Mr. Williams?"

"Yeah?"

"You need anything from me before I leave?"

"Why would I need anything from you? You know anything about air-conditioning?"

"No, but . . ."

"Then I don't need nothin' from you. Your missus home?"

"Yes, but . . ."

"I need some coffee or somethin', I'll rap on the door and ask her. Bet she don't make coffee so it tastes like motor oil."

"Actually, she makes it just the way I do."

"I can't believe that."

"Well, she does. Ask her to make you some coffee if you don't believe me. I'd stick around and chat, but I know you're anxious to get started on our system, and I've got a whole bunch of places to go, so . . ."

"Only reason I come out here today with Gus was because your wife was such a nice lady. Other people I work for — well, they're not so nice. Especially them Jews. What is it with them people — money, money, money, money. Jeez! And they want everything right away. Don't even give me a chance to talk. Just order me around like I was some stupid dog or something."

"You can be assured we won't treat you like that here, Mr. Williams."

"And that's why I come out here at the crack of dawn. With Gus no less. And it ain't like I got nothin' else to do. Like I told you yesterday — I go so much work I don't even know where to start. That bed-and-breakfast on Blue Star Highway is having all kinds of problems with their system — and I'll probably have to run over there this morning to see what I can do, and I got a system on my dining room table that I'm working on for a guy in Glenn, and . . ."

"I'm outta here, Mr. Williams," Jimmy said, heading for Angel Car. "I'll look forward to having air-conditioning when I come back this afternoon."

"Yeah, sure," Mr. Williams said in a voice that wasn't so sure.

Jimmy ignored the note of uncertainty because he was desperate for air-conditioning. He had lived his whole life without it, chiefly because his alcoholic father had squandered the family fortune on weekly caseloads of good scotch, gin, vodka, tonic, club soda and ginger ale. "Big Jim" Clarke didn't have a dime to spare to air-condition the big, brick house at 322 Forest Drive in Wynnwood, Pa., much less heat the damn brick pile. The old man had been too pickled through the year to experience the changing of the seasons in suburban Philadelphia, much less feel the heat or cold.

Never mind that the neighbors on both sides had
air-conditioning. Never mind that they both had big, brick houses
that also seemingly defied modern air-conditioning.

James Gordon Clarke II decreed that it was good enough for his
father not to have air-conditioning, therefore it was good enough for
him, his long-suffering wife, Louise Maye Clarke, and for his
worthless, no-good, lay-about, lout of a son, James Gordon Clarke
III, to endure without. Stiff upper lip and all that.

Then James Gordon Clarke II would pour himself another gin
and tonic, repair to the living room where the neighborhood drunks
had assembled for the nightly "grown-up time" and listen to their
overly generous host do his pathetic best to bring Winston Churchill
back to life.

Jimmy was merely expected to be "seen and not heard" and to
greet the "guesties" at the door, take their coats, and be sure their
drinks were filled at all times and then just go off and die
somewhere.

Jimmy shuddered and got in his car. He shifted into reverse,
backed away from the Dunery, shifted into first and puttered up the
road to the land beyond Havencrest.

He was muttering to himself about air-conditioning when he
pulled alongside Mildred Mackermyer. She was out for one of her
constitutionals and couldn't help but notice that Havencrest's most
famous playwright was talking to himself again.

"Oh, you writers," she exclaimed. "Always writing out loud. How
interesting."

"Yes," Jimmy said, blushing and accelerating.

He blanked his mind, cranked up the local classical music station
to a zippy Tchaikovsky tune, and drove directly to the speed-o-print
where he had copies of his two plays made. While he waited, he
wrote a letter to Martin Gregory explaining that he was charging $20
for the first performance of *The Last Haircut* and $15 for each
subsequent performance. He made a copy for himself, paid for the
scripts when they were ready and left one bundle at the doorstep of
the Blues Star Players on Blue Star Highway and the other in the red
mailbox outside the last house on Dune Meadow Lane in Dunewood
Acres. The one with the green roof and belonging to the noteworthy
Dr. Peter Phillips, Ph.D.

Jimmy then treated himself to a sensible, low-cost luncheon at the South Haven Subway franchise, carefully saving all appropriate coupons.

Satisfied with all he had accomplished and certain of his impending success and fame as a playwright, Jimmy drove back to the Dunery to join Joyce in celebrating the advent of air-conditioning.

What he found, however, were: Mr. Williams' tire tracks, a huge pile of sandy soil beside the house, two discarded shovels, and a thoroughly un-air-conditioned house.

"Where'd they go?!?" Jimmy asked Joyce as he came in the door.

"Somebody from that bed-and-breakfast on Blue Star called Mr. Williams here and said their system was completely down, plus their refrigerator was on the fritz, and all their meat was going to go bad, so they went over there. But he said they'll be right back."

Jimmy smiled gamely. It was still dry, but getting hot again. Degree by maddening degree.

"Right back?!? When was that?!?"

"Jimmy, we'll have air-conditioning. All right?"

"No, Joyce, it's not all right. The guy said he'd have our system in in no time, and I come back and he's already gone. Just a pile of sand out there and some shovels and tire tracks. Maybe I was wrong to call him. Maybe I should call a real air-conditioning contractor."

"Maybe you should just stop trying to get produced as a playwright."

"What?!?"

"You heard me."

"Thanks a lot, Joyce."

"All I'm saying is you're setting yourself up for some major disappointments."

"How can you say that? Yesterday, two complete strangers asked me to write plays for them, and Blue Star Players commissioned me to write an original work which . . ."

Jimmy's phone rang.

It was Martin Gregory, and he had stopped by Blue Star Players and found the package containing copies of *The Last Haircut* and Jimmy's note.

"Everything looks great," Martin Gregory said. "I see no problem with your terms. Just a formality for the board to approve. And from what I've seen skimming through your play, it looks like a real blockbuster. We're going to have a real hit on our hands."

"You think so?"

"I know so. Well, I've got to run. Eight thousand things to do today, but I'll see you on August 18th."

"Yeah, I'm looking forward to it."

Jimmy cradled the phone and turned to Joyce. "See. The phone rings, and it's destiny."

Joyce exhaled and just walked away.

"Where are you going?"

"For a walk."

"Can I come?"

"I'd prefer to walk alone."

"Fine. Have it your way."

Joyce exited stage center, and Jimmy went to his computer. The damn thing booted up on the first try, and he set right to work on his cheery play for Jessica "call me Jess" Springer.

Cheery Christmas play, Jimmy thought.

About a young woman from Pennsylvania away from home for the first Christmas in her life because she's just gotten this job for this power company in Michigan and . . .

The phone rang or whatever sound the modern things make when they interrupt whatever you're doing. Whenever they damn well feel like it.

Jimmy answered to an ecstatic Dr. Peter Phillips, Ph.D. who had just found his packet of plays in his red mailbox.

"I'm skimming a script as I speak," Dr. Peter Phillips, Ph.D. said, skimming a script as he spoke. "And I must say — you've got a winner on your hands here. It'll work beautifully with the monologue we already have about the trials and tribulations of an African-American-lesbian-feminist Episcopal priest in an oppressive patriarchal society dominated by Euro-centric-Caucasian-heterosexual males. The whole point of the program is to attract more young people to Saint Giles by the River Episcopal Church here in South Haven, and I now feel, after skimming your fine little play here, that we have just the program to accomplish our goal. Now all I need to do is get a cast for your play. Any suggestions?"

"Don't you have anyone at Saint Giles who could . . ."

"Not really."

Jimmy thought for a moment and then offered: "How about Maye Michaels? She's an Episcopalian and she's . . ."

"I'm quite familiar with Maye Michaels. You can't go to a diocesan conference and not be harangued by Maye Michaels about the need to end oppression of women right now."

"Yeah, that sounds like good-old Maye. But she did one hell of a job in my play *No Dice,* and I was thinking if you're having a hard time casting *Common Prayer*, you could ask Maye to play the queen, and you and I could take the other roles."

"That sounds doable."

"Yeah. So let's do that."

"Fine. I'll phone Maye today and set something up. Then I'll firm up the date for the program at Saint Giles by the River Episcopal Church here in South Haven and get back with you."

"Great."

"Bye for now."

"Bye for later, too."

Jimmy gave the phone a high-five and returned it to its cradle.

Then he set to work on his cheery Christmas play for Jessica "call me Jess" Springer. He began by giving it the zippy title of *Carol's Christmas* and then pounded out the following:

THE PLACE: Carol Kane's efficiency apartment, 2C, in Sweetbriar Village in Johnsville, Michigan.

THE TIME: Christmas Eve in the present

THE PLAYERS:

Carol Kane, 23, "road tech" at the Bakertown Nuclear Plant in Bakertown, Michigan. Single. Short hair. From Paoli, Pennsylvania. A brainy jock — played soccer at Lehigh University.

Julio the pizza deliveryman, 33. Mexican-American. Looks like an Aztec warrior in an old overcoat. Has a pronounced Midwest accent.

Mrs. James S. (Consie) Kelly, 78, lonely widow who lives downstairs from Carol. Only relatives are her husband's kids by a previous marriage, and they refuse to see her. Has to sort checks at a bank to supplement social security and husband's paltry pension.

(It is a cold and lonely Christmas Eve in Johnsville, Michigan in the efficiency apartment of Carol Kane. She is a "road tech" temporarily assigned to the Bakertown Nuclear Plant where she is assisting with a refueling project. Her apartment is just up the Green Arrow highway from the plant. Apartment consists of a living/room bedroom where Carol sleeps in a hide-a-bed, an adjoining kitchenette with a small table and a small bath off to the side. Carol has decorated her "flat" with a silly ceramic Christmas tree and her childhood Christmas stocking. She has pinned the latter to the wall. The apartment is otherwise undecorated.

At rise, Carol Kane is sleeping on the hide-a-bed. The only illumination comes from a nine-inch TV showing *It's A Wonderful Life* with the sound off and the Italian lights strung around the ceramic Christmas tree. There is one lonely present under the tree. The cordless phone, which is in the kitchenette, rings. And rings. Carol Kane awakens slowly and grumpily. She answers the phone wearing "pajamas" consisting of a University of Michigan t-shirt and Michigan State sweatpants. She wears a red sock and a green sock.)

Carol Kane: (Rubs face and puts phone to ear) Merry Christmas; Happy New Year — now go away and let me sleep.
(Shocked)
Oh hi, Mom. I thought you were somebody from work. Sorry.
(Listens and yawns)
Yeah, Merry Christmas to you, too. And Dad, and Karen and Rick. Is Andy there? Can you put him on so his Aunt Carol can wish him a Merry Christmas from Michigan?
(Listens)
Well, when he's not playing with the dog.
(Listens)
Yeah, it's snowing here, too.
(Listens and stretches)
No, there's hasn't been any sun here for a month. I think it's against the law in Michigan.
(Listens)
Jimmy stopped writing and listened to the past voice of some pompous drama professor at Penn State telling him that the cardinal

rule of theatre is to never have a scene in which a character is alone on stage talking into a telephone.

"Fuck the cardinal rule of theatre," Jimmy muttered, "and fuck the pompous professor from Penn State. Whatever the hell is name was, and I sure haven't seen it in the NEW YORKER or AMERICAN THEATRE lately."

Jimmy got right back to writing his play with the following:

Yeah, I wish I was back home in Paoli with you guys but . . .

(Listens and picks brown workshirt off back of chair and sniffs at it. Shrugs and puts it on over t-shirt.)

No, I haven't been to church yet. I'm going tomorrow morning after I get off work. There's an 11 o'clock service at the Episcopal Church in Saint Joan.

(Listens)

I think it's low church, Mom. Just like our church in Paoli.

(Listens)

No, I haven't been there yet, Mom. But I'm going tomorrow for sure.

(Listens)

Right.

(Listens)

Saint Joan? It's this cute little town north of here. Kind of like Ardmore or Villanova, except it's got this huge lake. I mean it looks more like the Atlantic Ocean than a lake. You can't even see the other side.

(Listens and buttons shirt which has a red atom and her name emblazoned on it.)

It's called Lake Michigan. It's one of the . . .

(Listens)

That's right, Mom — the Great Lakes.

(Listens)

No, it doesn't have any sharks — it's fresh water, Mom.

(Listens)

Well, I suppose there could be some freshwater sharks in there, but it's all covered with these big ice mounds right now, so I'm not about to go swimming, or . . .

(Listens)

No, I'm not going to walk out on the ice. All the locals at work say it's real dangerous.

(Listens)

Mom!! I won't — all right?

(Listens)

What?

(Listens)

No, I was just going to throw something in the microwave before I go to work.

(Listens)

Yeah, I have to be there at 11:30.

(Listens)

I know it's terrible, Mom, but you can't stop a refueling project at a nuclear plant just because it's Christmas.

(Listens and takes brown work pants off chair and goes into kitchenette to change out of sight of audience.)

Mom, we've been through this before. I told you I was going to have to be away for some holidays when I took this job. It's like when Dad was in the navy. I mean they didn't bring his ship home from the Mediterranean just because it was Christmas.

(Listens and emerges from kitchenette wearing brown work pants. Searches for work shoes.)

I know. I wish I was there, too. This is my first Christmas away from home.

(Listens and finds steel-toed work boots. Cradles phone against ear and puts them on.)

No, there's really nobody around. I mean this place is a ghost town. I guess everybody in the complex went to be with their families.

(Listens and laces boots)

No, I'm fine, Mom. It's not dangerous. It's just — well, it's where all the road techs from the nuclear plant rent while they're here. And I guess a few retired people or whatever.

(Listens)

No, but I think I saw a light on in one of the apartments in the first floor.

(Listens and goes back into kitchenette. Takes frozen dinner out of freezer, laughs at label and pops it in the microwave.)

No, I don't know who lives there, Mom. I think it's some old lady, but I'm never awake during the day to meet her, so . . .

(Listens)

Mom, I work the graveyard shift. I'm a vampire. I feed at night and sleep during the day.

(Listens)

It's a joke, Mom. The guys at work think it's real funny.

(Listens)

Right. Well, look, I just popped dinner in the microwave, so I'd better wrap this up. Could you put Andy on, so I can wish him a Merry . . .

(Listens)

It's a turkey dinner. With all the trimmings.

(Listens)

That's what the package says.

(Listens)

Mom, my diet is fine. Do we have to go through this again?

(Listens and looks impatiently at microwave)

Right. Could you put Andy on?

(Microwave beeps)

There's my dinner.

(Gets dinner out of microwave and sets on table)

I love you too, Mom. And give Dad a big hug for me.

(Listens and searches drawer for knife and fork)

Okay. Merry Christmas to you, too. Now would you please put Andy on.

(Listens and finds knife and spoon. Shrugs and sits down to eat.)

Hi, Andy! This is your Aunt Carol.

(Listens and smiles)

No, I'm in Michigan.

(Listens and frowns)

No, Andy, it's a long, long way from Pennsylvania.

(Listens and tears cover off turkey dinner)

Because I have to work, Andy.

(Listens and laughs)

Well, if we all stopped working everybody's Christmas lights would go out, Andy. And I don't think they'd like that — do you?

(Listens and spoons portion of turkey dinner into mouth. Makes disgusted face.)

Did you open the present I sent you?

(Listens and frowns)

Well, it's okay if you open it now. Tell your mommy and daddy that Aunt Carol says it's okay to open it now.

(Listens)

I know they told you you're not supposed to open it until Christmas morning, but I'd like you to open it now.

Jimmy leaned back in his chair and beheld all that he had written.

"Not bad considering you don't have air-conditioning," he said.

Jimmy wiped sweat from his brow and plunged ever onward, writing:

(Listens)

Why? Because it's more blessed to give than to receive.

(Covers phone with hand)

And I'd like to get *some* pleasure out of this miserable holiday.

(Uncovers phone)

Why don't you put your daddy on, Andy, and I'll tell him to tell you to open your present now? Okay?

(Listens and rolls eyes)

Hi, big brother. Yeah, Merry Christmas and a hundred ho-ho-hoes to you, too.

(Listens)

Yeah, I love you too, Rick. Now, why don't you be a sport for once in your life and let the kid open my present while I'm on the phone with him.

(Listens)

Rick, it's not like I'm stuck in Michigan by choice. And, big brother, last time we compared paychecks, wasn't I the one who had pulled ahead. Now indulge your little sister and let Andy open his present while I'm . . .

(Listens)

Right — don't listen to me. Nice to see that some things don't change.

(Listens and spoons food into mouth. Grimaces.)

It means that the older you get, the more set in your ways you
are. You were just like this when we were kids. Nobody could open
a single present until Christmas morning, and you always had to be
the first — and the last — to open a present.
(Listens)
Like I said, Rick . . .
(Listens)
Right.
(Listens and eats)
No, that's all right. I'm sure you would have sent me more than a
card if you weren't so busy at work. By the way, how many people
did you fire this month. Sorry. That's right — you never say "fire," do
you? How many did you "out-place?"
(Door buzzer sounds)
Rick, somebody's at the door. Can you hang on half a sec?
(Listens)
Rick, for pete's sake, I'm just going to answer the door. Can't
you just . . .
(Listens as she goes to the door)
All right. I'll call back after I answer the door. I'm sure it's just
some . . .
(Listens)
Right. You have a good life, too.
(Clicks off and pushes in antenna. Goes to door and looks
through peephole. Yells through door.)
Do I know you?!?
Pizza Deliveryman: (Yells from other side of door) I got your
pizza, lady.
Carol: Pizza?!? I didn't order a pizza. (Peers through
peephole) Hold it up so I can see it. (Nods) That's a pizza all right,
but I didn't order it. You sure you've got the right apartment
number?
Pizza Deliveryman: It just says Sweetbriar Village. It don't say
which apartment.
Carol: (Sniffs the intoxicating pizza aroma and looks askance at
miserable microwave meal on table) Well, why don't you come in
for a second, and we'll figure this out.
(Carol admits pizza deliveryman.)

Pizza Deliveryman: (Stomps snow off boots and surveys humble apartment with a sympathetic eye) Home alone for Christmas, huh?

Carol: Look, don't get any ideas, pal.

Pizza Deliveryman: (Extends hand) My name's Julio.

Carol: (Stuffs hands in pockets) That's nice. Now who put you up to this — was it Erikson in containment, or Klein in radiation control, or . . .

Pizza Deliveryman: (Drops hand) Lady, I'm just doing my job — okay? There was an order for a deluxe spinach pizza at Sweetbriar Village, and I . . .

Carol: Did you say a deluxe spinach pizza?

Pizza Deliveryman: Yeah. So?

And so it went until later in the play when Mrs. Kelly appeared at Carol's door bearing the deluxe spinach pizza Carol had directed Julio to take to her. She hadn't ordered it either, but seeing Carol's light on, she brought it up, and the two lonely women shared the true meaning of Christmas together.

Or something like that.

Actually, Jimmy ended Carol's Christmas thusly:

Mrs. Kelly: (Beckons Carol to take a seat) No, dearsie, it's just the two of us. Everybody else has gone off to be with their families. Even Mrs. Brandt got up the nerve to call that no-good son of hers, and, do you know, he finally came and took her to his house for Christmas. He lives in South Bend, you know.

Carol: (Slides slowly into chair) So what about your family, Mrs. Kelly? I mean, Consie.

Mrs. Kelly: (Pats Carol's hand) That's the ticket, dearsie. Call me Consie, all my friends do. That's what I always say.

Carol: Right. So what about your family? Don't you have any relatives to . . .

Mrs. Kelly: Woody and I never had any children, and his kids by his first marriage wouldn't give me the time of day if their lives depended on it. I can't say that I blame them — I'm not a blood relative after all, and their mother is still alive. Not that *she* gives them the time of day, but whatever she does give them is enough to keep them coming back for more — but — oh, don't let me get started on *her!* My last living blood relative was old Uncle Charley in Texas, but he passed on the year after I lost my Woody, so I've been pretty much on my own for holidays ever since.

Carol: (Pats Mrs. Kelly's hand) Well, Consie, you've got me for two hours. And this pizza — oh, that's right — your dentures. You can't bite through . . .

Mrs. Kelly: You get me a knife and fork, dearsie, and I'll work around the crust. (Opens box) Look, it's still warm. It's amazing — the things they do these days. Why, in my day, we never even heard of pizza. And the idea of somebody actually delivering dinner to your house — land's sake. Of course, in my day there was the iceman, and the milkman. And somebody who brought eggs to the back door — maybe things haven't changed all that much.

Carol: (Relaxes) Well, they say that the more things change the more they stay the same. (Goes to kitchenette) Here, I'll get some silverware and plates. (Opens refrigerator) All I've got is Diet Coke. Is that okay with you?

Mrs. Kelly: (Impishly) I know you atomic people aren't allowed to drink before work, but I don't suppose you have a little red wine for a silly old woman? When my Woody was alive, we always had red wine on Christmas Eve.

Carol: (Shoulders droop) I'm afraid I'm not much of a drinker, Mrs. Kelly, so I don't have any . . .

Mrs. Kelly: Oh, that's just fine, dearsie. Silly me — always demanding. No, Diet Coke will do just fine. When in Rome, do as the Romans do. Right?

Carol: Right. (Returns to table with Diet Coke, plates, glasses and silverware) I could run out and get some wine for you.

Mrs. Kelly: No, don't be ridiculous. I'm fine. Absolutely. You just sit and enjoy. Growing girl like you needs all the pizza she can eat. Now come on and eat before it gets cold.

(Carol pours the Diet Coke; Mrs. Kelly serves the pizza, and then they eat — Carol with her hands and Mrs. Kelly with a knife and fork.)

Carol: This is to die for! I've never had pizza this good.

Mrs. Kelly: Neither have I, dearsie.

Carol: (Chews contentedly) It doesn't get better than this, does it, Consie?

Mrs. Kelly: No, it doesn't, dearsie.

Carol: So who do you think ordered the pizza? I'm thinking maybe it was this guy at work who did it as a practical joke, but then I . . .

Mrs. Kelly: Ours is not to reason why, dearsie. That's what my Woody always said. And do you know that that delightful man who brought the pizza — that Julio — wouldn't let me pay for it. No, sir. He said somebody back at the pizzeria must have made a mistake, and they'd just have to pay for it. Wasn't that nice of him?

Carol: Yeah, considering he offered to sell it to me for half-price.

Mrs. Kelly: Well, you're a working girl, dearsie. Me, I'm trying to scrape by on social security and what's left of Woody's pension. Oh, that awful company! Why, do you know I actually had to go out and get a part-time job sorting checks at the bank to make ends meet? Can you imagine sorting checks at my age?

Carol: I hear you. Well, it was nice of that guy to give you the pizza. And it was sure great of you to bring it up here. (Grabs another slice and begins devouring it) Consie?

Mrs. Kelly: (Finishes chewing before replying) Yes, dearsie?

Carol: Would you like that bathrobe? You really seem to like it. (Playwright's note: Carol's family had sent her a bathrobe which she opened earlier while on the phone with them. She pretended to like it, but indicated to the audience that she did not.)

Mrs. Kelly: Oh, dearsie, I couldn't take your robe.

Carol: No, please. I insist.

Mrs. Kelly: But . . .

Carol: You like it, don't you?

Mrs. Kelly: (Touches robe) Well, yes, dearsie. It's quite lovely. But wasn't it a gift from . . .

Carol: My parents? Yeah, but I wear sweats and stuff around the apartment. I'm not the robe type.

Mrs. Kelly: Then why did they send you a robe?

Carol: (Shrugs) They've always said I'm difficult to shop for, so they always give me practical stuff. I think they think Michigan is like near the Yukon or something, so they sent me this. Actually, they had L.L. Bean send it. My mom loves to shop out of the L.L. Bean catalog. I think she owns stock in the company or something. She should if she doesn't.

Mrs. Kelly: (Gets up and picks robe off back of chair) Oh, I don't know, dearsie. It's so . . .

Carol: Please, Consie. It would make me real happy if you'd accept it. And you can lend it back to me when my parents come to visit. How's that?

Mrs. Kelly: (Giggles girlishly) It could be our little secret, couldn't it?

Carol: (Gets up and helps Mrs. Kelly into robe) Yes – our little secret. How's it feel?

Mrs. Kelly: (Sighs) Like ranch mink, dearsie. Do you have a mirror?

Carol: On the back of the closet door.

Mrs. Kelly: (Heads for closet door) Oh, that's a clever idea. Did you do that yourself?

Carol: Yeah, I'm pretty handy when I want to be. If you want, I'll put a mirror on the back of your closet door. It's real simple.

Mrs. Kelly: Would you?

Carol: Sure. Now take a look at yourself, Consie.

(Mrs. Kelly opens closet and examines herself in mirror for the longest time. She sighs and her shoulders shake.)

Carol: You okay, Consie?

Mrs. Kelly: (Dabs at eyes with back of hand and faces Carol) I'm fine, dearsie. It's just that it's been so long since anyone's given me anything for Christmas. And something so lovely. I just don't know what to say. I don't have anything to give you in return. I feel so . . .

Carol: You brought the pizza, Consie. You see how I'm chowin' down on that thing. This is the best pizza I ever ate.

Mrs. Kelly: But Julio brought the pizza.

Carol: So? you brought it to me, and we shared it. Isn't that what Christmas is all about?

Mrs. Kelly: (Sighs) I suppose.

Carol: What's wrong, Consie?

Mrs. Kelly: I just wish we had some red wine. I know you can't drink before you go to work, but we could enjoy a glass together tomorrow when you get home. My Woody and I always had red wine for Christmas.

(Door buzzer sounds)

Carol: Who could that be? (Goes to door and looks through peephole) It's that pizza guy again. He probably straightened out who ordered the pizza and wants it back.

Mrs. Kelly: Let him in, dearsie.

Carol: You sure?

Mrs. Kelly: Yes!!

Carol: All right, but get ready to hit him with a chair if he tries anything.

Mrs. Kelly: I don't think he's going to try anything, dearsie. He's not that type.

Carol: How do you know? I thought you never saw him before tonight. And he's not wearing a uniform or anything like the guys from the big pizza companies.

Mrs. Kelly: I'm an excellent judge of character, dearsie. That's what my father always said. Even my Woody admitted I was an excellent judge of character. That's why I married him – that's what he always said. No, you go on and let that nice Julio in. He's probably lonely too, and just looking for some Christmas cheer.

Carol: All right, but if we end up in the headlines of tomorrow's paper, it's your fault. (Opens door and admits Julio) You forget something?

Pizza Deliveryman: (Steps into apartment with hands behind back and approaches Mrs. Kelly) Guess which hand?

Mrs. Kelly: Oh, I've always hated this game. I don't know – how about your right hand?

Pizza Deliveryman: Right you are. (Displays bottle of red wine) I forgot to leave this before. Sorry. (Presents it to Mrs. Kelly with a flourish) Make sure she doesn't have any before work – I wouldn't want her getting fired. (Turns and goes to door. Hesitates at door and turns.) Oh, yeah, you probably need a corkscrew. (Tosses one to Carol) You don't look like the type who'd have a corkscrew. Feliz Navidad and all that good stuff. (Departs)

Carol: (Runs to door and looks down corridor) Hey, wait a minute! Come back!! (Comes back into apartment and closes door. Shakes head.) He's gone – he like vanished or something. You don't suppose he's an . . .

Mrs. Kelly: Like my Woody always said: "Ours is not to reason why, dearsie." Now come on and eat the rest of that pizza before it gets cold. You're a growing girl, and you can't keep all those little atoms hopping around all night on an empty stomach.

Carol: (Grins and ushers Mrs. Kelly back to table) This is turning out to be an okay Christmas after all.

Mrs. Kelly: Of course. Now could you be a dear and open that wine for a sentimental old woman?

Carol: My pleasure. Dearsie.

(Carol turns off TV, and they resume seats at table. Lights fade as Carol opens bottle of wine. Plays ends.)

Jimmy sat back in his ergonomic chair and sighed the contented sigh of the playwright who has just written a play that he knows, just knows, is going to be produced.

Then he fired up his trusty Epson FX-185 dot matrix printer and ran off a copy of *Carol's Christmas* for Jessica "call me Jess" Springer and his adoring public.

Chapter Nine

Fasten your seatbelts, gentle readers. And not-so-gentle readers.

Because we're gonna hit the old fast-forward button here and put some nitro in the tank. Get this old dog off the couch and out chasin' rabbits.

Or something like that.

Anyway, here's how it all shook out with Jimmy Clarke's three plays, *Common Prayer, Carol's Christmas,* and *The Last Haircut.*

First and happiest, Jessica "call me Jess" Springer summoned Jimmy to a meeting and told him she just loved *Carol's Christmas* and had only a few minor changes in mind. Basically just a superfluous line cut here and a fatty phrase lopped from the body theatric there.

Null problemo.

Then she actually told him that his play along with selected scenes from "that nifty book by this woman in Oregon—Paula Peters or Petra Paulson or something will grace the stage at the Glenn Consolidated High School on Saturday, November 20 and then again on Sunday the 21st."

All in the year of Our Lord 1993. The very same year Jimmy wrote, produced and co-directed his very first play, *No Dice.*

"Thank you, Saint Genesius," Jimmy muttered.

"What was that?" Jessica "just call me Jess" Springer said.

They were dining at a trendy restaurant on the Blue Star Highway. One with lots of hanging plants and whole-grain thises and thats and "servers" who insisted on telling you their first names and all about the daily specials.

"Oh, I was just giving thanks to Saint Genesius."

"Saint Genesius? I'm afraid I'm not familiar with that particular saint. I was raised a Methodist, you see."

"Ah, that explains it. But as a professional actor, Jessica, you should . . ."

"Please, call me Jess."

"Sorry. Jess, you should know that Saint Genesius is the patron saint of actors. Even of method actors and Methodist actors."

"Oh, you are witty. No wonder you write such sparkling dialog."

"Sparkling dialog? Did you say sparkling dialog?"

"Oh yes. Your play just zips right along. It will be a pleasure to produce, and I have just the young woman in mind for the part of Carol. And if I can twist his arm, maybe I'll get Justin Ward to play the pizza person. He's half Puerto Rican, so he would be perfect. Plus, he's a wonderful actor. Although his friends all want him to go out for basketball. But I think that would be a waste, don't you?"

Jimmy shrugged and said: "I was on the swim team in high school, but my senior year I auditioned for the fall play and got the lead."

"What were they doing? Something by O'Neill? Chekhov? Tennessee Williams?"

Jimmy looked around to be sure nobody was listening and whispered, "It was *Oklahoma* actually."

Jess Springer sprang into laughter.

Jimmy couldn't help but join her and they had a jolly good luncheon together. After which she promised to get back to him with a "solid rehearsal schedule and a commitment from the school to pay you."

On that happy note, Jimmy went home and phoned Dr. Peter Phillips, Ph.D. to see how preparations for producing *Common Prayer* were proceeding.

They were not.

"But I thought you were going to call Maye Michaels and offer her the part of the Queen," Jimmy said.

"I did," Dr. Peter Phillips, Ph.D. replied.

"And?"

"Well, she read the script and liked it. Quite a lot actually. She's quite an admirer of your work, you know."

"Yes, she said I was the new Eugene O'Neill. In print no less."

"Yes, well, I wouldn't go that far, but she did read *Common Prayer,* and she told me she was perfect for the part of the Queen, and she wanted to do it."

"So, what's the problem? You and I flip a coin for the two male parts, and we're off to the races. It's not that long a play—we could be off book in a week. We could even do it as reader's theatre if we wanted."

"Yes, that would certainly work. But there's one slight problem."

"What?" Jimmy said.

"The fall musical at Lake Michigan College," Dr. Peter Phillips, Ph.D. said.

"What about it?"

"They're doing a musical adaptation of WORKING by Studs Terkel, and Maye told me she'd just die if she didn't get a part. So she's doing some back study for all the female parts and says she won't be able to make any commitments until at least November 15th. At the earliest."

"But I thought you wanted to produce this program in August. Certainly before Labor Day."

"Absolutely."

"So maybe you need to find another actress."

"Please, they prefer to be called actors."

"Yeah," Jimmy mumbled, "just like there are no waitresses and waiters anymore. Just fucking *servers* who insist on telling you their entire fucking life stories and then rolling off some list of daily specials that's a mile long, and all you want to do is eat a fucking hamburger."

"What was that?"

"Nothing."

"You were talking to yourself again—weren't you? You really should make an appointment with me for some hypno-therapy. I could really help you process a lot of buried issues from your obviously troubled childhood. For example, I'll say with absolute assurance that your father was an alcoholic. Wasn't he?"

"Yeah, but who's old man wasn't?"

"Mine for one. That is: my adopted father. I don't actually know who my birth father was, but I've joined a nationwide support group of people searching for their birth parents, and I feel that closure is near."

"Good for you, doc."

"Please, don't call me that."

"That's right. You're not a real doctor."

"I am too."

"Are not."

"Am too."

"Look, can we get back to the play?"

"If you insist," Dr. Peter Phillips, Ph.D. said.

Jimmy insisted.

"All right. What are you proposing?"

"I'm proposing that you find another actress — excuse me — actor/creature to play the Queen."

"I've already run a notice in the church bulletin and come up with nothing. Maye Michaels is our only hope, and she won't be available until November 15. Of course, she said something about auditioning for the Christmas play at Blue Star Players, so that might mean she won't be available until after the holidays."

"Let's not forget Broadway and Hollywood," Jimmy muttered.

"What was that?"

"I said let's forget it. It doesn't sound like this is going to get off the ground."

"Oh, no. It'll fly. You'll see."

"I bet," Jimmy said, certain he would never see *Common Prayer* produced at Saint Giles by the River Episcopal Church here in South Haven.

And he was right.

So enough of Dr. Peter Phillips, Ph.D., Maye Michaels, and the rest of Jimmy's erstwhile Epis-co-pals.

And on to that fateful evening of August 18th when Jimmy drove Angel Car to the home of the Blue Star Players for what he had been told by Martin Gregory would be an amicable meeting with the board to "just dot a few T's and cross a few I's."

That was Martin Gregory's big attempt at humor, and Jimmy had made a reasonable effort to laugh.

Hey, the guy's theatre was going to produce *The Last Haircut* and make them all rich and famous. And maybe Jimmy would win the Pulitzer Prize for drama, and pigs would fly, and mosquitoes would stop biting, and Ireland would become a leading industrial nation.

The meeting was set to begin at 7:30, and Jimmy was there promptly at 7:20. Complete with extra scripts of *The Last Haircut*, a fresh haircut for himself, a clean shirt, and a contract stating that he was charging $20 for the first performance of his play and $15 for each subsequent performance.

He had prepared the latter with help from a book he found in the ever-helpful South Haven Public Library and saw no reason it wouldn't be properly signed and dated within the hour.

But when he whipped down the dirt drive that veered off the Blue Star Highway and came upon the ramshackle shack that was the Blue Star Players playroom, he sensed trouble.

No cars in the unpaved parking lot.

Nobody.

Nothing.

Nada.

Just some crows driving off a turkey vulture.

Jimmy watched the black birds duke it out in the sky and took that as a bad omen.

Then a troubled old Toyota rumbled up the drive, coughed to completion and emitted a total tight-ass with a clipboard, retractable key ring, and photo ID clipped to her button-down shirt that proclaimed her as "Margaret Anderson, P.S.W."

She fingered the mini MACE applicator on her key ring and eyed Jimmy warily. Clearly, she was of the "all men are rapists" school of feminist logic and was ready to do this creep grievous bodily harm.

"May I help you?" she said in a particularly pinched voice.

Jimmy knew right then and there that the P.S.W. just had to stand for Psychiatric Social Worker. This was one of the helping professionals, and she was addressing him just as she would her charges at whatever miserable psychiatric hospital employed her.

Jimmy dropped his shoulders so as not to look like a demented, sexist, male rapist with only one thing on his mind, coughed up a friendly smile and said, "I'm Jim Clarke. I'm the playwright Martin Gregory invited to the board meeting tonight, and . . ."

"Martin didn't say anything to me. Oh wait," the woman backed away from Jimmy and consulted her clipboard. "Oh yes, I have a phone message. Martin called and said you'd be coming."

"Good."

"Yes. Good." The woman kept her distance and professionally observed the sexist male rapist who clearly had only one thing on his mind.

Jimmy nodded gamely and glanced at this Margaret Anderson creature and thought, who in his right mind would want to crawl in bed with that thing with the ratty red hair and coke bottle glasses?

"Did you say something?" Margaret Anderson said.

"No."

"Your lips were moving."

"They were?"

"Yes, they certainly were." Margaret Anderson backed farther away from Jimmy and put her trigger finger on her mini MACE.

Jimmy exhaled and backed away from the woman who still hadn't introduced herself.

They remained like that until another car crunched up the dirt road.

Seeing that help was on the way, Margaret Anderson nodded curtly at Jimmy and said, "Well, I suppose we can go inside now."

Jimmy nodded and waited while the newly arrived car disgorged its driver. She was none other than Stephanie Rezmore. The one who Jimmy had seen show her tits in the Blue Star Players' production of *Elephant Man*. Wife of fellow stage star Carl Rezmore, occupant of an architecturally insignificant pile of rubble in the dunes, and a woman just way too busy to take a part in *No Dice*. But not too busy to come and critique it with her husband.

Jimmy forced himself to smile at her, and Carol Rezmore gave him a toothy greeting complete with, "I see you've met our secretary, Margaret Anderson."

"Oh yes, we've been having a friendly little chat," Jimmy said.

"You could say that," Margaret Anderson said, clearly meaning not to say that. "Well, shall we go inside? I want to get the table ready for the meeting. Maybe you could help me."

Of course, Jimmy could help, and he did. He and the two women schlepped an incredibly heavy and cumbersome folding table up to the stage, set it up, and then festooned it with folding chairs.

By 7:40, the other board members were beginning to straggle in.

First, there was Jimmy's old pal, Douglas Iglesia. The Spanish grandee himself who had helped Jimmy "develop" *No Dice* and brought new meaning to the role of Christopher Kurtin.

"Hey, boss," he said as the others took their seats, "How're they hangin'?"

"Good," Jimmy said. "How's about you?"

"Can't complain. So what are you doing here?"

"Didn't Martin Gregory tell you?"

"No. All he said was he can't make the meeting tonight. Which is par for the course. And which means I'm running it since I'm vice president. Which I took because I thought it meant I wouldn't have to do anything, but with Martin as president, it means I have to run practically every meeting."

"You love it, Douglas," Margaret Anderson said in a manner that could almost have been mistaken for flirting.

Almost.

Because we're talking about a woman who's sex drive was suctioned out of her nostrils at birth. Just like that bun-head at the University of Michigan and her fat dyke "companion" who have devoted their lives to ridding the world of evil, male-inspired pornography. But don't get the author started on that.

All right?

Right.

Now, where the hell were we?

Right, in hell.

The world headquarters of the Blue Star Players actually, but old Dante would certainly have regarded the dingy rathole as one of the lowest levels of his INFERNO.

We're talking a hot, dusty, stuffy awful place on a hot, dusty, stuffy, awful August evening. And we're talking about a table full of total tightasses. Including the great and wonderful Douglas Iglesia.

The latter finally called the meeting to order at 8 p.m., totally ignored Jimmy, and allowed things to disintegrate into a shambling discussion of: the minutes from the last meeting, various and sundry correspondence, problems with the the plumber who had screwed up the plumbing, problems with the electrician who had screwed up the wiring, the shrinking patronage base, and the need for new talent.

Always the need for new talent.

Then, finally at 8:30, Carol Rezmore had the decency to clear her throat and say: "Isn't it rather rude to keep our guest waiting here all this time while we argue about ways to get more people into our theatre? I'm sure he has better things to do than sit here and listen to us bicker."

"We're not bickering, Carol," Douglas Iglesia said. "We're discussing the very survival of this theatre. Of theatre in general. Of art. Of truth. If the Republicans seize control of Congress next year, which I fear they may do because they've got all of corporate America behind them, then we're toast. History. The only art you're going to see in this country is what those morons at Disney dish out. Unless everybody wants it, nobody's going to get it."

"That's all very well and good, Douglas," Carol Rezmore persisted, "but what about our guest?"

Douglas Iglesia faced Jimmy Clarke and flicked his mane of jet-black hair for the benefit of the women folk. Then he smiled ever so slightly and said, "You're right, Carol. Time to introduce the world-famous playwright, Jim Clarke. Stand up and take a bow, boss."

Jimmy half rose and and waved weakly at the total tightasses. Then he dropped back to his back-breaking seat and wanted to crawl in a deep hole and die.

But he didn't.

He should have, however.

Because it got much worse from there.

Much worse.

So much so that it is indeed difficult and painful for the author to recreate this awful moment in the annals of theatre history. But it is the duty of authors everywhere to recreate painful moments so society can learn from its mistakes and repeat them over and over until we finally get it right and just wipe ourselves off the planet, leaving Mom Earth to its rightful owners, the cockroaches and rats.

Let them fight it out, right?

Sorry.

Slight digression.

Slap to the forehead.

There, much better.

Much, much better.

So, where were we?

Ah, yes, at the meeting of the board of directors of the Blue Star Players on August 18, 1993.

Douglas Iglesia pointed at the blushing playwright and said, "As some of you may know, Jim Clarke here wrote the play that I helped develop and starred in at the Glenn Art Studio back in July. Really packed 'em in, didn't we, boss?"

"We sure did," Jimmy croaked.

"It was because of my stellar performance and world-class art on the program," Douglas Iglesia modestly allowed. "Anyway, Martin invited Jim to our meeting for some reason, so I'll let Jim explain why he's here. It's all yours, boss."

Jimmy cleared his throat and passed copies of *The Last Haircut* around his table. He handed his contract to Douglas Iglesia and said, "Well, Martin Gregory called me the morning after we closed *No Dice* and invited me to write an original play for your theatre. He said you wanted to do more cutting-edge theatre along the lines of what we did at the Glenn Art Studio, and so he suggested I write something original for you that you could produce here at . . ."

"Let me see that!" a man at the end of the table said, grabbing the contract out of Douglas Iglesia's hands. He had the rough hands and look of a tradesman, complete with untrimmed beard and faded flannel shirt.

Douglas Iglesia surrendered the document without protest and waited for the tradesman to peruse it.

The tattered tradesman donned a taped-together pair of reading glasses, glanced quickly at Jimmy's carefully prepared contract, tore it in half and said, "This is totally unprofessional! Totally unprofessional! Martin didn't say a word to me about this, and as your treasurer, and I assume you still want me to be your treasurer since no one else will take the fucking job, then it is my duty to inform you people that we can't run out and drag in every Tom, Dick and Harry who thinks he's a playwright and promise to pay him ridiculous amounts of money for something we haven't even seen and don't know will work. Not when we can barely keep our heads above water, people, and retire our debt to that stupid plumber and electrician the last board hired to do work we could have done ourselves and five times better, for a third of the price. But then I wasn't on the board then, but I am now, and I'm telling you people this is totally unprofessional! Totally unprofessional!!"

There was a huge, groaning silence.

Then Margaret Anderson looked up from her minutes, smiled her pinched smile at Jimmy, and said: "Stu is absolutely right. This *is* totally unprofessional. Martin has no business making commitments on behalf of the board when he knows the financial difficulties we are facing."

Jimmy waited for Douglas Iglesia and Carol Rezmore to rise to his defense.

They remained seated and silent.

So Jimmy rose in a fury, gave them all the finger, ordered them all to eat shit and die, and flew from that rathole of a theatre in a blind rage.

Never to return!!

NEVER!!

Chapter Ten

Joyce was a great comfort to Jimmy that night.

After he vented his venom and vowed to quit writing forever, Joyce told him he was the best.

"The best," she repeated. "And those morons at Bull Shit and Piss don't even deserve to shine your shoes."

"I'm not wearing shoes. I'm wearing my Birkenstocks."

"Well, they're not worthy to wipe your sandals, and you can't let the actions of a bunch of petty, small-town, community theatre jerks tell you what to write. They're not the judges of your worth, Jimmy."

"Yeah, you're right. Maybe I should get a shoulder-fired rocket and take that fucking place out. With all of them in it."

"Maybe you should just go for a swim and put this all behind you. And then get up tomorrow morning and write to your heart's content. Whatever you want. However much you want, and about anything you want. You don't have to please anybody, Jimmy. Least of all a bunch of petty, talentless community theatre jerks. I mean, these are the kind of people who think *The Sound of Music* is great theatre."

"Tell me about it."

"Go for a swim."

"I think I'll go for a run."

"Do you think that's a good idea?"

"What do you mean?"

"Well, you're looking a little — you know."

"What, Joyce?"

"When was the last time you stepped on the scale, Jimmy?"

"Joyce, I'm not going to enslave myself to some stupid bathroom scale that's wrong 99 percent of the time. My weight fluctuates. I'm sure I'm mostly muscle right now. Maybe a few pounds of excess fat. But I can get rid of that anytime I want."

Jimmy stomped into the bedroom and changed furiously into his running togs.

Joyce followed at a safe distance and said, "I'm just going to say one more thing, and then I'm going to leave you alone."

Jimmy looked up from lacing his New Balance 580 running shoes, known to the cognoscénti as "Bricks," ground his teeth, and said, "Lay it on me, Joyce."

Joyce sighed and looked at the love of her life. The man she thought she would never find. And feared desperately she would lose to a sudden and fatal heart attack. All because he had eaten and drunk his grief.

"What, Joyce? Spit it out. I want to get out and run before I explode."

"I didn't say anything."

"Well, your lips were sure moving. You're getting as bad as me. Maybe we should both go and see that Peter Phillips asshole and have him hynotherapize us or whatever the hell he does. Probably put us out and then strip us naked, and put us in compromising poses with his goldfish, or something, and take dirty pictures of us, and sell them on the schoolyard. The guy's a fucking pervert if ever there was one. God, I should have realized that the first time I met him. Then he blows off *Common Prayer* because that stupid bitch Maye Michaels is so fucking busy, she . . ."

"Jimmy!!"

Jimmy looked up at his distressed wife and said, "Sorry."

"Go for a run."

"But I thought you wanted to tell me one last thing."

"Just go for your run."

"Come on, Joyce. Don't leave me hanging. What did you want to tell me."

Joyce sighed and said, "I just want you to be happy, Jimmy. That's all."

"Happy and thin?"

"Yes. If you want to know. I'm afraid you're going to eat and drink all your grief, Jimmy, and have a fatal heart attack, and leave me a widow. Then I'll have no one. Absolutely no one. I'll die of loneliness and grief." Joyce sobbed and collapsed into Jimmy's arms.

Jimmy held her tenderly and said, "How about if I go on a diet tomorrow?"

Joyce swallowed, wiped her tears with the back of her hand and looked at her husband with new hope.

"Maybe I'll even call Diet Center. They just opened an office in South Haven. In fact the lady came in the other day to take out an ad in the HIGHLIGHTS, and she gave me some literature which I saved."

"You did?"

Jimmy shrugged. "Yeah. I filed it away for a rainy day. And I think it's going to rain tomorrow, so maybe I'll go over there and see if I can work out some kind of deal. Maybe write a feature on them or something in return for . . ."

"No, you pay her whatever it costs, Jimmy. I don't care what it costs, because we always have money for our health. Do you hear me?"

"Loud and clear."

"Good. Now go for your run and don't overdo it."

Jimmy kissed his wife and went for a long and glorious run through the twilight. He ran until he could run no more and then cast himself into the lake, and crawled far out into the sweetwater sea, and backstroked back to the beach with his eyes on the twinkling firmament.

All was right with the world, and on the morrow he would call Diet Center and start a new and improved life and not leave Joyce a lonely widow with no one to turn to.

In fact, Jimmy thought, I'll call Diet Center from the HIGHLIGHTS because I'm going to be working there tomorrow anyway. And they're right around the corner, and Tiffany won't mind if I pop over there for an hour or so.

With that plan firmly in mind, Jimmy let himself into the world headquarters of the weakly weekly HAVENCREST HIGHLIGHTS the next morning and called: "Tiffany. Are you here?"

Nothing.

Then he cocked his ear and heard a familiar noise emanating from the rear of the home/office. A wet, slapping noise he hadn't heard since the days of the great and magnificent L. David Hinchcliff.

Jimmy wondered if the dynamic director had returned from California to recast his fate with his beloved Tiffster.

"Tiffany? Are you back there?" Jimmy called.

There was a muffled noise, then Tiffany calling back: "Jimmy, come on back. I want you to meet somebody."

Jimmy wanted to run away. Right away.

But a morbid curiosity drew him deep into the dump.

He figured the source of the saucy sound could be Tiffany's vibrator and some K-Y Jelly.

Yeah, Jimmy thought, that'd do it.

But no, he decided, cocking his ears, this is the sound of two genitalia slapping. Not one. Two.

And as he drew into the back bedroom where he had first laid eyes on the glistening nether regions of Tiffany Ann Starbuck and the erect member of the great and magnificent L. David Hinchcliff, he now saw again the glistening nether regions of Tiffany Ann Starbuck and an erect member.

The later, however, did not belong to the great and magnificent L. David Hinchcliff. Its owner was a fat fellow to be sure, just like the portly editor and director who had split for the West Coast, but this bloke had decidedly red hair. Red curly hair, and a great red beard that was absolutely gleaming from its dive into Tiffany's moistened muff.

"Jimmy," Tiffany said, lifting her mouth off the man's pole, "I want you to meet Brian O'Malley. He's from Chicago, and he's going to be the new editorial and feature writer. He used to work for the DAILY NEWS before it folded. And he worked at Muni News. Just like you. Didn't you, Brian?"

Nonplussed by the circumstances, Brian O'Malley lifted his great gaelic head off the bed and winked at Jimmy. "Glad to make your acquaintance, sor," he said in a great blustery Irish brogue that sounded more practiced than real. "I'd shake your hand, sor, but I'm afraid me fingers are a bit sticky at the moment. If you're about catchin' me drift."

Jimmy nodded and averted his eyes. Then he cleared his throat and said, "Uh, Tiffany, why don't I come back later? I was thinking of going downtown and doing some business."

"You don't have to leave, Jimmy. Stay and watch. You don't mind, do you, Brian?"

"As long as he doesn't throw peanuts and popcorn on us, I'm fine with an audience. God knows, I've had enough audiences in me day.

Anyway, if you worked at Muni News like Tiffany says you did, then there's nothing that's going to shock you, is there?"

"No, that's for sure," Jimmy said, thinking of the memorable time he had surprised that immensely fat cop from women's lock-up, O'Something-or-Other, and fellow Muni News reporter Norma Jankowski going at it like gigantic gophers on the couch in the press room at police headquarters in Chicago.

"So," Brian O'Malley said, matter-of-factly, "when did you depart from the sacred portals of Muni News?"

"I was there in 1976."

"Ah, a fine year, but a bit after me time. I was there in the Dark Ages of journalism during the reign of the great Margolis. City editor to be feared by all who came within the sound of his terrible voice. He made you stand for inspection at the beginning of your shift. And if your tie wasn't knotted properly or your shoes not shined to a grand, high gloss, he'd boot you back to the stairwell and kick you down. Ah, them was the grand old days of me dissipated youth. And the drinkin' we did in them days at that celebrated public house on North Avenue — O'Rourke's. Where a man could curl up with a fresh pint of Guiness Stout and a pack of Marlboro's finest and while away the night with tales of derring do. Ah, them was the grand old days, but now I've taken the pledge and joined that dear fellowship of those who stay sober one day at a time."

"Yeah," Tiffany said, "that's where I met Brian. At an A.A. meeting."

"But you're not in A.A., Tiffany."

"I am now," she said. "I was lonely, and I heard the best place to meet men is at A.A. meetings so I went last night, and Brian was there, and now he's here, and he's going to be our new editorial and feature writer starting with this next issue. Isn't that right, Brian?"

"As sure as Ireland is a free and fair land, me love."

"But what about me?" Jimmy said, finally realizing what all this really meant for his future on the cutting edge of American journalism.

"What about you?" Tiffany said, taking Brian O'Malley's member back in her mouth.

"Well, I thought I was the editorial and feature writer for the HIGHLIGHTS."

"You can still — lick — write features — slurp — and editorials — lick — when there's room — slurp — isn't that right — lick — Brian? Lick, slurp, lick, slurp . . ."

"That's — lick — right — slurp — my angel — lick, slurp, lick, slurp, slurp . . ."

"I'm outta here," Jimmy said, turning on his toe.

He turned on his toe and fled from the carnal carnage that represented the wreck of his career in journalism.

But he did not go to Diet Center as he intended and as he had promised Joyce.

Rather, he drove to Chaser's Lounge on the edge of town where he mounted a serious assault on the "Wall of Foam."

Chapter Eleven

Joyce raced out to the car when Jimmy finally returned home that evening and said: "Jimmy! Where have you been?!? I was ready to call the state police."

Jimmy released his death grip on the steering wheel and smiled drunkenly at his wife. Then he said, "I was climbing the 'Wall of Foam.'"

"What?!?" Joyce said, sniffing.

"I was at Chaser's Lounge climbing the 'Wall of Foam.' What's so unusual about that? Now get out of the way so I can get out of the car and go in the house before these mosquitoes eat me alive."

"Jimmy, you smell like a brewery."

"Not just any brewery, Joyce. Some of the best breweries in the world. See, to get on the 'Wall of Foam' at Chaser's, you have to drink 365 different beers from around the world. Including America, of course, and I sampled some really good beer from these microbreweries I never even heard of. Like this one called 'Red Pete' or 'Sneaky Pete' or something like that. Anyway, it had superior body and a fine fruity finish with a nose that just didn't quit and . . ."

"Jimmy, you're so drunk you can't even talk. I thought you were going to go to Diet Center today. Instead, you come staggering home an hour past dinner-time so drunk you can't even make sense. And don't ask me how you drove in that condition, because I certainly don't want to know, and I certainly don't want to know why in God's name you would even go in that crummy hillbilly bar."

"It's not a crummy hillbilly bar, Joyce."

"What do you mean — all we ever see when we drive by that place are pick-up trucks."

"Yeah, but the people are really friendly, Joyce. Like this guy I was sitting next to at the bar. I mean, he's a chimney sweep and a roofer, but he's also a hang-glider pilot and he restores old motorcycles. And he reads all kinds of writers I like. Pete Dexter and people like that."

Joyce shook her head in disgust and went in the un-air-conditioned house.

Jimmy just sat there letting the mosquitoes drink his pickled blood.

"Get drunk on me, you little fuckers," he muttered. "Then you'll all be easy prey for the next passing dragonfly, and there'll be no more of you little fuckers to . . ."

"Oh, you writers! Always working in the strangest places."

Jimmy whipped around and saw that it was old Mildred Mackermyer. She was out for an evening stroll through the bug-infested forest and had stopped to marvel at the man of letters muttering to himself in his car.

"Oh, hi, Mrs. Mackermyer. I was just, uh . . ."

"Oh, you don't have to explain. I know how the creative process works. I took a course in creative centering back in Ann Arbor at the Universalist Learning Center. I know all about it. No, you just go on working, and I promise not to interrupt again."

Jimmy nodded gamely at the nosy old bat and decided to head on into the dump in the dunes. "No," he thought aloud, "not the dump in the dunes — the Dunery."

"What was that, dear?"

"Nothing, Mrs. Mackermyer."

"Oh, you don't have to explain. I know how the creative process works. I took a course in creative centering back in Ann Arbor at the Universalist . . ."

Jimmy fled into the Dunery before the crone could croon another refrain.

Joyce was already settled on the couch with a thick book with tiny print and tried to ignore him as he came in. But she did manage a tight, "Your dinner's in the oven if you're hungry. All you have to do is heat it up. Otherwise, just cover the plate with aluminum foil, and I'll give it to you for lunch tomorrow."

Jimmy was tempted to say he had eaten his fill of salty, greasy popcorn along with his eight — no, nine — no, ten — bottles of designer beer from around the world at Chaser's Lounge, but he knew that could lead to grievous bodily harm, so he muttered a meek: "Okay. I'll heat it up. I'm sorry, Joyce. I should have called."

Joyce stared a hole through her thick book, sighed, and clapped it shut. She looked up at her husband and said, "Jimmy, what's wrong?"

Jimmy was about to tell her when his phone rang.

It could be destiny, he thought.

It wasn't destiny.

It was Tiffany Ann Starbuck, and she was all sweetness and light as she poured her soul into Jimmy's answering machine and begged him to come back to the weakly weekly HAVENCREST HIGHLIGHTS.

"Aren't you going to pick up and talk to the woman?" Joyce said.

"No," Jimmy said, feeling quite the coward.

"Jimmy, pick up your phone and talk to the poor woman. She sounds hysterical."

Indeed, she did.

". . . can't go on without you, Jimmy. You're the one who helped me hold this paper together after David left, and I don't know what I'm going to do if you . . ."

Jimmy turned the sound off and stomped out on the deck.

Joyce followed at a safe distance and said, "Do you mind telling me what's going on?"

Jimmy angrily swatted a mosquito and said, "I don't suppose that stupid air-conditioning guy was here today."

"No, he wasn't here. Jimmy, would you . . ."

"Did you call him?"

"No, I didn't call him. I assume he'll come back when he's ready to come back. He'll finish our system. Don't worry. Now tell me what's going on with you and Tiffany. Did you quit your job at the paper? We could use that money, you know."

Jimmy ground his teeth and swatted another mosquito. "Little fuckers," he cursed loud enough for half of Havencrest to hear. "Why don't they bring back DDT and spray the shit of these little fuckers? But no, all these stupid tree-huggers say DDT is harmful to the little birdies, so we can't spray with DDT anymore, so instead we're just going to be eaten alive by fucking mosquitoes. And they call this progress. I call it horse shit!!"

"Jimmy, come inside."

"Why? It's cooler out here. It's like an oven in there."

"Jimmy!!!"

"Joyce!!!!"

Joyce went inside and returned to her book.

Jimmys stewed with the mosquitoes for as long as he could stand it and went in and erased Tiffany's message. Then he turned off his answering machine and phone and collapsed into his chair in the living room.

Joyce looked up from her book and frowned.

"God, it's hot in here," Jimmy said, waving his hand in front of his face.

"Why don't you take a shower? That'll cool you off."

"Why don't I just call that Klaus Williams jerk and see when the hell he's going to finish our air-conditioning system so we don't have to roast alive in our own house?"

"Call him. If it'll make you feel better — call him."

"I will."

Jimmy jumped up and staggered over to his phone. He picked it up and was about to dial Klaus Williams' number which he had written in red ink on his blotter when Tiffany Ann Starbuck said: "Jimmy? Jimmy, is that you?"

"Yeah, it's me."

"Oh, good. I didn't want to get your machine again. Jimmy, I know you have every right to be mad, but it's not like what you think it's like with me and Brian."

Jimmy tried to count to ten but only got to two. Then he said, "Tiffany, I don't care about your personal relationship with that phony Irishman."

"What do you mean, phony?" Tiffany said, taking a turn for the worse.

"I've heard high school actors do a better Irish brogue than that guy."

"Jimmy, he's from Galway. He came over here when he was a teen-ager, so of course his accent is fading a little, but . . ."

"The guy's a fucking fraud, Tiffany. I could smell that a mile away."

Tiffany went ballistic. "You're just jealous," she screamed. "You're just jealous because you can't fuck me, and he can."

"Tiffany, that's . . ."

"It's the truth. I know how hot you are for me. Don't think I don't see you looking at me over the light table when we work late. Like you just want to tear my clothes off and fuck me right on the floor. I know how men think. I know how men operate. You're all the same — let your damn dicks do all the talking and thinking. And that's all you think about. And don't think just because you're married you're any different. Because you're not. You're not a bit different than any other man I've ever met. Except . . ."

"The great and magnificent L. David Hinchcliff."

"What?!?"

"You heard me."

"Yeah, I heard you all right. And let me tell you, Jimmy Clarke, you can't even hold a candle to David. Nobody can."

"That why did he walk out on you like that? And leave you holding a whole bunch of debt, and a newspaper that's going nowhere, and all of his . . ."

"FUCK YOU, ASSHOLE!!!! Do you hear me?!?"

"I could have heard you without the phone, Tiffany. And if that's the way you feel then . . ."

"FUCK YOU, ASSHOLE!!!!!!!!!!!!!!!!!!!!!!!!!"

Slam!!!

Click!!!

Buzz.

Then some obnoxious recorded message from the phone company of the day.

Jimmy slammed his phone down and punched himself in the face. A really good one that raised an immediate welt.

Joyce rushed to him and grabbed his arm before he could strike another blow.

"What are you doing?" she said, frantic.

"I'm giving myself the beating I deserve, Joyce. Now let go of my arm so I can hit myself again."

"No!"

Jimmy looked at his wife and a semblance of sobriety crept into his beer-besotted brain. He lowered his arm and let Joyce hug him.

Then he told her all his hurts and disappointments and allowed her to feed him dinner. It just happened to be his favorite — meatloaf, broccoli and baked slices of potato. With a great garden variety salad and Joyce's homemade yogurt dressing.

Jimmy did the dishes, and went to bed drunk but well-fed and happy in the knowledge that he still had a wife who loved him no matter what.

Chapter Twelve

Jessica "call me Jess" Springer entered stage right, marched to center stage, smiled at the assembled parents, grandparents, siblings and neighbors of the cast and unfolded a prepared statement.

Jimmy stood backstage and got goosebumps.

"This is it, buddy boy," Saint Genesius said. The patron saint of actors everywhere gave the playwright an ethereal pat on the back and added: "This might be a blustery Sunday afternoon in November in the ratty gym/auditorium of some backwater little dump of a school in Michigan known as Glenn Consolidated High School, but it doesn't get any better than this. Drink it up. Soak it up. Eat it up. Make it up. You deserve it. You've worked your butt off to get to this moment, and it's arrived. The great here and now. And how. Way to go, buddy boy."

Jimmy nodded and gazed fondly at the high school students who had labored so hard to learn every last line of *Carol's Christmas:* freshman Jane Burton as Carol, freshman Justin Ward as Julio, and senior Heather Lipsom in a brilliant turn as Mrs. Kelly.

Plus good old Jess herself as director.

Jess Springer cleared her throat and said in a stentorian voice: "Good evening, ladies and gentlemen. On behalf of the Glenn Consolidated High School Drama Club, it gives me great pleasure to welcome you to what I believe will be a delightfully entertaining and uplifting evening of theatre.

"We wish to thank all who helped; the administration, clerical, maintenance staff, the adults who agreed to be actors and backstage crew, the teachers, the parents of these fine young actors and actresses and crew and students who assisted with music, sets, props, publicity and tickets.

"We are honored to present the premieres of the works of James Clarke, a local playwright who is just coming into his own. Originally, I planned to just premiere his wonderful one-act play, *Carol's Christmas,* along with some scenes and skits from this nifty woman in Oregon — Petra Paulson.

"But when we began rehearsals, we realized we needed another ten minutes in the program, and Mr. Clarke graciously agreed to write another short play—just for us. It is called *Summer Love,* and you will be privileged to see its premiere here tonight in Glenn.

"We are very grateful for Mr. Clarke's willingness to write this extra play and to make changes and work with us from auditions to the present moment. And now, with no further ado, let the show begin."

Jess Springer sprightly exited stage left, and the guy she had hired to do the lights, lowered the house lights and darkened the stage.

Jane Burton appeared next to Jimmy and whispered: "Do you think I'll be all right, Mr. Clarke? This is such a wonderful play you wrote, I don't want to mess it up."

"You'll be great," Jimmy whispered back. "Break a leg."

The young woman took a deep breath, wended her way through the dark to her "spot," and when the lights came up on Jess Springer's marvelous make-do set, she *was* Carol Kane. Carol Kane and nobody else.

Jimmy stood enthralled in the wings and gave silent thanks to Saint Genesius.

"It doesn't get better than this," he prayed.

"Nope," the old saint said, a bit misty-eyed himself, "it sure don't."

As Jane Burton charmed the audience into believing that she really was a nuclear power worker away from home for her first Christmas, Jimmy helped Justin Ward with his "moment before."

"It's snowing to beat the band," Jimmy whispered, sprinkling stage snow on Justin's head and shoulders. "You're only a second-class angel which means you don't have your wings yet which means you have slog along on the ground like mere mortals. Basically, you're an angel with attitude. You want to move up and get your wings, but your feet are cold and wet, and you could do with an assignment in Florida or Arizona or somewhere warm. Delivering pizzas on a cold, snowy night in Michigan is the last thing you want to do for Christmas. Especially when all the first class angels are having a big do in the Crab Nebula."

Justin Ward nodded sagely and slipped into his stage persona.

Little Lisa Lambert heard Jane Burton say: "That's right— you never say 'fire,' do you? How many did you 'out-place?'"

Little Lisa Lambert pushed the stage buzzer with elan, and Jimmy whispered in Justin Ward's ear, "This is your big moment. Knock 'em dead, champ."

And Justin Ward did just that.

He was wonderful.

Didn't drop a line or skip a beat.

Ditto with Heather Lipsom as Mrs. Kelly. She had the grandmas in the audience reduced to continuous weeping by the end of the play.

Jimmy hugged them all as they came off, and then became lost in the swirl of Jess Springer's fast-paced program.

He even did a turn of acting himself by appearing with Justin Ward in one of Petra Paulson's scenes.

It was called "A Normal Father-Son Conversation" and had Jimmy play a sports-obsessed father who is too involved in watching the ballgame to listen to his son talk about his first date. Jimmy and Justin acted rings around one another, and the audience ate it up.

As they did all of Petra Paulson's other scenes for teens.

"How did you ever get this past the principal?" Jimmy whispered to Jess Springer as they watched a talented threesome tell the tale of two friends who help another with a drug problem.

"It was a battle royal," Jess replied. "And I'm afraid it means I won't be back to do this next year."

"You mean . . ."

"I mean I threatened to pull out entirely if they didn't let me produce the program as is, and the principal said it was too late to get somebody else to come in and do a brain-dead musical, but I'm afraid they won't be renewing my contract which means you're going to have to find another venue for your work."

Jimmy looked up at Saint Genesius and muttered, "Now I know what you meant when you said it doesn't get any better than this. Because this *is* as good as it's ever going to get."

"What?"

"Nothing. Just thinking out loud."

"Occupational hazard, eh?"

"I'm afraid so."

"Well, just sit back and enjoy the premiere of your work. Maybe there's a big Broadway producer out there in the audience tonight disguised as somebody's grandmother."

"Don't I wish?"

"Well, it's a nice thought anyway. And you should really be proud of yourself. The kids love your work, and I must say you've been a delight to work with, Jim. I'm just sorry it has to end here."

"Me, too."

"Well, *Summer Love* is next. Sit back and enjoy."

"I will."

And Jimmy did as senior Morgan Schumacher as Mary Hope and sophomore Carl Stremel as Francis Ignatius "Frank" Phelan filled the cold, dark gym/auditorium with the vibrancy of a summer afternoon at the beach.

To wit:

THE PLACE: A private beach on Lake Michigan near Old Bison, Michigan.

THE TIME: A summer day in the present.

THE PLAYERS :

<u>Mary Hope</u>, 18, of Old Bison, Michigan. Mary has just graduated from Old Bison High School where she was in the National Honor Society and lettered in three sports. She plans to attend the University of Michigan in the fall. She is working for the summer as "beach director" at Willow Run Camp near Old Bison. She is a Lutheran and a "strict" vegetarian. Wants to do something with her life that will "like totally change the world for the better and make a lot of money."

<u>Francis Ignatius "Frank" Phelan</u>, 18, of Rolling Lawns, a suburb of Chicago. Family has summer place at Willow Run Camp where Mary Hope is beach director. Just barely made it through high school and has no immediate plans for college. Might go to a community college in fall, but doesn't know. Only grade better than a C he got in high school was in Art. Did not participate in high school athletics. He is a Roman Catholic and will eat anything that's been dead for ten minutes. Wants to be a rich and famous artist who does all his work on the beach. Failing that, maybe he'll go into something like Coastal Land Management.

(At rise on that Saturday in November 1993, Heather Lipsom as Mary Hope was seated on a high stool standing in for a lifeguard perch and facing the adoring audience. She wore sunglasses, a sun visor, swimsuit and a t-shirt with "beach director" hand-lettered by the playwright on it. She had a backpack at her side with various real food items. That's right, sports fans, real food items. If this was to be Jimmy's crowning night of theatre, then his leading lady would be supplied with real food items and nothing else. Carl Stremel as Frank Phelan sat on a towel beneath Mary Hope drawing in a sketch book.)

Frank: (Finishes drawing) There, I finished it.

Mary: (Glances down) I beg your pardon.

Frank: I finished the sketch I've been working on. Would you like to see it?

Mary: Can't you see I'm on duty? I'm not supposed to talk to anybody while I'm on duty.

Frank: There's nobody in the water right now but my little sister, and she knows how to swim. Come on, let me show you what I just drew.

Mary: No, I'm on duty. I'm protecting your sister from drowning.

Frank: (Stands up and waves arms) Yo, Annie! Time to get out of the water!! Come on—there's a shark alert today. (Listens) Yeah, they spotted a Great White off Saint Joe, and it was last seen heading this way. And everybody knows Great Whites love to eat bratty little kids. (Listens) Yeah, I'll tell you when it's safe to go back in the water. (Listens) Yeah, I'll come and look at your sand castle when you're finished. (Turns back to Mary) There, now there's nobody in the water. How about looking at my drawing?

Mary: That was mean.

Frank: It worked, didn't it.

Mary: I still think it was mean. It was just the kind of thing my older brother used to do to me when were kids. He had me believing that there were freshwater sharks in Lake Michigan until I was twelve.

Frank: You've got an older brother?

Mary: That's what I just told you, didn't I? Something tells me you weren't exactly the valedictorian of your class.

Frank: Actually, the only B I got in high school was in Art. I'm real good at Art. That's why I want to show you this sketch I just did.

Mary: I'm not supposed to talk to people while I'm on duty. The guy who hired me said he'd fire me if he caught me talking to people while I'm on duty.

Frank: The guy who hired you is my father. Don't worry, I won't let him fire you.

Mary: That guy's your father?!?

Frank: Yeah—so?

Mary: Well, he's kind of ...

Frank: Strange?

Mary: Well, yeah.

Frank: What can I say—he's a teacher. That's why he spends all summer going up and down the beach looking for money. He's always complaining that they don't pay him enough at school. Last summer, he found $99 in one day—all in paper money. I can never find it, but he's got a real eye for it. He had the whole family down on the beach looking for that last dollar so he could say he found more than $100 in one day, but we never found it. He's still mad at us.

Mary: That's kind of ...

Frank: Weird?

Mary: Yeah.

Frank: Yeah, I guess it is. So, you want to see my sketch?

Mary: What is the big deal with this sketch?

Frank: It's of you. (Tears sketch out of book and hands it to her) Here, you can have it.

Mary: (Looks at it for a long time) It's—it's, you know.

Frank: No, I don't know.

Mary: Well, it's good. I mean like really good. Are you famous or something?

Frank: (Laughs) No, but I want to be. My goal is to be like this totally famous art dude who does all his work on beaches. Rich people would like pay me to do their portraits on the famous beaches of the world. In winter, I'd go down to Florida and Brazil and places like that. And Australia, of course. Did you know their winter is our summer and versa vice?

Mary: It's vice versa, and, of course, I knew that. I was in National Honor Society, and I was *the* valedictorian of my class.

Frank: That's because you went to a little school around here, right?

Mary: How'd you know?

Frank: Because I know a local when I see one.

Mary: And I know a stupid Chicago person when I see one.

Frank: I'm not from Chicago — I'm from the suburbs.

Mary: It's all the same to me. What a stupid place — all that traffic and pollution.

Frank: Yeah, but I bet you and your girlfriends love to go shopping on Michigan Avenue. Don't you?

Mary: Sometimes. Well, thanks for showing me your sketch. Here, you can have it back.

Frank: No, it's for you to keep.

Mary: Really? (Looks at it again)

Frank: Yeah, really, Mary.

Mary: How'd you know my name?

Frank: My father hired you — remember? Your name's Mary Hope, and you're going to the University of Michigan in the fall. Hey, do you think you could like get some extra tickets for the Notre Dame game? My father went to Notre Dame, but I'd cheer for Michigan. I promise. I think Michigan has the coolest helmets in all of football. You know, maybe that's what I could do — design really cool football helmets. I bet there's a lot of money in that. What do you think, Mary? .

Mary: I think you're the weirdest boy I've ever met, and I think I hear your mother calling, Frank Phelan.

Frank: How'd you know my name?

Mary: Your father hired me — remember?

Frank: Oh, yeah.

Mary: So, are you like a vegan, or what?

Frank: A what?

Mary: You know — do you eat strictly vegetables and grains, or are you like one of those disgusting people who still eat eggs and dairy products?

(Frank laughs)

Mary: What's so funny?

Frank: I saw you eating yogurt yesterday. And I bet you've got some in your backpack right now.

Mary: So what if I do?

Frank: Well, where do you think yogurt comes from — a yogurt tree?

Mary: I know where yogurt comes from.

Frank: And I bet you eat ice cream, too.

Mary: Sometimes. Mackinac Island Fudge. On occasion.

Frank: Yeah, like any occasion you happen to be hungry.

Mary: Are you saying I'm fat?

Frank: No, I'm just saying you make exceptions to your own rules.

Mary: What's wrong with that?

Frank: What's the point of principles if you're not going to stick with them?

Mary: I stick with my principles.

Frank: No, you don't. You just told me you're this totally righteous vegetarian who . . .

Mary: I did not! I just asked if you were a vegetarian. But I can tell from talking to you that you're one of those disgusting meat-eaters. Do you know how much farmland is wasted growing feed for cattle, not to mention all the methane they release into the atmosphere, and have you ever been to a slaughterhouse?

Frank: No, have you?

Mary: No, but I've seen pictures of them.

Frank; Well, so have I, and I still brake for McDonald's.

Mary: I'm not surprised.

Frank: Well, it's been real nice talking to you, but I'm ready to head out on the water.

Mary: I suppose you have one of those disgusting jet-skiis.

Frank: No, actually I have a kayak. (Points) That yellow one over there's mine.

Mary: You own a kayak?

Frank: Yeah, I worked the last three summers and saved up for it. I bought it mail-order from this company in Seattle. It's a sea kayak. Perfect for Lake Michigan. And it's a great work-out.

Mary: I know.

Frank: You have a kayak?

Mary: No, but I have a friend who has a kayak, and she lets me use hers. Plus, I'm going out for the rowing club at Michigan in the fall. I've already talked to the coach and everything.

Frank: That's cool. So maybe you'd like to use my kayak sometime this summer. You know, like when you're off duty and everything.

Mary: Maybe.

Frank: Well, it's been a slice, lifeguard dude.

Mary: I'm not a lifeguard, and I'm not a dude.

Frank: That's right — we're supposed to call you beach director because the insurance company says we're liable if we call you lifeguard. Later, beach director dude.

Mary: Do I look like a dude to you?

Frank: (Gazes up at her in awe) No, you sure don't. You look like — you know . . .

Mary: No, I don't know, but I'm sure you'll tell me.

Frank: I don't know if I should. You'll probably say it's sexist.

Mary: Try me.

Frank: Okay, here goes — you look like Aphrodite.

Mary: Who?!?

Frank: I thought you said you were valedictorian of your class.

Mary: I did, and I was.

Frank: Then how come you don't know who Aphrodite is?

Mary: I know who Aphrodite is.

Frank: Who is she?

Mary: She's like on MTV or something.

(Frank laughs)

Mary: What's so funny?

Frank: You.

Mary: What about me?

Frank: You look just like Aphrodite — the goddess of love and beauty. There, I said it. Now, who do you think I look like? Apollo, god of beauty, youth and poetry, or . . .

Mary: No, you look like some stuck-up, meat-eating boy from Chicago. And I thought you were going kayaking.

Frank: I am.

Mary: Good. So go.

Frank: I will. (Starts to exit, stops and turns to her) Hey, there's this new espresso place in town. How'd you like to like hang-out there tonight after you get off? I've heard they've got some great espresso places in Ann Arbor, so you'd better start getting in training.

Mary: Maybe I don't drink espresso.

Frank: They've got steamed milk with honey and that kind of stuff. I bet you'd go for that.

Mary: Maybe.

Frank: Good. I can borrow my parents' car.

Mary: I've got my own car.

Frank: That's cool. We can go in your car.

Mary: Maybe.

Frank: Maybe?

Mary: Maybe.

Frank: Okay, maybe. I'm off to sea, Aphrodite. (Exits)

Mary: (Gazes fondly at sketch and Frank, and self-consciously fluffs hair) Watch out for sharks!

The guy Jess Springer hired to do the lights brought down the lights, and the audience burst into robust applause.

Followed by an ethereal reappearance by Saint Genesius who whispered in the playwright's ear: "That was it. Drink it up, buddy boy. Soak it up. Put it in your pipe and smoke it for a good long while, because that's as good as it gets."

"But, what about . . ."

"Later, dude."

"Talking to yourself again?" Jess Springer said, appearing at Jimmy's side.

"Just a spiritual moment."

"Right. Well, come on, it's time for us all to go out and take a bow."

Which they did.

And then, miracle of miracles, Tiffany Ann Starbuck appeared backstage and planted a big kiss on Jimmy's cheek.

"That's to make amends for the beastly way I behaved," she said. "And I'm going to write the best review you'll ever get of your plays."

"You're kidding."

The Tiffster wasn't kidding, and she would have stayed and talked but she had another story to cover.

She dashed off, leaving Jimmy to help Jess Springer strike the stage and tear down the black-out paper he had taped to the top windows in the gym.

"Who says theatre is for wimps," Jimmy said, hoisting a heavy table off the stage.

"It's certainly not all glamour," Jess Springer said, helping him.

"So what are you going to do next?"

Jess Springer shrugged. "More calls in Chicago and Detroit. Maybe get some hand modeling if I'm lucky or some commercial work. Probably end up doing some of my best work for a line of adult diapers."

"That's awful."

"It's a living."

"Yeah, I suppose."

"What about you, Jim? I'd think after last night and today you're hungry for more."

"Yeah, but I really don't know what to do next. I was thinking of writing some more plays and maybe sending them to theatres in New York or something, but that's probably not the best way to go about it. What would you suggest?"

"If I were you, I'd continue trying to make a name for myself locally, and then branch out."

"Yeah, but I haven't exactly been having much luck on the local scene." Jimmy summarized his unhappy experience with the Blue Star Players, concluding with: "And they're really the only ones around here — except for you, and you're not going to be able to do anything more here — who are interested in original theatre. Everybody else just wants to endlessly put up the old war horses."

"Have you thought about the Fennell?"

"The what?"

"The Fennell Art Gallery."

"You mean that old dump off the Blue Star between here and South Haven?"

"Precisely that old dump off the Blue Star. Did you know that it was built in the '20's as a vaudeville house?"

"No."

"Yes, and Al Capone allegedly frequented it. But you should go and see it. It's just waiting for somebody young and ambitious to restore it to its former glory."

"Last time I looked, they were operating an archery range in there."

"Not anymore. I've heard through the grapevine that there's a new owner, and he's looking for somebody like you to restore it as a theatre. I've heard there's an enormous fly space in there, a dressing room under the stage, an orchestra pit, and even a raked floor."

Jimmy gazed dreamily across the darkened gym/auditorium. "New owner, you say?"

"So I've heard. Why don't you check it out? It's right on your way home."

"Maybe I will."

"Go for it. O'Neill started his own theatre, and so did O'Casey in Dublin. What have you got to lose?"

"Nothing. Say, would you be interested—I mean if it looks like something could be done with the old place?"

"Sure. You can count on me."

"Good. Well, thanks again for giving me so much of your program, Jess. It was a playwright's dream come true."

"And your work was a director's dream come true. I just wish we could extend the run."

"Yeah, me too. But it was really great. Really great."

"Don't worry—there'll be plenty more. Just stick with it, and do go and see the Fennell. I have a good feeling about it."

Jimmy looked at Jess Springer and saw that she was sincere.

So he sincerely wished her all the best with her acting career (what there was left of it, that is), and went with a brave heart to investigate the old dump off the Blue Star known as the Fennell Art Gallery.

Chapter Thirteen

Jimmy could barely make out the old barn of a vaudeville house in the November gloaming.

But there was just enough lingering light in which to see the soaring fly space.

Jimmy got out of his car and stared up at it. "Wow," he exclaimed to the elements, "They sure don't make 'em like that anymore."

"Nope, they sure don't."

Jimmy looked around.

No one.

Nobody.

Just the slashing November wind.

Jimmy conked his head with the butt of his hand and wondered if maybe it wasn't time to make an appointment with Dr. Peter Phillips, Ph.D. Have a little hyno-therapy and get to the bottom of the barrel that his former therapist, Judy, had only begun to scrape.

But then again, Jimmy thought, it could be Saint Genesius talking to me.

"Right?"

"Wrong."

Jimmy looked around again.

No one.

Nobody.

Then a dark figure stepped into what little light was left of the late November day. He wore a thick beard, flannel shirt, worn jeans, shitkickers, and a relaxed and ready manner.

"Evenin'," he said, laconically.

"Evenin'," Jimmy said. He wasn't sure if he should extend his hand or run away. Saint Genesius told him to extend his hand, so he did.

The dark figure took it, gave Jimmy a quick, hard squeeze and dropped his hand.

Jimmy cleared his throat.

The dark figure nodded his head.

Jimmy said, "Uh, I'm Jimmy Clarke. I uh . . ."

"You were the one who did that play at GAS this summer."

"Yeah, that's me."

"My wife and I were all set to come and see it, but then her relatives from Scotland showed up, and we had to entertain them. But I heard it was a great success."

"Yeah, we did all right. All things considered."

"I'd say you did more than all right — considering all the write-ups you got in the papers."

"Well, it helped that a member of the cast was a reporter for the HERALD-PALLADIUM."

"Yeah. So, you stop by to have a look at the old Fennell?"

"As a matter of fact, I did. Are you ..."

"Oh, didn't I introduce myself?"

"Uh, no, you didn't."

The bearded man laughed, showing his weathered creases. "Boy," he said, "if my wife was here, she'd kill me. She says I have the manners of a snake. But then that's not fair to snakes, because most snakes have better manners than me."

"Well, I wouldn't ..."

"No, it's true. Anyway, my name's Larry. Larry German. And me and my sister Julie just bought this old dump. We're planning on moving our woodshop — *Out of the Woods* — into what was the lobby of the old theatre, and we've been thinking of fixing up the old theatre and maybe putting on some plays in there again. You interested in helping out?"

Jimmy waited for Saint Genesius to whisper some heavenly advice in his ear.

Saint Genesius was strangely silent.

Jimmy waited two more beats, then licked his lips, shuffled his feet, rubbed his hands together for warmth and finally allowed as how he "just might be interested in helping out a little bit. But I have to be honest, I'm all thumbs when it comes to doing handy work."

"Well, you don't have to be handy to push a broom or operate a paint brush," Larry German said.

"No, I suppose you don't."

The two men stood in the descending darkness and gazed up at the brick theatre that allegedly had hosted Al Capone. Along with every other theatre, restaurant and hotel in southwest lower Michigan.

Then Larry German said, "How about coming in and having a look around? Unless you're in a big hurry to get home."

Jimmy was in a big hurry to get home because it was dinner-time and Joyce was making meatloaf, but, damn it, he had the theatre bug, and he had it bad, and it bit him right on the ass right then and there outside the decrepit old Fennell Art Gallery.

"And Theatre," Jimmy muttered.

"What was that?"

"Oh. Sorry. Just thinking out loud. But, yeah, let's go in and have a look. As long as you're inviting."

"I'm in no hurry to go anywhere. Now what was that you just said about a theatre?"

"I was just thinking—if we fix this place up again—and it sounds like you're already well on your way with your woodworking shop and all—then why not call it the Fennell Art Gallery and Theatre? I mean, I assume your shop is basically going to be a showroom for your woodwork, so that's the gallery part, and the theatre would be the theatre. So it'd be appropriate to call it the Fennell Art Gallery and Theatre."

Larry German rolled that around his noggin for a moment and said, "The Fennell Art Gallery and Theatre?"

"Yeah. Why not?"

"Yeah. Why not? But wouldn't the initials be F-A-G-A-T. I mean, everything is initials these days, and we'd end up calling it FAGAT. There's a lot of gays around here in the summer, and I don't think they'd go for that."

"On the contrary, Larry. I think they'd get a hoot out of it. It might even work to our advantage. A little reverse publicity, if you know what I mean."

"Sounds like you've done a lot of marketing."

"Yeah, I've been around the track a few times."

"Well, we're having an organizing meeting next Saturday morning—maybe you'd like to come. We could use somebody to do some marketing and publicity."

"Let me see the theatre first."

"All right. But don't expect much."

"I won't."

Larry German shouldered open the warped door and fumbled around in the dark for the one good light switch.

Jimmy sniffed in the smell of abandonment, decay and industrial abuse.

"What in God's name were they doing in here?" Jimmy asked.

"What in God's name weren't they doing in here," Larry German replied. He found the one good light switch and illuminated the various vicious vicissitudes visited on the old vaudeville house. For starters, there was a lifelike rubber likeness of a deer posed front of the stage. With a target arrow embedded it its lifeless heart.

And, as Jess Springer had warned, a level floor covering the old raked theatre floor. And pipes and discarded duct work, and junk, and dust and clutter, and stains, oil spills, foul smells, decay, rotted wood, broken windows, mouse droppings, dropped mouses, leaves, heaps of desiccated insects, a dead opossum or two, and insult of insults — a toilet installed at center stage.

"What in God's name is that doing there?!?" Jimmy said, pointing at the offending object.

"After the theatre closed in the 1940s, a machine shop bought it and put in the level floor for their equipment, and that toilet for their employees. The deer is from the archery range — I've been trying to get those people to come and pick it up, but they don't seem to care."

Jimmy laughed in spite of himself.

"What's so funny?"

"I was just thinking — you could do a great absurdist comedy here just the way it is. That rubber deer with the arrow in it would be the perfect prop. Hell, it could be the protagonist. And the toilet at center stage. The perfect statement about the state of American theatre and the world in general."

Larry German stroked his beard and nodded enthusiastically. "Yeah, I can dig it. So what do you think?"

"I'd like to see the fly space."

"The what?"

"The space over the stage where props could be hoisted up and out of sight. It's called the fly space."

"Well, there's nothing over the stage now but a ceiling."

"Let's have a look."

Larry German had a handyman's flashlight handy and shined it up at the ceiling over the cluttered stage.

"That's a false ceiling," Jimmy said at once. "Let me borrow your flashlight."

"Sure."

Jimmy used the flashlight to find a long piece of scrap iron, and handed the flashlight back to Larry.

"Shine it up there."

"Okay."

Larry put a beam of light on the false ceiling, and Jimmy perforated it with the scrap iron. Shredded newspapers showered down on the two men.

Larry German picked up a yellowed scrap and read the headline: "'JAPS ATTACK PEARL HARBOR!!' Wow. This is incredible. We'll have to start a scrapbook or something."

Jimmy continued poking at the false ceiling until he had made a decent hole. Then he took the flashlight and shined it up into the abyss.

"Yes!!" he hissed. "Just as I suspected—a perfect fly space and the pulleys and support beams are still up there."

"Let me see."

Jimmy let Larry German see, and then Larry German let Jimmy see the dressing room beneath the stage. From there, he let him see the orchestra pit that had been covered over by the level industrial floor.

"It's perfect," Jimmy said. "It's almost like they were unconsciously preserving it for future use."

"Yeah, it's karma. It's meant to be. And your coming by tonight was meant to be. I could feel it in the wind."

"You could?"

"Oh yeah."

"Larry?"

"Yeah?"

"You, ah, do a lot of—well, you know—back in the '60s."

"Who says the '60s are over?"

"Yeah. Right."

"Want to fire up?"

"Excuse me?"

"Smoke a bowl. I've got some dynamite homegrown. Knock your socks off."

"I don't know — if I start smoking that stuff again, I'll go back to cigarettes and end up getting lung cancer."

"Not from my homegrown. Goes down mighty smooth."

Jimmy looked around to see if Saint Genesius was watching. The old Roman actor and Christian martyr had business elsewhere, so Jimmy allowed as how maybe he'd just have a toke or two.

"For old time's sake."

"For old time's sake," Larry German said, loading a brass pot pipe straight out of a '60s headshop and firing up with a Zippo lighter with an actual peace sign on it.

Larry took an enormous toke, and handed the pipe to Jimmy, saying, "Peace and love, man."

"Yeah, peace and love, man."

Jimmy took a toke and wondered what Joyce was going to say. It was bad enough that he had had a major marijuana slip with the illustrator of his ill-fated children's earlier in the year. Joyce got over that, Jimmy thought, but only because I promised on a stack of bibles to be on good behavior for the rest of my life, and I was going to go to Diet Center the other day or something, but . . .

"What'd you say, man?"

Jimmy blinked and could suddenly see in the dark. "Wow," he said, handing the pipe back to Larry, "this is some dynamite shit."

"Yeah, the harvest just came in. Why buy imported when you can smoke homegrown that'll knock your socks off?"

"Right on."

The two men smoked the bowl down to ash.

Then Larry asked the inevitable question: "Wanna smoke another bowl?"

And Jimmy gave the inevitable answer of potheads the world over: "Sure, man."

* * *

The meatloaf was chilling in the refrigerator and Joyce was steaming over a thick book with tiny print when Jimmy finally rolled through the door.

Joyce took one sniff and knew at once that Jimmy had been smoking pot. Despite Jimmy's having stopped at the truck stop and doused himself with cheap aftershave and eaten an entire roll of Certs.

"You're stoned," she declared, clapping her book shut.

"No, I'm not!"

"Yes, you are! I can smell it. And I can see it in your eyes. Your pupils look like a couple of hockey pucks, and you've got that goofy 'life of the party' look on your face."

Jimmy sighed enormously and willed himself to be sober.

No can do, old man cannabis said, busily coursing through his veins.

"Jimmy!!"

"What?"

"Aren't you going to say something?"

"What do you want me to say?"

"Why did you smoke pot? I thought you were never going to smoke pot again. Especially after that awful time you had with Chuck Dawson and his hillbilly friends at that Timber Lounge or whatever it was called."

"It's the Plywood Palace, Joyce," Jimmy said, heading for the bathroom.

"Where are you going?"

"To take a piss. If I don't take a piss immediately, I'm going to explode."

"Were you drinking, too?"

"Just a few beers. Larry had a six-pack in his truck and, they were cold, and, well, my throat was pretty parched from the, ah, you know, and . . ."

"Who the hell is Larry?" Joyce demanded, following her husband into the bathroom.

Jimmy ignored her, unzipped his unit and let splash with a mighty stream of beer piss.

"Jimmy, I asked you a question."

"Joyce, I'm trying to take a leak. Do you mind?"

"I mind that you show up two hours late for dinner; you don't call; you're stoned, and now you're talking about some guy named

Larry. Who the hell is Larry — some local pothead you met at the truck stop?"

"Joyce, would you let me piss in peace?!?"

"Not until you give me an explanation for why you're behaving like an idiot. I thought this was supposed to be such a great day for you — they did your plays at the high school. Wasn't that enough?"

"Yeah, it was great," Jimmy said, squeezing out the last golden drops. "But then Jess told me she's out for next year. Which means I've got to find somewhere else to get my plays produced, and she suggested I stop by the Fennell Art Gallery on the way home and talk . . ."

"You mean that old dump off the Blue Star?"

"It's not a dump, Joyce," Jimmy said, shaking and zipping in one practiced motion.

"Jimmy, the place looks likes it's ready to cave in from decay. What do you mean, it's not a dump? And who is this Larry creature?"

Jimmy sighed enormously and stomped into the kitchen to get his cold meatloaf. He had a powerful case of the munchies and was ready to eat everything in the refrigerator and then start in on the kitchen shelves.

Joyce followed on his heels and watched in horror as her husband began devouring her meatloaf cold. And with his fingers.

"What are you doing?"

"Eating," Jimmy said, chewing and smacking his lips in a most disgusting manner.

"Heat it up first."

"No, Joyce. I'm hungry. I'm starving."

"Well, you wouldn't be starving if you would have come home for dinner on time. And you wouldn't be starving if you hadn't run off with some jerk named Larry and smoked pot like some stupid teen-ager or something. God, Jimmy, I can't believe you did such a childish thing. What's going on with you anyway?"

Jimmy slammed down the plate of cold meatloaf, potatoes and broccoli and pounded into the living room.

Joyce followed, demanding: "Answer me."

Jimmy slapped his forehead.

"Stop that!"

Jimmy made a fist and punched himself in the cheek.

Joyce rushed to him and grabbed his arm before he could strike himself again.

Jimmy looked at her wildly and then bolted out of the house into the November night thinking he would never be seen again.

Well, he thought, maybe some bird-watcher at the state park will chance upon my bloated corpse on the beach in the spring. The crows will be pecking out my eyeballs and the . . .

Bummer man.

Too depressing.

Yeah.

Go back to Joyce and say you're sorry, asshole.

Why?

Because I said so.

Who're you to tell me anything?

Saint Genesius. Roman actor supreme and principled Christian martyr. One of God's holy messengers.

Yeah right. It's just this fucking pot, and I'm hearing voices — that's all. Mental breakdown. Runs in the family. Look at poor old Uncle . . .

"That's enough," Saint Genesius said, enfolding the troubled playwright in an ethereal embrace.

Jimmy immediately felt calm and tingly.

He sighed.

Saint Genesius sighed.

Then the latter led the former back to the Dunery and stood by as Jimmy said to his beloved wife: "Joyce, I'm sorry. I really am."

Having returned to her thick book with tiny print, Joyce was not easily mollified. So she pretended to continue to read about the ruination of the Roman Empire.

Jimmy slipped off his shoes and padded over to the couch. He settled quietly next to his wife and sighed.

Joyce's resolve retired for the night. She closed her book and slowly turned her head to her husband. "What's the matter, Jimmy?"

Jimmy threw up his hands and said, "I just — well — I ran into this guy at the Fennell. His name is Larry German and he and his sister Julie bought the old place and want to restore it into a theatre again and . . ."

"And they want you to do all the work."

Jimmy felt a flash of anger and waved it away. Then he took two beats in which to compose himself and said, "No, not at all. In fact there's a meeting next Saturday to organize the whole thing. And Jess Springer said she'd help, and Larry said there are all kinds of people interested in restoring the old place to its former glory—even some bigshot architect from Chicago who's apparently done a lot of restorations like this."

"Sounds like you and this Larry creature smoked a lot of pot together."

"Well . . ."

"Let me guess—he said: 'How about another bowl?' And you said: 'Sure, man.'"

"Joyce, you know me better than that."

"Which is exactly why I know exactly what happened. Now why don't you you go finish your meatloaf—it's heating up in the oven. Go eat—you must be starving."

"I'm not really hungry now."

"Jimmy, you were eating it cold with your fingers five minutes ago. Now go eat."

"Maybe I'll just have some coffee."

"Jimmy, you can't live off of coffee."

Jimmy realized he was reverting to total jerkness, so he held his breath for a second and said, "You're right. I'll go eat. And thanks for making meatloaf, Joyce. And I'm really sorry I was so late for dinner. And that I came home stoned."

Joyce could see that he was sincere, but she was still hurt so she just nodded grimly and went back to the ruination of the Roman Empire.

Jimmy went glumly to his meatloaf and cleaned his plate in silence.

Joyce went to bed early, and Jimmy stayed up half the night channel surfing. He finally settled on the umpteenth airing of *Victory at Sea* on one of the PBS stations, and fell asleep in his chair with Japanese kamikazes dive bombing through the earphones on his head.

Chapter Fourteen

Jimmy was so excited about the impending organizing meeting at Fennell Art Center that he got on the horn and cajoled Jess Springer and Burt Babbington into coming.

He even called Maye Michaels, but she said she had an assignment for PEOPLE MAGAZINE she was not at liberty to discuss.

"Besides," Maye added, "my agent has a deal in the works that will soon require me to move either to the east or west coast."

"Right. Good for you, Maye."

"Have fun with your little theatre project, Jimmy," Maye said, clicking off.

Jimmy was going to call Douglas Iglesia and his emotional bat-girl, Constance Myers. But there were limits, and the ill memory of his dreadful drubbing at the hands of the Blue Star Players' board of directors was still fresh in his head.

So he said fuck it and started in on a new play.

One he was sure would be a raving great hit at the Fennell Art Center.

"Correction: The Fennell Art Center & Theatre."

"Jimmy, keep it down over there — I'm trying to write."

"Sorry, Joyce. Just writing out loud again."

"Well, write in silence. Like me."

"Yes, dear."

Jimmy focused on his Samsung amber monitor and saw a world where justice applied only to white folk. A world in which there was — "Criminal Justice."

"Jimmy!!"

"Sorry, Joyce. I just thought of the title for my new play. Remember that exhibit we saw at the mall in Benton Harbor about the black migration north before, during, and after World War I and how there was practically a lynching every day in the South in those days, and even a few cases where they burned blacks to death because they thought they had been messing with some white woman and . . ."

"Jimmy!!"

"Sorry, Joyce."

"Just write. In silence. And you can read it all to me later."

"Right."

Jimmy wrote the following:

CRIMINAL JUSTICE

One Act, Three Scenes

For those who really died this way

THE PLACE: Town jail in Hope, Alabama

THE TIME: A sultry summer night in 1914

THE PLAYERS:

Leader of posse – (Maynard Pickens) Burly white man in factory clothes.

Five posse members – Burly white men in factory and farm clothes.

Isaiah Washington, 22, African-American. Handsome, well-proportioned, well-dressed. Self-educated, well-read. Dignified. Astute. Considered "uppity' by blacks and whites. A cynical optimist.

Sheriff Morris, 37. Timid white man who has never raised a blister in his life. Slight build, sallow complexion. Prefers paperwork to policing the town. Just doing his job. Not well-read or educated.

Mr. (George) Rutledge, 28. Reporter for the HOPE TRUTH. Local boy who hopes to make a name for himself and move up to a big city paper in Montgomery or Atlanta or maybe even Baltimore. Has bachelor degree from the University of Alabama. Considers himself open-minded.

The Reverend Mr. Pinckney, 56. Rector of All Saints Episcopal Church. Only local clergyman willing to come and see the condemned man. Well-educated and well-read but has hidden behind his books and church from the terrible brutality around him.

SCENE ONE

(It is a sultry summer night at the town jail in Hope, Alabama. The jail is a simple affair: a desk with a telephone and some chairs on one side, and a jail cell on the other. There is a portrait of Robert E. Lee on the wall and a calendar from the local feed and mill. Sheriff Morris is seated at the desk completing a form when a posse of six white men barges in with a black prisoner. Five of the posse hold the prisoner while their leader talks to the sheriff.)

Leader of Posse: We got us a prisoner for you, Sheriff. Open up your jail cell, and we'll put this young buck on ice 'til we arrange the proper punishment.

Sheriff: (Rises) Wait a minute. What is this?!? I'm the sheriff here! Judge Wallingford didn't tell me to go and arrest anybody.

Leader of Posse: If you was a proper sheriff, you'd a known that this uppity nigger here done raped and ravished Miss Margaret Sherwood. And if you was a proper sheriff, you'd of arrested his black ass by now and hung him from the nearest tree. But on accounta you ain't nuthin' but a desk-bound little weasel what's afraid of his own shadow, me an' the boys here took it upon ourselves to perpetrate justice. Now open the damn cell, Sheriff, an' lock up this menace to civilization. We gots to go out and alert the good citizens of this here town so we can deliver the proper punishment.

Jimmy shuddered at the thought of what the proper punishment in such situations had been. Then he continued creating:

Sheriff: (Opens drawer and gets key) I don't rightly know about this, Maynard. Ain't that Isaiah Washington? The colored preacher's boy?

Leader of Posse: Don't matter what his name is or who his daddy is, Sheriff, because this time tomorrow he ain't gonna be nothin' but a pile of ashes sittin' at the gates a hell.

Sheriff: You mean to burn the boy?!?

They did, and the play ended thusly:

SCENE THREE

(Three hours later in the same jailhouse. The Sheriff is still pretending to be sleeping on his desk where Mr. Rutledge placed him in the preceding scene. Isaiah Washington is at the window with his hands on the bars. His tear-stained face is uplifted and bathed in the first blush of dawn. He is quietly muttering the Lord's Prayer for the umpteenth time as the now formidable lynch mob outside gives voice to its fury.)

Isaiah Washington: ". . . and forgive us our trespasses, as we forgive those who trespass against us, and lead us not into temptation, but deliver us from evil. For thine is the kingdom, and the power, and . . .

(The door bursts open, and the Reverend Mr. Pinckney is shoved into the jailhouse. He wears an Anglican collar and a fine linen suit from one of the better stores in Montgomery. He collects himself and approaches the cell.)

Rev. Pinckney: Forgive my rather abrupt entrance, Mr. Washington. I, ah, well, the, uh, committee thought it proper that you should, uh, have some spiritual guidance before you, uh, well before they, uh . . .

Isaiah Washington: Burn me to death? (Turns and advances to front of cell) That what you tryin' to say, Reverend?

Rev. Pinckney: Actually, I prefer to be called the Reverend Mr. Pinckney. If it's all the same to you, Mr. Washington. I am the rector of All Saints Episcopal and . . .

Isaiah Washington: I know who you are, Reverend. If they want me to have spiritual guidance, why didn't they let my father come and see me? He's more of a Christian minister than you'll ever be.

Rev. Pinckney: (Clears his throat) Well, it seems as though your, uh, family and neighbors have, uh, well—

Isaiah Washington: Have what?!? Say it!!

Rev. Pinckney: Well, shall we just say they've been placed under the benevolent protection of the Knights of the . . .

Isaiah Washington: Ku Klux Klan's got them surrounded? That's what you mean—don't you?

Rev. Pinckney: (Laughs nervously and mops brow with silk kerchief) It's for their own good, Mr. Washington. Folks are a might agitated right now, and it wouldn't do for your people to be comin' down here to see you. If you follow my meanin'.

Isaiah Washington: Oh, I follow your meanin', Reverend. Only too well. (Studies the clergyman) So, you the only one brave enough to come in here and give the darkie a proper Christian send-off?

Rev. Pinckney: Well, in a manner of speakin', I suppose you could say that.

Isaiah Washington: And in a manner of speakin', Reverend, I'm sure you'll tell your bishop all about your heroic mission. Won't you?

Rev. Pinckney: Mr. Washington. Please. This is no time for sarcasm. Not with . . .

Leader of Posse: (Kicks open door) Come on, Reverend! Hurry it on up!! Folks is gettin' mighty restless.

(Cries of "burn the nigger" are heard.)

Rev. Pinckney: (Rubs elbows) Very well, Mr. Pickens. I'll just be a moment more. Now, if you'll please leave us in peace for five minutes, I'll say the Litany for the Dying with the prisoner here.

Leader of Posse: Prisoner?!!? (Spits chaw of tobacco on floor) That's good, Reverend. That's real good. You hurry on up with your little ceremony. You hear?

Rev. Pinckney: I hear you, Mr. Pickens.

Leader of Posse: Good. Real good. (Grins malevolently, retreats and closes door)

Isaiah Washington: You heard the man, Reverend. Best get on with it. Wouldn't want to keep such important people waiting.

Rev. Pinckney: (Withdraws leather-bound BOOK OF COMMON PRAYER from inside coat pocket and approaches the cell) Would you care to bow your head, Mr. Washington?

Isaiah Washington: If it's all the same to you, Reverend, I like to look at the Lord when I pray.

Rev. Pinckney: Very well. (Carefully opens prayer book to page marked by ribbon. Clears throat and bows head slightly.) "O Almighty God, with whom do live the sprits of just men made perfect, after they are delivered from their earthy prisons; we humbly commend the soul of this thy servant, our dear brother, into they hands, as into the hands of a faithful Creator, and most merciful Saviour; beseeching thee, that it may be precious in they sight. Wash it, we pray thee, that it may be precious in thy sight. Wash it, we pray thee, in the blood of that immaculate Lamb, that was slain to take away the sins of the world; that whatsoever defilements it may have contracted, through the lusts of the flesh or the wiles of Satan, being purged and done away, it may be presented pure and without spot before thee; through the merits of Jesus Christ thine only Son our Lord. Amen."

Isaiah Washington: Amen.

(Leader and five posse members burst through door. Two of the posse members care carrying coils of rope.)

Leader of Posse: You done save his soul, Reverend?

Rev. Pinckney: That was hardly five minutes, Mr. Pickens.

Leader of Posse: It was more time than this nigger deserved. (Looks at sleeping sheriff and laughs) Looks like ol' justice is sleepin' on the job. Ain't that right, Jimmy boy?

(Sheriff emits another loud snore.)

Leader of Posse: Hell of a damn actor, ain't he boys?

(Posse members grunt and guffaw as one)

Leader of Posse: (Fetches keys from desk drawer and pushes clergyman aside) Okay, boys, don't let him get away when I open the cell.

Isaiah Washington: Don't worry, Mr. Pickens. I'm not going to run away.

Leader of Posse: (Laughs) That's what they all say. (Puts key in lock and turns it) Okay, boys, grab 'im!!

(Five posse members rush into cell and seize prisoner and bind his arms behind his back with rope. A posse member puts a rope around prisoner's neck and hands end to leader.)

Leader of Posse: (Yanks rope) Come on, you black devil dog, and meet your old master Satan!

Rev. Pinckney: (With all the dignity he can muster) Wait!!

Leader of Posse: Wait for what?!? This here buck's got an appointment with the devil, and I sure don't want to be the one to keep old Lucifer waitin'.

Rev. Pinckney: (Raises hand over prisoner) "The Almighty and merciful Lord grant thee pardon and remission of all thy sins and the grace and comfort of the Holy Spirit. Amen. Depart, O Christian soul, out of this world . . ."

Leader of Posse: We heard enough outta you, Reverend. (Shoves clergyman aside and pulls a choking Isaiah Washington out of the jailhouse.)

(Five posse members follow eagerly, and there is a great guttural shout from the mob.)

Rev. Pinckney: (Goes to door and continues solemnly) " . . . In the Name of God the Father Almighty who created thee. In the Name of Jesus Christ who redeemed thee. In the Name of the Holy Ghost who sanctifieth thee. May thy rest be this day in peace, and thy dwelling-place in the Paradise of God." (Makes sign of cross and slowly departs.)

(There is a great tumult outside and then a frenzied cry as the fire is ignited. The jailhouse is bathed in the eerie light of it. The Sheriff slowly rises and goes to door and watches in horror for a long moment.)

Sheriff: (Sings softly) "Mine eyes have seen the glory of the the coming of the Lord; He is trampling out the vintage where the grapes of wrath are stored. His truth is marching on."

(Lights fade as Sheriff is singing. His face is bathed in the light of the fire for a long moment, then total darkness. Play ends.)

Jimmy pushed his ergonomic chair away from his computer and surveyed all that he had written.

In thought, word, and deed it was very good.

Indeed.

But he knew in his heart of hearts that it would never be produced.

Never.

And that hurt him deeply.

Still, he resolved to give it his best shot, and the nascent Fennell Art Gallery & Theatre certainly seemed like the logical target.

So Jimmy flicked on his Epson FX-185 dot matrix printer and started typing in the necessary print commands.

"Jimmy!!" Joyce howled from her writing booth, "I'm not finished writing yet."

"Sorry."

Jimmy climbed into his running togs and took off around their wooded "block." Seeing on the second loop that Joyce had finished writing her "real stuff" for the day, Jimmy jogged into his office and, without breaking stride, ordered his computer to print his new play.

Then he galloped off into the autumnal splendor dreaming of fame and glory at the Fennell Art Gallery.

"Correction," he told himself, "The Fennell Art Gallery *and* Theatre. Yeah!!! Now shut up and run."

He shut up and ran for his life.

Chapter Fifteen

Jimmy arrived for the organizing meeting of the Fennell Art Gallery (and Theatre) with his new play in hand and hope in his heart.

It was a cold, clear November morning and the earth tones were ascendant. Jimmy took in the subtle brown beauty before him and stomped his feet and rubbed his hands.

Then he looked around and wondered where the hell everyone was.

Hadn't Larry German said the meeting was set to begin promptly at 8:30?

Yes, of course. I just talked to the guy last night to confirm. He said 8:30 because he and his sister open their woodshop promptly at nine o'clock. With the emphasis on promptly.

Jimmy glanced at his watch and saw that it was 8:29.

Jimmy glanced around.

No one.

Nada.

Jimmy tried the door.

Locked.

Jimmy got back in his car and turned on the engine. When it was sufficiently warm, he fired up the heat, cranked up his favorite NPR station and settled back for an in-depth discussion of the day's news.

He was bouncing around someplace called Bosnia when he heard the crunch of steel-belted radials on crushed stone.

An enormous, black, German car with vainglorious Illinois license plates braked to a precision stop and disgorged a woman with preternaturally black hair and great gobs of clanking silver and turquoise jewelry. And, oh yes, a pair of ostrich-skin cowboy boots from some mail-order boutique in Dallas. Home of the truly brain-dead.

The woman gestured theatrically at the Fennell and seemed prepared to deliver herself of a stirring soliloquy on the true meaning of truth and meaning when a little butterball of a man burbled out of the great Nazi staff car.

He actually wore a cape, bow tie, and a monocle.

Jimmy was aghast. God, he thought, central casting for the truly wretched B movies of the '50s couldn't have come up with such a couple of clichés.

The woman with the great clanking jewelry admitted Jimmy and his little car into her sweeping vision. She put on a prepared smile and strutted over to Angel Car.

Jimmy hurriedly rolled down the window.

Having never been in the presence of royalty before, Jimmy was unclear as how to proceed.

The woman with the great clanking jewelry proceeded for him by demanding: "Would you please open the door? Myron and I are freezing out here."

"I don't have the key," Jimmy stammered.

"Then call somebody who does."

"But I don't have a car phone."

The woman raised her powdered nose and penciled eyebrows in contempt. She had heard about these Michigan rustics who lived on less than $200,000 a year. Had heard about them, but had never actually met one.

Until now.

And now she was all icy contempt.

"You don't have a car phone?!? In this day and age?!?"

"Sorry. I . . ."

The woman dismissed Jimmy with a rude wave and went to confer with the caped butterball.

More tires crunched the crushed stone, and three lost youths emerged from a battered Ford pick-up. One was a fat farm boy who ate only Hershey Bars and french fries; one was a skinny farm boy who ate only Diet Coke and cigarettes; and one was a plump little thing from South Haven who looked like she lived off jelly donuts, M&Ms, and pizza. Which she did, of course.

The threesome said nothing to no one and proceeded directly to the door. When they found it locked, they retreated to the comfort of their truck cab and listened to loud, raucous rap music.

Jimmy glanced at his watch.

8:32 and counting.

And no sign of Larry German.

But there were signs of other life as a whole host of cars came crunching up the unpaved drive.

In no time flat, Jimmy was confronted with a crowd of fat, pretentious twits all wondering why he didn't have the key.

8:35 and counting.

And no sign of Larry German.

Jimmy got out of Angel Car and tried to mingle. But by being naturally courteous and friendly, he positioned himself as someone with true leadership potential.

A wrinkled wreck of a middle-aged woman with a great dusky crop of red hair and green eye shadow said Jimmy should be president. "You're a natural leader," she said in a thick Brooklyn accent. "You're the one who can make this a truly great art center."

"But you just met me," Jimmy protested.

The woman seized Jimmy's forearm and said, "But I can feel your psychic energy."

Jimmy nodded grimly and reclaimed his arm.

He retreated to the edge of the artless art crowd and was prepared to escape when Larry German and a woman who just had to be his sister Julie crunched into view in a late-model forest green van of alleged American manufacture. Well, so what if a few parts were made in Malaysia and some assembly had happened in Honduras.

It was 8:38 and at least Larry German had arrived.

Larry German conferred with his sister for the longest time, and then the couple leisurely got out of the van and regarded the assembled multitude with pleasant surprise.

"Wow," Larry German said, "I didn't expect so many people. This is great. Just great."

Jimmy peered into Larry German's eyeballs and saw that his pupils were seriously dilated. 8:38 in the fucking morning, and the man was already stoned.

The woman who was Larry German's sister Julie gathered up a load of ledgers and files and followed her brother to the door.

Larry unsnapped his retractable key ring from his belt and pondered the vast array of hardware. He nodded and grunted for the longest while but seemed unable to reach a decision.

The Illinois woman with the clanking jewelry snapped, "Come on. We're freezing out here."

"Yeah," the blowsy Brooklyn redhead said, "Come on already."

Larry's sister Julie looked sharply at the two women, as if to say: Mess with my dear brother, and I'll tear your fucking ovaries out with my teeth.

The fat farm boy stepped forward and pointed to a key with a distinctive scratch on it. "I bet it's that one," he said.

Larry German gazed in wonder at the scratched key and nodded. "Yeah," he said, "I bet that's the one."

And, you know, it was.

And in no time flat, the crowd of fat art swells was assembled around a couple of ratty old picnic tables Larry had scrounged from somewhere and was attempting to organize as the first board of directors of the Fennell Art Center . . .

"And Theatre," Jimmy said.

"What was that?" the blowsy redhead from Brooklyn said.

Jimmy cleared his throat and smiled at the assemblage. "What I said was — why not call it the Fennell Art Center and Theatre. I mean, what we're talking about is restoring this as a theatre, so it should have the word 'theatre' in its name."

"That's brilliant," the aging Brooklyn bombshell exclaimed. "Simply brilliant."

The clanking Illinois woman concurred, and the caped butterball grimaced mirthfully.

"You realize of course," the butterball pronounced, "that the initials come out to F-A-G-A-T."

"Yeah," Jimmy said, "that had occurred to me. Why, do you think it's homophobic?"

"On the contrary," Myron T. Ackerman said. "I think the local gay community will find it quit kitschy. Provided it's presented in the right way."

The ostrich-booted woman nodded thoughtfully and said, "You know, everybody, Myron's right. And he's always right because he's a world-renowned architect in Chicago, and his home here in Michigan was featured in ARCHITECTURAL DIGEST."

"Not quite, Harriett," Myron said. "It was actually THE MIDWEST ARCHITECTURAL RECORD. A trade publication of somewhat more modest means."

"What's the difference, Myron? You're famous. Everybody who's anybody in Chicago knows who you are, and if you people have any sense, you'll listen to every word that Myron says because Myron has been intimately involved in innumerable theatre restoration projects including the Jaspers in Chicago and that one in Ludington I can never remember."

"The Rialto."

"Thank you, dear," Harriett Lawford said, patting Myron's hand. "Anyway, I want you people to know how blessed we are to have an architect as great as Myron T. Ackerman in our midst. And Myron has promised to donate his considerable talents to this restoration. Haven't you, Myron?"

Myron T. Ackerman adjusted his monocle and gazed around the cold, dark, and dusty theatre. Then after five theatrical beats, he proclaimed, "This is a jewel."

A hush fell over the crowd.

And then Larry German looked at his watch and said, "Well, it's practically nine o'clock. Julie and I have a business to run. Customers to serve. Money to make. You people are welcome to stay. In fact, I think Chip and his friends want to organize a work party to start clearing off the stage."

The mere mention of "work" prompted a mass exit that would have made Maynard G. Krebs blush with envy.

Chip Gooch, the fat farm boy who lived off of Hershey Bars and french fries, scratched his goatee indifferently and shrugged at those who had remained—his two friends and Jimmy.

Jimmy the desperate playwright.

Desperately seeking a theatre, any theatre, in which to produce his work.

"Oh well," Chip Gooch said, "probably better with just the four of us. Some of them people didn't look like they was in too good of shape to do the kind of work we're gonna do today."

"Uh," Jimmy said, "what kind of work are we going to do today?"

The chubby young woman giggled and said, "We're all in the theatre program at the college and we're doing this for a class credit.

In fact Kathy from our class is supposed to come with a camera and videotape this so we can get credit. And our professor — well, he's not really a professor — but he said it's okay if we do this and all, but we like have to document it and show what a mess it was when we started and how great it is when we finished. And all. Like. You know."

Jimmy wondered where that patron saint of his was when he needed him.

He was about to utter an intergalactic call for help when a familiar voice echoed through the dim and dusty space: "Say, old sport, I thought you'd have this place fixed up and ready to go by now."

It was none other than Burt Babbington, and he was dressed for a casual day of kicking through the leaves and a spot of "antiquing." He was accompanied, of course, by the ever-saftig Zoe "Z.Z." Zell. She, too, was dressed to casually kill and also wondered why the restoration work wasn't completed.

The three youths ignored the newcomers, so Jimmy went and tried to make them feel comfortable.

"You haven't done very much," Burt said. "I thought you'd at least have a coat of paint slapped on by now."

"Burt, we're just getting started. In fact, the meeting was at 8:30 and I thought you were going to . . ."

"It's only 8 o'clock," Z.Z. said, glancing at her designer watch.

"That's Chicago time, Z.Z.," Burt hissed. "They're on Michigan time here."

"Well, I don't know why. It's so stupid. I don't even bother to change my watch when I come up here. I mean it's not like going to New York or anything. Now, if I was flying to New York, I'd set my watch ahead an hour." Z.Z. scratched her pancaked forehead. "That's right — you set your watch ahead when you fly east to New York, and back an hour when you fly west to Chicago. And don't even begin to ask me about flying to the West Coast. Two time zones are way too much for me to deal with. Not to mention all that silly business with daylight savings time. All I know is I just got an extra hour of sleep a few weeks ago, and when you're on your feet as much as I am selling high-powered real estate, then you need all the extra sleep you can get, because there are some days I'm lucky if I get three hours. I live off coffee, you know. Go into Starbucks and just open up a vein and tell them to pour in one of those yummy double latte things with mocha whatever. To die for. And I tell you, I'm going to need all the Starbucks I can get come spring when we have to—let's see, fall back, spring ahead—that's right, when I lose an hour of sleep because we set our clocks ahead an hour before we go to bed Saturday night. See, Sundays are my biggest day. In fact, I have to race back to Chicago tomorrow for about eight zillion showings. The only reason I came up here at all is because Burt wanted to show me this gorgeous theatre. He said it was a real jewel and that Myron T. Ackerman was involved, but I don't see him."

"He just left," Jimmy said.

"Well, no wonder," Z.Z. said. "You've let this place deteriorate completely. You should be ashamed. And like Burt said, I would have thought you would have had the place all fixed up by now. How do you think you're going to attract investors if you show them a dump like this? Nobody's going to part with a dime. Believe me. They'll walk in a second. I see it all the time in Chicago. You can have the best brochures in the business—four color—the works—but if the customer comes in and sees a dump like this—they walk, and you're history. Word gets around, and you're done for."

Jimmy nodded thoughtfully and said, "I understand. Well, as long as you're both here, how about helping us? I think Chip over there has some plans for clearing off the stage and . . ."

"Sorry, old sport," Burt babbled, "but we didn't come here expecting to have to get our hands dirty. I just thought I'd sit on the edge of the meeting and act as a senior advisor. That sort of thing. Must have been a short meeting, huh?"

"Yeah. Larry and his sister had to open their gallery in the front at nine, and everybody else split. There were a ton of people here, but nobody wanted to stick around for the work party."

"Can't say as I blame them," Burt said, eyeballing the old wreck of a theatre. "Well, I think Z.Z. and I are going to head off and do a spot of antiquing and then check out that new winery in Fennville. Maybe even head on up to Holland and do a bit of window shopping on 8th Street. When's the next meeting?"

"I don't know. We never got that far on the agenda. Why don't you go around to the gallery and ask Larry?"

"No, you call me, old sport. If I'm not in, leave a message on my machine. Toodle-loo."

With that Burt Babbington squired his lady off into the sublime November sunshine for a spot of antiquing and a visit to that new winery in Fennville. And maybe even a bit of window shopping on Holland's trés chic 8th Street.

Leaving Jimmy to the devices and desires of Chip Gooch and his inchoate sidekicks.

Jimmy went to the stage where the threesome were already hard at work and said, "What do you want me to do?"

"You got a Saws-All in that Jap car of yours?" Chip Gooch said, trying to wrestle a section of ductwork off the brick wall.

"Actually, my car was made in Ontario, which was in North America last time I checked, and, no, I don't have a Saws-All."

Chip shrugged and continued tugging at the stubborn ductwork.

"Want me to help you get that off?"

"No. What we really need is a Saws-All. Why don't you go ask Larry if he's got one."

"Fine."

Jimmy gladly went to the gallery in front where Larry German and his sister Julie were already playing gracious host and hostess to a herd of well-heeled weekenders with fat wallets.

He waited the longest time while Larry and Julie did their ever-loving best to sell a pair of plump weekenders, or Tunas, a bedroom set carved from a big sugar maple that had met an untimely end back in the woods out by Larry's place.

The Tuna couple almost bit, but then didn't.

She had heard there was a new Wal-Mart opening up off Phoenix Road and was sure their prices were much lower.

He had heard the same, but whispered that they should support local "artisans" like Larry.

She whispered that she would bite his balls off next time they scheduled a quarterly screw, and he quickly caved in.

Big money waltzed out the door, and Larry crumpled inside of himself. Sister Julie rushed to his side and cooed and comforted him back to life. Then she kissed him on the lips. Not a little peck mind you, but a full-blown kiss on the lips.

Jimmy tried not to look, but, hell, he was a trained reporter, so he just had to look and what he saw—yes, he was sure it was what he saw, and he was prepared to swear under oath that he had seen it— was that Julie had slipped her brother the old proverbial tongue.

Jimmy wondered if that constituted an "Arkansas Kiss."

As opposed, of course, to a French Kiss.

He cleared his throat, and the siblings separated at the lips and looked at him with annoyance.

"Problem?" Larry said.

"Ah, that guy Chip was wondering if you have a Saws-All."

"A Saws-All? What's he need a Saws-All for? All you need to do is rip that stuff off the walls. It'll come right off if you pull hard enough."

"Yeah," sister Julie said, anxious to resume her intimacy with her beloved brother.

"Not really," Jimmy said.

Larry let out a lungful of air and went to the phone.

"What are you doing?" Julie said.

"I'm gonna call Pete. Pete's got a Saws-All. Pete's got everything." Larry dialed and waved Jimmy off. "You go on back there and do something else until Pete gets here. When Pete gets here, he'll be able to get what you couldn't get. Okay?"

"Yeah, sure."

Jimmy headed back into the cold, dark recesses of the abandoned theatre and reported to Chip Gooch and his sidekicks.

Chip Gooch shrugged indifferently and continued tugging at a section of stubborn ductwork.

"Need some help?"

"Nah. Grab a broom and help Susie and Gerry."

Jimmy grabbed a broom and helped Susie and Gerry with the sweeping job from hell.

After a few minutes of inhaling God-knows-what kind of toxic dust, Jimmy offered, "Hey, maybe I should make a run to the hardware store and get some masks and gloves."

Gerry and Susie looked at Jimmy in amazement.

"Well, it was just a suggestion. I mean, it's awful dusty in here, and I can hardly breathe. Plus, I'm getting blisters."

"You want gloves and masks, go get 'em," Gerry said. In case you forgot already, he was the skinny farm boy who lived off Diet Coke and cigarettes. He was none too concerned about the condition of his not-so-tender young lungs. Didn't figure on living much past 40, so what was the point of store-bought masks and such.

"Yeah," Susie said. "We don't need 'em, but if you're not used to getting dirty and working with your hands, then maybe you should get them for yourself."

Stung by that feminine rebuke to his manhood, Jimmy dropped the subject and wielded his broom with new authority, raising an unholy cloud of dust composed largely of industrial solvents and rodent excrement.

He was raising some unholy blisters on his desk-bound hands when a taciturn fellow arrived with a Saws-All.

"You must be Pete," Jimmy said, looking up.

The man nodded.

Chip Gooch nodded.

Gerry and Susie nodded.

Then the man called Pete looked at all that had to be done and set to work with his Saws-All in a singular effort that forever shall be enshrined in the annals of the Fennell Art Center and Theatre, or FAGAT for short.

The man called Pete worked with such a feverish intent that even the hard-driven farm boys stepped back and watched in awe.

Watched in awe as decades of debris were cut away from the once sacred stage.

Watched in awe as the man called Pete busted the toilet at center stage with three fell blows from his sledgehammer, and gaped in wonder as he poked a gaping hole in the false ceiling over the stage and then inserted a ladder into the breech and scrambled up into the heights with his trusty Saws-All.

In no time flat, he was handing sawed-off support beams to the foursome below. The false ceiling gave way from its unsupported weight, cascading the stage with shredded newspapers from the 1940s.

Chip Gooch shined a flashlight up into the reclaimed fly space and let out a rebel yell that would have done old George Pickett proud.

A fat woman with bad hair and a blinking videocamera appeared as if on cue and began shooting close-ups of Chip Gooch as he did his victory dance.

"You're so wonderful, Chip," she said, aiming and shooting what for her was the only subject in the world worth aiming and shooting at.

You see, she was Kathy Walker, and she was finding herself in mid-life as a doyenne of the theatre. Never mind the messy divorce, and three neglected kids at home, and nagging mother in the next town and a phone call away—she was really Bethel Merriday, fresh from the Sinclair Lewis novel of the same name, and she had fallen for the amazing Chip Gooch the first day of Theatre Arts Class out at the college. The very same course taught by the professor who wasn't really a professor, one Tim Daniels.

More on that moron later.

For now, suffice it to say Jimmy was irked that this hefty heifer was shoving everyone aside so she could get the ultimate shot of Chip Gooch in action, all the while totally ignoring the herculean efforts of the man called Pete and his Saws-All.

Jimmy tapped the video vixen on the shoulder.

"Can't you see I'm shooting?" she snapped in a high nasal voice designed to shatter diamonds.

"Well, you ought to shoot Pete up there. He's the one who's doing the real work."

The woman deactivated her videocamera and turned on Jimmy. "Who the hell are you?!?" she demanded.

"I'm James Clarke. The playwright."

The woman turned up her porcine nose. "Never heard of you."

"What a coincidence," Jimmy said, smiling grimly, "because I've never heard of you—whatever your name is."

"Kathy Walker. Now get out of my way and let me shoot. I've got to get all the work Chip and Gerry and Susie are doing on camera for our Theatre Arts class out at the college with the amazing Tim Daniels. He's a real director. And a real actor. And a real producer. And a real drama teacher. And a real playwright. Unlike you. Who I've never heard of."

Jimmy exhaled.

Is it always to be thus in the theatre?

"What?"

"I didn't say anything."

"Yes, you did. You just moved your lips and whispered something. Very strange. My ex-husband used to do that. Before he beat me. Which is why I left him. God, what an animal."

Jimmy nodded.

The woman named Kathy Walker whipped her videocamera back on her shoulder and shoved Jimmy aside. "Now step back, and let me shoot Chip in action."

Jimmy stepped back and prayed to Saint Genesius for guidance.

"Punt," the saint seemed to suggest.

"What?"

"Punt," quote the saint and nothing more.

Jimmy backed up to punt and bumped into Jess Springer. She had come bearing a sheaf of flyers announcing an acting class she intended to teach at the "beautifully restored Fennell."

"Sorry I'm late," she said, looking around with alarm, "but I've just had one of those mornings. Say, things don't appear to be as far along as I had imagined."

"You should have seen it a half hour ago. But look at all that fly space we just opened up."

Jess Springer was too old and too tired to look.

"If I were 30 years younger, I'd jump in with both feet and help you, but this looks overwhelming." She contemplated her flyers and sighed. "I had these printed up thinking this place would at least be ready for some acting classes, but there isn't even any heat in here."

"You know; you're right."

Chip Gooch overheard them and said, "No, there's an industrial blower over there back where the balcony used to be. But Larry doesn't like to turn it on because it sucks up the electricity like crazy, and it sounds like a jet engine."

That did it for Jess Springer.

"You know," she said, exiting stage right, "there's that adult education center in South Haven. I bet they'd let me have acting classes there."

She was gone before Jimmy could burble a "but Jess," and that was the last anyone ever saw of Jess Springer at the Fennell Art Center and Theatre, aka: FAGAT.

But her exit segued with the dramatic entrance of a wide-beamed woman who introduced herself as Wendy Filbaitus and let it be known to all within earshot that she had indeed "been that lady who took Harrison Ford's fingerprints in *The Fugitive*.   Some of my best work, if I don't mind saying, and I've been in more than 500 stage productions in Chicago. Not to mention commercial work which, of course, included that prize-winning piece I did for Wendy's posing as the winner of the Soviet fashion show. But that was back during the Cold War when a girl still had her figure. Anyway, I don't want to blow my own horn or anything—but God, if you don't blow your own horn these days, who's going to blow it for you—I was in on the ground floor of every theatre that's a theatre in Chicago, including the Organic, Victory Gardens, and, of course, Steppenwolf.

"And did I tell you I just had lunch with Malkovitch the other day, and Dennis (Franz) and I go way back. All the way to *Bleacher Bums*, and Dennis was just saying the other day how much he misses the good old days of Chicago theatre even though he's got every TV producer who's anybody begging him to play the lead in their new series. He could probably get me a gig if I wanted it, but I'm rooted in Chicago. Plus, I just bought a darling little place in the country near here, and when I heard through the grapevine that there was an effort to restore this old jewel of a theatre, why I came running."

Kathy Walker was impressed enough to turn her videocamera on the genuine Chicago theatre celebrity.

Chip Gooch nodded thoughtfully and handed Wendy Filbaitus a broom. "Got a lot of newspaper and junk to sweep up," he said.

Wendy, God bless her, accepted the broom without protest and started sweeping like a Lithuanian charwoman. Which is precisely what her ancestors had been. Why, one toothless old Filbaitus had even emptied and washed the Czar's personal chamber pot. Imagine that.

Jimmy got back to work and decided that maybe this Fennell thing wasn't such a waste of his time after all.

He figured he'd get to idly chatting with this Wendy Filbaitus creature while they were sweeping and casually mention that he just happened to have the script of his latest play handy, and, in no time flat, he'd be winning his very own Joseph Jefferson Award for excellence in playwriting. In Chicago, of course.

Theatre capital of the world.

"So," Jimmy said after they had been sweeping for a while, "you were in on the ground floor at the Organic."

"Oh yeah," wide Wendy Filbaitus said, sweeping with a vengeance. And the Jaspers, the Grant, and the Thornton. We lived, ate, and breathed theatre in those days. God, there was this French restaurant next to the theatre where we used to go for coffee, but it seemed like every time we were there, whole plates of food would just sort of mysteriously appear at our table. It was the restaurant's way of supporting the arts. Which you don't see today. The arts are dying in this country. It's turning into a cultural wasteland."

"Yeah, unless everybody wants it, nobody gets it."

"You just make that up?"

"No, my wife read it somewhere in one of her thick books with tiny print."

"You've got a smart wife. She must be Lithuanian."

"Part. On her mother's side. Her great-grandfather played in the Czar's orchestra."

"Yeah? My great-grandmother cleaned his friggin' chamber pot."

"Well, there you go. Say, uh, do you still have connections with the Organic and Steppenwolf and . . ."

"What — you got a play in your pocket you want me to put on some A.D.'s desk? That what you're asking?"

Jimmy looked to his sweeping for a moment and wondered if he shouldn't just bail out completely from the whole stupid playwriting gig. Go to trade school and become a plumber or something useful. Unblock people's toilets all day. Deal with their shit. Keep it flowing.

"What'd you say?" Wendy said.

"I didn't say anything."

"What — you always mumble to yourself?"

"Acid flashback."

"Tell me about it. God, it's a wonder any of us are still alive.
And there's even one of us in the White House. That's really scary.
Course, he didn't inhale, but I heard through the grapevine that they
called him 'brownie Bill' at Oxford because he always ate his pot
instead of smoked it. Which isn't a bad way to go. We used to make
these marijuana brownies back in the old days that would knock
your friggin' socks off. We had one guy who actually went and got
married on us. I gave him some brownies and told him not to eat
them, but he did anyway and he ended up practically tripping while
he was driving to the wedding. He was on the Eisenhower in a VW
Beetle and he thought the steering wheel was a snake. I wish I could
have been there. Musta been a riot."

"Yeah. So, you know some A.D.s at the big theatres in Chicago?"

"Sweetheart," Wendy said, sweeping, "if there's somebody I don't
know in Chicago theatre it's because they've been hiding under a
frigging rock for the last 30 years. I've been on the Jefferson
Committee for the last five years, and I've seen more rotten plays
than I can remember. I don't even know what the point is of most of
them. No plot, no character development — and the only people who
come to see most of them are relatives of the A.D. and cast. It's
pathetic."

"So why stay in theatre?"

"Because it's in my blood. It'd be like having my heart and lungs
ripped out of my chest if they made me stop going to the theatre."

"Yeah, I hear you."

"So, you got a play?"

"A couple actually."

Jimmy proceeded to tell Wendy Filbaitus all about *Criminal
Justice, No Dice* and even digressed back to 1976 when he had the
lead in the Stonebridge Theatre's production of *Playboy of the
Western World.*

"We were in this third act," Jimmy recalled, "and this guy I knew
from another life came stumbling into the house with his wife and
daughter. He was this big, fat guy dressed up like a priest because
he was actually a deacon in the Episcopal Church, but it was by far

the worst moment in my theatrical life because he actually told the usher that he had paid to see this 'Playboy Bunny' thing and . . ."

"You're kidding?!?"

"No. True story."

Wendy Filbaitus proceeded to share some of her true stories from the annals of Chicago theatre, and by the time Chip Gooch decided they had done enough work for one day, Jimmy and Wendy were fast friends.

Or so Jimmy thought.

In all events, Wendy Filbaitus accepted his script of *Criminal Justice* and promised to "shop it around in Chicago" when she returned on Monday.

"And if nothing else," she said, "I can bring some of my old theatre friends out from the city and we can produce your masterpiece here at the Fennell next summer when we have this place up and running."

Jimmy blinked and nodded happily and didn't mind one bit that Kathy Walker hadn't once aimed her videocamera at him.

Didn't matter.

Not one jot, for as Jimmy climbed into Angel Car and headed for the Dunery, a familiar ditty danced in his head: "Oh, I'm gonna be in the movies, mm hm, they're gonna make a big star outta me, mm hm . . ."

Chapter Sixteen

"Jimmy!" Joyce exclaimed when Jimmy came through the door, "what have you been doing?!?"

"Just sweeping," Jimmy said, feeling his merry mood go bust. "Why?"

"You look like you've been working in the sulfur mines of Ancient Rome."

Jimmy looked down at himself and realized he was absolutely filthy, rotten dirty. "I'm just a little dirty is all."

"A little dirty?!? Go and take your clothes off on the deck, and I'll give you a plastic garbage bag to put them in. Then I'm going to drive them straight to Palisades and have them irradiate them for about five years. God, I've never seen you so dirty."

"Well, it's an old theatre, Joyce, and we made a lot of headway today. This guy called Pete showed up with his Saws-All and did some amazing things. Plus, there was this woman who knows everybody who's anybody in Chicago theatre, and she took *Criminal Justice* and is going to shop it around in Chicago. And probably even help me produce it next summer at the Fennell when we get it up and running."

Joyce just stared at her dirt-caked cavalier.

"What's the matter, Joyce?"

"Couldn't you just go to trade school and become a plumber or something? Unblock people's toilets all day? I mean there'd always be a challenge, and plumbers make good money."

Jimmy ground his teeth and declined to tell Joyce he had been thinking precisely the same thing back before Wendy Filbaitus promised him fame and glory. Well, not promised exactly, but . . .

"Jimmy, stop talking to yourself and get out of those filthy clothes and take a shower. You must be miserable."

"I'm not miserable, Joyce. In fact, I couldn't be happier. I have a really good feeling about this Fennell thing."

Joyce groaned inwardly and outwardly.

"Joyce!!"

"What?"

"What kind of attitude is that?"

"It's a realistic attitude, Jimmy. Haven't you had enough theatre for one lifetime?"

"No," Jimmy said tightly. "The theatre is in my blood. I'd sooner have my heart and lungs ripped out than be made to quit the theatre."

"Did you just make that up?"

"Actually, Wendy said it, but it's a good line, and it's exactly the way I feel, Joyce. And you know it."

Joyce looked at her ditzy dreamer of a determined husband and sighed.

"What's that supposed to mean?"

"It means there's no stopping you. You're going to do what you want no matter what I say, so what's the use of me saying anything?"

"Joyce, you know I value your opinion."

"To a point."

"What do you mean: to a point?"

"I mean, you value my opinion to the point where it clashes with what you want to do, and then you just ignore my opinion. That's what I mean."

Jimmy looked at Joyce.

Joyce looked at Jimmy.

Then they both laughed uncontrollably.

When they stopped laughing, Jimmy climbed out of his filthy clothes and took a long, hot shower.

Then they made mad, passionate love and got on with their lives.

In Joyce's case it meant maintaining her main client, Jerry Mappers. The Northwestern University alumnus, world-traveler and bon vivant "edited" 10 newsletters for a marginally managed Chicago accounting firm and phoned Joyce that day complaining that Joyce had "never once taken me to lunch. Not once in all the years I've been giving you thousands and thousands of dollars of free-lance work that I could just as easily could have given to other free-lancers."

Never mind that the ever-conscientious Joyce had never missed a deadline, and always went out of her way to add depth and interest to the stories Jerry Mappers assigned her. Never mind that every senior partner she interviewed absolutely adored her and complimented Jerry Mappers for hiring such a delightfully professional free-lancer.

Jerry Mappers never relayed these positive messages back to Joyce. No, she only commented on Joyce's work when Joyce misspelled someone's name or split the occasional infinitive. And now the aging harridan was hot about the fact that Joyce had not only never taken her to lunch but "never in the nearly 10 years you've been working for me, have you ever once sent me a birthday card or a Christmas card."

Joyce was ashen when she got off the phone with her main client, Jerry Mappers.

Actually, it was their only client at the moment, because Jimmy hadn't heard diddly-squat from his main client, Kathryn Stavakitis at FLS Corporation in Chicago. He had done a fine job for her on his last assignment, but she just hadn't gotten around to calling with another.

And, truth be known, Jimmy was thrilled and delighted because the poor, deluded fellow actually believed he could make a living as a playwright in modern America.

"We're screwed," Joyce said, cradling her phone.

"What's wrong?" Jimmy said, rushing to her writing booth. He had a keen nose for financial ruination.

"Jerry Mappers is on the war path again. Now she's all pissed off because I've never taken her to lunch or sent her a birthday card. I don't even know when her stupid birthday is."

Jimmy picked up Joyce's phone and handed it to her. "Call her back and find out. And ask her to lunch."

"But I can't do that — it's unethical. Most companies have rules against such things. It's bribery."

"Obviously not at her company. Call her, Joyce. We can't afford to lose the account. At least not yet."

That got Joyce's attention. "What are you talking about?"

"Well, I just have a feeling about this Fennell thing."

"Jimmy, instead of wasting all your time and energy on that bottomless pit, why don't you look for new free-lance accounts?"

Jimmy sighed so massively that their dump in the dunes shifted on its foundation of rotting beams and impacted sand.

"Joyce, I'm a playwright!"

"Yeah, and I'm the Queen of Sheba, but we both have to eat, and if I lose Jerry Mappers, we're totally screwed. I mean you don't even have the HIGHLIGHTS anymore, and I don't know why you won't call Kathryn Stavakitis and get another assignment. She likes your work."

"Yeah, that's not all she likes."

"She's dealing with that, Jimmy. Why don't you call her? And make some cold calls. We need the business."

"Why don't you call Jerry Mappers back and ask her to lunch?"

Joyce looked at Jimmy.

Jimmy looked at Joyce.

Joyce called Jerry Mappers and invited the menopausal woman in management to lunch. She even went as far as finding the bitch's birthday.

"Oh goody," she said when she got off the phone, "her birthday is next week. I still have time to send her a card."

"Was she happy?"

"Oh, she's delighted. And she's going to pick out the restaurant. Probably cost a fortune."

"It's the price of doing business, Joyce. And it's tax-deductible."

"I knew that."

"I know you knew that, but I just wanted to . . ."

"You sound like some corporate wife coaching her husband from the sidelines. It'd be a lot easier if you'd go out and get some free-lance accounts."

Jimmy went to his chair and collapsed.

Joyce thought he had had a heart attack.

"Are you all right?" she said, waving her hand in front of his face.

Jimmy gazed glassily at his wife.

"Jimmy! Jimmy! Can you hear me?"

Jimmy rolled his eyes and groaned.

"Jimmy, if you don't answer me, I'm calling 911."

Jimmy snapped out of his funk and said, "Joyce, if you want me to get free-lance work, I'll get free-lance work. You're absolutely right — it's not fair that you're bearing all the financial burden. And it's hardly like The Dunery Press is taking up all my time like it used to when I was stupid enough to think that we could actually make

money publishing our own books." Jimmy slapped his forehead.
"God, was that ever deluded or what?"

That tact worked.

Joyce threw up her hands and said, "All right, pursue your dream
of being a playwright. Why not? We've driven over the edge
before—let's do it again. It's so much fucking fun."

"Joyce!"

"What?"

"You don't have to take that tone of voice."

"Why not? Am I supposed to be happy that our only income is in
the hands of a crazy woman who ignores all the great work I've done
for her over the years and extorts a free lunch out of me?"

"Why don't you write a play about it?"

"What?"

"A play. You should write plays, Joyce. You're a natural-born
playwright—what with your love of dialog and all."

"But I hardly write any dialog. My books are all exposition."

"Well, the dialog you do write is brilliant."

"You think so?"

"I know so, Joyce. Plays would just fall out of you if you started
writing them. Just like when you started writing novels. I remember
you and Judy (their ex-therapist) both telling me I was crazy for
wanting to write novels, but now you pound them out like the village
blacksmith or something. The transition to writing plays would be a
piece of cake for you, Joyce. Trust me on this. And then we could
both have our plays produced at the Fennell and move on to bigger
and better things. I mean, one day there, and I've already met a key
player in Chicago theatre."

Joyce kicked it around in her head and instead of telling her
husband he was totally nuts, she softened and said, "So you think I
should try writing plays?"

"Oh, yeah. You're a natural playwright, Joyce. Trust me on this."

And, dumb bunny that she was, Joyce trusted Jimmy.

And Jimmy thrust himself into the Fennell Art Center and
Theatre, aka: FAGAT.

At the very next meeting, which was held the following Saturday
morning promptly at 8:45, Jimmy allowed himself to be elected to

the board of directors and made chairman of the publicity and marketing committee.

And when the blowsy Brooklyn broad with the red hair from a bottle bubbled on about the need to "do something really big, really soon," Jimmy suggested a gala open house for Saturday, January 15, 1994.

That hit the assembled fat art swells (minus Myron T. Ackerman who had pressing business in Chicago and, of course, Burt Babbington and Zoe "Z.Z." Zell who were off doing a spot of antiquing) like oil on a hot griddle.

Spattered with excitement, Jimmy was compelled to explain: "Well, it's about a month and a half away which gives us time to line up a program, and . . ."

"Oh," said Harriett (of the clanking jewelry) Lawford, "I know this absolutely wonderful poet with a summer place near here who I am sure I could get to come and recite from his new book."

"And we'd have to have Elizabeth Aimes do a piano recital with one of her students," said Margaret Carlson, the Brooklyn woman with flaming red hair.

"But wouldn't we need a piano?" said Larry's sister Julie.

"Piece of cake," Larry German said. "In fact, I've been in touch with a guy in Fennville who restores old pianos and he practically guaranteed us a baby grand for only $500. In fact we can go and get it today if anybody's available after the meeting."

Silence.

Then Jimmy inched up his hand. As did Chip Gooch and Gerry and Susie.

"So," Larry German, "it's decided we should have a big open house on Saturday, January 15th to get this place off the ground. All in favor say aye."

All said aye, and Margaret Carlson nominated Larry German for president for showing "such decisive leadership qualities in a time of great need."

Larry's sister Julie quickly seconded the nomination, and Larry was unanimously elected president of the board of directors of the Fennell Art Center and Theatre.

As his first official act, he nominated his sister, Julie German-Cooper, as treasurer.

Harriett Lawford seconded, and all signaled their assent by saying "aye."

Jimmy wondered if this was such a good idea what with the way he had seen the two of them exchanging an Arkansas Kiss the previous week, but he held his counsel. They'll work closely together, he thought, and that's good.

Isn't it?

Everyone else seemed to think so, and before adjourning, they elected Harriett Lawford as vice president and a large woman in a purple shawl as secretary. After all, she had a notebook and pen handy and said she was a poet, so why the hell not? Her name by the way was Beverly Mantinkus, and she, God bless her, said maybe there should be more to the gala program being planned for January 15th than just a poetry reading and a piano recital.

"Jim here's a playwright," she said. "He had a play at Glenn Art Studio this summer that was real successful, or so I heard. So maybe we could do a reading of one of his plays for the open house. Would that be okay with you, Jim?"

"Jim" was jubilant. "Yeah, that'd be fine."

"Good," Larry German said, "we'll have a reading from one of Jim's plays. And I think my friend Taylor Griffith should perform. Anybody who's ever heard Taylor Griffith sing the blues he's the best."

"Oh, yeah," sister Julie seconded, "the absolute best blues singer this side of the Mississippi Delta."

Never mind that Taylor Griffith was a fat, balding honkie from an affluent all-white Chicago suburb. Well, not all-white. There was that black biochemist and his Asian wife, but they sure acted white on Sunday at All Saints Episcopal Church. Anyway, as Julie said, Taylor Griffith is the absolute best blues singer this side of the Mississippi Delta.

"So it's decided," Larry German said. "We're going to have a big open house on—what was that date again?"

"Saturday, January 15th," Jimmy said.

"Right. Write that down, Bev. And next week we'll devote the entire meeting to planning it."

"I think we should start planning it right now," Margaret Carlson mewled. "Every second is precious. We've got to start working on it right now. If we lose the momentum we've built up this morning and last week, we'll never get this place off the ground. Never!"

Everyone looked at Margaret Carlson.

Margaret Carlson looked like she was going to explode. The woman's entire identity seemed to be riding on the success of the Fennell Art Center and Theatre, aka: FAGAT.

Jimmy totally sympathized since he had just told his wife in so many words he was going to support them as a playwright in modern corporate America.

So he said: "Margaret's right. We've got to get the ball rolling now, or we're never going to pull this thing off."

"Fine," Larry German said, rising from the wobbly picnic table, "you and Margaret and anyone else who wants to can stay and discuss the open house, but me and Julie got a business to open. Otherwise we're not going to be able to afford to pay the rent for this place."

"Rent?" Jimmy said. "I thought you guys owned this place."

Larry and Julie exchanged a secret look and Larry turned to Jimmy and the others. "A mere technicality having to do with a land lease or something, but we'll discuss it at another meeting. Now, if you'll excuse us, we've got to go and open the gallery and make some money. Come on, Julie."

"What about the piano?" Chip Gooch said.

"Oh yeah. Come and see me when you're ready to go and get it. I'll give you instructions how to get to the guy's house."

"But how are we going to pay for it?" Harriett Lawford said. "We haven't even incorporated yet. We don't have a bank account or anything. We can't run out and buy a $500 piano."

"YES WE CAN!!" Margaret Carlson said, popping tendons and blood vessels in her neck, "WE ABSOLUTELY HAVE TO GET THIS PIANO!! ABSOLUTELY!! DO I MAKE MYSELF CLEAR?!?"

Absolutely, Margaret.

Still, Jimmy wondered if the guy in Fennville was going to need some cash in hand before parting with the piano.

"It's all taken care of," Larry said. "Just go and get it, and me Julie will deal with him. Right, Julie?"

"Right, Larry."

And with that the happy siblings went to open their gallery to the hordes of waiting Tunas and their fat wallets.

Margaret Carlson wanted to keep the meeting going to discuss the gala open house, but everyone else had other plans and quickly exited stage right.

"How about us meeting some night this week to get this thing organized?" Margaret said, grabbing Jimmy's sleeve.

"Yeah. Sure. Why not?"

"Wednesday night be good for you?"

"Yeah. Sure. Why not?"

"Wednesday night at 7:30 at my place. I'll get Harriett to come. She looks like she's got lots of good ideas. Anyway, we're the antique shop on Blue Star at Prairie Road. You know where that is?"

"You mean Lakeside Treasures?" Jimmy said, referring to the notorious dump that had been repeatedly cited by the township as a "an eyesore."

"Yeah, you should come early and browse. And meet Allan. He's an actor. Did a lot of theatre in Kalamazoo, which is really a major theatre town. Allan knows anybody who's everybody in Kalamazoo theatre. Maybe you could get him to help you with the reading of your play at the open house?"

Actor in Kalamazoo? Hmmm.

"What'd you say?"

"Nothing. Just thinking out loud."

"Allan does that, too. All the time. Well, you be sure and come early and browse. We have tons of wonderful stuff. I mean treasures. Allan would kill me if he caught me referring to it as stuff. It's not stuff. It's treasures."

"I'm sure. Well, I'll see you Wednesday night at 7:30. At your place."

"Right. And be ready to work, because we've got so much to do, and I really want this to work. I really, really do." Margaret seized Jimmy's forearm and squeezed the blood right out of it.

"I believe you, Margaret. I believe you."

Jimmy somehow reclaimed his arm and reported to Chip Gooch and his sidekicks who were ready to go fetch the piano.

They got instructions from Larry German and set off in Chip's pick-up for a destination on the outskirts of Fennville. Not far from where fat factory workers in ridiculous camouflage outfits, or "camos", were standing out in the middle of a harvested cornfield blasting defenseless Canada Geese out of the sky with shotguns.

Ah, America.

If it didn't exist, you'd just have to make it up for the amusement of the rest of the world.

Which is why it probably exists in the first place, but that's the subject of another book, and we're all committed to this story, so let's stay the course.

Right, everybody?

Right, Mr. Author.

Good.

So anyway, back to the story.

"This it?" Chip Gooch said, slowing from 75 to 45 in two seconds.

"I think so," Susie said, looking at Larry German's scribbled map. She was scrunched up next to Jimmy, and try as she might, she could not dislodge her ample bosom from the crook in his arm.

"Looks like it," Gerry said.

"I don't think so," Jimmy said.

Chip Gooch went for it and executed a flying right turn onto a rutted, overgrown dirt road that would have done Daniel Boone proud.

Overhanging branches battered Chip's windshield, but he didn't care. He was on a mission for theatre and that was all that counted.

Presently, they came upon a clearing in the bush and brambles and encountered a great wolf/dog tethered to a tree. It howled furiously for a few moments and then collapsed in a whimpering heap.

"Nice dog," Jimmy noted.

The others hardly noticed.

Chip Gooch braked opposite a double-wide house trailer mounted on cinderblocks and adorned with bits of purloined Styrofoam "blue board" insulation and duct tape. A handyman's special that only Red Green and the guys at Possum Lodge could love.

The four of them sat squeezed in the front seat of Chip's truck and waited for something to happen.

Nothing happened.

Except the wolf/dog struggled to its forelegs, howled pitiably and collapsed in another whimpering heap.

"Dog outta be put down," Chip observed.

"Yeah," Gerry said, "was my dog, I'd take it out behind the barn and put a bullet in its head."

"What's wrong with it?" Susie said.

"Probably got the heartworm," Chip said.

"Yeah," Gerry concurred. "Probably got the heartworm."

Jimmy digested this brilliant bit of dialog and said, "But aren't there heartworm pills you can give your dog?"

The farm boys simply stared at the stupid, animal-loving city slicker.

Then a door on the double-wide creaked open and a crab-legged fellow with a big bald patch and a scraggly beard emerged into the unshaded November sunlight.

He shielded his deep-set eyes from the sun and said: "You come for the piano?"

Chip nodded and got out.

Susie popped her door and dislodged her breast from the crook in Jimmy's arm. Jimmy unlocked his left knee from Gerry's right knee, and they followed Chip to the double-wide.

En route, they encountered two gutted cars, three engines, five stacks of tires, a golf cart with no battery, and a mound of paving material.

"Don't mind the dog," the man at the door said, "he got the heartworm. 'bout on his last legs."

Chip and Gerry nodded in agreement.

Susie said, "That's awful."

The man at the door said, "Life sucks and then you die."

Jimmy said nothing. This was too much like his experience with the "rustic" illustrator of his ill-fated children's book to warrant further comment. He zipped his lip and determined to let Chip Gooch do all the talking.

But Chip Gooch wasn't a man of many words. Not after a childhood on the farm with an abusive father who treated the

Mexican migrant workers better than his own son. And that ain't saying much.

The man at the door advanced into his yard and said, "Which one of you's got the check?"

Chip and his sidekicks said nothing, leaving Jimmy to sputter: "Larry said he'd take care of you later. Or something."

The crab-legged man chewed his lip and shook his head. "You don't give me a check, I don't give you no piano. It's that simple."

Chip and his sidekicks said nothing, leaving Jimmy to sputter: "But Larry said he'd take care of you later. Or something."

The crab-legged man chewed his lip and shook his head. "You don't give me a check, I don't give you no piano. It's that simple."

The wolf/dog struggled pitiably to its forelegs, uttered a brief howl and collapsed in another whimpering heap.

The crab-legged man hobbled over to the dog and kicked it sharply in the ribs. "Shut the fuck up!" he raged.

Susie sobbed quietly and Chip and Gerry nodded thoughtfully.

"They get like that when they got the heartworm," Chip Gooch observed.

"Yeah," the crab-legged man said, "I reckon I ought to put that damn bitch down, but you know what the price of bullets is these days."

Chip and Gerry nodded thoughtfully.

Jimmy looked up for the mother ship.

No sign of it.

And Saint Genesius was maintaining radio silence.

So he cleared his throat and said, "What exactly did Larry tell you about paying for the piano?"

The crab-legged man hobbled over to the foursome and got right in Jimmy's face. Jimmy was reminded of the seminal scene in *Deliverance*. Except there was no Burt Reynolds sneaking up behind the hillbilly with a wicked bow and arrow to save his city-slicker ass.

"He said he'd come and get the piano hisself. And he said he'd pay me cash for it when he took delivery. That's the way I do business. The only way I do business. You people don't like it, you can turn tail right now, and get the hell off my property."

Jimmy looked to Chip Gooch for support.

Chip Gooch looked to a booger hanging off his nose and tried to get it with his tongue.

Jimmy looked to Gerry and Susie for support.

Gerry and Susie looked to their shoes with sudden interest.

Jimmy exhaled and looked to his breast pocket where resided the checkbook for the joint account he and Joyce "maintained" at the South Haven Lakeside Bank. Maintained is the operative word here, because they barely kept the balance in the black.

Jimmy knew Joyce would kill him if he went and wrote a check to this crazed dog abuser for a piano that would probably only be played once or twice and then allowed to rot away in the Fennell Art Center and Theatre, aka: FAGAT. He knew in his heart it was all destined for failure – all he had to do was take a quick glance at his present company for proof. But in his heart of hearts – that crazy core of miscreant cells that lies somewhere between the left and right ventricles – he knew he had to go for it.

Go for it all and become the next – what was it Maye Michaels had written – that's right, the next Eugene O'Neill. It was up to him and no one else.

And the Fennell Art Center and Theatre, aka: FAGAT, was his best chance. Probably his last chance, but it was a chance, and, damn it, he was going for it. No punt at 4th and 15. Hell no. He was going long for the fucking touchdown.

"YES!"

Everyone looked at the sputtering city slicker.

Jimmy looked at all of them and said, "How about if I write you a check, Mr. uh . . ."

"That'd be fine. But I'd prefer cash. That Larry guy said he'd pay cash. All $500. That's what he said. Give me his word. How come he ain't come out here with you? He backin' off his word?"

"He had to open his gallery, so he sent us."

The crab-legged man launched a lunger that just barely missed Jimmy's shoe. Then he said, "He ain't much of a man if he can't come out here and face me. Still, if you got a check, I'll take it. For the full amount, or you don't get no piano."

Chip, Gerry, and Susie looked to Jimmy and his golden checkbook.

Jimmy looked to the sky for a sign from the mother ship, Saint Genesius, or whoever was on duty.

A red-breasted nuthatch flitted overhead on its way to find the last bugs of fall.

That's the sign, Jimmy thought. There was a red-breasted nuthatch in my children's book. Nancy. Yeah. And she saved the day, so . . .

"You got the shell shock, don't you?" the crab-legged man said, waving his hand in front of Jimmy's face. "I seen cases like yours in Vietnam. You got yourself a bad case. What war was you in — the Gulf? Grenada? Panama?"

Jimmy blinked and shook his head. "I was defending the home front. Look, how about if I write you a check for $50, and we'll have Larry come back out here and . . ."

"You write me a check for the full amount, or you don't get no piano."

Jimmy took the checkbook out of his pocket, cracked it open and squinted at the balance: -$435.26. More of Joyce's infamous "negative numbers," meaning that they weren't really overdrawn because she had set aside a pile of checks for when the utility bills and such like came. Jimmy calculated and came up with a new negative: -$935.26.

Nice number.

Not round exactly, but nice.

Jimmy emptied his lungs into the November chill and said, "All right — I'll write you a check for $500, and we'll take the piano. As long as we're here, we might as well take the piano, and I can just settle up with Larry and Julie when we get back."

The crab-legged man nodded, spit and said, "You can settle up with whoever the hell you want, but if you write a rubber check on me, me and my dog'll come lookin' for you. And believe you me, we'll find you. And I'll tear your heart out and eat it right in front of your face while you're dyin'."

Jimmy bit his lip and wrote a check for the full amount: $500. Nice number. Round and rubbery.

Chapter Seventeen

They loaded the baby grand piano in Chip Gooch's truck and motored back to the Fennell Art Gallery and Theatre where Kathy Walker awaited them with her blinking videocamera.

She pushed Jimmy aside as he struggled with his end of the stubborn piano so she could have a clearer shot of the truly magnificent Chip Gooch. Fat farm boy with a grand future in American theatre.

"How about lending us a hand instead of standing there with that stupid camera?" Jimmy said.

Kathy Walker continued filming her hero and snapped, "I have a bad back. Besides, I am helping. Helping to create a video record of all the amazing things Chip is doing to single-handedly restore this theatre."

Jimmy knew there was no use in arguing with the fat head, so he simply grunted and lifted and shoved and heaved his end of the piano into the dank, dusty, dreary old wreck of a theatre. He was careful, of course, to remain off camera. He didn't want Kathy Walker's amazing professor (who wasn't really a professor) pal at the college to think for one second that the totally wonderful Chip Gooch had had any assistance whatsoever in single-handedly restoring the Fennell.

Well, it would be all right if Gerry and Susie appeared briefly on videotape, but they were subsets of the amazing Chip Gooch. Mere appendages of the great man. Who doubtless would one day adorn the cover of AMERICAN THEATRE MAGAZINE.

Why not?

"Why the fuck not indeed?" Jimmy wondered aloud as they set the piano on the stage.

"Don't mind him," Chip Gooch said to Kathy Walker. "He's got the shell shock. Ain't that right?"

Jimmy nodded grimly and went to settle up with Larry German and his sister Julie in their gallery, *Out of the Woods.*

Larry and Julie, of course, were busy trying to unload the still-unsold bedroom set Larry had carved from a big sugar maple that had been poached out of the woods.

The would-be buyers, a plump pair of Tunas from Chicago, almost bit, but then they didn't.

She had heard there was a new Wal-Mart opening up off Phoenix Road and was sure the prices were much lower there.

He had heard the same, but whispered that they should support local "artisans" like Larry.

She hissed that she would boil his balls for breakfast if he didn't shut the fuck up, and he did.

And they left, taking their precious-metal credit cards with them.

Jimmy watched discreetly as brother and sister reprised their scene from last week:

-Larry crumpled inside of himself.

-Sister Julie rushed to big brother's side and cooed and comforted him back to life.

-Then she kissed him on the lips. Not a little peck mind you, but a full blown kiss on the lips.

"The full Arkansas," Jimmy muttered in spite of himself.

Brother and sister unlocked their lips and looked at the so-called playwright with annoyance.

"Problem?" Larry said, more than a little irritated.

"Ah, yeah," Jimmy said, not sure how to start. So he just dove into the deep end with, "Uh, we got the piano."

"Good," Larry said.

"Great," Julie beamed, hovering close to her beloved brother.

"Chip and Gerry and Susie are setting it up on the stage and their friend's filming it for their course at the college."

"Good," Larry said.

"Great," Julie beamed, hovering even closer to her beloved brother.

Jimmy cleared his throat and shifted his stance. What is it about these two, he wondered, that makes me so goddamned nervous? So unable to just fucking spit it out.

"Spit it out," Larry said, grinning, "don't just stand there sputtering."

"Yeah," Julie said, rubbing her brother's neck, "spit it out."

"All right. I'll spit it out—that guy we got the piano from—"

"His name's Doug."

"Yeah, right. How could I forget? Well, Doug wouldn't give us the piano unless we gave him a check for the full amount."

Larry and Julie nodded happily, seeing no problem with that.

So Jimmy said: "I wrote him a check. With my own money. With money I don't have."

Larry and Julie nodded happily, seeing no problem with that.

Another Tuna couple waddled into the gallery, and Larry shooed Jimmy away toward the theatre.

"But I have to be reimbursed," Jimmy whispered. "My wife'll kill me if you don't reimburse me."

"You heard Harriett at the meeting this morning," Larry muttered, grinning enormously at the Tunas, "we don't even have a checking account yet. What are we going to reimburse you with?"

"But you said you'd take care of that guy. Doug or whatever the hell his name is."

"Keep it down," Larry said, pushing Jimmy toward the door to the theatre. "We've got a business to run here. Why don't you go back and help them get the piano set up, and we'll talk about it next week at the meeting? Call Bev and have her put it on the agenda. Or better yet, just consider it your donation to the Fennell."

"But we don't have $500 to give to the Fennell," Jimmy squawked.

Larry pushed him all the way into the theatre and closed and locked the door behind him.

Jimmy stood in the dark and shuddered.

"Now what?" he asked of his suddenly silent saint.

Saint Genesius wanted to respond, but he had been informed by his superiors that this poor playwright had been raised a Protestant. And Protestants simply didn't believe in saints, so why bother?

So Saint Genesius didn't bother. Except to lay a vaporous hand on Jimmy's shoulder.

Jimmy felt oddly comforted and left Chip Gooch and his adoring acolytes to the care and feeding of the Fennell Art Gallery and Theatre's new-old baby grand piano.

As he was leaving, he collided with Wendy Filbaitus, the wide-bodied wonder woman of Chicago theatre.

"Sorry I'm late," she said, all out of breath. "But I've had one of those mornings. Plus, I always forget to change my watch when I come over here. You'd think I'd get used to the different time zones by now, but it's been one of those weeks. The casting call from hell, plus I had this big run-in with the principal."

"The principal? You're a teacher?"

"Didn't I tell you?"

"Uh, no. You never said anything about being a teacher."

"Oh. Well, I teach drama and some other classes at Diego Rivera High School on the southwest side. Right off the Stevenson. It's a reverse commute, and I take the Drive down to the Stevenson, and I can be there in 30 minutes or less. Except when there's some truck turned over on the Stevenson. Which happens all the time. A month ago it was chickens. Can you believe it? A million chickens running around the Stevenson."

"Yeah, I can imagine. So you teach to support your acting habit?"

"Something like that. It's the hope of American theatre. We don't get these kids interested in attending plays, there's not going to be any theatre left in this country because there won't be anymore audiences."

"So what was your hassle with the principal?"

"I wanted to do *West Side Story* but he put the kibosh on it – big time."

"You mean censorship."

"I mean we got a gang problem at Rivera like you wouldn't believe, and the powers to be at the Board of Ed said no way, José. Figured doing a play about the Sharks and the Jets would get our little Latin Eagles and Crips and Bloods boiling. So he's making me do *Sound of Music* instead."

"Gag me with a spoon."

"My sentiments exactly. But what're you going to do, eh?"

"Yeah. So, uh, you have a chance to look at that play I gave you last week?"

"Huh?"

"*Criminal Justice.* It's a one-act about this black guy in the South who gets burned alive by a lynch mob for just talking to this white woman at the library."

Wendy Filbaitus shrugged. "Sorry, I don't remember."

"You said you were going to shop it around some Chicago theatres." Jimmy felt his heart slip into his pancreas. "You know—like the Steppenwolf and the Organic and some of the other theatres where you have connections."

Wendy looked vaguely at the brick walls and said, "You know, when we started the Organic, we raised money by selling bricks. For like $50, you could get your name painted on a brick. It was your brick, and you could visit it everytime you came to see a play. We raised a hell of a lot of money that way. You guys should do that here. I'm telling you—it would work. You got some very rich people with summer places around here—hell, there're not summer places any more. Not the way these people are fixing them up and winterizing them and everything. It would get interest going, and people would feel they have a piece of this place, and it would give you the money to get this place restored properly. But in the meantime, you got to get work up right away. You can't wait until everything is all nice and pretty. We didn't wait when we started the Organic. We were putting up plays in some of the worst conditions imaginable, and the public loved it. Felt like they were in on the ground floor, because they were standing on the ground floor. Literally. So what do you say?"

Jimmy told Wendy all about his plan for the gala open house on January 15.

"You can't have it then!"

"Why not?" he wondered.

"That's Doctor King's birthday."

"Yeah, so?"

"So? So, nobody's going to come to an open house on Doctor King's birthday. Not unless the program's devoted to him."

"Well, I suppose we could invite Coretta King, but I doubt she's available on such short notice."

"Are you trying to be funny, or are you just another garden-variety racist?"

Jimmy ground his teeth and said, "Well, we're going to discuss it at the meeting next week. Maybe you should bring up that point about King's birthday . . ."

"Oh, I won't be here next week. Or for the next month, actually. Not with *Sound of Music* in production at the high school. And whatever commercial work I can get at my advanced age."

"Yeah. Right. So, you haven't had a chance to read my play or shop it around?"

"Look, if you want to get a play produced, you should get an agent. And forget Chicago. Unless you know somebody big like the A.D. at the Goodman or something. It's not like the good old days when we started the Organic and everybody was young and full of energy and ideas. Now you've got too many theatres chasing too few patrons. Who wants to go to a play and deal with parking and all the crap when you can run out to the video store and rent five movies for what it costs to see a play. Hell, I do it myself half the time. And why not? A lot safer sitting in your living room watching some slasher movie than going out at night in Chicago. You wouldn't believe all the crime there is now. Even in places like Lincoln Park. Everybody's either a criminal or a victim. I'm telling you."

Jimmy nodded thoughtfully and wondered if he should hit Wendy Filbaitus up for a donation for the piano.

Forget it, he thought, looking at the wide-bodied wonder woman of Chicago theatre. She's got cheap written all over her.

So he simply bid her a broken leg with her exciting production of *Sound of Music* and headed for home.

But this time when Joyce asked how things had gone at the Fennell, Jimmy remained mum. In fact, he held on to the checkbook for the rest of the weekend and into Monday morning lest she see it and discover his perfidy.

No need for Joyce to see the nice new negative number he had created by writing a $500 check to some deranged Michigan hillbilly for a restored baby grand piano that would probably only be played once or twice and then allowed to warp and rot.

No need at all for Joyce to see the rubbery -$935.26 he had entered in the check ledger.

No need because he had a plan.

A plan that would be brilliantly executed Monday morning at 10:16 a.m.

Not 10:15 mind you, but 10:16.

Precisely.

Chapter Eighteen

At precisely 10:16 on Monday morning, a young woman with a clipboard and a professionally perky smile opened the door to the waiting room and said: "Mr. Clarke?"

Jimmy looked up from PEOPLE MAGAZINE and replied: "That's me."

The young woman motioned for Jimmy to enter the inner sanctum of David R. Zahnbuerste, D.D.S. and said, "We have a chair ready and waiting for you."

"But I'm not even halfway done with PEOPLE MAGAZINE."

"You can watch the soaps while Dr. Zahnbuerste examines you," the young woman said, brightly. "We have TVs in all the examination rooms now."

"Well, in that case, let me in there."

The young woman smiled even wider and ushered Jimmy into an examination room where she arranged him in one of those wonderfully comfortable dental chairs that lull you into instant sleep. Then she put a dental bib around his neck and switched on the wall-mounted color television.

"Any soap you want to watch in particular?"

"No. I'll take whatever comes first."

What came first, of course, was a commercial for adult diapers. Then one for the social situation denture-wearers fear the most. Followed by an "important message from nine out of ten leading physicians" who preferred one brand of anal cream over another because it "really shrinks those unsightly hemorrhoids fast. And without a prescription."

"Imagine that," Jimmy said, interacting as always with the television.

"Talking back to the TV, I see." It was David R. Zahnbuerste, D.D.S. Fresh out of dental school and full of himself and good ideas for building the already successful practice dear old Daddy was bequeathing him. Putting TVs in the examination rooms was "Doctor Dave's" idea, as was the hearty handshake and shoulder squeeze he insisted on giving each and every patient, regardless of gender, age, racial persuasion and or sexual bias.

Jimmy squeezed back as the burly dentist mashed his hand in manly earnest and then settled back to set his trap.

"I've been hearing good things about you," Doctor Dave said. "My folks went and saw your play this summer. Said it was a riot. Bonnie and I wanted to go too, but we were at a dental conference in Hawaii. Tough life. But they had some great sessions on patient enhancement which is where I came up with the idea for putting TVs in the examination rooms. You like it?"

"Oh yeah, Doctor Dave. Great idea. Really great."

Doctor Dave Zahnbuerste nodded and snapped on a pair of spiffy latex gloves. Then he assembled the necessary instruments for examining his patient's mouth and said, "Why don't you open real wide and let me have a look-see?"

Jimmy opened wide, and Doctor Dave went to work on his mouth.

"So what are you up to now?" Doctor Dave said as he probed one of Jimmy's remarkably remaining wisdom teeth with a pronged instrument.

Jimmy gagged and choked out a garbled message about restoring the Fennell.

"Oh yeah," Doctor Dave said, fidgeting with a filling, "I've been hearing good things about what you're trying to do with that old place. So you really think you can get that old place going again? Gee, that'd be great, because one thing this area really needs is a concert hall and theatre. I mean as it is now, Bonnie and I have to drive to Kalamazoo or Grand Rapids or South Bend if we want to hear a decent concert or see a good play. Or even Chicago, and that's a long way to go to hear a concert. Especially this time of year when the weather gets dicey. Don't you think?"

Jimmy mumbled a hearty agreement, and then when Doctor Dave withdrew temporarily from his mouth he said: "You know, Doctor Dave, one thing we really want to do at the Fennell is have some really serious concerts. I mean top musicians from around the world and all. Local artists too, but the acoustics in that old place are really great, and with the right piano, we could . . ."

"Open please."

Jimmy opened.

"Piano, huh?" Doctor Dave said, heading back into Jimmy's mouth. "Yeah, I bet you get the right piano for that old place, and you could have some really decent concerts. And Bonnie and I wouldn't have to drive all the way to Kalamazoo or Grand Rapids. Or Chicago. Not that we don't mind going to Chicago. We usually stay at this hotel right off Michigan Avenue. You can practically roll out of your room and into Bloomingdale's. I mean, it's a shopper's paradise. Not that I like to shop as much as Bonnie, but I guess you could say I am something of a clothes horse."

Jimmy eyed the silk turtleneck protruding from the good dentist's smock and decided to hit the horseshoe while it was glowing.

So when Doctor Dave withdrew temporarily to get another instrument, Jimmy said: "We have a chance to get a restored baby grand piano for the Fennell for only $500, and we're looking for donors. All donations, of course, would be tax-deduct . . . "

"Open please."

Jimmy opened.

"Tax-deductible you say?"

Jimmy nodded as best he could under the circumstances.

Doctor Dave chewed on that for a moment and then offered: "You know, Bonnie and I met with our tax planner the other day, and he was saying we needed some more deductions if we don't want to take a big hit next April 15th. I mean a really, really big hit. Five hundred dollars, you say?"

Jimmy nodded eagerly at the well-fed dentist in the silk turtleneck. The one who had jetted off to Hawaii for a dental conference without a second thought. The one who was rumored to have a totally huge palace on choice dune acreage. Right on the fucking lake.

"When could you get the piano if I were to help you out?"

Jimmy rolled his eyes as if to say — no problem, Doctor Dave. Done deal, Doctor Dave.

Doctor Dave Zahnbuerste smiled and said, "I suppose you'd like me to write you a check today."

Jimmy nodded and tried not to weep.

"And you say it's tax-deductible? You've got non-profit status?"

"We're about to," Jimmy mumbled. "We're going to incorporate in the next week or so, and . . ."

"Good. I'll write you a check before you leave. How's that?"

Jimmy nodded and wept. Then he mumbled, "Uh, you might want to make that out to me, because we don't actually have an account yet."

That stuck between Doctor Dave's teeth, and he said so.

"I know it sounds awfully crazy, but we're just getting started, and, well, you see — I ended up paying for the piano out of my own pocket on Saturday when we went to get it from this guy in Fennville who restores pianos, and, anyway, I, uh, don't really have $500 in my account, and . . ."

"You post-dated the check and hoped like hell you'd find some rich sucker to cough up 500 big ones on Monday?"

"Well . . ."

"Consider your problems over, my friend." Doctor Dave peeled off his latex gloves and gave Jimmy's shoulder a manly squeeze. "In fact, I'll write you a check right now."

And darned if he didn't.

And darned if Jimmy didn't race right over to the bank and deposit that sucker in the joint checking account he and Joyce "maintained."

Then he sighed so big and so wide he feared he would split and be two people, side by side.

But he didn't, and life went on as it has a way of doing, and in no time flat, Jimmy found himself braking for the dump on Blue Star Highway known to antique-hunting Tunas everywhere as Lakeside Treasures. He had come, as you may recall, to meet with the blowsy redhead from a bottle from Brooklyn, Margaret Carlson (not her given name, of course), to plan the gala open house at the Fennell Art Center and Theatre set for Saturday, January 15, 1994.

Jimmy regarded the makeshift sign that was falling off its moorings and the ratty little house with attached garage that served as Lakeside Treasures. Many had been the times he and Joyce had zipped right past on a Saturday or Sunday in summer and marveled at all the BMWs and Mercedes with Illinois plates parked out in front. The Clarkes, of course, had never stopped. Never had the slightest urge to paw through all the leavings of past lives that attracted such regular hordes of bored Tuna broads and their dickless husbands.

But now Jimmy had no choice.

Now he actually had to enter the little green house that doubled as showroom for the amazing Lakeside Treasures and as a residence for the amazing Margaret Carlson and this man of hers, the mysterious Allan Q. Hovington.

It being nearly 7:30 on a November night in Michigan, it was dark. Inkily and absolutely so.

But brilliant light radiated from the Lakeside Treasures showroom that was housed in the attached garage, and Jimmy was drawn to it.

Upon closer inspection, however, he found that the brightness was due to a clever contrivance of a naked 35-watt bulb shimmering against sheets of aluminum foil stapled to the walls. The effect was at once magical and depressing as hell for it shed light on a vast collection of worthless junk.

"I like Ike" campaign buttons, and milk bottles from the Depression, and bits of this, and scraps of that, and piles and piles and piles of yellowing old magazines, and it was just overwhelming, and Jimmy had no choice but to sigh enormously.

"Pretty awesome isn't it?" a man's voice said.

Jimmy looked around and saw no one.

Maybe, he surmised, the junk is alive. Been rotting away together for so long, that it's taken on a life of its own and is able to start to . . .

"Speak?"

"Huh? Hey, who's there? Come on, where are you?"

A portly man with a ready smile and a hand-me-down sweater emerged from behind a stack of aging rock albums and said, "You must be Jim Clarke. The playwright I've been hearing so much about."

Jimmy smiled. No faster way to the boy's heart than to start off calling him a playwright one has been hearing so much about.

"And you must be Allan."

"That's me. Allan Q. Hovington. At your service."

The two men shook hands, and then Jimmy said, "So, uh, Allan, Margaret tells me you're an actor. Did a lot of theatre in Kalamazoo."

"Yeah. The whole bit. I was a drama major at Western (Michigan University) along with the rest of the world, but then I dropped out my senior year and became a resident at the PIT."

"Excuse me?"

"You've never heard of the PIT?"

"No, but then I've lived a sheltered life."

Allan smiled pedantically and explained that the PIT was an acronym standing for the Performance Initiative Theatre.

"And it really is a pit," he added, "because it's in this basement in downtown Kalamazoo below this dry cleaner. The place leaks and smells like dry cleaning solution, but it's the gutsiest little theatre this side of the East Village. Hell, they don't have anything in the East Village half as ballsy as the PIT. And it's all because of one man."

"And who might that be?"

Allan Q. Hovington paused for three full beats. Then he delivered the line with perfect modulation and enunciation: "Donald C. Adams, S.O.D."

"Who? What?"

"You've never heard of Donald C. Adams, S.O.D.? And you call yourself a playwright?"

"Well," Jimmy said, shifting uneasily and balling his fists, "I'm kind of new to the game."

"I'll say," Allan Q. Hovington said, with a derisive laugh. "Everyone who's anyone in Michigan theatre knows who Donald C. Adams, S.O.D. is."

"Good. Well, I guess I'm not everyone who's anyone in Michigan theatre. So pray enlighten me. And, pardon my ignorance, but what the hell does S.O.D. stand for? Sounds like some Irish agricultural organization or something."

Allan Q. Hovington sighed at the simpleton. "S.O.D. is the Society of Directors."

"Oh. Yippee. So this Adams guy direct something really big to get put in the SOD?"

Allan Q. Hovington motioned for Jimmy to move closer.
Jimmy moved closer.

"Actually," Allan whispered, "anybody can join. All you have to do is send them ten bucks a year and you can belong. Your dog could belong if he sent them ten bucks."

"I don't have a dog."

"Well, if you did."

"So this Donald C. Adams guy isn't all that he . . ."

"Let's just say his bark is worse than his bite. But if you're serious about breaking in as a playwright, he can help you. He's very interested in putting up work by regional playwrights. They even have a yearly competition for regional playwrights."

"Really?"

"Yeah, it's known as 'It's the PITs,' but they come up with some really good stuff. I even acted in a few a couple of years back. Before Margaret and I got together. God, that seems like another life. Where does the time go?"

"You're in your 40s too, huh?"

"Pushing 50."

"Oh, my God. Halfway to a hundred. I thought my parents were dead when they hit 50. I couldn't imagine anyone living beyond that ripe old age, but now even our fabled generation is heading for it. And you're the advance guard. Are you ready for it?"

"Fuck no."

"Yeah. Me either. But what choice do we have?"

"I don't know—I listen to a lot of these old albums and smoke the old devil weed. Keeps me young."

Jimmy regarded Allan Q. Hovington's sallow complexion and sagging gut and wondered what kind of youth that was. But he didn't share his thoughts. Rather he said, "So, I guess Margaret's probably ready to get the big meeting started."

"Margaret's not here."

"She's not? But we're supposed to be meeting tonight to discuss the big open house at the Fennell. Excuse me, the Fennell Art Center and Theatre."

"Margaret mentioned that you might be coming by sometime this week, but she didn't say anything specific. Certainly nothing about tonight, but then that's par for the course with her."

"Oh. Well, is she . . ."

"She's out selling real estate. Or trying to. She doesn't think we make enough money from Lakeside Treasures, so she went and got her real estate license, and she works on commission for one of those sleaze merchants out of South Haven who are trying to chop up every last inch of dunes into some overpriced condominium development. With Tunas crammed in cheek-to-jowl."

"Well, it's a living. Right?"

"She has yet to earn one single dime of commission."

"Sounds like you're a little bitter."

"A little?!?" Allan Q. Hovington huffed. "If she spent half the energy here that she does out trying to interest those damn Tunas in worthless real estate, then we'd be rich. I know we would. We've got the best antiques on Blue Star Highway. Bar none."

Jimmy looked at a genuine bar set from the 1950s and nodded approvingly. Then he said: "Well, I guess I'll just head home. Would you tell Margaret I was here?"

"Sure. Should I have her get back with you?"

"Yeah. That'd be good." Jimmy turned to go and then turned to stay. "Say, as long as I'm here I'd like to get . . ."

"Hey, browse all you want. And we take checks."

"Yeah. Sure. Well, actually, Allan, my wife and I are on kind of a tight budget, and . . ."

"We take lay-away. You see something here you really like – like that 'Kennedy for President' pennant, which is in mint condition I might add – I'll be happy to let you buy it on lay-away."

Jimmy regarded the pennant in question and saw that it was indeed in mint condition. And he had been a big Kennedy fan and had even built a model of PT-109. Which he ritualistically burned and sank the day after JFK was assassinated in Dallas.

(That's right, remind everybody that Kennedy was assassinated in Dallas. Drag the poor home of the Cowboys and truly wretched architecture into the discussion every chance you get.)

"How much is it?"

"For you," Allan said, "fifty bucks. Normally, I'd sell if for $75, but since you're a starving playwright, I'll knock $25 off the price. And you can start your lay-away with as little as five bucks. Come on, what do you say?"

Jimmy dug deeply into his pocket and came up with three crumpled singles, five quarters, six dimes, four nickels and four pennies. Jimmy dug deeper and failed to find another penny. He blushed as he counted out his money and said, "Sorry, but I seem to be a penny short."

Ever a man of magnanimity, Allan Q. Hovington dismissed the missing penny with a wave and a smile.

"What's a penny between fellow starving artists? Although I'd hardly say either of us are starving."

"Yeah, you got that right."

Allan wrote Jimmy a receipt for $5 and added a notation that he had $45 to go before he could claim the fabulous "Kennedy for President" pennant for his very own. Then he took the pennant in question off the wall and said, "Say, as long as you're here, you want to smoke a little wacky tobaccy?"

"Thanks, but I'm trying to cut down."

"How about a drink? I've been nursing a bottle of single-malt scotch one of our rich customers gave us last Christmas. How about a wee dram, laddie?"

"Twist my arm."

"Consider it twisted."

Jimmy nodded and followed Allan into the little house that was attached to the garage. It contained a living room that was crammed with "treasures" and served as an annex to the garage showroom. There was also a tiny bedroom with no closet, a bathroom barely big enough to burp in, and a kitchenette with an honest-to-God linoleum table and two wobbly aluminum-frame chairs.

"Make yourself comfortable," Allan said, rummaging for the scotch and two glasses.

"Nice place you've got here," Jimmy said, trying not to laugh.

"Margaret wants to sell it and move to a bigger house, but I think she's nuts," Allan said, continuing to rummage. "Ah, here you are."

He seized a dusty green bottle and plunked it on the table. Then he found two filthy glasses with Alvin and the Chipmunks emblazoned on them, ran them quickly under the faucet and set them out for action.

"Alvin and the Chipmunks," Jimmy marveled. "God, that takes me back."

"Yeah, me too," Allan said, pouring them each a generous shot. Then he lifted his glass and said, "May you live as long as you want to, and want to as long as you live."

"I'll drink to that," Jimmy said, clinking Allan's glass.

They drank their scotch whiskey neat and with great pleasure for it was truly one of the great malts of the Highlands.

Both men, you see, had more than a few wee drams of Scottish blood between them, so why the hell not take a big bite out of the November cold and gloom with a dram or two of the "honey of the Highlands?"

"So," Jimmy said after they had drunk to one another's health, long life, prosperity, and absolute avoidance of prostate cancer, "do you happen to have the address of this PIT place in Kalamazoo?"

Allan Q. Hovington made a sour face and said: "What, you have some plays in your drawer you want to send the great and wise Donald C. Adams, S.O.D.?"

"Well, yeah — a few. Why, is that a bad idea?"

"The great and wise Donald C. Adams, S.O.D. never produces anything that comes in over the transom."

"But what about that contest he has?"

"You mean — 'It's the PITs'?"

"Yeah."

"Yeah, they produce stuff from that — obviously. But it's all stuff by playwrights Donald knows. He makes it out to look like there was blind judging and everything, but he plays his favorites. And the entry fees keep them alive for half the year. It's great work if you can get it."

Jimmy sipped his single-malt scotch and let it slide goldenly down his tongue. His Scottish ancestors called to him from glen to glen. Something about not burning the oatmeal and poaching more salmon. Then he came back to the present and faced the florid Allan Q. Hovington. His genial host.

"So what's the best way to approach this Adams guy?"

"Go and see one of his plays. And flatter him afterwards. Flattery will get you everywhere with the great and wise Donald C. Adams, S.O.D."

"Yeah?"

"Oh yes. In fact, your karma must be on tonight, because they're doing a play sometime early next year about President Kennedy. At least that's what I've been hearing through the grapevine, and rumor has it that the great and wise Donald C. Adams, S.O.D. himself will star as Kennedy. No, as Jack. He always refers to Kennedy as Jack.

Like they were personal pals or something. But hell, he might as well play 'Jack' because he's always walking around boring anyone within earshot about where he was on November 22, 1963. Like the rest of us were on fucking Mars or something."

"So where was he on November 22, 1963?"

"At some youth theatre program in New York getting buggered by the artistic director."

"Jeez, no wonder he went into theatre. I guess you wouldn't forget that, would you?"

"No, I guess not. Well, how about drinking to your success as a playwright? Both at the Fennell and in the PIT."

"Set me up, barkeep."

Allan Q. Hovington was about to set them up when the door burst open, admitting a blast of cold November night and the ever-blowsy Margaret Carlson. She wore a tight-fitting navy blue business suit and had two women in tow. One was immediately recognizable as the jewelry-bedecked Harriett Lawford, and the other was an unrecognizable aging harpy with preternaturally blonde hair.

"The way these women glop up their hair I'm gonna have to go out and buy some stock in Dow Chemical," Jimmy muttered to himself.

"What was that?" Margaret Carlson demanded, angrily eyeballing the two men and a bottle.

"Nothing," Jimmy said, feeling his testicles ascend protectively into his abdominal cavity.

"I heard what you said," Margaret Carlson said. "You said you're going to have to go and buy some stock in Dow Chemical. Because of the way women glop up their hair or something. That's what you said — isn't it?!?"

Jimmy blushed and looked for a quick exit. The three ball-chewing women had it blocked.

Oh boy!

"Stop muttering and answer me."

Jimmy cleared his throat and took the offensive. "I thought we were going to meet at 7:30."

"We were. But I had a showing. A dream house on the Black River. To die for, right, Laura?"

The aging bottle blonde in the distressed leather bomber jacket smiled tightly. She had clearly looked but not bought.

"After I showed Laura the dream house to die for on the Black River, which I know she's just dying to buy, I took her over to the Fennell and told her all about our gala open house on January 15. And she volunteered to be on our committee, didn't you, Laura?"

Laura Downs smiled tightly and tried not to breathe through her nose. She had heard about places like this, but had never actually been in one.

"Laura's from Chicago. Aren't you, Laura?"

Laura Downs smiled tightly and tried not to breathe through her nose.

"Laura's going to start a catering business here. She catered to Oprah Winfrey in Chicago. Didn't you, Laura?"

Laura Downs smiled tightly and tried not to breathe through her nose.

"She knows all the celebrities in Chicago. Gene Siskel, Michael Jordan, Roger Ebert, Walter Jacobson, Bill Kurtis — all of them. Don't you, Laura?"

Laura Downs smiled tightly and tried not to breathe through her nose.

"Laura's going to cater to them all in their summer places in Michigan and Indiana. And bring all kinds of exciting people to our area and increase our property values. Aren't you, Laura?"

Laura Downs smiled tightly and tried not to breath through her nose.

Jimmy cleared his throat to break this cycle of banality, and Allan Q. Hovington padded off to the showroom with a fleeting: "I'd better leave you to your meeting. Besides, I've got lots of treasures to organize for the weekend."

"Bring us some more chairs," Margaret called.

Allan dutifully brought them some more chairs, cleared off the bottle and glasses and disappeared.

Then Margaret and Harriett began organizing the gala open house set for January 15, 1994 at the Fennell Art Center and Theatre, aka: FAGAT.

Laura Downs smiled tightly and tried not to breathe through her nose. She listened as long as she could stand hearing the other women blither on and on about the poetic genius of Dan Andreas, the poet laureate of the local community college, and then she just swept all conversation aside with a wave of her haughty hand and a terse: "You're not going to get a living soul in that dreary old place on January 15th unless you offer them decent food and drink. And you've got to get invitations out. To anyone who's anyone around here. And I mean the Robert Ebert's and Oprah Winfrey's — real people who have country places in Michigan and Indiana. If you don't get them, why even bother? It's not worth the effort. I mean, have you people done anything besides buy some old broken-down piano? I mean, what's going on here? What's the use of proceeding if you're not ready to work, and I mean work hard, and do a massive mailing and real marketing, and I mean real marketing and . . ."

Margaret and Harriett were in awe.

They had been bested by a *real* bitch. A woman who ate plates full of balls for breakfast and spit them out on the roadside as she roared through life in her black BMW with her oversized designer dog (as her only companion in and out of bed) in pursuit of being better than everyone else and having the biggest portfolio and the heftiest resume when she died.

Jimmy just sat on his hands and looked for the exit.

Seeing that it wasn't blocked, he used it and headed for his little dump in the dunes in his little gas-pinching car.

He summoned his patron saint as he drove.

"Yo, Saint Genesius. We need to talk."

Saint Genesius got the call but did not answer. It's that stupid Protestant again, he thought. Protestants don't believe in saints, so what's the use? Besides, I've been ordered. And when you've been ordered up here, you don't take individual initiative. Stick your neck out up here and He'll whack it off in a twinkling with that mighty flaming sword of His. So noodle it out on your own, Protestant playwright. That's what He gave you a noodle for in the first place. Use it or lose it, and all that good stuff.

That came in garbled, and Jimmy asked for a retransmission.

But the line went dead.

Jimmy exhaled and painfully realized he would have to work all this out by his lonesome.

One thing he knew for certain: Laura Downs gave him the creeps. And she looked like she was ready to take over the whole project. Hell, she already has.

And if it's not her, then it'll be the next sharpie from Chicago. They'll let suckers like me and that amazing Pete guy and his trusty Saws-All do all the work and then step in and take all the glory. And the money.

What money?

Exactly.

What money?

Still, Jimmy dreamed as he drove through the inkwell that was November night in western Michigan.

A six-point buck bounded before his car, and Jimmy swerved expertly and instinctively to avoid it.

The buck disappeared into a dark field, and Jimmy continued on his way home to the dump in the dunes he and his wife called the Dunery.

With his heart fluttering madly.

And not just because he had nearly crashed headlong into a mighty deer. But because his future as a playwright was on the line.

And because he was running away.

Running away from perhaps the best and probably the last chance for success and glory.

"Success and glory," Jimmy said, braking and executing a daring U-turn.

He drove straight back to Lakeside Treasures, apologized to the assembled harpies for his abrupt departure earlier, and then he wedged his way into the discussion with a terse: "I have a play that would work perfectly as a reader's theatre for the open house, and Harriett, Allan and I could read the parts. And you, Harriett, would get to play the queen."

Harriett liked that.

A lot.

So much so that she clanked her jewelry and actually defied the mighty Laura Downs to question the man's suggestion.

Laura Downs simply smiled tightly and tried not to breathe through her nose.

Then she allowed as how she could cater the whole sorry affair for a "reasonable price" as long as "everyone was willing to chip in and help a little with my costs."

Jimmy was the first to agree.

Hell, they were going to read his play to the assembled multitudes at the gala open house on January 15, 1994 at the Fennell Art Center and Theatre, aka: FAGAT. He was going to be rich and famous beyond measure.

So why not a measure of money he and Joyce didn't have for the greedy girl caterer from Chicago?

Chapter Nineteen

Hang on to your brewskies, sports fans, because we're going to fast forward here for a while.

At least to get us up to the seminal night of Saturday January 15, 1994. The night of the gala open house at the Fennell Art Center and Theatre, aka: FAGAT.

First the intervening events in the order they occurred:

1. Joyce's main client, Jerry Mappers, decided to summarily fire Joyce as her main free-lancer, because Joyce had had the temerity to actually call accounting and inquire about a check that was more than 90 days past due. A big check that Joyce was counting on to pay most of the major bills piled on her desk.

Upon hearing that her main free-lancer had gone behind her back to get her check, Jerry Mappers blew up ballistically and told Joyce she was through.

Joyce panicked and ordered Jimmy to save the day by finding free- lance clients.

Jimmy bit his tongue and called Kathryn Stavakitis at FLS Corporation in Chicago to see if he could cadge an assignment or two for the next exciting issue of IN DEFENSE OF AMERICA, or IDA.

Nada, said Kathryn, but she promised to call as soon as something came up.

So Jimmy did a big mailing to every business in western Michigan, northern Indiana, and Chicago.

He came up with exactly zero until a man named Barkley Gordonson phoned to invite him to write a brochure for the home health care business he was operating out of a converted school house on Phoenix Road.

Jimmy dutifully donned his only tie and jacket and went to meet his prospective client. But as he was about to emerge from Angel Car, a one-tone Ford screeched up and emitted four men in blue nylon windbreakers. As the grim-faced men fanned out, Jimmy could see the letters "FBI" emblazoned in yellow on the backs of their jackets.

One of the agents crunched over to Jimmy's car and rapped on the window.

Jimmy rolled it down, and the agent said: "You have business with Mr. Gordonson?"

"I'm just a free-lance writer he wanted to talk to about some brochures, and . . ."

"Well, he won't be talking to anyone today. I suggest you look for other clients."

"Yes, sir."

And thanks for not shooting me. Thank you, thank you.

Jimmy fumbled with the ignition, clutch, and gas pedal for what seemed like God's lunch hour and finally got underway. He tried not to stare at the FBI agents as they entered Barkley Gordonson's home health care business through all available doors.

And later, when the weakly weekly HAVENCREST HIGHLIGHTS revealed that Mr. Gordonson had bilked Medicare out of $3.4 million and was soon to be lodged in a federally funded rest home for criminally inclined white collar types, Jimmy wondered if somehow Saint Genesius hadn't been trying to send him a message after all. Even though the saint was under strict orders not to talk to Protestant playwrights.

Anyway, when Jimmy got home, Joyce was just getting off the phone with Jerry Mappers. Turned out that Jerry Mappers had been so upset about Joyce's going behind her back because Jerry Mappers' doctor had wondered if a mole on her check was malignant. The "life-and-death mole," as it came to be known in Jerry Mappers' office, was removed; a biopsy had been performed, and the results had just been phoned to Jerry Mappers.

No cancer. Just a benign, benighted colony of friendly facial cells hanging out on her cheek for all the world to peek.

Life as Jerry Mappers knew it could continue complete with two-hour lunches, "the errands" at 3 p.m., daily mid-day sessions at the health club, and delegation of virtually every task to underpaid underlings and helpful, loyal, thrifty, brave, clean, and reverent free-lancers like Joyce Clarke.

"We're saved!" Joyce proclaimed as Jimmy came in the door. "You don't have to free-lance after all! That was Jerry Mappers, and she still wants me to be work for her. Of course, she had to chew me a new rectum just to show what a real woman in

management she really is, but she still wants to use me for all her
newsletters, so . . ."

"I can go ahead with being a playwright?"

"You can go ahead with being a playwright."

Jimmy said that was good and told what had just occurred at
Barkley Gordonson's home health care business on Phoenix Road.
He left out the bit about it being a sign from Saint Genesius, because
he knew Joyce had cashed in her Catholicism along with her Girl
Scout cookies and Archie and Jughead comic books.

Still, Joyce was inspired to say: "I guess this must be a sign from
above or something."

Jimmy just smiled.

2. Klaus Williams, the wizened heating and air-conditioning man
with the glowing eyes and Lucky Strikes, appeared one December
night at the Dunery to assure Jimmy and Joyce he was thinking of
them every day.

Every day since the hot, muggy summer day he and sozzled old
Gus were supposed to have returned to begin work on Jimmy and
Joyce's heating and air-conditioning system employing the very
latest geothermal technologies. Obviously, they hadn't returned that
day or any other day until that December evening when Klaus
Williams showed up on their doorstep.

"You know that $6,000 you give me for your system?" Mr.
Williams said, hat in hand.

Jimmy and Joyce looked at one another in alarm. They were
heating their little house with electric baseboard units and were
running up enormous electric bills. Mr. Williams' amazing system,
which he had assured them would be up and running months ago,
was supposed to be saving them big bucks on energy bills by now,
but here was the little Slovak fucker obviously trying to con them out
of more money.

Money they didn't begin to have.

Jimmy wanted to take the little D.P. out and brain him with his
splitting maul, but Joyce took pity on the man.

He was, after all, a fellow artist.

A genius.

And a soulful one at that.

And like Jimmy and Joyce, Klaus Williams was a misunderstood genius.

So Joyce looked deeply into Klaus Williams' rheumy eyes and said: "What about the $6,000 we gave you for our system? You said in August that was supposed to cover everything. Parts, labor, the whole works."

Klaus Williams relayed to a fresh Lucky Strike from the one he had smoked down to nearly nothing, and sighed so big and so wide the entire cottage shook. Trees bent and coyotes howled. Well, a dog in the next subdivision yapped at a squirrel.

Anyway, Joyce felt the cold hand of guilt grip her heart. Like she had personally let down this amazing man. Like he was her father or something.

Ever the perceptive genius, Klaus Williams picked up on that right away, saying: "Well, yeah, it was supposed to pay for all that, but, uh, well, you see I been trying to get this system patented. With the U.S. Patent Office, you know, and them people want a whole heap of paperwork, and the application fee ain't nothin' to sneeze at, and I was thinkin' of using your system as the prototype for my patent. See, I got it all laid out at home on my dining room table — can't even eat at my own dining room table because I got your system all laid out there — not that we ever eat at my dining room table because business ain't been all that good lately, but you bein' in business for yourselves like me — well, you know what that's like. Hand to mouth. And sometimes you ain't got nothin' in your hand to put in your mouth."

Klaus Williams handed his mouth a glowing Lucky Strike and took a long, satisfying pull. Right out of some 1950s commercial when ballplayers fired up in the dugout to ensure faster fastballs and heartier homers.

"So what are you saying, Mr. Williams?" Jimmy said, fighting desperately to remain calm.

"He's saying he needs more money, Jimmy. Isn't that right, Mr. Williams?"

Klaus Williams thanked the patron saint of heating and air-conditioning men, Joan of Arc. He was a good Catholic after all, so she answered when he called. Besides, she knew all about heating. As for air-conditioning, well she had gone to a much cooler place after her fiery martyrdom.

Klaus Williams coughed out smoke and lung particles and said: "Well, yeah, I could use some more money. To get your system up and running. Because I know how important it is to you people to have proper air-conditioning and heating in here what with them computers you got for your business. And speaking of them computers, I was wondering if maybe you couldn't help me with this patent application because . . ."

"Shouldn't you just hire a patent attorney to do that?" Jimmy asked.

Klaus Williams coughed out smoke and lung particles and sadly shook his Slovak head.

Joyce jumped in with an immediate and heartfelt, "Don't worry, Mr. Williams. We'll help you with your application. We're fellow artists and we know all about filling in complicated applications. God, that one we did for the National Endowment for the Arts took days to do."

(And they still didn't get it, nor did Jimmy and Lynda Johnson get a dime out of the Michigan Council for Arts and Cultural Affairs when they applied for a project grant for producing *No Dice* at the Great Hall of GAS in July. But that's neither here nor there and hardly relevant to anything except that it was fun to write, and why write if it's not fun? *N'est-ce pas?*)

"Joyce, we don't have time to . . ."

"Jimmy!!"

Jimmy knew Joyce had the moral imperative here because she controlled the purse strings, so he shut the fuck up and went into a deep funk as his wife volunteered their writing services to the deadbeat D.P. who was never going to finish their heating and air-conditioning system in their lifetime. Or in God's lifetime for that matter.

Suffice it to say Jimmy was right, and despite the couple's best efforts and "gift" of an additional $1,000 to help the poor man get by, Klaus Williams never received a patent for his amazing geothermal system. Klaus Williams never received a patent for his amazing geothermal system because he never got around to filing for a patent. Despite Joyce's best efforts to nudge him toward the post office.

Klaus Williams eventually drifted south to Berrien County where he was crushed to death by a contraption of his own making under the cottage of Christopher and Kathleen Kurtin. (But that's another story, and luckily for you, gentle readers, you can soak up all the juicy details in TALES FROM THE OTHER SIDE by Charles McKelvy. Available, of course, from The Dunery Press.)

3. The board of directors of the Fennell Art Center and Theatre, aka: FAGAT continued to begin their 7:30 meeting every Saturday morning promptly at 7:45. For a frantic 15 minutes each week, they daringly went ahead with plans for the gala open house set for Saturday, January 15, 1994.

In other business, the board:

-Admitted the wise and wonderful Laura Downs to its membership and elected her chairperson of the newly created Strategic Planning Committee.

-Opened a checking account at the same bank where Larry German and his sister banked and asked each board member to contribute $10 to create an opening balance. Jimmy was the only contributor, but Margaret Carlson was sure their coffers would overflow after January 15.

-Asked the wise and wonderful Laura Downs to create a "business plan" for the next five years of operation.

-Determined to find a local attorney to provide pro bono services such as incorporation, tax-exempt status and other minor matters. In return, said attorney and his/her significant other would be given front row seats for all FAGAT events for life. (FAGAT's life, not theirs).

-Approved Harriett Lawford's motion that the celebrated Myron T. Ackerman, A.S.A.E. be invited to provide architectural renderings of how the Fennell Art Center and Theatre would appear after restoration. Said renderings to be prominently displayed at the gala open house set for January 15, 1994. Harriett assured said board that although said architect was currently "servicing" a client in Germany, "he'll be delighted to do some drawings for us. I know, because all he talked about last time I saw him was the Fennell. It's on his mind constantly."

-Appointed Larry German and his sister Julie German-Cooper to "Liaison with Building Owners Committee" after Larry German let it be known that he and his sister didn't really own the building but were in fact renting it from a shadowy couple who were behind the project "one hundred and fifty percent and then some." Said shadowy couple were never named by said brother and sister and declined an invitation from the board to appear in person and bless the restoration venture.

-Appointed the amazing Chip Gooch as "chairperson" of the restoration committee and directed him to proceed post haste in restoration efforts. Chip Gooch asked for volunteers and got the usual suspects — Gerry, Susie, and Jimmy Clarke. Kathy Walker, bless her bulging heart, volunteered to videotape their efforts for posterity and for full credit in Tim Daniels' drama class out at the college.

-Created a committee to line up local artists and dealers for a gallery program. Margaret Carlson volunteered to be the "chairperson."

-Created a committee to line up plays for a theatrical season in the summer of 1994. Jimmy Clarke, the playwright with plays coming out of his pores, volunteered to be chairman and promised to "come up with some great original work."

-Created a concert committee and voted to dedicate the Fennell's first concert to "Doctor Dave" Zahnbuerste, D.D.S. who had nobly bought the theatre's restored baby grand piano. Jimmy moved that the board reimburse Doctor Dave for the piano, but no one seconded. Doctor Dave, everyone agreed, was just a generous donor whose recompense would come in heavenly music. On the fully restored piano at the fully restored Fennell Art Center and Theatre, aka: FAGAT.

-Created a grants committee to apply for every grant imaginable, including a bricks and mortar grant for restoring the old wreck of a theatre. Never mind that the latter grants were awarded only to arts organizations that either owned their buildings outright or had secured 99-year leases. Never mind that the FAGAT fellows would never own their building outright much less even get a lease in writing from the shadowy couple who actually owned the old dump.

-Elected to get a new furnace and air-conditioning system as soon as financially feasible. "Probably," Margaret Carlson assured everyone, "right after we raise tons of money at the open house on January 15."

-Created a publicity committee and begged Jimmy Clarke to head it. After Jimmy reluctantly agreed, the wise and wonderful Laura Downs ordered him to "get cracking immediately," and the wide and woe-begotten Kathy Walker said, "And be sure and mention Chip Gooch in the first paragraph because he's the one who's single-handedly killing himself to restore this theatre."

-Moved to adjourn promptly at 8 a.m. every week so Larry and Julie could rush to open their gallery and pander to Tunas with fat wallets.

* * *

Had enough fast-forwarding?

I thought so.

Okay, go to the fridge, get a fresh brewski, add some chips to the bowl, and sit back and enjoy the show.

Specifically the gala open house on Saturday, January 15, 1994 at the partially restored Fennell Art Center and Theatre, aka: FAGAT.

Emphasis on "partially" because Chip and his sidekicks had finals and farm chores in late December and early January, not to mention family responsibilities and gift buying and all that other Christmas crap that informs American life, so the weekly work details wilted down to Jimmy Clarke and Larry German when he had a second or two.

Margaret Carlson persuaded Allan Q. Hovington to come over and help one afternoon, but after a few turns on the old push broom, he developed a debilitating back problem that sent him howling off to a nearby bar, the Blue Chip Lounge.

Still, Jimmy and Larry managed to get the old wreck of a place reasonably respectable-looking for the open house. Why, Larry even went so far as to fix up the old bathroom and actually got the ancient toilet working again. (Which was a must considering the township was not going to allow the open house if modern plumbing wasn't provided. Jimmy went out and bought a pack of good toilet paper for the occasion. Out of his own pocket, of course.)

Jimmy won the wise and wonderful Laura Downs' approval for his press releases and sent them to every media outlet in Michigan, northern Indiana and Chicago. Kathy Walker blew a fuse when the HAVENCREST HIGHLIGHTS failed to include a photo of Chip Gooch in its story about restoration at the Fennell.

Jimmy gently reminded the woman that Chip had been absent the day that Tiffany Ann Starbuck had dispatched her new "newsboy" over to take photographs of the Fennell, but that wasn't good enough for Kathy Walker.

Oh no.

Not by a country mile. She went ballistic, as modern American woman are want to do when faced with the stubborn resolve of modern American men, and told Jimmy Clarke in no uncertain terms that he was "a typical, stupid, stubborn male."

Jimmy just swallowed it, thinking there was no sense alienating a woman with a videocamera. A woman who could be persuaded to videotape the reading of his play at the gala open house.

But when he couldn't persuade her to videotape his play at the open house, he took her aside and said, "Stay the fuck out of my way, you fat bitch! You hear me?"

The fat bitch heard. Oh, she heard all right.

And she vowed never to speak to Jimmy again as long as they both shall live.

Which was fine with Jimmy because he had had quite enough of the Kathy Walkers of the world.

And when Laura Downs organized a "stuff and lick the invitations" party at a failing Turkish restaurant she was selling marked-up produce to, Jimmy avoided Kathy Walker entirely. And Kathy Walker avoided Jimmy Clarke entirely. But they both worked along with the others to put 1,556 invitations in the mail the next morning.

Meaning that a huge crowd was expected for the gala open house set for Saturday, January 15, 1994.

Expectations were further heightened when Jimmy wangled an interview on Michigan Public Radio out of Ann Arbor and got the

KALAMAZOO GAZETTE to do a major feature with color photos in the Sunday paper prior to the open house.

Now all they needed was good weather.

And as they all assembled at the Fennell on the morning of Saturday, January 15, 1994 to make final preparations, they were greeted by a snow-covered fire plug who came stomping and cursing into the cold and drafty old theatre. The ice creature came to a coughing stop at the wobbly picnic table that served as the board's board and said: "There's one hell of a blizzard brewin' out there, folks, and it followed me all the way from Chicago."

The speaker was none other than the irrepressible Wendy Filbaitus, and she was nearly frozen because the heater in her little Chicago Public School teacher's beater-car was on the fritz. Plus, she had been unable to afford new tires, so she had nearly flown off the road on several occasions when her balding tires failed to grasp the pavement.

Margaret Carlson stared at the stomping Wendy Filbaitus for an eternal second and then went into a complete and total panic attack.

"We've got to cancel!!" she sputtered, her face turning redder than her preternaturally red hair. "Jim, you've got to call all the newspapers and radio stations right now and tell them we've got to cancel, because we can't have all these hundreds of people we're expecting—some of them my prospective real estate clients from Chicago—driving in a blizzard. What if somebody ends up in the ditch?!? What if somebody freezes to death in their car?!? It's happened. I've read about it. I've heard about it. And it could happen here!! Tonight!!!! And we'd be to blame. All of us. God, it would be horrible!! The Fennell would never recover. We'd be ruined—our dream down the drain!! Jim, you've got to get on the phone right now. Call all the papers and tell them to put something in right away and tell everybody to stay home, and we'll cancel, and we'll reschedule for another date in the spring when there aren't ice storms and blizzards and . . ."

"Freezing temperatures," Wendy Filbaitus said, rubbing her hands together. "God, you wouldn't believe how cold it's getting out there. And with that wind that's whipping across the lake, we're talking about a wind chill of minus . . ."

"See!!" Margaret Carlson screamed. "People are going to be frozen in their cars!! Packs of wild dogs are going to eat them!! It's going to be terrible. Awful. Horrible!! The worst nightmare of my life." She reached across the wobbly picnic table and seized Jimmy's arm. "Jim, you've got to get on the phone right this second, and I mean right this second and call all the newspapers, and all the radio stations, and all the TV stations and the wire services, and CNN, and anybody else you can think of, and tell them that the open house is canceled because we can't have people getting frozen in their cars and being eaten by packs of wild dogs. Do you hear me?!? Are you listening to me?!?"

Jimmy yanked his arm free and shook his head. "No way, Margaret! We can't cancel now. No way! It's too late to get anything in the newspapers, and we can't count on people hearing an announcement on the radio or seeing it on television. Provided the stations even decide to run it. It's way too late to cancel. We've made our bed, and now we've got to sleep in it no matter what the weather is." Oh, was he hot. Oh, was he ready to strangle the hysterical broad from Brooklyn.

But he didn't have to because Wendy Filbaitus calmly positioned herself behind Margaret Carlson and placed an icy hand on her shoulder. Then she said in a measured voice: "You cancel this open house at the last minute, and the Fennell is down the toilet. We had our first big fund-raiser at the Organic in the middle of one of the worst ice storms Chicago's ever had, and we packed the place. And people loved us for it and gave us tons of money. It made all the difference, and it's going to make all the difference for the Fennell. You go ahead tonight, and whoever shows up will love you for it. You cancel, and you're history."

The rest of the board took that to mean that the show must go on, and Laura Downs immediately motioned to that effect.

Jimmy instantly seconded, and all were in favor except for Margaret Carlson who moaned for the rest of the morning about the disaster that was waiting to happen.

There was nothing to do but ignore her and give the old place one more good sweeping and then go home and pray all afternoon for a break in the weather.

Which didn't happen, of course.

The winter storm advisory became a warning which became a reality of driving snow, plummeting temperatures and frequent white-outs on all local roads and highways. A real mess. And a great night to stay home in front of a fire with a thick book with tiny print.

Which is what Joyce fervently urged Jimmy to do.

"They can carry on without you," she said. "Why do you need to go out there and get Angel Car stuck in a ditch and freeze to death?"

"You sound just like Margaret Carlson."

"Who? Wait, you mean that phony red-head from Brooklyn you told me about?"

"Yeah. You should have heard her going on and on about the weather. I mean she had one of the most massive panic attacks in history. It was truly legendary. Too bad that stupid Kathy Walker didn't have her videocamera. It would have made a great film. Or a monologue. That's it—I'm going to write it up as a one-woman horror show. Something like that, and we'll produce it at the Fennell in the summer during our first big theatre season and . . ."

"The cold's gotten to you, Jimmy. You're delusional. Come on, eat some hot food and take a hot shower and make a fire, and we'll just settle in for a night of reading thick books with tiny print."

"No!"

Joyce looked at her reeling husband with alarm. The man was clearly committed to his crazy course, and she knew instinctively that she either had to support him or sit on her hands. Any further opposition would surely result in the melt-down of a major organ system in her beloved's body.

Being too young for widowhood, Joyce notched back and said: "You're really committed to this thing, aren't you?"

"Joyce," Jimmy said, pacing before her, "it's my big chance to break in as a playwright. You never know who's going to be there tonight. We sent invitations to tons of Chicago people, and you just know one of them is got to have some big-time theatre connections in Chicago."

"What about that Wendy creature you're always talking about? I thought she was going to get you produced at a Chicago theatre. You even gave her your play, *Criminal Justice,* to shop around."

"She's been real busy. But she'll be there tonight, and I'm sure she'll introduce me to whatever bigshots show up. And you know they're going to come, because Wendy said the Organic was in the exact same situation when they first started, and they went ahead and had this big fund raiser right in the middle of the worst ice storm Chicago's ever had, and all these people showed up anyway, and gave them a ton of money, and . . ."

"Even if a whole bunch of people show up tonight and give you a ton of money, who's going to know where it goes? Have you thought of that?"

"What do you mean?"

"I thought you told me that that Larry German creature and his sweet little sister have control of the bank account. He's president, and she's treasurer. Right?"

"Yeah? So?"

"Yeah, so you said you saw them kissing like a couple of horny teen-agers on more than one occasion."

"Yeah? So?"

"Yeah, so they're in cahoots, Jimmy. You guys could end up collecting a ton of money tonight, and you'd have no idea where it ended up because your little kinky pair controls the purse strings. There's no oversight. Like with the ownership of the building. You still don't know who really owns the building, do you?"

Jimmy exhaled forcefully and collapsed in his chair.

Joyce was a born realist and found it hard not to tell the truth. But she was also deeply in love with her mad dreamer of a husband, the perpetual adolescent. And she could not bear to see him suffer.

And she was certainly seeing him suffer now, so she poured syrup on her voice as she said: "I'm sure everything will be fine tonight. In fact, I was thinking of calling Marlene Small and talking her into going. She has a four-wheel drive and I could hitch a ride with her so I don't have to go early with you."

Jimmy came back to life. "I think her father's visiting. If he came too, that'd be an extra person."

"Don't worry, Jimmy, it's going to be fine tonight. You'll get a big turn-out tonight. You'll see."

"You really think so."

Joyce didn't think so at all, but she smiled and said, "I know so."

Chapter Twenty

Well, there is one good thing to report about the gala open house at the Fennell Art Center and Theatre, or FAGAT, on Saturday, January 15, 1994:

Angel Car started right up both going and coming and didn't even think about getting stuck in a snow drift. And the little hard-working Honda threw all the heat she could muster on her delusional owner.

And as an addendum to the above item, Marlene Small's four-wheel drive wonder vehicle was up to the task of transporting Marlene, her father, and Joyce to and from the Fennell.

So there were no familiar characters frozen in cars or eaten by packs of wild dogs.

For that matter, not one of the more than 300 people who braved the worst winter storm in memory to attend the open house was frozen in his or her car. Or even looked at funny by a domestic dog much less menaced by the feral variety.

From a purely mass transit standpoint, it was a brilliant undertaking. Foolhardy as hell, but brilliant nonetheless.

And that's something, considering Margaret Carlson's very real concerns that the whole thing could have been an unmitigated disaster with frozen blood on the hands of a board of directors with only $10 to its name.

Okay, that's the good news bit.

Now on to the rest of the evening which was fucking dire.

It began, of course, with Jimmy arriving at the door to the Fennell with armloads of foodstuffs. Wendy Filbaitus, you see, had pulled up next to him, and had brought the fixings for her patented "killer open house punch," and gentleman Jimmy gallantly volunteered to help her hump the bags into the theatre.

Kathy Walker greeted them at the door with her activated videocamera. She totally ignored Jimmy and focused on Wendy. And, of course, she was too busy filming to hold the frigging door.

Figures.

And it only got worse from there.

Like when Jimmy asked the clanking Harriett Lawford what had become of Myron T. Ackerman's architectural renderings of how the Fennell would appear after the miracle of restoration.

"Are they still in your car or something? I've still got my boots on so I can go and . . ."

"Oh, Myron just didn't have time," Harriett said, arranging a bauble. "You can't begin to imagine how busy he is. It's a wonder he even has time to sleep what with all the work he has. And the mega-clients he's working for. But we're so lucky to have him involved here at the Fennell. Just his mere presence is an inspiration to us all."

"So is he going to inspire us all tonight with his mere presence?"

Harriett Lawford made a sour face and said, "Myron is in the city."

"You mean Chicago?"

"No, I mean London. He's lecturing on architecture at some big international symposium. Prince Charles is going to be the keynote speaker. It's quite the do."

"I bet. Well, I guess he'll get to the drawings when he gets back."

Harriett Lawford gave Jimmy a frosty look as if to suggest she was not accountable for what she said from one board meeting to the next. And as if to suggest the playwright could just go soak his head in the punch bowl and leave her to her mingling with the high society of South Haven that was expected any minute.

Jimmy shrugged and said, "So, you ready for the reading tonight?"

"You mean am I ready to be the Queen?"

"Yeah."

"Darling, I don't have to prepare for a role I was born to. Now run off and make yourself useful, and leave me to my public."

Jimmy nodded and shuffled off to help Wendy Filbaitus make the punch. Then he helped Chip Gooch and his sidekicks set up the stage for the gala open house. Kathy Walker filmed the latter, carefully excluding Jimmy from every shot and actually telling him at one point to "move out of the way so I can get a close-up of Chip."

Julie German-Cooper grabbed Jimmy as he was working on the stage and said, "You've got to be the M.C. tonight."

"But Larry's president. He should be the M.C."

"I know, but he hates to get up in front of lots of people."

Jimmy glanced at the empty ice house and said, "Doesn't look like there is going to be a big crowd."

"Even if nobody shows up, you should do it. You're a natural. You're from Chicago, and Larry's just a shy woodworker who grew up around here."

"But I don't have anything written. And everybody in the community knows Larry. I mean, he's a home boy. I'm just another despised Tuna who moved over here and drove up the real estate taxes."

"I know," Julie said, heartily agreeing. "But I still think you should do it. What do you say?"

"Julie, I really think your brother should be M.C. Unless he's sick or something. I mean, where is he?"

Julie tightened her face and whispered, "He's out in his van with Taylor Griffith."

"You don't mean they're smoking . . ."

"Shuuusssh!!"

Jimmy nodded. "I get it. Okay. Stupid me. Well, look at it this way, Julie, he'll be totally relaxed up on stage. Now, if you'll excuse me, I've got to go and talk to Allan Hovington over there about our reading."

Jimmy dashed over to Allan Q. Hovington who was holding up a completely hysterical Margaret Carlson.

"Where is everybody?!?" she demanded. "I told you, Jim. I told you. People are sliding off the road and freezing in their cars!! I knew this would happen. It's supposed to start in 20 minutes, and there's nobody here. It's a complete disaster!! A complete disaster!! It couldn't be worse. This is my worst nightmare come true. My whole life I've been waiting for this moment, and this stupid storm comes in and ruins everything. We never had storms like this in Brooklyn. My God!! What kind of place is this?!? Michigan!! I knew you should have called the media and canceled. I knew it!! But you wouldn't listen to me. You . . ."

"That's a lovely dress you're wearing tonight, Margaret."

"You think so?" she said, fussing with the vintage black satin number Allan had fished out of some dumpster for her.

(In truth, she looked like some blood sausage gone bad, and her ample bosom was about to bound free for all the world to see, and she had enough make-up on her puss to keep the International House of Pancakes cranking 'em out for a week, but, hey, the old girl had put her all into it. And she was proud. Damn proud. And that's why she was so totally upset.)

"I know so. And don't worry — they will come. Just like that movie with Kevin Costner — build it and they will come. Well, we rebuilt, and they will come."

And, right on cue, they came.

All 457 of them.

In one great steaming, tramping, moaning, shivering mass of cabin-fevered humanity bent on having one hell of a good time at somebody else's expense.

"Now are you happy, Margaret?" Jimmy said.

Margaret Carlson brightened perceptibly but then let her crest fall. "Oh God," she moaned, "we won't have enough food for all these people. I knew we should get more food. That was the one thing I was worried about — that we wouldn't have enough food for all these people. And — oh, there's that couple I've been trying to reach about that darling little hide-a-way on the Black River — excuse me."

Allan Q. Hovington and Jimmy watched Margaret sashay off to sell real estate. All was well with God in His Heaven and on earth below in the frozen confines of the Fennell Art Gallery and Theatre, aka: FAGAT.

"She's happy," Allan said, smiling.

"Yeah, it certainly would appear so. And it sure looks like we hit the jackpot. God, would you look at all these people."

They looked at all those people move as one to the refreshment counter where a beleaguered Wendy Filbaitus attempted to serve them.

"We'd better go help her," Jimmy said.

Allan Q. Hovington winced and touched his tender back. "You go," he said, "I'd better give my back a rest for the big reading."

Jimmy nodded and went and helped Wendy Filbaitus feed the hungry horde. Being true freeloaders, the revelers were pushy, demanding, and highly opinionated about what they saw as the serious lack of progress in restoring the Fennell.

"Oh," opined one rich broad with big hair, "I thought you'd be much farther along by now. And where's the heat? What kind of theatrical program do you think you can offer when the only heat you have is that awful thing up there making all that racket?"

"Would you care to make a contribution?" Jimmy said, pointing to a jar marked "donations."

The rich broad with big hair shook her head. "I'd make a contribution if I thought it would make a difference, but I don't think you people have the slightest idea what you're doing. I mean, you haven't even done anything with the floor. Look at all those stains. What have you people been doing here — twiddling your thumbs?"

"Shall we flip a coin to see who gets to strangle her first?" Wendy whispered.

"How about if we just pour the punch bowl on her head?" Jimmy hissed back.

They did neither because the press of pushy people demanding free goodies was perpetual.

At one point in the general mayhem, Jimmy looked up and saw Stephanie and Carl Rezmore standing before him. If looks could say it all, they were saying that they were thoroughly amazed that so many people had turned out on the most wretched night in history for an open house at an old wreck of a theatre. A theatre they clearly thought would never rival the great and wonderful Blue Star Players. The very same Blue Star Players, or Bull Shit & Piss, that had spurned Jimmy so utterly just a few short months before. And don't forget, gentle readers, that these were the same sneering Rezmores who had declined Jimmy's offer to perform in *No Dice*. The sole function of these fulminating fops, it would seem, was to appear after the fact and pass condescending judgment. Which they did at that precise moment at the gala open house.

"Well," Carl said, "you've certainly got a lot of people in here tonight, but they won't be back. Will they, dear?"

"Oh, no," Stephanie said, shaking her head assuredly. "Not with the appalling condition of this place. No way."

Jimmy nodded, and when they weren't looking, spit in their punch glasses. Then he handed them their "flavored" grog with a servile smile and a heartfelt: "You folks have a nice evening now."

The Rezmores mingled off, and the expensive and hopelessly complicated sound system Taylor Griffith had brought to amplify his amazing musical moments crackled into an annoying half-life of loud, obnoxious hisses and buzzes.

Jimmy looked and saw Chip Gooch fiddling with a handful of wires and nobs as Kathy Walker dutifully videotaped every golden moment for posterity and full credit in Tim Daniels' drama class out at the college. Jimmy saw a little man in a cheap suit watching Kathy film Chip and decided that must be the amazing Tim Daniels himself. Come to witness first-hand the rebirth of the Fennell Art Gallery and Theatre, aka: FAGAT.

After much fussing, Chip Gooch got Taylor Griffith's sound system working properly, and Larry German stepped to the fore.

He wore a tan corduroy sports jacket, black turtleneck, and a totally glazed look. The man was seriously toasted, and as he gazed out at the assembled multitude of leeches, lay-abouts, and laggards, he grinned so big and so wide his brain cracked and spilled a warm, sticky fluid all down his spinal column.

That made him feel real good, and his began his remarks with a heartfelt: "Like, wow, man!!"

The assembled multitude hooted and hollered.

"Like, wow, man!!" Larry German repeated.

The assembled multitude hooted and hollered again. Then everybody headed back to the refreshment counter for more goodies. Enough listening to long, boring speeches.

Larry German dimly sensed he was losing his audience, so he said, "Uh, on behalf of the board of directors of the, uh, Fennell Art Theatre and Gallery and . . ."

"It's the Fennell Art Gallery and Theatre, Larry," Margaret Carlson called from the crowd.

Larry German cupped his ear and squinted into the spotlights Chip Gooch had rigged up for the occasion. Big mistake. Now he was totally dazed and confused.

"What?" he said, tapping the microphone with his finger. "Huh?"

Margaret Carlson rushed to Jimmy's side and demanded that he "go up there this instant and take over. You can talk — he can't. It's going to be a complete disaster if he continues any longer."

Jimmy moved away from Margaret, saying: "It's his show, Margaret. He has to sink or swim on his on."

And Larry German did.

Sink, that is.

To wit: "Uh, so like, on behalf of the Fennell, uh board of, uh, well, it's really a gas to see all you fine people like out here on the totally worst night of the year, man. I mean, I barely got here myself, and my truck ain't never been stuck nowhere. And I grew up here." Larry paused for the laughter that never came.

Further dazed and confused, he plunged ahead with: "Well, anyway, I'm not one for long, boring speeches, so I won't stand up here and give you a long, boring speech, because I'm sure you didn't come out here on the worst night like in the whole history of the world or something to listen to me stand up here and give a long, boring speech. Because I hate to give long, boring speeches, and I'm like sure you hate listening to long, boring speeches because like who wants to stand in a cold, drafty old theatre like this on the worst night in history and listen to some guy give a long, boring speech when all you want to do is eat, drink and be merry. And speaking of merry, I hope you all had a real merry Christmas, because I know me and my family sure did.

"My wife gave me a new chisel for Christmas, and I gave her some bath oil that she really likes, and the kids — don't get me started on the kids — but anyway, I don't want to stand up here and give a long, boring speech because I know you didn't drive through the worst storm in history to listen to me give a long, boring speech. Especially when we have such a great line-up of entertainment for you tonight here at the reopening of the Fennell Gallery and Art Theatre. Or something like that. Anyway, with nothing further to do, I give you the great Taylor Griffith who is going to play — what are you going to play Taylor?"

"A whole heap of down and dirty Delta blues," Taylor Griffith said, striding on stage adjusting his guitar strap and grinning enormously at the biggest crowd he had ever played for. And would ever play for. Never mind that they were all fighting over the free food and punch and basically turning their backs on the stage, he had people out there, and, damn, he was gonna give 'em something to remember.

So the fat, balding baby boomer of a white suburbanite gave the inattentive crowd more than 90 minutes of highly amplified music by poor blacks from the miserable Mississippi Delta. Music, by the way, he didn't have to pay royalties to play. Why bother when the old black guys who originally wrote the songs of despair and misery were dead and gone. And their survivors weren't organized enough to protect their artistic property.

So the fat, balding baby boomer of a white suburbanite got down on the Delta and howled and strummed and just had a great old time in the freezing old Fennell. Never mind that nobody was listening. Never mind that Jimmy Clarke and the other performers were being made to freeze their heels. Never mind that Taylor Griffith had been told to keep it short. As in 30 minutes max so as to allow each performer an equal slice of the audience's tiny pie of attention.

Joyce, Marlene Small, and her father arrived halfway through the wailing white boy's blues blast, and Joyce immediately sensed her husband's upset. He was standing off by himself stomping and snorting and trying to be a sport.

Joyce readily saw he wasn't succeeding and said, "Has he been up there since 7:30?"

"Pretty much."

"Then why don't you go up there and get him off the stage? It's not fair to you and the other performers."

"Joyce, I can't do that."

"Why not?"

"Because I'm not the M.C. Larry's M.C., so it's his job."

"Then tell Larry to get him off. He's losing the audience. In fact, I'd say he's lost the audience."

Jimmy looked at the crowd mobbing the refreshment stand and sighed. His last chance of becoming a famous playwright was slipping away, and it was all Taylor Griffith's fault.

"All right," Jimmy said, "I'll go talk to Larry."

Jimmy went and talked to Larry, and Larry went up on stage and stood behind Taylor Griffith for a full 15 minutes before he got up the courage to actually interrupt the great white boy of blues. And all he did really was whisper something in Taylor's ear and hurriedly retreat.

Taylor Griffith nodded thoughtfully and smiled at the backs of his audience. He figured they were facing away from the stage because the acoustics were better that way. Plus, he figured, *I sound so friggin' good, they really think I'm some Mississippi blues guy, and they don't want to spoil the magic by actually looking at me. Yeah, that's it.*

"Well, blues brothers and sisters," Taylor announced through his rich boy's amplifier, "Larry German has just informed me that there are other performers waiting to dazzle you with their amazing talents — I hear one of them has a flea circus but had to cancel because all the fleas froze."

Taylor paused for the laughter that never came.

He nodded grimly and continued: "Larry wants me to wrap things up here and share the stage. Which I don't mind doing. Hey, I'm a generous guy. And to show just how generous I really am, I'm willing to let the other performers use my sound system. For a small fee, of course."

Another pause for another round of laughter that didn't come.

Taylor Griffith shrugged his soft teddy bear shoulders and said: "All right, I'm not a comedian. I didn't come here tonight to do stand-up, I came here to testify to all you blues brothers and sisters, and I think I've done a damn fine job, if I don't mind saying so. And now I want you all to put on your dancin' shoes and help me close out my set with *Sweet Home Chicago.*"

As Taylor Griffith launched his buttery body and soupy soul into the blues classic, a few people broke away from the chow line and actually began to dance. Hell, it was the only way to keep warm, so why not?

Jimmy asked Joyce if she wanted to dance, but she declined, saying: "This is the most ridiculous thing I've ever seen in my life. I hope this has cured you of wanting to be a playwright."

Jimmy watched Laura Downs squire a bald little man in a tuxedo with red tie and cummerbund out onto the solvent-stained dance floor to get down to Taylor Griffith's funky music. Jimmy could see that the great and wonderful Laura Downs was quite taken with the little penis head, and he could further see that the dandy was quite in love with himself.

"You watch," Jimmy said more to himself than Joyce, "he'll be at the next board meeting wanting to take over. Just look at the way he's strutting around the dance floor."

"Jimmy, what are you talking about? I asked you a question about your future as a playwright, and you start blithering about somebody taking over at the next board meeting. I don't think this has been good for you, Jimmy. If you ask me —"

"Joyce, would you please give it a rest. Just for one night."

"God, what a night."

"Yeah, tell me about it. Look, why don't you take Marlene and her father over and get them some punch or something?"

"They're capable of taking care of themselves."

"Yeah. Then just chill out, okay?"

"Chill out is the understatement of the century. I've never been so cold in my entire life, and I'm wearing everything I own."

Indeed, Joyce appeared to be wearing the entire contents of a Goodwill Store, and all that could really be seen of her as she stood stomping in the ice palace that was the Fennell that night was her radiantly red nose.

Jimmy wanted to hum *Rudolph the Red-nosed Reindeer*, but he knew that wouldn't win him any points, so he said, "Joyce, I really appreciate you coming tonight. I know it's hardly the kind of thing you'd want to do on any Saturday night, especially one like this."

"I'm here because you're here, Jimmy. And I'm here to hear your play. You're next, right?"

"Actually, this poet guy from the college is next. Dan Andreas or something."

"Well, I just hope he's is the soul of brevity."

Hah!

When Taylor Griffith finally bid farewell to his "Sweet Home Chicago" and lumbered off the stage, Larry German introduced a balding man in an incredibly expensive Italian sweater as "one of the like great poets of all times or something. So with nothing further to do, I bring you all Andy Dandruff."

Dan Andreas smiled gamely at his indifferent public, and rather than correct Larry German, launched right into a reading from his "little chapbook of recent poems."

Recent as in the last fucking 50 years.

Jimmy, Joyce, Marlene Small, her father, an adoring Harriett Lawford, and a handful of others actually heard the portly poet compare the meat department at the local supermarket to the state of western civilization. Then they followed him on a metered tour of his inner life and were touched by his tormented (yet fully tenured) soul.

"This is the worst poetry I've ever heard," Joyce whispered. "There should be a law against letting idiots like that read in public. And he's going to go on all night. God, look how thick his little chapbook is."

Jimmy couldn't help but see how the well-thumbed volume resembled the New York phone book.

Oblivious to the fact that the audience was either ignoring him or heading for the exit, Dan Andreas read one boring, pointless poem after another.

Larry German stood behind him and watched in waco-weed wonderment.

"I guess you've really got to be seriously stoned to appreciate this guy's work," Jimmy whispered.

"More like brain dead," Joyce said in full voice. "God, these academics are going to be the death of American letters yet."

And speaking of death, Dan Andreas took his dwindling audience back to the meat department for a discourse on the true meaning of death, which he saw as a metaphor for a slice of balony, or some such thing which didn't make any fucking sense, except that the man had tenure and could gas on like this all he wanted because nobody was ever going to fire him, and there was Kathy Walker with her videocamera filming his every golden pronouncement for posterity and full credit in Tim Daniels' drama class out at the very same college where Dan Andreas dithered and blithered semester after semester in a state of semi-comatose "creativity."

God, it was awful.

God, it was endless.

But God knew that.

Which is why God had nothing to do with the gala open house at the Fennell Art Center and Theatre, aka: FAGAT.

No, The Big Guy had more important things to do out in the ever-expanding universe that night than worry about some stupid old theatre on a little pinprick of a planet hidden away in some forgotten galaxy.

So God wasn't listening when Jimmy moaned, "Oh, God, when will this ever end?"

Without divine intervention, it ended when the pompous poet damn well wanted it to end. Which was when the food and goodies had run out, and he had driven even the adoring Harriett Lawford to distraction and warmer climes.

Jimmy chased after her, whispering: "Harriett, you can't leave. You've got to read the part of the queen in my play."

"If I stay another second, I'm going to freeze to death. God, I've never been so cold in my entire life."

And with that Harriett Lawson was gone. As were 99.9 percent of the 475 fools, fops, and fogheads who had come out on the coldest, nastiest night in history to sponge off the Fennell. They had eaten everything that wasn't nailed down, exchanged all the latest gossip, and now it was time to slip and slide their collective way home.

And, miracle of miracles, no one froze to death in his car. Or her car. Or its car.

But back to the Fennell where Larry German was asking the few remaining souls to "like put their hands together for Andrew Dandruff."

The few remaining souls did just that, and then Larry squinted at Jimmy and said, "Uh, isn't your play like next?"

Jimmy nodded but said that he had lost his leading lady.

"Well," Larry said, "Elizabeth Aimes is here, and she's ready to charm us all on our beautifully restored baby grand piano."

"That was paid for by Doctor Dave Zahnbuerste," Jimmy called from the chicken gallery.

"Right," Larry German said. "Yeah, let's all hear it for Doctor Dave. Heck of a fine dentist, which reminds me — I've got to make an appointment with him to get some root canal work done. Man, I'm not looking forward to that — I'll tell you. Anybody out there's had any root canal work done, I'll tell you — I'm not lookin' forward to that. Well, I know all you fine people who came out on the coldest night in history to help us officially reopen the Fennell Gallery of Theatre and Art Happenings didn't come out on the coldest night in history to listen to me talk about my friggin' root canal. Not that root canal is boring. Believe me, root canal is never boring. Well, it's boring because the dentist bores into your head. Hey, no pun intended."

Larry German waited for the laughter that never came.

He rolled his glassy eyes and said, "So, uh, with nothing further to do, I proudly present on behalf of the board of directors of the Fennell Art Whatever the incomprehensible Elizabeth Aimes. Take it away Elizabeth."

The aged chanteuse spiked over to the baby grand piano in a pair of six-inch heels. She actually wore an evening dress that had first seen active duty in World War II, and an absolutely amazing mane of red hair that put Margaret Carlson's measly mop to shame.

Elizabeth Aimes tickled the ivories for a few swelling moments and then turned to the audience.

"I'd like to introduce one of the most gifted voice students it has been my privilege to work with in quite a few years. And as you all know, I've been around for a quite a few years. But I must say that rumors that I played the piano at President Washington's first inauguration are completely exaggerated. Although I must admit, the Lincolns certainly enjoyed my performance. Anyway, enough talk. Ladies and gentlemen, may I present the talented and lovely Laura Zinkowski."

The talented and lovely Laura Zinkowski took the stage wearing a white dress that showed her frozen cleavage to full advantage.

"Somebody should cover those poor women with horse blankets," Joyce whispered.

"Shuussh," Jimmy hissed.

Joyce gave her husband a frozen look and fell into a silent contemplation of how far she had gone in supporting her husband's delusional pursuit of fame and glory in the arts.

"Why couldn't I have married a nice accountant with a good, big job?" she wondered aloud, moaning.

"Joyce!!"

"Sorry. I'll be quiet."

Joyce was quiet, and Elizabeth Aimes and Laura Zinkowski filled the frozen Fennell with all the warmth and glitter that was the Big Band era. Real toe-tapping stuff that made Marlene Small's old-fart of a father audibly attempt to hum along and remark, "Now that's what I call music."

It was what Jimmy politely referred to as songs for those who had had their brains sucked out their ears, but, hey, the boy was just moments away from fame and glory, so he sat on his hands and wondered if he could get away with reading the part of the queen in Harriett Lawford's absence.

Nah, he thought as the Aimes/Zinkowski team got into a Glenn Miller mood, I really need a female to read the part.

Jimmy looked at the remaining women — Joyce, Margaret Carlson, Julie German-Cooper, Marlene Small, and Wendy Filbaitus.

Joyce was definitely out, and so were Margaret and Julie, but, hey, Marlene and Wendy were for-real actresses.

Problem solved.

Jimmy sidled over to Marlene Small and whispered: "Say, Marlene would you like to help me out and read the part of the queen for our staged reading?"

"I can't read a part I haven't rehearsed."

"Come on, Marlene — for old time's sake. You were so great in *No Dice* as Mary Alice, I know you'd be a natural in this. You get to be the Queen of England. And it's not that long a reading. I promise."

Marlene chewed her lip and shrugged. "All right. Why not? But this is it. You understand — I'm not available for anything else for the foreseeable future. Not with all the extra hours I'm working now."

"Fine. No problem." Jimmy handed Marlene his script and said, "We can share my script. You read all the parts marked 'Queen' and . . ."

"No kidding."

"Yeah, no kidding."

Yeah, and there was no kidding on stage as Elizabeth Aimes led her star student Laura Zinkowski on a magical tour "of all the great show tunes from back when they knew how to write great show tunes."

The twosome ended their celebration of yesteryear with a touching performance of *Over the Rainbow*, and yielded the stage to the perpetually stoned Larry German.

"Hey, everybody, put your hands together for our very own Elizabeth Aimes and her star student Lana Klinkowski. They're on their way to Broadway for sure, and we're sure lucky to have had them perform here at the Fennell tonight on the coldest night in history. Ladies and gentlemen, let's all give a big hand to Elizabeth Aimes and Lonnie Zlimowitz."

The diminished audience clapped lustily to keep warm, and then Larry German cleared his throat into the microphone to signal that it was finally time for the long-awaited final act.

Namely, a staged reading by Jimmy, Allan Q. Hovington, and Marlene Small of a portion of Jimmy's play, *Common Prayer*.

"Uh," Larry said, by way of introduction, "the next, uh, thing is going to be some play or something by our resident playwright and head broom pusher, Jack Clarke."

"It's Jimmy," Joyce called from the peanut gallery. "Jimmy Clarke. Not Jack Clarke."

"Uh, yeah. Sure," Larry said, scratching his chin. "All I know is like this is the dude who kind of helped get this whole big ball of wax rolling. Not that he did it all alone, mind you. Chip Gooch actually did most of the work. Chip, are you still here?"

Chip Gooch, his two sidekicks, Kathy Walker and her videocamera, and the great and wonderful Tim Daniels were long gone to Tim Daniels' fully heated living room where they were busily discussing the spring play out at the college. A happy musical with toe-tapping tunes and good, old-fashioned family values that would be sure to keep the voters approving more millage increases for the college.

Larry German made hand binoculars and surveyed the crowd. "Come on, Chip, I know you're out there. Stop hiding and come on up here and take a bow."

"He went home, Larry," Margaret Carlson said, shivering to death. "Now can you just get on with Jim's play and let us all go home before we freeze to death? God, I knew we should have waited until spring to have this open house. I knew this was a big mistake. I knew it would turn out like this. And nobody put any money in the donation jar."

"No," Wendy Filbaitus corrected, "that Pillsbury Doughboy who owns the Goshington Gallery put in a pledge for $2,000."

"A pledge?!?" Jimmy said.

"Yeah," Wendy said, unfolding the hand-scrawled note, "Mr. Goshington pledges $2,000 to the Fennell provided another individual or individuals match it."

"Well, he's off the hook," Jimmy said. "And I'm sure the bank's not going to be too thrilled when we try to deposit a scrap of paper with some flakey promise on it that's never going to be met. That Goshington guy's notorious around here for promising the sun, moon and stars to people and never delivering. He probably just wants us to display his flower paintings."

"I think he does lovely work," Margaret Carlson said. Besides, she was hoping to interest the gay butterball and his lover of the moment in an absolutely gorgeous hide-a-way out along the Black River. Perfect for fresh-air fisting and other happy homo hijinks. Ah, the gay life!

"And," Margaret added, "he has such a wonderful sense of aesthetics. I think his work would be a real asset to the Fennell. In fact, I plan to call him next week and . . ."

"Can we get on with Jimmy's play?" Joyce said, ready to strangle Margaret Carlson.

"Yeah," Larry German said, "we should probably wrap this thing up. I know I hate to leave because I've been having so much fun being M.C. You know I didn't think I'd like being M.C., but once you get over the initial stage fright, it's really a gas. And what a night we've had. God, some of the best entertainment money can buy, and it was all free. I mean, it doesn't get better than this. And can you believe Taylor Griffith? Does he know how to belt out the blues or what? Taylor, why don't you take another bow?"

"He's gone, Larry," Margaret Carlson called, her teeth chattering.

"Oh, well, I guess he'll come back tomorrow for his amp and stuff. Great sound system — you know. The best. That's what I like about Taylor — he's a class act all the way. 'From his first cigarette to

his last dyin' day.' Hey, that's pretty snappy. I think I just had a
brain fart or something. That's from . . ."

"*West Side Story*," Wendy Filbaitus called from the goodie
counter. "The friggin' Board of Ed wouldn't let me produce it at my
high school in Chicago because of the gang content. So I had to do
The Sound of Music instead for the fall production. Talk about
sickening pap. But don't get me started on the Board of Ed and
censorship, or we'll be here all night."

"Yeah, we don't want to do that," Larry German said, starting to
shiver. The pot was wearing off and, damn, if he wasn't frozen stiff.
"So, uh with nothing further to do, let's get to the last act of the
night — uh, Jack — no, sorry, I mean Jim Clarke and his little skit or
something. Everybody put your hands together if they're not frozen
and help me welcome the best broom pusher this theatre's ever
seen, or probably is ever going to see. Take it away, Jack. I mean
Jim."

"Oh, Jimmy," Joyce whispered. "I'm so sorry."

Jimmy smiled bravely at his long-suffering wife, and led his two
troops up to the stage where they gamely read from *Common Prayer*.

When they were finished, Joyce, Margaret Carlson, and Julie
German-Cooper clapped lustily. Wendy Filbaitus "hipped" and
"hoorayed" and continued cleaning up the refreshment counter, and
Marlene Small's father loudly wondered why they hadn't "done the
skit with English accents. I mean," he persisted, "what's the point of
doing a skit set in England if you're not going to do it with English
accents?"

Jimmy looked the lummox of a retired navy captain (who never
made admiral) right in the eye and said, "You're right, Admiral,
there is no point."

Joyce grabbed her husband's arm and said, "Take me home."

And Jimmy took her home. But not before lingering at the door
and taking one last loving look at the frozen old Fennell where he
was just sure that good things were still to come in his dazzling
career as a playwright.

Dream on, Sweet Prince, dream on.

Chapter Twenty-One

So many shysters showed up for the next board meeting of the Fennell Art Center and Theatre that Larry German didn't know where to put them all.

"I guess some of us will just have to stand," he said, taking a seat. He eyed his watch and added, "But don't worry, we won't have to stand for long, because my sister Julie and I have to open our gallery right at 9. So that gives us exactly 15 minutes, and I can see we have a lot of things on the agenda which our very own Beverly Mantinkus has so graciously drawn up for us on her spiffy new computer that she got for Christmas."

Larry paused and smiled paternally at the enlarged poetess who had been too shy to share her innermost thoughts at the gala open house. "We really appreciate all the fine work you're doing for the Fennell, Bev. Don't we?"

Jimmy led a polite round of applause that caused Big Bev to blush bright crimson.

"Way to go, Bev," Larry said, smiling the smile of a man who had smoked some excellent homegrown on the way to the meeting. "I mean, forget Maui Wowie and Panama Red and Lebanese Gold and all those other leading brands. Forget 'em the fuck entirely when you got your very own homegrown that you like care for and cultivate and like dry and then roll into the fattest, most exquisite like totally awesome joints this side of Haight-Ashbury, and from all accounts, man, they didn't really have such good shit out there, at least . . . " Larry said, taking in all the bright, shining new faces on this like totally bright and sunny and snow-clad January morning like sometime in the 1994th year of Our Lord A.D. or something, and . . .

"Larry," Harriett Lawford said, "could we get on with the meeting? Whatever it is you're trying to say, it's not coming out very clearly."

"Oh," Larry said, scratching his chin. "Must have been a brain fart. Been gettin' a lot of them lately. I wonder if it's the brand of coffee my wife buys. Yeah, that's it. I'm gonna tell her to switch brands. Or maybe try some of that fancy Starbucks stuff my good buddy Taylor Griffith has at his place. Man, that stuff'll put hair on your chest. But is it ever expensive — wow. What's the point of paying that much for a pound of coffee?"

"Because it's the best money can buy," Laura Downs said, impatient to advance her agenda. "Can we get on with the meeting, Larry? We got some tremendous momentum going at the open house, and now we've got to keep it rolling. Just look at all these people here — including my friend Dominick McGrath who's come to tell us about an exciting event he has planned for the Fennell for Memorial Day weekend. Dominick —"

Dominick McGrath was the very penis head Laura Downs had squired onto the ersatz dance floor during the eternal open house on Saturday, January 15, 1994. The very strutting little peacock who had actually appeared in the frozen Fennell wearing a tuxedo with red cummerbund and bow-tie. Now, for this mere board meeting, he was "dressed down" in a buff sports jacket, black turtleneck, casual (but not too casual) slacks, argyle socks and penny loafers. The country squire out surveying all that he owned, and from the look in his beady little eyes that morning, he *owned* the Fennell Art Center and Theatre.

Dominick McGrath nodded graciously at the truly amazing Laura Downs, girl caterer to the stars, and paced dramatically to the head of the wobbly picnic table. There he stretched to the fullness of his 5'5" frame and said: "The name Reb Yankell mean anything to you people?"

Margaret Carlson coughed nervously.

Larry German sort of like nodded and scratched his chin. He started to say something, then stopped. "Another brain fart," he said, grinning boyishly.

Dominick McGrath smiled smugly at the assembled art swells. "Well, since no one seems to know who Reb Yankell is, let me tell you who Reb Yankell is. Reb Yankell just happens to be *the* premiere Mississippi Delta Blues musician left alive in this country, and through some connections which I am not at liberty to divulge at this moment, I am able to tell you fine people that he's coming to the Fennell for the the Bach and Blues Festival I'm planning for Memorial Day Weekend."

Larry German nodded. "Bach and Blues, huh? Sounds like that old group — what was it — Bachman Turner Overdrive or something."

Dominick McGrath pursed his little lips and actually winked at Laura Downs. Like the fix was in. Like they knew all along it would be easy getting what they wanted from this bunch of dummies who thought they were actually a board of directors of a going theatre and art center.

Jimmy cleared his throat and raised his hand.

Larry German nodded at Jimmy.

Jimmy smiled at the dome-headed Dominick McGrath and said, "How much is this going to cost?"

"Cost?"

"Yeah, you know — money. Even old Blues guys from the Delta have to be paid something, and since you mentioned Bach, I presume you're talking about an ensemble or ..."

"Actually, I'm talking about the Grand Rapids Symphony Orchestra," Dominick McGrath boldly proclaimed.

"That's wonderful," Harriett Lawford gushed. "Bach and Blues. So there would be classical music one night and blues the next. Is that what you're proposing?"

"Precisely. Now, I don't mean to brag or anything, but with my extensive media background, I know exactly what the American public wants at any given time, and I can tell you the demographics here are perfect for a weekend that includes classical and blues. See, what we've got here in this area is a whole bunch of aging baby boomers with tons of disposable income. On one hand, they're striving to culturally enrich themselves. So we give them a night of the best classical music money can buy. But at the same time, they are heavily into nostalgia and want to get down every now and then — so we give them a night of the best blues money can buy. The incomparable Reb Yankell. And we support all this with a major media campaign which I will gladly orchestrate. But first thing, we have to come up with a better name than the Fennell Art Center and Theatre. The acronym is absolutely homophobic, and whoever thought of it should be publicly castrated."

Larry German made a snipping gesture at Jimmy, and everyone held Jimmy in utter contempt for daring to be such a homophobe in the New Age of acceptance of the unacceptable.

"So," Dominick McGrath said, sneering at Jimmy, "it's agreed that we'll drop the offensive acronym and simply refer to this place as the Fennell. I've even gone to the liberty of having one of our graphics people at the television station where I work in Holland do a few rough sketches of a logo and typeface for the Fennell."

Dominick McGrath produced an easel out of thin air, assembled it, and was soon pointing at a bigger-than-life rendering of the "Fennell" logo and typeface. It was all done in a flashy red with the initial "F" looking like it had been swashed onto the page by a swishy French swordsman.

"Oh, that's absolutely brilliant, Dom," Laura Downs effused. "I move that we accept it as our official logo."

Harriett Lawford seconded.

Larry German called for discussion, and Jimmy said, "Uh, I hate to point this out, but Laura's not a member of the board, so she can't really . . ."

"Then I move to make Laura a member of the board," Margaret Carlson said. "Laura's absolutely right — we've got to get moving on these things while we have the momentum from the open house. Otherwise, we'll sink. Absolutely sink."

"Do I hear a second for the motion?" Larry German said.

"Which motion?" Big Bev said, scribbling furiously.

"Uh, the one that — wow, this is all going so fast, and . . ." Larry looked at his watch, ". . . the time is really flying, sports fans, so we'd better start winding this up, because me and Julie got to open our gallery right at nine — so I vote that we pass both motions unanimously. All in favor raise their right hand and repeat after me — aye."

Everyone but Jimmy raised his or her right hand and repeated after Larry German: "Aye."

"There being no further business before the board, I entertain a movement for adjournment so me and Julie can go and open our gallery and make some money so we can pay the rent and keep this place going until we finally bring in some real money."

"But Larry," Laura Downs said, "there is lots of further business before the board. Dominick isn't done yet, and I've got people here to talk about: the Shakespeare Festival this summer, which we're going to call 'Midsummer at the Fennell,' and a big band from Saint Joe that will pack the house for only $750, plus the most brilliant pianist in all of Lithuania who we can get for a mere $500 in March.

And I know Margaret Carlson wants to get started on the gallery idea, and I've already been in serious discussion with Ed Goshington about doing a retrospective of his work."

"Speaking of the great and wonderful Ed Goshington," Jimmy said, "is anybody going to match his pledge?"

Silence.

"So if nobody matches his pledge, does that mean that the great and wonderful Mr. Ed is going to renege on his promise to give the Fennell $2,000?"

Laura Downs gave the nobody from nowhere a withering look and said to the others: "As I was saying, I have been in serious discussions with Mr. Goshington about a retrospective of his work, and I think we are close to a final agreement. He is famous, you all know, for his sensitive renderings of flowers."

"Yeah," Jimmy muttered, "pansies by a poofter."

"What was that?" Laura Downs said, arching her eyebrows.

"Nothing. Just a brain fart."

Larry German gaveled the meeting to a close and rose from his seat. "Well, Laura, you're free to stay and discuss all those fine ideas with anyone who wants to stay, but me and Julie got to open our gallery like right now because I'm sure there's a ton of Tunas with big fat wallets waiting out front."

"What about a work party, Larry?" Jimmy asked.

"Oh, yeah. Anyone who wants to stay and work to fix this old place up, stick around and talk to our head broom pusher, Jack. I mean Jim."

"Where's Chip? And his pals?"

"They're working on the spring play out at the college. So I guess we won't be seeing much of them for a while. Okay, everybody, me and Julie are outta here. Last one out, be sure and turn out the lights."

Larry and his beloved sister Julie raced off to open the gallery, and Laura Downs seized control in their absence.

Well, tried to at least.

Without the wise counsel of Larry German, the assembled art swells became a mob of competing egos all talking over each other and demanding that his or her program get the most attention.

"This isn't a meeting," Big Bev said, "this is chaos."

"You got that right," Jimmy said, putting his coat on.

"Where are you going?"

"Home."

"But you can't go home. You've got to stay and work."

"Right, Bev. How silly of me." Jimmy cupped his hands over his mouth and called: "Anyone who wants to sweep, chip paint, and haul trash, report to me."

The place cleared out in a twinkling, leaving only Big Bev and Jimmy to turn out the lights.

"Like I said," Jimmy said, "I'm going home and taking a long nap."

"But there's so much work to be done. Painting and sweeping and . . ."

"Be my guest, Bev."

"But I have a bad . . ."

". . . back. I know. Must be an epidemic around here or something. Don't forget to turn out the lights."

"But, but . . ."

Jimmy left before Big Bev could belch out another but.

He drove straight home to the Dunery in Angel Car and told Joyce that he was taking a "vacation from the Fennell."

"Why not just quit entirely?"

"You think I should?"

"Yes."

"But then what would I do?"

"How about getting some clients?"

Jimmy kicked off his shoes and settled on the couch. "Joyce, I've been looking, but I haven't had much luck. Besides, you said before the open house that I could go ahead with being a playwright."

"I know that's what I said, and I meant it. But I think you should keep looking. I mean, you never know what Jerry Mappers is going to do from one day to the next."

"That's true." Jimmy sighed so enormously that the Dunery shifted on its foundation of sand and rotting wood.

Joyce wanted to tell her husband that he didn't have to work, that he could forever pursue his dream of being a rich and famous playwright, novelist or whatever, but she was tired. Oh, so tired. Tired of being the sole breadwinner. Tired of watching her husband hurl himself into brick walls. Tired of watching him be rejected time and time and time again.

But then she thought of how happy he had been at the close of *No Dice.* The man was absolutely ecstatic, she thought. Maybe he just needs a little more time. Maybe a break from the Fennell will recharge his batteries. He'll get all refreshed and everything and come up with some brilliant new scheme for making us both rich and famous.

"Maybe you should go back to writing novels," Joyce suggested.

"I've been thinking I'd write a novel about all the hassles I went through producing *No Dice.*"

"Why not start Monday?"

"Yeah. Maybe I will. And I will keep looking for clients, if you think . . ."

"Well, you do what makes you happy. We've got enough money for the time being with what Jerry Mappers pays me, and even though she's crazy, she's not going to fire me completely. Her secretary said I make her life so easy."

"You do, Joyce. She's really lucky to have you."

"You think so?"

Jimmy gave her his winningest look and said, "I know so."

"You're right. I do make her life easy. And she is lucky to have me. And we are lucky to have a client like her. God, she's basically kept this whole show afloat all these years."

"I know. You don't think she's going to do something weird in the near future?"

"You never know with her."

"Yeah." Jimmy sighed. "So do you think we're crazy for being so dependent on one client?"

"Oh, probably."

"Should we worry?"

"Oh, probably."

"Are we going to worry?" Jimmy asked.

"No," Joyce replied.

They both sighed and Jimmy took a long, refreshing nap while Joyce happily baked a whole bunch of bread. When it was baked, they ate an entire loaf, loading each slice with real butter and jelly.

Life was good in the Dunery that day.

And it got even better on Monday when Jimmy called Larry German and told him he was taking a sabbatical from the Fennell to pursue "artistic interests."

"We'll really miss you," Larry said. "Nobody pushes a broom like you, Jack. I mean Jim."

"Yeah. Well, it's not like I'm falling off the face of the earth or anything. I'll still be around."

"Yeah, don't be a stranger."

"I won't. I'll still support the Fennell."

"You better."

"I will."

And that was that.

Or so Jimmy thought.

Anyway, he didn't give it another thought that Monday morning as he set about starting a novel about his exploits as the playwright, producer and assistant director of *No Dice*. But in writing a fictional account of his beginnings as a playwright, he felt a yearning for further adventures on the boards. The spotlight of fame was still burning brightly in his heart, and that afternoon, he started writing a sequel to *No Dice*.

He titled it, *Cottage Industry,* and set it a year later in the Boona Vista cottage in the mythical town of Greenbush, Michigan. Across the lake from Chicago.

And, since things weren't working out at the Fennell the way he had hoped, Jimmy made a mental note to call Lynda Johnson at the Glenn Art Studio, or GAS, and see if she might be interested in doing another play.

Hell, Jimmy thought, of course she's going to be interested. I did all the work, packed the house for her both nights, and, in fact, her very words after the final performance of *No Dice*, were: "Of course you can do another play here next summer. It's a done deal, Jim. Look at all these people flocking in here. We haven't had this kind of crowd in years."

Jimmy sighed at the thought of new crowds coming in the summer of 1994 to see the world premiere of his dazzling sequel to *No Dice*. Appropriately titled *Cottage Industry* and concerning itself with the adventures, or misadventures, of the scion of the Kurtin family, Christopher, and his Irish-Catholic wife, Kathleen Fitzpatrick-Kurtin.

"It'll be a year after the big family fight in *No Dice* when they all said unspeakable things to one another. Christopher hasn't found another job to support his Yuppie lifestyle, and he and Kathleen are so broke, they had to sell their big house in the Chicago suburbs and actually move into the family cottage in Michigan. Just like a lot of people do here at Havencrest. Use the old family cottage as a dumping ground for all the rejects and losers and mental defectives who nobody . . ."

"Keep it down over there," Joyce called from her writing booth. "I'm trying to work on a really boring article about banking prospects in Hong Kong after 1997."

"Fucking dire," Jimmy called back.

"What?"

"I said there are no banking prospects in Hong Kong after 1997. Because when those red bastards take over, it's curtains for any capitalist dumb enough to stick around."

"Can I quote you on that?"

"Sure."

Joyce laughed. "I just might. Now keep it down over there."

"Okay. Sorry."

"Just don't let it happen again."

"I won't."

"Promise?"

"Promise."

Jimmy phoned Lynda Johnson at GAS and was told she was in Nova Scotia or some other third-world country recruiting artists for GAS's residency program. Her trip and the program, of course, were funded by your tax dollars, funneled through a sub-department of the U.S. State Department.

"She'll be back in a few weeks," the helpful woman at GAS said.

"Well, if she happens to call in the meantime, tell her Jimmy Clarke . . ."

"You're the did the play here last summer."

"Yeah, that's me."

"Oh, we're still talking about that. It was the most wonderful thing that's happened at the Glenn Art Studio in a long time."

"Really?"

"Oh, absolutely. I hope you're calling to tell Lynda that you're planning another play for this summer."

"As a matter of fact I am."

"Oh, she'll be thrilled. I know I am. What's it called?"

"*Cottage Industry*. It's a sequel to *No Dice*. It's a year later in the same cottage . . ."

"The 'Boona Vista.'"

"Yeah. And the son . . ."

"Christopher. Oh, I loved him. He was such a whiner. God, but I hope you give his wife more to say. I'm Catholic, and I think she should have more to say."

"Oh, she will. Trust me."

"I can't wait to read it."

"I can't wait to write it."

"Well, don't let me keep you from your keyboard. I'll tell Lynda when she phones in from Nova Scotia, and when she comes back, I'll have her call you and set up a meeting so we can get the ball rolling. Oh, I'm so glad you called. Your play was the greatest thing that's happened to the Glenn Art Studio in a very, very long time."

"Thanks. Well, I'd better get cracking on the play so I can have something to show Lynda when she gets back from darkest Canada."

"Oh, I'm so glad you called."

"Me, too."

Jimmy gave thanks to Saint Genesius even though the old Roman actor had no time for non-Roman Catholics, and hit his keyboard with a vengeance.

In no time flat, he had created the following:

THE PLACE: "The Boona Vista" cottage in Greenbush, Michigan.

THE TIME: The present

THE PLAYERS:

Mr. ("Call me Jeff") Schmedley, 39. Balding, paunchy, intense hustler. Has sold everything from whole life insurance to shoes out at the mall. Lives on coffee, cigarettes, and donuts. Over-extended. Hasn't paid off student loans. Has wife, three kids and a home he can't afford in a pricy subdivision outside South Bend. Desperate to be rich like his older brother. Currently regional sales manager for the Eterna-Skin Corporation. Wears a green blazer with the company logo sewn on the pocket, gray dress slacks and tasseled loafers.

   Kathleen Fitzpatrick-Kurtin, 37. Third child and first daughter of an Irish-Catholic family of 11 on "da Sout' Side" of Chicago. Raised the seven siblings who followed her because her mother was shot after three and her father, the famous orthopedic surgeon, was never home. Educated by Catholic Church from first-grade to DePaul University. Earned bachelor degree in Irish-American History and went to night school to become qualified as a paralegal. Hobby—Irish history and music. Plays tin whistle and would love to start an Irish music group. Mother of two sons who are away at camp. A "cafeteria" Catholic—thinks the Pope is swell but practices birth control and favors ordination of women. Currently working as paralegal at law firm in St. Joseph, Michigan. Married to Christopher Kurtin.

   Christopher Allen Kurtin, 37. Married with two sons. "Out-placed" more than a year ago by large conglomerate in Chicago area. Forced to sell brick house in Wilmette and move into family cottage in Michigan. Has Marketing degree from Northwestern University and got about halfway through MBA program before quitting. Has had a succession of jobs since he was fired, including delivering pizzas out of what his father called his "Nazi staff car." Finally sold the Mercedes and bought a Honda Civic, which was a bitter pill for him to swallow. Moody, embittered, hen-pecked, and drinking and eating more and enjoying it less. Wondering if he should have a mid-life crisis, but not sure how to go about it.

   Commerce Chorus. Six civic boosters who act and "speak" as one. Three women (soprano, alto-soprano, and alto) in smart business ensembles with pearls, gold earrings, pumps, and shoulder pads; and three men (tenor, baritone, and bass) in navy blazers, rep ties, button-down shirts, gray slacks and tasseled loafers. Ineffably cheery. Life never rains on this sweet little parade.

SCENE ONE

   (Mid-morning in mid-summer in the living room of the Boona Vista cottage in Greenbush, Michigan. Kathleen and Christopher Kurtin are seated on the sofa facing Mr. Schmedley who is seated in Dad's favorite chair. The Kurtins are dressed in casual summer

attire; Mr. Schmedley wears a forest-green blazer with the
Eterna-Skin logo on the pocket, gray dress slacks, and tasseled
loafers. His brown leather briefcase stands ready at his side. The
coffee table that lies between them is covered with brochures and
product samples. There is also a plunger-pot of coffee, three cups
and a basket of Kathleen's blueberry muffins.)

Mr. Schmedley: I tell you: THIS IS THE MARKETING
OPPORTUNITY OF HISTORY!! If you want to be a millionaire
by the time you hit 40, this is the only way to fly. So what do you say,
Karen and Ken? Do you want to be part of the Eterna-Skin
adventure and see all your financial dreams come true, or do you
want to be left in the ditch with all the other has-beens?

Kathleen: (Clears throat and arches back) Actually, Mr.
Schmedley, our names are Kathy and Chris.

Mr. Schmedley: (Slaps forehead) Have I been calling you Karen
and Ken all morning? Stupid me. My wife had to put name tags on
our three kids for years so I could get their names straight. I'm an
idiot when it comes to names. What can I say? My apology. Uh . . .

Kathleen: Kathy and Chris.

Mr. Schmedley: Right. Kathy and Chris. That's easy enough.
The trick is to say a name out loud, and then you've got it. Kathy
and Chris. Right. I learned that at the last Eterna-Skin convention.
Speaking of which, that's another perk — as an Eterna-Skin
distributor you get special discounts on all seminars at the national
convention. And we're talking high-powered sessions led by
nationally recognized motivational experts. I'm so excited about
Eterna-Skin as a company, I can hardly sit still. The whole concept
is so totally unique and ahead of its time. The people who started
this company . . .

Christopher: They're Mormons from Utah aren't they?

Mr. Schmedley: (Laughs nervously and quickly recovers)
Exactly. And look at the fabulous marketing job those people have
done with the Mormon Tabernacle Choir. Uh, how'd you happen to
know that?

Christopher: Saw it on *60 Minutes.*

Mr. Schmedley: Oh, you saw *that* story?

Christopher: Yes.

Mr. Schmedley: Not the most flattering piece that's been done on us, but then everybody knows those people are out to kill anything that doesn't come out of New York or Los Angeles. They hate success stories in the heartland. And they've really got it in for the religious minorities. But that's neither here nor there. If you believed *60 Minutes,* you wouldn't have invited me to your cottage today to present the Eterna-Skin program, would you?

Kathleen: (Glances at husband) Actually, it was my idea. Chris wasn't really too keen on it.

Mr. Schmedley: (Reaches forward and pats Christopher on forearm) Ah, but we'll bring you around, won't we, Chrissy?

Christopher: It's Chris, not Chrissy. Okay?

Mr. Schmedley: Hey, just trying to be friendly is all. You want to call me Jeffy, that's fine by me. Just don't call me late for dinner. (Forces laugh) So, Chris and Kathy, what do you think of the Eterna-Skin program? Remember, I'm ready to offer you all of western Michigan as your exclusive sales territory. And we're talking virgin territory here.

Christopher: Then how come I saw a car in St. Joe with an Eterna-Skin bumper sticker?

Mr. Schmedley: (Forces another laugh) Must be one of our mail-order customers. I mean, our line of total skin-care products is so effective, people are seeking us out even in places like this where we don't have established sales reps. Look folks, what I'm offering you is probably your only chance to be rich by the time you hit 40. And face it, if you're not rich by the time you hit 40, you're never going to . . .

Christopher: I don't know. Colonel Sanders did pretty well for himself at a ripe old age, and there was Ray Kroc, and . . .

Mr. Schmedley: Is he always this difficult?

Kathleen: Christopher!

Christopher: What, Kathleen?!?

Kathleen: (Smiles tightly) Would you please cool it, and let me handle this?

Mr. Schmedley: You two are just like me and my wife. Maybe I should take a walk around the uh – path or whatever that is out there and let you two sort things out.

Kathleen: No, we're fine. Aren't we, Christopher?

Christopher: Just peachy, dearest. Pray continue, Mr. Schmedley. Tell us more about this amazing marketing opportunity of history. I'm all ears.

Kathleen: Christopher, why don't you make some more coffee? He makes the best coffee. Don't you think?

Mr. Schmedley: (Lifts cup) No kidding. I was thinking of taking some of this home to strip my deck. Wow! What's your secret?

Christopher: I buy good, whole-bean coffee, and grind it just before I brew it.

Mr. Schmedley: See. I could tell the minute I walked in here that you two appreciate the finer things in life. That's why you're perfect for the Eterna-Skin program. I mean, I love what you did with your cottage. (Looks around) It's really kind of—what's the word?

Kathleen: Kitschy?

Mr. Schmedley: Exactly.

Kathleen: Well, it's not exactly our cottage. It really belongs to Chris' parents, but they just went through a rather difficult divorce, and . . .

Christopher: My father found a new cookie out on the golf course and ran off with her to California. I mean she's younger than my sister. It's unbelievable.

Mr. Schmedley: Hey, it happens all the time. My parents—now they're still happily married after 45 years—but they've got these friends who went through the same thing. You know—the guy running off with the new . . .

Kathleen: Could we get back to Eterna-Skin? I'd like to know exactly what you meant by western Michigan? Does that mean all the way up to the bridge?

Mr. Schmedley: The bridge?

Kathleen: The Mackinac Bridge.

Mr. Schmedley: You mean all the way up there?

Kathleen: Well, yes. To a lot of people, western Michigan means from the state line all the way up to the bridge.

Mr. Schmedley: Actually, we've got somebody in Grand Rapids who handles that area. A couple of people in Grand Rapids actually. But you two'll have a huge territory all to yourselves.

Christopher: How huge exactly?

Kathleen: Chris, why don't you make some more coffee?

Christopher: I'm caffeined out. Now, how huge exactly, Mr. Schmedley? Are we talking Kalamazoo, Grand Haven, Saugatuck, South Haven—what?

Mr. Schmedley: Actually, we have some people in Kalamazoo who cover . . .

Christopher: Grand Haven, Saugatuck, and South Haven.

Mr. Schmedley: Right.

Christopher: So what does that leave us? The greater Greenbush metropolitan area? We're not talking major population here, Mr. Schmedley.

Mr. Schmedley: Please, call me Jeff. Chris.

Christopher: Right. So what exactly is our territory going to be? Assuming we sign on with you.

Mr. Schmedley: Oh, you will. After you see this. (Produces a document from briefcase and waves it in front of couple) This is a statistical abstract for Berrien County. Do you have any idea of the kind of money that's moving in here?

Kathleen: Tell us about it. We've got a movie critic down the beach who spends more on his Fourth of July party than we spend on our entire food budget for the year. And we've got two sons who eat like horses. Thank God they're away at camp, or they'd be eating us out of house and home as I speak.

Mr. Schmedley: All the more reason to sign on with Eterna-Skin. Plus, we have the best acne products in the world. We can set your sons up as exclusive distributors at the local high school. We've had kids work their entire ways through college selling our Blasto-Blem products in their spare time to their friends.

Christopher: Blasto-Blem?!?

Mr. Schmedley: Laugh all you want, but that name was tested on 20 teen-aged focus groups around the country. That's what sets Eterna-Skin miles above the competition—we're totally market-driven.

And so the pitch went until Mr. Schmedley finally convinced Christopher and Kathleen to sign on as Eterna-Skin distributors, generously giving them all of south Berrien County Michigan as their exclusive territory. He summoned the Commerce Chorus on his car

phone and they appeared at the Boona Vista to make a great show
of cutting an enormous pink ribbon as they sang:

> We are the Commerce Chorus,
> Oh yes we are,
> And we welcome you to
> The country so quaint and
> The harbor so snug.
> Oh yes we do!!

Here a snip—there a cut, and now you're a member of our
growing fam-i-lee.

> Dues can be paid in
> Low monthly installments,
> Low monthly installments,
> Or at the end of your fiscal year,
> Fiscal year,
> And are completely tax-deductible,
> Tax deductible,
> Tax deductible.
> Oh yes they are!
> And there's a mixer
> Every month;
> Don't forget to bring

(Here, Jimmy directed that the chorus form a circle and pass
business cards)

> Your business cards,
> Your business cards, oh
> Your business cards, and
> Network, network, network!!
> Now clap your hands and join the
> Jubilee . . .
> It's the marketing op-por-tun-i-ty of
> His-tor-ee!!

And so on and so forth until Jimmy had the Commerce Chorus
rush to the bewildered new business owners, give them fakey hugs,
and depart in a burst of blazing boosterism.

Scene two, found the Kurtins failing in their attempt to sell
Eterna-Skin products to their neighbors. Kathleen called Mr.

Schmedley, and he was back in a flash to sell them on an even better marketing opportunity of history: Colon-O-Cleanse.

To wit:

Mr. Schmedley: We believe in total harmony. By that we mean body, mind and spirit. And to achieve total harmony, we believe one must be cleansed both from without and from within. Yes, to be in total harmony, you must be pure of mind, spirit, and body. And you certainly can't have a harmonious body if you're carrying a load of rotting meat around in your colon. So . . .

Christopher: You want me to go out and give rich jerks enemas on their yachts in New Buffalo?

Mr. Schmedley: (Laughs) That's a rather crude way of putting it, Chris. I'd prefer to say that as part of the Colon-O-Cleanse concept you'll have time to pursue your dream of becoming a famous cartoonist while restoring true harmony to people who have lost touch with their Inner Teachers.

Kathleen: You really want Chris to go out and use that thing on people? On women? But he's not a nurse. He's not able . . .

Mr. Schmedley: He won't touch a soul until he has completed the Colon-O-Cleanse home study course. And as for cleansing members of the opposite sex, Colon-O-Cleanse believes that we are all children of the universe – women and men alike. And it's not like you just go and – you know. There's a whole procedure – it's all there in the literature. (Pulls cassette tape out of briefcase) And you play this scientifically designed relaxation music while you're cleansing your client, and Colon-O-Cleanse provides a year's supply of latex gloves and discounts on medical attire.

It was entirely too kinky for Christopher to resist, and he persuaded Kathleen to sign on to THE CLEANSING OPPORTUNITY OF HISTORY!

In no time flat, according to Jimmy's script, Mr. Schmedley phoned the Commerce Chorus, and they returned to the Boona Vista to end the play with a rousing reprise of their immortal "We are the Commerce Chorus" chorale.

Only this time, they substituted "cleansing" for "marketing" when singing of the "op-por-tun-i-ty of his-tor-ee!!"

Jimmy sighed and wrote: (Lights fade, play ends)

Then he pushed away from his desk and wondered who in the hell he was going to get to write the music and choreography for the Commerce Chorus.

Not to mention who he was going to get to perform and direct the damn thing.

Chapter Twenty-Two

For starters, Jimmy named himself director.

What other choice did the poor boy have?

Especially when the great and wonderful L. David Hinchcliff had fled to California, and especially when Jimmy didn't know another soul in the area who could direct. And he was not about to call those assholes at Blue Star Players who had so grievously insulted him.

But what, you may ask, about Doctor Peter Phillips, Ph.D. of Saint Giles by the River Episcopal Church here in South Haven, or Jessica "call me Jess" Springer who directed *Carol's Christmas* with such aplomb?

Well, for starters, Jimmy wanted nothing further to do with the good doctor after the way he had totally trashed *Common Prayer*, and hadn't Jess Springer said upon first meeting Jimmy that the reason she hadn't attended *No Dice* was because it was too close to home, what with her ex-husband having been a raging alcoholic, and she being a faithful member of Alanon, and her Alanon sponsor telling her that it wouldn't be such a . . .

See what I mean.

So what Jimmy clearly saw was that he had to direct and produce his play at the great hall of GAS in the summer of 1994. That is if he wanted *Cottage Industry* produced at all, and he did.

Oh, he did.

Poor boy.

So, after appointing himself director and producer, he phoned Constance Myers, emotional bat-girl to the great and magnificent Douglas Iglesia, and invited her to be musical director for *Cottage Industry*.

"Plus," he told the woman who had played Kathleen in *No Dice*, "you and Douglas have right of first refusal on the parts of Christopher and Kathleen. They're there for the taking, and, Constance, I really beefed up the part of Kathleen in this play. I mean she gets as much dialogue as Christopher. If not more."

"Really?"

"Oh yeah."

"Well, I'd have to see a script before I can decide."

"I'll put it in the mail today and then call you in a week. What do you say? If you agree to be musical director, I'll split the box with you — 50/50."

"That's more than generous."

"Hey, I want to get my work produced, and you and Douglas are the best."

"You think so?"

"I know so, Constance. So take a look at the script when you get it, and I'll talk to you next week."

"This actually is a good time, because I'm between projects, and things have been a little slower at work for Douglas, and we've been able to have more free time together."

"Good." Jimmy declined the temptation to inquire as to Douglas' mental health and had to bite his tongue to stop from suggesting that Constance keep her troubled wonder boy away from the Black River and sharp objects. "Well, I'm really thrilled that you and Douglas are interested."

"Oh, we had such fun with your play last summer. It's too bad David isn't around to direct."

"Yeah, a real pity. But the man's finding himself in California, so what are you going to do?"

"Maybe he'll come back and direct your play. I mean he was such a brilliant director."

"Definitely, but I really don't think there's much chance of luring him back from California. I ran into Tiffany not too long ago, and she said he's really ensconced out there."

"Well, you really should try. Because, no offense or anything, but I really don't think playwrights should direct their own plays. They don't have the perspective that a real director like David has."

"Right. Well, I'll throw the script in the mail and talk to you next week."

"Sure. Bye."

Jimmy threw the script in the mail, waited a week and phoned Constance Myers.

She had gotten so busy, she hadn't even opened it. But she would. "Promise."

Jimmy waited two more weeks and phoned her again.

This time he got her answering machine.

Constance's voice informed the world that she and the great and magnificent Douglas Iglesia were attending a drama conference in Minneapolis and wouldn't be back for two weeks.

While he awaited the return of the great and magnificent Douglas Iglesia and his emotional bat-girl, Jimmy phoned Lynda Johnson at the great hall of GAS to enlist her support for the production.

Lynda had heard all about it while she was junketing around the Maritimes, and now that she was back, she was behind the project "100 percent. And I mean 100 percent. But I'm not going to be able to meet with you for the next couple of weeks because I have to arrange an art show for my father in Chicago."

"Right. But it's okay that we do the play at GAS this summer?"

"Oh, definitely. And I'll be there beside you, every step of the way. Just like with *No Dice*. Oh, that was such a rush. People are still talking about it here. You really breathed new life back into GAS."

"Great. Well, maybe we should set a date for this summer for *Cottage Industry* and . . ."

"Good idea, but I've got to run. Call Christine. She's the lady you talked to while I was in Canada. She'll set it up. Gotta run. Bye."

"Bye."

Jimmy dutifully called Christine, and they established the second weekend in August as the ideal date for staging *Cottage Industry* at the great hall of GAS.

Christine was ready.

Christine was eager.

Christine was competent.

She even volunteered to help Jimmy hang lights. "And I'll get after Martin and make him help you."

Martin, you may recall, was the elusive figure at GAS who finally came through in the clutch and helped Jimmy and L. David Hinchcliff get the proper power for the lighting system. A real miracle-worker that Martin.

"Well, one good thing," Jimmy said, "I remember exactly where I put everything after we struck the set for *No Dice*. So putting up *Cottage Industry* this summer should be a piece of cake."

WRONG!!!

For starters, Constance Myers completely flaked out. Jimmy was only able to get her answering machine after she and her great and magnificent lord and master returned from their dramatic conference in Minneapolis. He left message after message imploring her to please call back, but she never did.

How could she possibly find the time when she was personally doing whatever it was she did with the physically challenged of half of southwest lower Michigan, acting her bosoms off at Blue Star Players, teaching voice, piano, flute, piccolo and God knows what else to musically challenged racial minority members from Michigan's only enterprise zone, and, of course, single-handedly upholding the fragile mental health of the truly great and magnificent Douglas Iglesia, Spanish grandee supremo?

Alas, Jimmy got lucky one evening and actually reached the frenetic Constance.

"I've got a student," she said, all out of breath from running halfway across her studio to the phone.

"Oh, then I won't keep you. This is Jimmy Clarke, and I was just going . . ."

"I'll call you back. I've got a student." Click.

Constance Myers never called back.

Jimmy grimly sought other assistance. Namely in the form of Marlene Small, his Havencrest neighbor who had taken such a stellar turn as Mary Alice Kurtin.

"You can play Kathleen this time," Jimmy said, holding his breath. "What do you say?"

"I can't make any commitments, but, sure, I'll think about it."

"Oh. Uh . . ."

"See, I'm taking this course in wound management systems — I mean I've had enough of scooping poop out of old men who can't look after themselves. I want to be on top of the medical scene, and people in wound management have the big picture — I mean we practically run the hospital, and that's what I can do if I take this course, because I would be more qualified than any stupid male

doctor — which reminds me — why is it that some dumb man who's
had abdominal surgery gets more attention from those stupid nurses
than a poor woman who's had a Caesarean section? I mean, if you
want to talk about about major abdominal surgery, go have a
Caesarean section some time and see how you feel. And then with
this new cost-containment business, the hospitals send the women
home the next day with no pain medication. They're just mere
women, right? They can cope with the pain, and the newborn, and
the raging hormones all on their own. But not the poor male who's
had his little, itty-bitty gallbladder out. No, he needs major
pharmaceuticals every time he rolls his baby blue eyes and moans or
does . . ."

"Marlene!"

"What?"

"Are you interested in being in my play or not?"

"Is David Hinchcliff going to direct?"

"No. He split for California. Didn't I tell you?"

"I don't remember. But you better get him back from California
if you're going to do this play. I mean you have to have a real
director, and you can't get a better director than David."

"Right. Well, I don't think there's any chance of getting him to
come back from California, so I thought I'd direct."

"You?!?"

"Yeah, me. What's wrong with that?"

Marlene laughed. Then she said, "You can't direct. You're just
the playwright."

"Right. Well, I thought I'd give it a try."

"Oh, I wouldn't if I were you. I'd send David a plane ticket and
put him up and do whatever it takes to get him to direct your play,
because you can't do your play without him."

"Right."

"Well, are you going to send him a plane ticket?"

"I don't have the money."

"Well, get a job and get the money."

"Right."

Jimmy got right off the phone and resolved to let *Cottage Industry*
die the quiet death it so unjustly deserved.

Later, after a good long run, he phoned Christine at the great hall of GAS and told her he had decided to cancel the play.

"But you can't," Christine said. "*No Dice* was the best thing that ever happened to GAS."

"I know. But I can't get a cast together."

"With all the talent lying around here there must be somebody."

"Do you know anybody? Especially somebody who can write music?"

A long silence, and then, "Gee, I'm afraid all the artists I know are . . ."

"Artists. I know. Well, it's better that we nip it in the bud now, rather than waiting until the last minute and having to appear in front of a full house and tell them that we can't do the play because we couldn't come up with a cast."

"No, I guess we wouldn't want that."

"No, we wouldn't. So this is for the best."

"Are you sure?"

"Yeah, I'm sure."

"You don't sound like you're sure."

"I know. But I'm sure."

"Well, if you change your mind, you know where we are."

"Thanks, Christine."

"Thank you, Jim. Thanks for giving us such a wonderful summer last year. I'm just sorry you can't get it together for this summer."

"I am, too. Oh well."

"Yeah, oh well."

They sighed and signed off.

Jimmy thought briefly of throwing himself into the Black River, but decided to leave that fate to Douglas Iglesia. He swallowed his hurt, disappointment, bitter frustration, and general resentment, and went into a flurry of playwright marketing.

He went to the South Haven Public Library and found a directory of theatres and sent a cover letter and synopsis of *Cottage Industry* along with a press clipping to virtually every theatre in Chicago, Detroit, Grand Rapids, South Bend, and Lansing. He even peppered in a few in New York, L.A. and Portland, Oregon for good measure.

And, just for a lark, he thumbed through to Kalamazoo and found an address for that PIT place that Allan Q. Hovington had mentioned a while back.

He spent a fortune on postage and envelopes and photocopying, but, oh, did he have a feeling of satisfaction that day in early March, 1994 when he took the bulging boxful of it all down to the main post office in South Haven and fired it off to the four corners of the American Theatre Empire.

"My manifest destiny," Jimmy muttered as he watched the postal clerk deal with his pile.

The postal clerk nervously eyed the silent alarm rigged directly to FBI headquarters. No telling when another nut was going to shoot up another Michigan post office. And this guy certainly looked like a total nutcase. Heavy, bearded, talking to himself, wearing ratty clothes. The works.

"I've got to hit with one of these," Jimmy said to the nervous postal clerk.

"Yeah. Well, you've certainly kept the Postal Service in business for another day. And speaking of days, you have a nice one, sir."

Jimmy took that as an indication to leave, and left. He proceeded directly to Clementine's where he treated himself to a lavish luncheon complete with designer beer with money he and Joyce simply did not have.

When he dutifully handed Joyce the receipt, she naturally went ballistic.

"Jimmy, what are you doing, spending $34.56 for lunch?!? Are you crazy?!? We don't have that kind of money!!"

"But Jerry Mappers just gave you that extra assignment."

"Yeah, but that money's already spent on bills we owe. Jimmy, we don't have the money for you to run around having $34.56 lunches at Clementine's!"

"I know, Joyce. But I felt like celebrating after I did that big mailing to all those theatres. With such a big mailing, you just know that I have to hit with at least one of them. I mean, it's simple arithmetic."

"You want to see some simple arithmetic—come and look at my budget."

Jimmy dutifully went and looked at Joyce's carefully constructed budget. It was all done in pencil on scraps of paper she had retrieved from his wastebasket, and there were multiple erasure marks and numbers on top of numbers.

"I can't make any sense out of this, Joyce."

"That's because you had a liquid lunch."

"I only had two beers."

"Two *designer* beers."

"Well . . ."

"What countries did you visit this time? Zaire and Sri Lanka?"

"Joyce, why are we fighting?"

"Because we're broke, Jimmy. And because I work and slave to create budgets, and then you go out and have $34.56 luncheons at Clementine's. You're turning out just like your father."

"How do you know? You never saw my father in action."

"I've heard you talk about him so much, I feel like he's part of our lives, even though he's been dead since 1985."

Jimmy carefully placed the budget back on Joyce's desk and said, "Well, maybe it's time I went out and worked construction. I could probably get a job scrubbing zebra mussels off the hulls of boats down by the river."

"Oh, brilliant. That's just brilliant. Here you are with a college degree, and tons of talent as a writer and actor, and you're going to scrape hulls. Give me a break, Jimmy."

"Well, what do you want me to do, Joyce?"

Joyce sighed and was about to say she just didn't know what Jimmy should do when Jimmy's phone rang.

"It's destiny," he said, rushing to answer it.

Joyce shook her head in frustration and looked at her negative numbers.

Jimmy answered the phone with a song in his heart and a bird of happiness in his brain.

"This is Jim Clarke," he chirped.

"Yeah, and this isn't Jim Clarke," Larry German chided. "How're you doin' over there, Jack?"

"Fine. Larry? Larry, is that you?"

"Yeah, man. It sure ain't Michael Jackson. Listen, you busy this Saturday night?"

Jimmy felt the sands of fate shift beneath his feet. There was a great sucking sensation as he felt himself drawn inexorably back into the masticating maw of the Fennell Art Gallery and Theatre, aka: FAGAT.

His body ached to flee. His bowels and bladder were ready to void on the spot, and his legs were juiced with high-octane adrenalin. His heart and lungs were fired for a full anaerobic burn.

But his brain was still programmed to the fame channel. Stuck on it, in fact. So it ordered his mouth to say: "Actually, Larry, we don't have any plans for Saturday night. What's up?"

Chapter Twenty-Three

You don't want to know what was up, but then you've read this far, so I might as well fill you in on the rest of the sad story of Jimmy Clarke's attempt to find fame as a playwright.

Here goes:

"Well," Larry German said in his lovely, laconic style, "we got us a little problem at the Fennell."

"Yeah," Jimmy said, "What's that?"

"Well, since you've been on your little leave of absence or whatever you called it . . ."

"Sabbatical."

"Yeah, that's easy for you to say. Anyway, a whole bunch of stuff's been happening at the Fennell. Makes my head spin just to think about it. I mean Laura Downs has just been a ball of fire. Every time I turn around, she's got some new event planned, or somebody new for me to meet or some project she wants me to do right away, and it's not like me and Julie don't got a gallery to run or nothing. Am I right or am I right?"

"You're right, Larry. You're always right."

"Yeah, that's what my kids are always telling me. You meet them at the open house?"

"No, I'm afraid I didn't."

"That's because they were out parking cars and helping people in and out of the theatre. We would have had a ton of lawsuits on our hands if it hadn't been for my kids and their high school friends. Did a heck of a job out there on the worst night in history. It's a wonder none of them got frostbite or nothin'."

"Yeah, it's a wonder. So, you were saying something about Saturday night. What's up?"

"Saturday night. Yeah, Saturday night. Well, you got any plans?"

"No, I don't have any plans."

"That's good. Because I got some plans for you."

Jimmy gulped and knew that if he were taking this call on a speaker phone, Joyce would disconnect at once. But he wasn't taking the call on a speaker phone, and Joyce was busy redoing her numbers over in her writing booth. And there was that little tickle of fame feathering his heart. The only solution was to go for it, and surely, Larry German had the solution. Just go along with whatever cock-a-mamie scheme he had, and there'd be one hell of a big . . .

"What'd you say, Jack?"

"Nothing. And the name's Jimmy, not Jack."

"Well, Jim not Jack, you was talkin' to yourself again. Or at least it sure sounded like you was because I sure heard words comin' outta the phone. It was like you were havin' a brain fart or somethin'. Yeah, that's what it was — a brain fart. You know, I guess that's what brain farts are — big, old gas bubbles that just kind of well up in your head and — pop! Words come bubbling out of your mouth, and you don't even know what you said. Am I right, or am I right?"

"You're always right, Larry."

"Yeah, that's what my kids are always telling me. You meet them at the open house?"

"No, but I heard they did one hell of a job parking cars and helping people in and out of the theatre."

"Yeah, if it hadn't been for my kids and their high school friends, we would have had a ton of lawsuits on our hands. Did a heck of a job out there on the worst night in history. It's a wonder none of them got frostbite or nothin'."

"Yeah, it's a wonder all right. So, you were saying something about Saturday night. What's up?"

"Saturday night? Yeah, Saturday night. Well, you got any plans?"

"No, I don't have any plans."

"That's good. Because I got some plans for you."

"Larry?"

"What, Jack?"

"Can we get off this conversational merry-go-round and cut to the chase?"

"'Cut to the chase' — oh, I like that. You just make that up?"

"No, it's an old cliché, but there's nothing like an old cliché when you want to cut to the meat of the matter."

Larry chuckled. "'The meat of the matter.' Oh, you writers — you guys just say the most amazing things. I wish I could be a writer. Never was too good at it. In high school, I had to get my girlfriend to write all my papers for me because I could never get them written myself. Course, it didn't help that I'd put them off to the very last minute and then expect her to come up with something that would guarantee me at least a C so I could get through high school and . . ."

"Larry?"

"What, Jack?"

"What do you want me to do on Saturday night?"

"Funny you should ask."

"Yeah. So what is it?"

"Well, you remember from the last board meeting you were at — just before your sabbatini or whatever you called it."

"Sabbatical."

"Yeah, that's easy for you to say. Well, anyway, Laura Downs was talking about bringing in this guy from Lithuania to plink on our piano. Which reminds me — I should probably go and see if that thing's frozen stiff from leaving it uncovered after the open house."

"Might not be a bad idea to get a tuner in to take a look at it. Especially if . . ."

"We can't afford a piano tuner. I'll get our good buddy Doug to come down from Fennville and fix it up good as new. Heck, for $500 he ought to take care of that piano for life. Am I right or am I right?"

"You're always right, Larry."

"Yeah, that's what my kids are always telling me. You meet them at the open house?"

"Larry, let's not get sidetracked again. What about this Lithuanian pianist?"

"Pianist? That what you call a fancy piano player?"

"That's what you call them, Larry."

"Sounds like a name for some pervert who goes around school yards showing his ying-yang to little kids or something."

"Well, it might sound like that, Larry, but it's not quite the same thing. I assure you."

"Good. Now where was I before you got me sidetracked?"

"You were about to tell me about the Lithuanian pianist, or should I say piano player."

"Say whatever you want. It's a free country."

"Right. So, I take it he's giving a concert at the Fennell Saturday night."

"Now you're with me. I can't even pronounce the guy's name, but Laura says he's the most famous piano player in Lithuania. Course, maybe he's the only piano player in Lithuania. Wherever Lithuania is. I mean, I've never seen it on any map I've ever looked at. Course, the only maps I ever look at are of Michigan and Ontario. Always looking for a good place to get away and fish, and you got to get a really good map to find a good place to fish these days, because everything's so fished out. You know what I mean?"

"Absolutely. So getting back to our Lithuanian piano player—"

"Right. Well, Laura says he's the most famous piano player in Lithuania, but I wouldn't really know because I can't even find the stupid country on the map, let alone ever been there. I mean, if I was gonna do some world-travelin', I'd go down to Brazil and look for that girl from Leepanema."

"You mean *The Girl from Ipanema.*"

"Yeah, that's just what I said."

"Right. But wouldn't your wife object if you went to Brazil and looked for the girl from Ipanema?"

"Ah, she's a good sport. She knows I like to look at the menu. As long as I don't order anything, she's happy. Look at the menu all you want, but don't order. That's what I always say."

"Words to live by. So what do you want me to do Saturday night?"

"There you go again, Jack. Chasing the cut."

"It's cutting to the chase, but that's close enough. So let me guess—you need an M.C.?"

"Yeah, you could say that."

"Why don't you do it, Larry? You did such a great job at the open house."

"No, I didn't."

"Yes, you did."

"No, I didn't."

"Larry?"

"What?"

"If I agree to be M.C. Saturday night, will you guys let me do one of my plays at the Fennell?"

"But you already did one of your plays at the Fennell. What do you call that little skit you and Harriett and that guy Margaret lives with did at the open house? Huh, answer me that?"

"I call that a staged reading, Larry. I'm talking about a full-blown production with lights and props and maybe even a real set, although I'm thinking black box because . . ."

"Black box? Sounds like them things they're always finding after an airplane crash. You know—some guy on the news says they recovered the 'black box,' and now they're gonna be able to hear the pilot's last words just before the crash. But I don't know why they need some fancy black box thing for that. I can tell you what the pilot's last words were before the crash: 'Oh, shit! We're gonna crash!' I know that's what I'd say. Or: 'Where the hell is the parachute?' Yeah, that's what I'd say. Which reminds me—why don't they give you a parachute when you fly on one of them big airliners? I mean, what's the point of tellin' you to fasten your seatbelt and to breathe through some stupid little plastic oxygen mask in case of an emergency when what you really need is a friggin' parachute. Am I right, or am I right?"

"Larry?"

"What?"

"If I agree to be M.C. Saturday night, will you let me do one of my plays at the Fennell?"

"Well, Laura and this friend of hers, Dominick McGrath, sure got a whole bunch of stuff planned. I mean after this piano guy from Lithuania, he's got some big band coming in April. And then, of course, the Blues and Bach thing on Memorial Day weekend, plus there's this guy Laura knows from Chicago who wants to do a whole big Shakespeare festival at the Fennell this summer. Have a whole Renaissance Faire to go with it and everything. I told 'em I want to rescue the damsels in distress."

Jimmy wanted to fling his phone through the window and run to the U.P. and howl at Lake Superior to give up her dead, but instead he said, "Well, that sounds like a pretty full program, but don't you think you could find a free weekend for my play? I'm only talking one weekend, Larry, because that's what we did last summer over at the great hall of GAS with my play, *No Dice,* and we . . ."

"That's right. I heard something about that. Me and my wife was gonna come but we had something else on that weekend. I don't remember."

"Yeah, well, you missed a great play. Let me tell you."

"The thing I like about you, Jack, is you don't mind promotin' yourself. Do you?"

"No, I guess not. So, is there a spare weekend left at the Fennell for my play?"

"I don't know," Larry said. "I'd have to consult with the board first. Heck, we're meeting Saturday morning. Why don't you just come and pitch your idea to them then? They'd love to have you back from your sabbatini or whatever you call it. We'd put you right back on the board like you never left, and I guarantee Laura'll put you right to work."

"Yeah, I'm sure she will. So you think the board will give me a weekend for my play if I agree to be M.C.?"

"I'd bet my mortgage on it. Course, this house was bought and paid for by my grandfather, so I ain't exactly got a mortgage, but you know what I'm talking about."

"Yeah. So . . ."

"So you come to the board meeting Saturday and tell everybody you're gonna save us all by bein' M.C. Saturday night, and I guarantee we'll give you a prime weekend for your little skit. You gonna do that same one you did at the open house or something else?"

"Well, since it'll probably be summer, I thought I'd do this play I just wrote about three men in a barbershop. It's only a one-act, so there wouldn't be any scene changes, and I already have the actors I want in mind, and I bet Allan Hovington could line up a barber's chair and . . ."

"You know, Father's Day weekend is open. Three men in a barbershop — boy, you couldn't get something better for Father's Day. We were talking at our last board meeting about doing something for Father's Day weekend. But nobody had any bright ideas. Not even that Dominick McGrath guy who seems to have an idea for everything. Just between you, me and the lamppost, that guy gives me a friggin' headache every time he opens his mouth. I mean, I make a point of gettin' along with everybody I meet, but that guy—I don't know. It's like somebody runnin' his fingers down a blackboard every time he opens his mouth. But he does have a lot of good ideas for the Fennell, and if we're going to make a go of it, I guess we need guys like Dominick McGrath."

"Yeah, I guess. So you think the board will give me the green light for my play?"

"I can't make any promises, Jack. But you come Saturday morning and tell them you're gonna be M.C. Saturday night, and I think things might go well for you."

"Okay. I'll come to the board meeting and tell them that."

"Good. And I know you'll do a great job Saturday night. You're a natural in front of people. In fact, some of the board members think you should have been president instead of me, but what do they know—right?"

"Exactly. Well, it's been a pleasure talking to you, Larry. I'll see you Saturday morning at the board meeting. Same time and place, I assume."

"You got it. Be there right at 8:30 because we've been running a tight ship with Laura Downs standing over my shoulder."

"No problem. See you then."

"Yeah, don't let your meat loaf."

"Yours either."

Jimmy did see Larry Saturday morning right at 8:30 right at the Fennell. Plus Laura Downs, Dominick McGrath and the rest of the board of directors of the Fennell Art Center & Theatre, aka: FAGAT.

When it came Jimmy's turn to pitch his play idea to the board after, of course, Larry had announced that Jimmy had volunteered to M.C. that night's concert, a tall, patrician fellow from Chicago cleared his throat and said: "I don't mean to sound rude or anything, but do we know anything about this play, or this playwright's track record? I know I certainly haven't heard of him in Chicago theatre circles, and there's nothing in Chicago theatre circles I don't hear."

The speaker was none other than Jeffrey Cantwell, a 34-year-old trust-fund twit living in Mommy and Daddy's guest house on their rather substantial spread in a secluded duneland setting south of South Haven. Just off the Blue Star actually, but you'd never see a thing from the highway except a rather sturdy gate and a yellow sign proclaiming that the whole area is under surveillance by a former CIA-trained death squad from El Salvador. And that you will indeed be drawn, quartered, terminally tickled, and beheaded if you even think about trespassing.

The speaker was the very same Jeffrey Cantwell who had gone off to some designer college in the east with Mommy and Daddy's full financial support to find himself in the theatre. After all, the dear boy seemed to show an aptitude for nothing but sitting in darkened theatres and watching tedious plays. Which was just fine because his out-of-sight-rich parents regarded the theatre as innocuous day care for their doltish boy. Plus, Daddy had no desire to bring the big galoot into the Fortune 500 corporation he directed as lord, master and CEO. The boy had no business sense, couldn't add, subtract, multiply or divide his life into manageable segments. And he couldn't express himself, except in long, loopy sentences such as the following:

"I don't mean any offense or anything, and I'm sure your little play has its place, but I really don't think we can risk doing amateur productions at the Fennell while we're trying to get it launched. I mean, it's absolutely crucial that we focus on top-drawer talent and material. Like Laura's brilliant program tonight, or Dominick's Blues and Bach festival on Memorial Day or my Shakespeare Festival this summer which, of course, I'm calling 'Midsummer at the Fennell' because we're bringing in the Melpomene Group from Chicago to . . ."

"She was the Greek goddess of tragedy," Jimmy interrupted.

Jeffrey Cantwell stared down his Roman aqueduct of a nose at the upstart and said: "You know who Melpomene was?!?"

"Sure, doesn't everybody? But why not name your troupe for Calliope? She was the chief of the Muses. I assume from the 'Midsummer at the Fennell' bit that you're doing *Midsummer Night's Dream*, and I'd hardly call that one of Shakespeare's heavy tragedies."

Jeffrey Cantwell forced his thin lips into a tight smile and said: "Touché. Well, I suppose there couldn't be any harm in you doing some little skit or something here on Father's Day weekend. After all—'Midsummer at the Fennell' doesn't kick off until the 4th of July and then, of course, it runs for the rest of the season. Concurrent, of course, with the Renaissance Faire which we will have out on the green."

"Out on the green?" Jimmy said. "You mean that mud pile out there that passes as a parking lot?"

Jeffrey Cantwell ground his perfect teeth and looked away from the ill-clad pest who had come to pollute *his* meeting. He settled his refined gaze on the lovely Laura Downs and said, "The Melpomene Group has agreed to come out from Chicago within the next month and spend a week landscaping and painting. And I'm talking about Equity actors with real careers in the theatre." Cantwell glanced at Jimmy and added, "I assume you have heard of Actors Equity."

"Yeah, but I think they've found a cure for that," Jimmy said. "At least in most first-world countries."

Jeffrey Cantwell locked eyes with the interloper, and the interloper locked eyes back.

Ever the leader, Larry German broke the impasse by clearing his throat and pounding the gavel his sister Julie had given him so he'd look more like a leader.

When all were quiet and attentive, Larry said: "Uh, so, like, uh, do I hear a motion that we move to accept the motion that somebody hopefully will make that we do Jack's little skit on Father's Day weekend?"

Julie German-Cooper dutifully took her brother's cue and moved that Jimmy be given Father's Day weekend with which to produce his play. "I mean," Julie said, by way of elaboration, "the whole reason we started restoring this place was to give local artists and writers a chance to showcase their work."

"I'll second that," Beverly Mantinkus said.

"I'd call for discussion," Larry said, looking at his watch, "but me and Julie got to open our gallery in exactly two minutes, so all in favor raise their right hand and say 'aye aye' or something, and all opposed just keep their mouths shut."

The motion passed with three mouths shut—those of Jeffrey Cantwell, Laura Downs, and Dominick McGrath.

Then Larry hurriedly called for a motion to adjourn, and he and his sister Julie raced off to open their gallery to the school of hungry Tunas waiting outside.

As everyone headed for the exit, Jimmy said, "Hey, maybe we should stick around and get this place cleaned up for tonight. It looks like it hasn't been cleaned up since the open house. And what about the piano?"

Laura Downs turned and said, "Look, honey, I have a business to run. You stay and clean up. And, yes, definitely do something about the piano. I've been after Larry for weeks to get the damn thing tuned, but I don't think he's done a thing. And we can't very well have the most brilliant pianist of Lithuania play on an untuned piano. Can we now?"

"No, I guess we can't. Not now or ever," Jimmy said.

Laura Downs nodded smartly, turned on her polished heel and was gone with her entourage.

Leaving Jimmy alone with his broom.

"Oh well," Jimmy said, taking a swipe at the embedded dust and grime. "Somebody's got to do it. Might as well be me."

And it was Jimmy who got to explain to Lithuania's leading pianist, a gentleman named Railfundus Matiliuskus, that no proper piano tuner had gotten around to tuning the piano which was why it sounded like total dreck every time it was streck. Excuse me, struck. Struck not streck.

"But I did get Larry to call this guy Doug in Fennville who restored the thing in the first place, and Doug actually came down this afternoon and did something with it, or at least that's what Larry said, and the thing should be . . ."

Railfundus Matiliuskus slammed the cover down on the keyboard and thundered something in his native tongue about eviscerating pigs and burning old Jews with beards. Something folksy and grounded in Lithuanian culture, myth, legend, and daily life.

Unable to understand a word of the colorful Baltic language, Jimmy looked to Mr. Matiliukus' "handler" for translation.

Mr. Matiliuskus' handler was a sinister-looking man named Steve who wore a floor-length leather coat and walked with a pronounced limp. Something to do with the war, no doubt, but it was best not to mention the war to Steve. He hailed from a Lithuanian-American enclave on the South Side of Chicago and said, "I don't think you want to know what Mr. Matiliuskus just said."

"No, I'm sure I don't." Jimmy sighed and glanced at his watch. Five minutes to curtain, and wonder of wonders, the old Fennell was actually filling up with aging Lithuanian-Americans who had come out on a cold, damp March night to hear the pride of their ancient homeland tickle the ivories.

"But I'll tell you something," Steve the handler said, taking Jimmy aside.

"Yeah."

"I been to a lot of theatres in this country and around the world, and this is the biggest dump I ever seen. That Downs broad promised us a real theatre with a green room, and decent seats, and a heating system — the works. We drove up from Chicago and what do we find — a dump. Makes the old Union Stockyards look like Caesar's Palace or something. You catch my drift?"

"Yeah. So what you want me to do?"

"I want you to tune the piano, or Mr. Matiliuskus don't play."

"But what about all those people out there?"

"It was me that got all them people out there. Every last one of them is a proud Lithuanian. Some of 'em don't even speak a word of English, and they been in this country since the war."

"Yeah," Jimmy said, wondering what Steve and his countrymen had done during the war. But, hey, what's a little country like Lithuania supposed to do when it's squeezed in between the German eagle and the Russian bear? Join the winning side and kick the fur or feathers out of the loser is what . . .

"What'd you say?"

"Nothing. I didn't say anything."

The handler named Steve looked closely at Jimmy. "You got shell shock. That's what it is. I seen it before."

"Yeah. So what about this concert? What about these people? What about the money?"

"We don't get our money," Steve the handler said, "and somebody's liable to get hurt. We didn't drive all the way up to this God-forsaken place for free. You catch my drift?"

Jimmy nodded thoughtfully and said: "And you won't get your money if there's no concert, and there won't be a concert if the piano isn't tuned to Mr. uh . . ."

"Matiliuskus. Railfundus Matiliuskus. And you'd better pronounce it right when you introduce him, or these people are gonna skin you alive. One thing Lithuanians can't stand is non-Lithuanians screwin' up their language. You catch my drift?"

Jimmy nodded thoughtfully and said: "I tell you what — I'm going to go over and get Larry German. He's our president, and I see him standing over there with Laura Downs, and I'll just go over and get him and have him come over here and take care of the business of tuning the piano. Okay?"

Before Steve could reply, Jimmy bolted over to Larry German who was idly chatting with the lovely Laura Downs about all the brilliant plans she had for the Fennell as, of course, Big Bev Mantikus handled the box office all by herself.

"Sorry to interrupt, Larry," Jimmy said, tearing Larry away from lovely Laura, "but we've got a little crisis on our hands, and you're going to have to deal with it."

"But you're the M.C." Larry said, his glazed eyes shimmering in the faltering light. "It's your show. If there's a problem, you've got to deal with it."

"No, Larry," Jimmy said, dragging the stoned woodworker back stage, "it's your problem, and you're going to deal with it."

Jimmy delivered Larry to Steve the handler and his fuming charge, the lion of Lithuania — Mr. Railfundus Matiliuskus.

"This is Larry German," Jimmy said, backing away, "he's our president, and he'll handle everything. Take it away Larry."

Jimmy backed into a corner and looked and listened as the aging pothead talked the Fennell's way out of a jam.

Steve the handler kept trying to interrupt, but once Larry got on one of his loopy loops, there was no stopping the natural boy.

Jimmy smiled and thanked Saint Genesius, even though he knew the Catholic saint discriminated against Protestants.

When Larry referred for the fourth time to the fine job his kids had done at the open house, Steve the handler threw up his hands and said: "All right, he'll play. He'll do the best he can with this piece of crap of a piano you got here. But you pay what that Laura broad agreed, or I'll do what I have to do to collect. If you catch my drift."

Stoned as he was, Larry caught Steve the handler's drift. "You'll be paid," Larry said. "Now let's get on with the show. Looks like everybody's getting restless."

Larry nodded at Jimmy, who went to center stage and said the only word of Lithuanian he knew: "Labas."

The old Lugans lapped it up.

And they loved the M.C. in the sharp Goodwill blazer even more when he said: "I know how long you have all waited for your homeland to be free and independent, and that great moment has finally arrived, and to celebrate it here at the Fennell Art Gallery and Theatre, we have brought the leading pianist of Lithuania here tonight for a special concert. A special concert celebrating the rebirth of Lithuania and the rebirth of the Fennell. Ladies and gentlemen, it gives me great pleasure to present the incomparable Railfundus Matiliuskus."

Railfundus Matiliuskus marched crisply to the Fennell's frost-heaved piano, nodded curtly at Jimmy and then bowed to his countrymen. They rose as one and applauded until their old hands ached. And then they continued applauding.

It was indeed a magic moment, and would have been even more magical if the Fennell board had gotten off its collective ass and actually helped Jimmy prepare the place properly for the event. But no, Laura Downs had a business to run, and Larry German and his sister Julie just had to get their gallery open at 9, and Dominick McGrath was . . .

Ah, forget it.

You don't want to hear it, and I don't want to rehash it.

So let's just say Mr. Railfundus Matiliuskus was a real player that night. Even when he had to declare a whole sector of the keyboard off limits during Mozart's *Piano Concerti Nos. 23 & 16.* Hey, he had been a conscript in the Soviet army. He knew all about making do with less, and he made the most beautiful music ever heard in the Fennell Art Gallery and Theatre using only two-thirds of a keyboard.

Jimmy was listening contentedly in the front row when Margaret Carlson appeared beside him and tugged at his arm.

"What?" he whispered.

"Jim," she said in a normal voice, "you've got to get up there during the intermission and personally thank all the members of the board. You didn't mention one member of the board during your introduction. And you've got to make an appeal for donations. You completely forgot to make an appeal for donations. We have a theatre full of people, and you didn't make one appeal for donations. If we don't get money, and I mean a lot of money right away, we're going to completely lose the momentum we built up during the open house, and I know Ed Goshington isn't going to want to have a show here of his wonderful flower paintings if there's no momentum. I mean, you haven't even started painting the place yet, and ..."

"Margaret," Jimmy said, putting his hand over her quivering lips, "you go up during the intermission, and you make an appeal for donations, and then you can tell the board that I quit."

Margaret pushed Jimmy's hand away from her mouth and sputtered, "But you can't quit. You're the life and soul of the Fennell. It'll collapse completely without you."

A formidable Lithuanian woman in the second row tapped Margaret on the shoulder and spoke sharply to her in biting Baltic phraseology.

Margaret knew a real threat to her person when she heard one, and retreated with a whispered, "Just go up there during the intermission and make an appeal for donations."

Jimmy nodded at the retreating blowser from Brooklyn and wondered what to do.

Railfundus Matiliuskus decided the question with his brilliant rendition of Mozart's sunny, spontaneously melodic *Concerto No. 23 in A major*. Minus a few keys, but, hey, who was keeping score?

Jimmy sighed and settled back in his broken seat. It's free, he thought, and it is truly wonderful. Even if it is freezing in here, but at least it's not really freezing like it was at the open house, and they are going to let me do my play on Father's Day, and they certainly won't if I abandon ship now and not get up there during intermission and ...

The formidable Lithuanian woman in the second row tapped Jimmy's shoulder and told him to shut the fuck up in her colorful native tongue.

Jimmy shut the fuck up and listened to Railfundus Matiliuskus pick his way through the rest of Mozart's sunniest concerto minus a third of the keyboard.

When Lithuania's most famous pianist was finished with Mozart's most spontaneously melodic concerto, the audience leapt to their feet and applauded new life into their arthritic old hands. Railfundus Matiliuskus bowed graciously, adjusted his tuxedo tails and marched backstage.

Jimmy gave him a few moments to regroup, and then gamely went back to see if he might like a cup of coffee or something.

"Coffee?!?" Steve the handler said. "You ask the greatest pianist in all of Lithuania if he wants coffee?!? Are you nuts?!?"

"No, I'm not nuts, I just thought . . ."

"Well, you thought wrong, pal. Pianists don't drink coffee during intermission. Affects their hands. Their minds. They don't need to be jittery out there. They're jittery enough as it is." Steve the handler turned to his charge and said in Lithuanian, "Ain't that right, Railfundus?"

Railfundus Matiliuskus nodded and then launched into a long complaint in Lithuanian about:

-The pathetic excuse for a green room Jimmy had patched together that afternoon,

-The lousy acoustics,

-The cold,

-The damp,

-The crummy lighting, and, of course,

-The sorry state of the piano.

"What'd he say?"

"You don't want to know," Steve the handler said. "Just go and get him a glass of water. That is, if you idiots got any water in this dump. I'm telling you, this place ain't gonna last the year the way you numbskulls are running it."

"Right. I'll get some water."

Jimmy got the pride of Lithuania some water, and the pianist signaled that he was ready to tackle the *Piano Concerto No. 16 in D major, K. 451.*

Steve the handler handed Jimmy the liner notes from an album and said, "Here, read this when you introduce the second concerto. Might as well say one intelligent thing tonight."

"Right."

Jimmy nodded grimly and marched to center stage and motioned for everyone to shut up and sit back down.

The ever-sharp Larry German looked up from his conversation with the lovely Laura Downs and actually doused the house lights. I tell you, that boy was showing all the signs for a brilliant career in theatrical management. Or at least in handling light switches.

"Ladies and gentlemen, before I re-introduce Mr. Matiliuskus, I wanted to put in a good word for this theatre in which you are enjoying tonight's concert. I know the seats are not the most comfortable, and the heat isn't what it should be, and the lights aren't as bright as we'd like, but we've only just begun to restore this old treasure. And we need your help. So, as you're leaving tonight, if you'd care to make a donation— however large or small—we'd greatly appreciate it. And now, I'd like to say a few words about the piece Mr. Matiliuskus will be performing next."

Margaret Carlson ran up the center aisle, hopped up and down and mouthed with those big Brooklyn lips of hers: "Don't forget to mention the board members."

Jimmy nodded indulgently at her and said, "Ah, yes, I am reminded to mention the board of directors of the Fennell Art Gallery and Theatre. Ladies and gentlemen, these are the volunteers who have worked tirelessly lo these many months to bring this dusky jewel back to life. Let's have a big hand for the board of directors of the Fennell Art Gallery and Theatre, aka: FAGAT."

The audience dutifully applauded, drowning out a further attempt by the frantic Margaret Carlson to get Jimmy to mention each member by name.

When all were still, Jimmy ignored the jittering jerk from Brooklyn and proceeded to read from the liner notes: "*The Piano Concerto No. 16 in D Major* dates from March 1784 and was written by Mozart for Mozart. A little early Christmas gift to himself I suppose. Anyway, the piano part is more difficult than that of the two previously composed pieces. 'I am sure,' Mozart wrote to his father, 'that the B-flat and the D are concerti that will make you perspire.' Ladies and gentlemen, prepare to perspire."

And sweat they all did as Railfundus Matiliukus returned to the out-of-tune piano and bravely made magnificent Mozartian music with it.

When the concert regretfully ended, a red-faced Margaret Carlson rushed up to Jimmy and demanded that he take the stage and make another appeal for donations.

"And you forgot to mention all the board members' names," Margaret gushed. "You've got to mention every board member's name. If people don't know who we are, how are they going to know who we are?"

Dumbstruck by that immutable logic, Jimmy patted Margaret on the shoulder and said, "There's the stage, Margaret. It's all yours."

"But I can't," Margaret said, melting. "I can't get up in front of a crowd of people! I break out and sweat, and have hot flashes, and then . . ."

"So do I, Margaret, so do I. Oh, Margaret, I almost forgot."
"What?"

"Be sure and see that Larry pays the nice piano player, or he might not be able to use his thumbs for a while, and he if can't use his thumbs, he's not going to be much good as a woodcarver, now is he?"

"I don't get it."

"Neither do I which is why I'm leaving. Bye."

"But you can't leave."

But Jimmy did. And, as we shall see, life went on. And on and on and on and . . .

Chapter Twenty-Four

Jimmy stayed away from the Fennell for all of a week, and then got sucked into joining the "theatre committee" at the very next board meeting. Which, of course, began promptly at 8:38 a.m. and ended precisely at 9 a.m. so Larry and Julie could open their gallery to the hoards of antique-deprived Tunas.

Jeffrey Cantwell graciously agreed to chair the theatre committee and set a meeting for the following Wednesday afternoon.

"I'm bringing the Melpomene Group up from the city, and we're going to get this old place painted and spruced up once and for all," Jeffrey told Jimmy after the board meeting.

"Good. Who's going to buy the paint and stuff, if you don't mind my asking?"

Jeffrey Cantwell's fine features darkened for a nanosecond and then the rich boy muttered, "My mother."

"I beg your pardon."

"I said, it's all taken care of."

"Good. Well, one thing I can do is paint. That's about all I did in the navy. I kept the world safe for democracy by painting bulkheads."

"Bulkheads?"

"That's salty sailor talk for walls."

"Oh." Jeffrey Cantwell regarded Jimmy Clarke with passing amusement. "Say, you've had quite a checkered career, haven't you?"

Jimmy wanted to crush the fatuous fool's instep, but, hey, this guy just might be the key to his theatrical success, so he said, "Oh yeah, I've been all over the map. I was even in a seminary once."

"What? You were studying to be a priest?"

"Well, an Episcopal priest."

"You're Episcopalian?"

"Yeah, and so is George Bush. So what?"

"So, I'm Episcopalian."

"Well, good for you, Jeffrey."

Jeffrey Cantwell chewed on his cheek lining for a moment and said, "Let me get this straight, you were in an Episcopal seminary, but you were also in the navy?"

"Right."

"Well, what were you doing in the seminary?"

"Avoiding the draft."

"But you were in the navy."

"Yeah, but that was after I quit the seminary. In fact, I went right into the navy from the seminary, because things didn't go so well for me while I was in the seminary. It was sort of the bottom of my sex, drugs and rock 'n' roll period. If you catch my drift."

"You were doing sex, drugs and rock 'n' roll in the seminary?!?"

"Something like that. Look, you been giving any thought to hanging lights here? I mean, you're going to need them for your 'Midsummer at the Fennell' extravaganza, and I'd sure like them for my play on Father's Day weekend."

"Lights are no problem. No problem whatsoever. You forget that I am the quintessential insider in Chicago theatre. If I want lights, all I have to do is snap my fingers, and we'll have the best instruments on the market. All virtually free."

"Hey, sounds great."

Jeffrey Cantwell shrugged. "When you've been a theatre insider as long as I have, things happen. So tell me more about the sex, drugs, and rock 'n' roll you did in the seminary."

Jimmy sighed and told Jeffrey Cantwell all about his short and sordid life as a student at Gatesbury Theological Seminary in Evanston, Illinois.

Cantwell couldn't get enough and asked for more details when Jimmy joined him and his illustrious Melpomene Group on the following Wednesday for a fun-filled afternoon of scraping and painting the old broken-down theatre.

"This guy was in an Episcopal seminary avoiding the draft, but then he went in the navy," Jeffrey told his "people." His people were four women, two of whom were young and impressionable and two of whom were old and jaded. Plus, there was a slight fellow of the gay persuasion.

"Really?" one of the young women said. She wore a t-shirt and was bra-less when she really shouldn't have been.

Jimmy wasn't a breast man, but who could resist when such an amazing pair was poised right under his noise. So young and tender and firm and ripe and . . .

"What did you say?" the young woman said, coyly covering her maidenly form.

"Oh, nothing. Just thinking out loud."

"He's a playwright," Jeffrey Cantwell explained. "Or says he is. They read a little piece of his at the open house. Say, that was about an Episcopalian wasn't it? That just dawned on me."

"Well, I'd hardly say Thomas Cranmer called himself an Episcopalian. The word was not used to describe a follower of a particular sect in 1556, but . . ."

"But he was the guy who wrote the Prayer Book, right? I do remember that from Sunday School at Holy Comforter."

"Yeah, he was the guy who wrote the BOOK OF COMMON PRAYER."

"Boy," the young bra-less actress said, "you know a lot."

"Yeah, I've been around the block a few times. So, I guess we'd better get to work. We didn't come here this afternoon for idle chatter."

"No, we certainly didn't," Jeffrey Cantwell declared, eyeing the vast wallspace awaiting fresh paint. "Well, let's see if we can't get this old girl — excuse me — old woman looking as good as new by sundown."

Moved by the cant of Cantwell, they set to work with scraper, drop cloth, roller, and brush and actually got about a fourth of the old wreck of a theatre painted a faintly agreeable lime green by sundown.

Then Jeffrey Cantwell and his people pranced off to the Cantwell estate for a sumptuous meal prepared by Mommy, followed by some serious theatre talk.

Jimmy, the mere playwright, was not invited.

But he was ordered to report for the next painting party the following Wednesday when the Melpomene Group would again grace the Fennell with its presence and finish the job it had started. Thus, the drop cloths, paint cans, rollers and brushes were left in the ready position. That is to say, they left the place in a paint-splattered mess.

The board spent a considerable portion of its next meeting congratulating Jeffrey Cantwell on the sterling job he and his people had done "restoring the Fennell to life."

And Jeffrey Cantwell spent the rest of the meeting feeding the board his high expectations for the dazzling "Midsummer at the Fennell" he had up one of his sleeves.

"It might be a little premature to announce this," Jeffrey confided, "but we're all friends here, so what the heck? Anyway, I've been in serious negotiations with the Society for Anachronistic Creativity in Evanston, and they see no problem in staging an actual tournament here on the green concurrent with our 12-week run of *Midsummer Night's Dream*."

The lovely Laura Downs beamed at her bright boy-toy and quickly calculated the obscene profit she would realize from catering such an affair.

Larry German was too stoned to do anything but nod enthusiastically, and the rest of the board just sat there like bumps on a log.

Except for Jimmy who cleared his throat and said, "You're talking about guys dressed up like knights — on horseback — the whole works?"

"Yes," Jeffrey Cantwell countered, clearly annoyed by the impertinent playwright. "Of course they will be on horseback. How could you possibly have a proper Renaissance Faire without knights on horseback?"

"Right. Silly me. And they'll be out on the, uh, green?"

"Yes."

"Which we're going to . . ."

"Prepare as soon as we get some decent spring weather. What's your point?"

Jimmy looked around the table for support, and finding none, decided to just drop it. But just for the hell of it, he threw in a: "I imagine the insurance for something like this is rather high. I mean if one of those so-called knights on horseback skewered some little kid or something, then . . ."

"The Society for Anachronistic Creativity provides its own insurance," Jeffrey Cantwell knowingly declared. In reality, he had no idea if said society provided anything of the sort, because he had never actually spoken with the pleasant people who lived for the past. He had been meaning to, and wanting to, and meaning to and wanting to in Jeffrey Cantwell's mind amounted to consummation. Fulfillment. Accomplishment.

"Don't worry," Jeffrey Cantwell assured the board, "it's all taken care of. All we have to do is dot the i's and cross the t's and we're going to have a summer festival of the arts here at the Fennell the likes of which will make them green with envy in London, Ontario. And I know all about London, Ontario, because my family has been going to the Shakespeare Festival there for years and years and years. There isn't a play by Shakespeare or Shaw I haven't seen. Not one."

Jimmy was tempted to applaud, but tactfully sat on his hands.

But he had his hands full the following Wednesday when he dutifully reported to the Fennell for the grand finale painting party with the estimable Melpomene Group.

"Hmm, they must be running a little late," Jimmy said, looking around the empty parking lot. "Excuse me — the village green. Site of the fabled Renaissance Faire."

Jimmy sighed and let himself into the theatre with the key Larry German had so graciously given him.

He figured he might as well get to work while awaiting their imminent arrival and was soon lime-greening another vast expanse of brick wall. The paint, of course, didn't want to adhere to the rough masonry surface, finding it much more fun to splatter merrily off the roller and all over Jimmy's clothing.

Fortunately, the playwright was wearing grubbies.

Like he owned anything else.

Jimmy was completely paint-splattered and exhausted three hours later when a harried Jeffrey Cantwell burst into the theatre and said, "Hey, looks like you kind of got started without me. But don't let me stop you. You're doing great. Really great. Keep on going, and I'll start on the trim around the stage doors. I got some more money from my — well, you know, and I got this really great dark green oil-based paint for those old doors, and it'll really look great in contrast to the lime green paint on the walls. Don't you think?"

Jimmy stopped splattering paint on himself and looked at the scion of Chicago theatre. "Jeffrey?"

"What?"

"Where's the Melpomene Group?"

"The what?"

"The Melpomene Group."

"You mean the Melpomene Group?"

"Yeah, that's what I said."

"No, you didn't. You put the accent on the first syllable. The accent goes on the second syllable."

"Right. Well, where are they, professor?"

Jeffrey Cantwell folded his thin lips into his mouth and chewed on them for a long moment. Then he put on a happy face and said, "They have other commitments in the city. I mean, we're talking about Equity Actors here, not rank amateurs with nothing better to do than paint old theatres in Michigan."

"Right. So, I guess it's just you and me."

"Yep, but they'll be here next week. You'll see."

All Jimmy saw the following week was a complete no-show, right down to the fearless leader of the Melpomene Group, the learned and masterful Jeffrey Cantwell, dean of Chicago theatre.

Jimmy took that as a sign to look after his own interests and abandoned the Fennell to the state of half-decoration he and Jeffrey Cantwell had left it in the previous week. Right down to the rollers in the pans and ladders leaning against the walls and paint-splattered drop clothes draped here, there and everywhere.

Not a pretty sight, but then somebody on the board would clean it up before the gala big band concert Laura Downs was planning for a Saturday in April. The one she had promised the board would attract hordes of well-heeled senior citizens longing for the day when you could swing your gal to the mellow tones of Glenn Miller and his Orchestra, and drink and drive all you wanted, and never even think about wearing seatbelts, and sure not worry one jot about what those Japs and Germans were up to because America had two great big oceans to protect her, and, and—

Anyway, the lovely Laura Downs was sure the big band concert was going to pull the Fennell out of the financial stall that had started with the open house and had continued unabated through the Railfundus Matiliuskus concert when Steve the handler basically ran off with every dime that was collected that night. Including the donations to the Fennell that had been made as a result of Jimmy's urgent appeal.

There being no further donations of any kind except the paint Jeffrey Cantwell's mommy had purchased, the Fennell was financially fucked. And Larry German and his beloved sister Julie occasionally let on at board meetings that there might, just might, be a teensy, weensy little problem with the rent and the people who really owned the building, but Julie kept forgetting to bring the books to the board meeting, and it was all getting quite murky, and Jimmy was getting ready to bail out and look for another theatre, but all he was getting as a result of his big mailing to theatres everywhere were rejections from theatres everywhere.

So he glumly stuck with the Fennell and actually began preparing to produce *The Last Haircut* on Father's Day weekend.

Two performances only, and admission was going to be $5 for adults and $3 for students and seniors. Tickets sold at the door. Come on down, and have a good time, and theatre agents, critics and producers take note, because the irrepressible James Gordon Clarke III is back on the block to stay.

Yeah, right, Jimmy thought, reaching for the phone.

He first called Allan Q. Hovington and after shamelessly flattering the actor's ego, got him to agree in principle, at least, to play the part of Pete the Barber. Jimmy sweetened the deal by offering to split the box, if there was any box, equally with the cast. Meaning, of course, the penny-wise Allan Q. Hovington would get a quarter of whatever was collected at the door.

Jimmy set the following Wednesday at 7:30 p.m. at the Fennell for the first rehearsal, and Allan Q. Hovington agreed to be there.

God bless Allan Q. Hovington.

Next, Jimmy called Justin Ward in Glenn. Justin Ward, you may recall, was the high school freshman who had played Julio the pizza deliveryman with such panache in the Glenn Consolidated High School Drama Club's production of Jimmy's *Carol's Christmas*.

Justin had also played opposite Jimmy in a scene called "A Normal Father-Son Conversation" by that nifty woman from Oregon.

The kid was good, and Jimmy wanted him to play the "Kid" in his play.

Justin answered and said, sure, he'd do it, but "like, I'm only 14, so you're like going to have to give me rides to rehearsals and stuff. Plus, I have track after school until the end of the school year, and then me and my mom are going to Puerto Rico after school's out to see her family and stuff, but sure, I can be in your play. When was it again?"

Jimmy patiently put the dates for the performances and the first rehearsal firmly in the boy's mind, and Justin noodled for a bit, and then decided it was doable.

"As long as you give me a ride to rehearsals, because my mom has like ten jobs, and she can't give me a ride anywhere. Okay?"

"Okay, Justin. No problem. I'll pick you up next Wednesday at 7."

"Yeah, okay, but wait around if I'm not home because I have track after school, and I think there's like a meet that day or something. But I should be home close to 7."

"Right. I'll wait around. How about the rest of the rehearsals? Are evenings best for you?"

"Sure. There's not much homework this time of year. The teachers have pretty much given up by now."

"Right. I'll see you next Wednesday."

"Yeah, sure."

Two down and one to go, Jimmy thought clicking off and dialing George Streznik's number in Allegan.

If you read CLARKE THEATRE (ACT I), you will recall George Streznik as the flu-stricken fellow who auditioned for *No Dice* and was subsequently rejected by L. David Hinchcliff. It represented a double rejection actually, because L. David Hinchcliff had previously dismissed George as his assistant editor of the HAVENCREST HIGHLIGHTS. Suffice it to say, Jimmy felt terrible about the whole affair, especially since he was the one who got to phone George and tell him he hadn't gotten a part in *No Dice*.

Truth to tell, George would have been great as Glenn Kurtin. In the short reading he did with Douglas Iglesia during his audition, he had the great and magnificent Spanish grandee going in all directions. But the great and wonderful L. David Hinchcliff simply wouldn't work with George. Not after he saw how wonderful Burt Babbington was as Glenn Kurtin, and there was no way L. David Hinchcliff was going to turn away Douglas Iglesia. So it was George Streznik who got the ax, and Jimmy got to be the headsman.

Jimmy listened to the phone ring at the other end and prayed for an answering machine.

Instead, he got a little cupcake who said: "Hello, this is Tracey Streznik."

"Hi, Tracey. Is, uh, your father there?"

"My daddy's outside fixing my bicycle. He's been teaching me to ride without training wheels, and I crashed into the garage. But I didn't hurt myself. Just my bike. So my daddy's fixing it, so I can practice some more riding without training wheels. But I wear a helmet. He makes me wear a helmet, and I think that's smart, because when I crashed into the garage, I landed on my head, and if I hadn't been wearing a helmet, maybe I would have brain damage, or be killed dead or something."

"Probably. Well, that's good you wear a helmet, Tracey. I wear a helmet too when I ride my bike."

"You do?"

"Oh, yeah. One time when I lived in Chicago I hit a man when I was riding my bike at night, and I flew right over the handlebars and landed on my head, and if I hadn't been wearing a helmet I might have been killed dead or something, too."

"You were smart to wear a helmet. Did your dad tell you to wear a helmet?"

"Actually, it was my doctor. Say, uh, could I talk to your father?"

"He's out fixing my bike. I ran into the garage, but I'm okay because I was wearing a helmet."

"Yeah, that's what you told me, Tracey. And that was a good thing you were wearing a helmet. Look, would you mind going and getting your dad and telling him I want to talk to him?"

"Do you want me to go get him so you can talk to him?"

"Yes please, Tracey."

"Okay. I'll go get him. But please don't talk to him long because I want him to fix my bike right away so I can ride some more. I'm really getting good. I can go the whole driveway without falling. Except for that stupid garage, everything was really, really easy."

"Right. Well I promise I won't talk to him too long, Tracey."

"Okay. Stay where you are, mister, and I'll get my daddy."

Presently, George Streznik himself came to the phone and said in a jolly voice: "Hello, this is George Streznik. Who's this?"

"George, this is, uh, Jimmy Clarke the playwright from near South Haven who . . ."

"Turned me down for his play. How could I ever forget you? I've never been turned down for a play in all the years of acting I've done, and I've done a lot of acting. Believe you me."

"I believe you, George, and I'm still really sorry about the way things worked out. It was really David's decision, but I guess I'm to blame, too."

"Yeah, you are. And it was a really rotten thing to do. I mean I dragged myself down to that audition with a 103 degree fever. I was at death's door, but I came anyway, because acting's in my blood. And if you ask me, I was perfect for that part. Actually either part, but especially the part of the father, because I sure had that Iglesia guy going for a ride. I mean, I really got under his skin. And that was just the first reading."

"Yeah, you were great, George. No doubt about it."

"So why didn't you give me the part? If you thought I was so great? Huh? Answer me that, Mr. Playwright."

"Look, I'm sorry, George. I really am, and to make it up to you, I'd like to offer you the lead in my new play, *The Last Haircut*."

"Hey, snappy title."

"Thanks. Anyway, it's a one-act, and you'd play this grumpy old guy who comes for . . ."

"His last haircut."

"Right. See, he's dying of cancer — he knows it, but he denies it, and his monthly haircut is the highlight of his dull and boring retirement, and . . ."

"Sounds like something I could sink my teeth into."

"Oh yeah. It's a great part, George. You could really have a lot of fun with it."

"How many other characters?"

"Two — the barber and a kid. But your character steals the show."

"Yeah?"

"Definitely, George. Plus, I'm planning to split the box office with the cast."

"And there's three in the cast, plus you so we'd each get a quarter of the box." George hummed a happy little tune and said, "Things are kind of tight around here right at the moment, and that's sure a better deal than they ever give you at the Copper Works in Allegan."

"The Copper Works?"

"It's a restored copper shop in downtown Allegan where we do a whole bunch of community theatre. I've been in practically everything they've done since we restored the old place and got it up and running again. Had the lead in *Arsenic and Old Lace* last summer. After you turned me down for your little play."

"Right. Again, I'm really sorry. And that's why I'd like to give you the lead in *Last Haircut*. To make it up to you for being such a shit to you last summer."

"Yeah, that really was a low point of my life. I had never been turned down for a part in a play before. Never. And I've done a lot of acting. Well, look, Tracey's tugging on my sleeve here, and if I don't get out there and fix her bike pronto, I'm gonna be in big trouble. So when's this brilliant play going to be? I assume you're doing this at the Glenn Art Studio this summer."

"Actually, we're doing it at the Fennell Art Center and Theatre on Father's Day weekend. Two performances only."

"The Fennell? Yeah, I've been hearing good things about that place. You guys had some big open house back in January during that blizzard."

"Yep, that was us."

"I heard you packed the place. On the nastiest night of the century."

"Yep, we're certifiable. And believe it or not, nobody got stuck in a ditch or had to resort to cannibalism."

"You sure made quite a splash having an open house on a night like that."

"Yeah, everybody came and ate all the free food and split. But for a while, we had more than 300 people in there. That body heat was the only thing keeping us warm. But don't worry, it'll be nice and comfortable for our play in June."

"And you're really going to split the box office? Four ways?"

"Yep. And I'm going to go all out to pack the place for both performances."

"What are you charging?"

"Five bucks for adults and $3 for seniors and students."

"That ought to pack 'em in. We charge more than that at the Copper Works in Allegan, and we get good turn-outs for everything we do, and I should know because I've been in practically everything they do, and I've never been turned down for a role. Not once. Except when you turned me down for your little play."

"Right."

"So, you say you're gonna pack the place both performances?"

"Yep."

"And you had more than 300 for the open house?"

"Easily."

George Streznik did a little mental arithmetic and said, "I figure if you pack the place both shows with mostly adults, I could make somewhere in the neighborhood of $700."

"Yeah, possibly."

George made a happy noise and asked when the first rehearsal was.

Jimmy told him, and George told him he would be there, and Jimmy and George clicked off.

Jimmy rushed right out to his favorite print shop to have rehearsal copies made of *The Last Haircut*, and George fixed Tracey's bike so she could ride it to her heart's content up and down the driveway. Wearing her helmet, of course.

Jimmy told the board that Saturday all about his big plans for *The Last Haircut*, and they listened politely, and then basically turned the meeting over to Jeffrey Cantwell, Laura Downs, and Dominick McGrath who regaled them with tall tales of the obscene fame, glory and profits that would soon accrue from the big band concert in April, the Blues and Bach extravaganza on Memorial Day weekend, and, of course, culminating in the fabulously fantastic "Midsummer at the Fennell" festival of fun and games set to stretch over the entire summer and guaranteed to bring out huge hordes of adoring Tunas with bulging wallets.

Jimmy listened politely because he knew his play would outshine everything. But thinking of shining made him think of lights, so he grabbed Jeffrey Cantwell after the meeting and said, "Say, Jeffrey, any word on getting lights for the theatre? I mean, if you're going to do Shakespeare here this summer, you're going to want . . ."

"The works?"

"Yeah."

"Don't worry. The fix is in." Jeffrey Cantwell smiled winningly at the aspiring playwright from nowhere and said, "Say, we should finish up the painting one of these days, don't you think?"

Jimmy looked at the paint litter that lay just where they had left it and nodded thoughtfully.

Jeffrey Cantwell nodded thoughtfully, too, and patted Jimmy on the back. "Well, no time like the present."

"You want to finish right now?" Jimmy shrugged. "Yeah, I'm basically free, although I was planning to run up to Holland to get some running toys, but . . ."

"I'd say painting the Fennell comes first, wouldn't you? I mean, do you want people coming in here for your little play and seeing a half-painted house?"

"No."

Jeffrey Cantwell gave Jimmy another pat on the back and said, "Well, then get to work. I'll join you in a bit because I've got a few things I've got to do for, er, uh, Mother."

"Right."

Jimmy shuffled over to the paint mess and watched Jeffrey Cantwell and the others vacate the premises. When Jimmy went to lift a roller from a paint pan, the whole thing rose as one because the paint had hardened around the roller. And so it was with everything. A total mess that would take hours just to set right before even a modicum of painting could be done.

And, Jimmy thought, I'll be damned if I'm going to do it all by myself.

And so he didn't.

He went instead to Holland and bought himself some expensive running toys with money he and Joyce didn't have. Then he treated himself to a double espresso and two whole-grain bagels at an artful little coffee house on 8th Street.

And then he went home and tried to sneak his running toys into the closet. But Joyce caught him, and they had a big fight about money.

Joyce said they were ruined financially and would both have to go out and work as farm laborers and ditch-diggers if Jimmy didn't curb his profligate ways, and Jimmy countered with a kiss and a hug and coo in one ear and then a coo in the other.

Joyce finally melted and they spent a thoroughly productive Saturday afternoon making mad, passionate love.

"At least," Jimmy said when they had consummated their lust, "that didn't cost anything."

"What do you mean?" Joyce countered, propping herself up on her elbow. "Have you seen what the price of condoms is these days? You don't know, because I always have to buy them because you're too embarrassed, but let me tell you . . ."

"Joyce?"

"What?"

"How about being real spendthrifts."

"What are you talking about?"

Jimmy boldly fetched another condom, ripped it out of its foil and said, "Let's live dangerously."

And they did.

Chapter Twenty-Five

Jimmy arrived at Justin Ward's house in gleeful Glenn, Michigan the following Wednesday promptly at 7 p.m. and rang the doorbell.

Nada.

He rang it again.

Nada mas.

He worked the brass knocker.

Nada.

He rapped his knuckles on the nearest window.

Still nada, so he sat on the front porch and waited a full 20 minutes for the young thespian to appear at full gallop from the big track meet at Glenn Consolidated High School.

"Sorry," Justin said, panting. "I thought I could get a ride with Michael's mom, but they were going up to Saugatuck for dinner or something. Should I change?"

"Nah, you're fine. But why don't you get a towel or something so you don't—you know . . ."

"What? Sweat all over your car and mess it up?"

"Yeah."

Justin Ward regarded Jimmy's aging Honda Civic with naked contempt. "Don't be like offended or anything, dude, but your car is already pretty messed up. I mean, who'd want to steal a little dorky thing like that?"

"Right."

"I bet you don't even have to lock it."

"As a matter of fact, we don't."

Justin Ward laughed. "Figures. Well, to make you happy, I'll get a towel and put on a clean t-shirt."

He did just that, and they were off to the Fennell for the first rehearsal of *The Last Haircut.*

Allan Q. Hovington was waiting for them when they arrived, but he had seen neither hide nor hair of George Streznik. Not that Allan knew what George looked like, but he knew that somebody was coming to play the part of Mr. Babbington, and nobody had come to play the part of Mr. Babbington.

"Well," Jimmy said, glancing at his watch, "he'll turn up. It's only 7:40. He's probably fixing Tracey's bike after the kid rammed it into the garage again. I just hope she was wearing a helmet."

Allan Q. Hovington and Justin Ward stared at the playwright, and then they looked at the congealed mess of rollers, brushes and paint stuff. Finally, they shifted their gazes stageward where there were no lights of any sort to illuminate the play.

Jimmy guessed what they were thinking and said, "Don't worry, this guy Jeffrey Cantwell's on the case like an attorney. He's a big shot in Chicago theatre, and he's going to get all kinds of lights for the Fennell. Any day now. Plus, he's got this group of actors out of Chicago—the Melpomene Group—and they're going to finish painting and decorating this place. Plus, they're going to landscape the parking lot so it looks like a village green in England. Anyway, Jeffrey was supposed to come back Saturday afternoon and finish up the painting, but I guess he got detained. He's a real busy guy, and anyway, it's all going to be terrific by the time we do our play. You'll see."

Jimmy sighed and slapped his thighs and looked at his watch which was inching its way toward 7:42. "Maybe I should read the part of Mr. Babbington until George gets here."

"Good idea," Allan said.

Justin just nodded.

"But maybe I should call George first. Just to be sure he remembered that there's a rehearsal tonight."

"Wouldn't hurt," Allan said.

Justin just nodded.

Jimmy phoned the Streznik residence in Allegan and got Tracey who said her daddy was out fixing her mommy's rosebushes that she had run over with her bike.

"At least I didn't hit the garage," Tracey said. "Plus, I was wearing my helmet, so I didn't get killed dead or anything. But my mom's rosebushes are kind of crushed down, but my dad says he can fix them before she comes home."

"Good, Tracey. Could you ask him to come to the phone?"

There then ensued another tedious conversational loop, finally culminating in the appearance of Mr. George Streznik at the telephone.

"George," Jimmy said, trying to remain calm, "this is Jimmy Clarke over at the Fennell Theatre near South Haven. Did you forget about our rehearsal tonight?"

"Rehearsal? What rehearsal?"

"For *The Last Haircut* — the play I wrote that I told you about last week when I called. Remember?"

"I remember that you turned me down for that play you did last summer. The one about the dice game or something. That was the only time I've ever been turned down for a part. The only time. The Copper Works has never turned me down for one of their plays in all the years they've been doing plays there. Never once."

"Well, good for them, and, George, I'm not going to turn you down this time. In fact, if you remember, I promised you the lead in this new play of mine."

George slapped his head and said, "Now it's coming back to me. Something about an old fart going to get his last haircut at his favorite barbershop. And you're going to split the box with the cast."

"Right."

"So when are rehearsals?"

"Well, the first one is right now."

"Right now? How can it be right now if I'm here in Allegan?"

"Right. Well, you must have forgotten."

George slapped his head again and said, "It's been a real zoo around here lately. I've been meaning to get a new message pad for the phone, but now that my wife's working the evening shift at the hospital, and what with me working two jobs, and the kids and — oh, you don't want to hear it, but I'm going to get a new message pad and write down all the messages from now on. Maybe get those little stick-em things and put notes on my forehead or something."

"Yeah, that would work. So, I guess it's a little late for you to come down here tonight."

"Tonight?!? Are you kidding?!? Tonight's a total disaster. Tracey just ran over the wife's rosebushes, and I haven't even gotten to any of the chores that I've been meaning to do, plus it's my turn to go to the grocery store and do the laundry, and I'm starting to memorize lines for the big part I'm going to have in *Lend Me a Tenor* at the Copper Works this summer. That's a really terrific comedy. I mean, you talk about a good play, that's a good play."

"Right. So, George, are you interested in being in my play about the barbershop or not?"

"Oh, sure I'm interested. If you're going to split the box like you said."

"Absolutely—four ways."

"And you're going to pack the place for—how many performances?"

Jimmy patiently played out the numbers and dates again for George and held his breath.

George did some more mental arithmetic and said, "Say, I could make somewhere in the neighborhood of $700. For two shows, right?"

"Right."

"Hey, count me in."

"Good, so when can you make rehearsals? What nights are good for you?"

"Any night is good for me. Except tonight. Tonight is no good for me. Obviously. And Thursdays are out, and, of course, weekends are a total zoo around here, but any night is good for me. Except Mondays and Tuesdays."

"How about next Wednesday?" Jimmy said, trying to keep his hopes afloat.

Allan Q. Hovington ran over to Jimmy and waved his hand in Jimmy's face.

Jimmy put his hand over the phone and said, "What?"

"Next Wednesday is bad for me," Allan said. "I'm picking up a load of furniture at an estate sale in Kalamazoo next Wednesday afternoon, and there's no way I'm going to be back in time for a rehearsal."

"What about you, Justin?" Jimmy said.

Justin shrugged and said he thought he remembered his mother saying something about a trip to Chicago to see her sister or something. But he wasn't sure.

Jimmy looked to Saint Genesius for an answer, but of course received none since the good saint wasn't taking calls from lowly Protestants. Much less lapsed Protestants who had only gone to seminary to avoid the draft.

In the ensuing silence, Jimmy listened to the beat of his own heart, and it told him to get the hell out of the Fennell and never come back.

But the flickering bug of fame countered with a foolhardy: Stay the course, and all will be well, and ye shall have riches and baubles exceeding all expectations. Yada yada yada yada. World without end, Amen.

Justin Ward and Allan Q. Hovington watched in wonder as the quivering playwright had a series of not-so-internal dialogues with himself.

"You okay?" Allan said, waving his hand in front of Jimmy's face.

Jimmy gulped oxygen and nodded. "Just having a little gaseous cranial episode is all. Nothing to worry about. The medicine should kick in any minute now. There. I'm fine. Okay. How about two weeks from tonight. Can you both make it two weeks from tonight?"

Allan Q. Hovington allowed as how he could unless something pressing came up, and Justin Ward just nodded.

Jimmy uncovered the phone and said: "George, how about two weeks from tonight? Allan and Justin can make it, and . . ."

"Hey, any time is good for me."

"Good. But specifically I'm talking about two weeks from tonight. That'll be a Wednesday, George. A Wednesday at 7:30 here at the Fennell."

"Yeah, I'm looking at our calendar here by the phone. Yeah, it's free as far as I can tell, but, boy, does the wife have a bunch of junk tacked to this thing. It's a wonder it doesn't fall off the friggin' wall."

"Yeah, I can imagine. So we can expect you in two weeks?"

"Hey, have I ever let you down before? I'm the one who came out to your stupid audition with a 103-degree fever and didn't get the damn part. So don't lecture me about letting people down. Okay?"

Jimmy rolled his eyes and muttered, "Mea culpa, mea culpa, mea maxima culpa."

"What was that?"

"Nothing, George. Just talking to myself again."

"Yeah, well you'd better get that checked out. I know I would if I were you. You let something like that go, and next thing you know you'll be standing in some post office with an assault rifle in your hands switched to full auto."

"Sounds like you've been there, George."

"Hah hah. Let's just say I've been around the block a few times myself, and I know it's not such a good thing when you start talking to yourself out loud."

Jimmy noted the growing impatience of Allan Q. Hovington and Justin Ward and said, "I'll work on it, George. So, we'll see you here in two weeks at 7:30."

"Unless there's a cataclysmic earthquake or something. I'm marking it on our calendar as we speak—oh, darn, the whole thing fell off the wall. I've got to go . . ."

Thunk. Clunk. Buzzzz.

Jimmy cradled the phone and looked at the two actors who had managed to make it to the rehearsal. "Well," he said, "shall we read through the play as long as we're all here? I'll take the part of Mr. Babbington."

"Why don't you just play the part for keeps?" Allan said. "I mean, this George guy sounds like a complete flake. Can't even make the first rehearsal. In real theatres, that would be grounds for immediate dismissal."

"I know, but . . ."

"But what? You can act, can't you?"

"Yeah. In fact I was a drama major at Penn State and did a spot of acting in Chicago. Heck, I even had the lead in *Playboy of the Western World* at the Stonebridge." Jimmy chuckled at the memory. "God, how could I ever forget—this guy I knew from my seminary days and his wife and daughter came barging in during the third act and started interacting with me up on the stage. It was one of the low points of my brilliant stage career, but we muddled through it somehow."

"See, you're a real actor. So you should take the part. Write, direct and act. There's a long tradition of it in the theatre."

"I know, but I'm afraid my brain capacity has been seriously impaired by all the drugs and alcohol—don't listen to that part, Justin."

Justin shrugged. "I think people who do drugs and alcohol are retarded."

"Good," Jimmy said. "Take it from a battle-scarred veteran — you're better off without that stuff. Anyway, Allan, I think I've lost the ability to memorize parts. It's been so long, and I just don't think I could do it any more."

"Well, let's just do a reading and see how you feel afterwards."

They read through *The Last Haircut*, and Jimmy, in spite of himself, felt like he could do a hell of job playing Mr. Babbington. A character of his own creation and dialogue of his own design.

"Well?" Allan Q. Hovington said. "You sounded pretty professional to me for somebody who's supposedly gotten rusty. I think you should take the part and forget this George guy. Don't you agree, Justin?"

Justin Ward just shrugged. What did he know? What did he care? He was going to be a happy camper just so long as his mother bought him a car when he was 16. Everything else that happened in the world was just background noise.

"Well, I'll think about it. If George flakes out in two weeks, I'll take the part. How's that?"

"If I were you," Allan said, "I'd fire George right now and take the part. You're a natural."

"You think so?"

"I know so."

"Well, we'll see in two weeks."

What they saw in two weeks was an actual appearance by George Streznik. He was a full 45 minutes late, mind you, but he did motor all the way down from Allegan and, by golly, did a creditable reading of Mr. Babbington.

And, Jimmy thought watching from the front row, he really looks the part. I mean, the guy's 43 going on 67. He's perfect: broken-down, spindly, losing his hair, God, we'll hardly need any make-up. Plus, he wears the kind of ratty old clothes that Mr. Babbington would wear.

When the cast completed the reading, Jimmy pronounced himself pleased and said he was going to have the programs printed on the morrow.

Allan Q. Hovington took Jimmy aside and said, "Do you think that's such a good idea?"

"Why not?"

Allan Q. Hovington arched his eyebrows at George Streznik who was dazzling young Justin with his tales of theatrical derring-do.

"He'll be fine, Allan," Jimmy whispered.

"All right," Allan said, "but don't say I didn't warn you."

Jimmy should have listened to Allan's warning, because George Streznik flaked out the following week. After, of course, Jimmy had shelled out some serious cash (that he and Joyce didn't have) for the programs and flyers.

When Jimmy phoned George to inquire as to his whereabouts, George slapped his forehead and said, "You know, I've really got to get those stick-ems for my forehead. Must be another brain fart. God, I've been having a lot of them lately. I know you told me last week we were having rehearsal tonight, and I know I wrote it down somewhere but — oh, here it is on the calendar — oh oh . . ."

Thunk, clunk, buzz.

Jimmy hit the switchhook and then the redial.

George Streznik answered on the first ring. "That you?"

"Yeah. You have a little accident?"

"Yeah, it's the wife's dumb calendar. I told her if she didn't stop tacking stuff to it, it was going to fall off the friggin' wall, and guess what — it fell off the friggin' wall. Again. Didn't this happen before when I was talking to you?"

"Yeah." Jimmy inhaled and slowly exhaled. Then he added: "George?"

"What?"

"Are you sure you want to be in this play?"

"Absolutely. You think I'm going to pass up a chance to make $800."

"Well, more like $700 if all goes well."

"I thought you said $800."

"No, I said $700, and that's provided I fill the house for both performances."

"What, now you think you won't fill the house? Before you about gave me a guarantee in writing that you'd fill the house both performances, and I'd make $800 as my share. I've already put it in our budget."

Jimmy wondered if life was worth living and death worth dying for. There being no apparent answers, he said, "How about next week, George? Can you be here next Wednesday?"

"Absolutely. And I would have been there tonight if the wife didn't insist on tacking all this junk to the calendar. How she thinks this thing is going to stay on the wall with all that junk tacked to it is beyond me. What is with women and the laws of physics? Huh?"

"I don't know — I think Sally Ride got it all figured out pretty well."

"Who?"

"The woman astronaut."

"Oh. Yeah, I should know that shouldn't I?"

"Not really. So, can you be here next Wednesday?"

"Sure, no problem. In fact, I'm going to write it on my hand, and then I'm going to get a new calendar tomorrow and put it on this wall, and the first thing I'm going to write on the new calendar is the rehearsal for your play."

"Good. By the way, have you started memorizing your lines? We're getting into April and . . ."

"No problem. You can count on me, Jack."

"The name's Jimmy."

"That's what I said — didn't I?"

"Whatever. So, we'll see you next Wednesday — same time, same place."

"You can count on me, Jerry."

What Jimmy counted the following Wednesday were minutes as they awaited the arrival of George Streznik.

"Can him," Allan said. "The guy's a flake. Just do what I said in the first place, and take the part yourself. It's the only way you're going to get this play up."

"Allan, I'm tempted, but I really don't think I can memorize that many lines any more. My brain just doesn't work that way. If he doesn't show up tonight, I'm thinking of just pulling the plug on the whole thing. I mean look at this place — nobody has bothered to do a lick of painting since the great and wonderful Melpomene Group came out, and Jeffrey Cantwell doesn't seem to be coming up with any lights for the stage. Despite all his lofty pronouncements."

"This is theatre," Allan said. "What do you expect?"

"Lights. Reliable actors. I don't know—I guess I'm asking too much."

"Probably. Maybe you should find another theatre. One that's established."

"That would be nice." Jimmy looked at his watch—George Streznik was more than an hour late. The fame bug flickered briefly and told him to stay the course, but Jimmy had had enough abuse. "Let's bag it," he said.

"You mean . . ."

"I mean cancel the whole damn thing. There's no way this is going to fly. Not with less than two months before we open, and the lead can't even show up half the time let alone get off book, or even find his way of out his God-damn driveway."

"Somebody say something about my driveway?" It was George Streznik, and he was all set to rehearse. But first, he had to explain that his tardiness was due to the fact he had spontaneously decided to blacktop his driveway that evening. "I'm afraid I got that gunk all over your script," he said, displaying his gunk-splattered script. "So you're going to have to give me another one."

Jimmy nodded grimly, and they proceeded.

Allan Q. Hovington and Justin Ward were completely off book, but George Streznik was not.

Never mind.

The show must go on.

Sure.

Right.

Why not?

Jimmy wanted to stay until George made some real progress, but Allan had a consignment of furniture to move in the morning, and it was a school night for Justin, and George said Jimmy could just come to his house and run lines with him until he got it.

Jimmy foolishly took George up on his offer and that Saturday afternoon was sucked into the malfunctions of the failing Streznik family.

It's too painful to recount in detail, but the low point came when some Jehovah's Witnesses appeared at the door, and instead of sending them on their holy path, George invited them in for a lively discussion complete with cookies and milk. Said discussion lasted for a full 45 minutes, and then George's wife came home sick from work, and Tracey wanted some lemonade before she went out to crash into the garage, and a teen-age son by a previous marriage — whose marriage it was not entirely clear — arrived with a bag of dirty laundry, and the phone rang incessantly and George just had to show Jimmy the new calendar he had tacked to the kitchen wall by the phone, and, sick as she was, George's wife suddenly decided to bake a peach pie, and, of course, George had to help her, and finally . . .

Jimmy ran screaming from the Streznik house in Allegan and told Joyce when he got home that he was through with theatre for all time. Except that there was a piece of junk mail from Kalamazoo awaiting him that changed his life.

Chapter Twenty-Six

Jimmy was so excited by the piece of junk mail from Kalamazoo he had to sit down at his desk to take it all in.

Joyce hovered behind him, clucking: "Throw it away, Jimmy. Throw it away before it's too late."

Jimmy shook his head in sharp disagreement and stared in wonder at the cheaply reproduced flyer from the Performance Initiative Theatre, or PIT, in Kalamazoo, Michigan. It advertised a "performance of our highly acclaimed original play, *Jack,* to benefit the resident company" on the morrow at 7 p.m. and promised plenty of good seating for $7. "Two dollars more at the door."

But that wasn't what really caught Jimmy's eye and made his heart thump.

No, it was the scrawled message next to the label bearing his name and address: "Got your play—hope to read soon."

"Got your play—hope to read soon" and nothing more.

But that was enough to palpitate the perpetual playwright's pituitary. Or some such thing. The result was a quickening of bodily functions.

Jimmy raced to the bathroom.

"What are you doing?"

"Taking a dump," Jimmy said, lighting a jasmine incense stick to hide the odor. "What does it look like?"

"If that's your reaction to that mailing, I'd say that's an omen from the gods to stay away from theatre entirely. In fact, this would be an excellent time to quit and get on with your life. I mean, isn't all this theatre stuff just a way of deferring your grief over the commercial failure of the Dunery Press?"

"Joyce?"

"What?"

"Do you mind if I move my bowels in peace?"

"No, go right ahead. But I still think . . ."

"Joyce!!"

"I'm going."

Joyce went and so did Jimmy, and when he had completed his paperwork he went back to his desk and reached for his phone. But it rang before he could uncradle the modern communication device.

"Destiny," he happily called.

"Yeah, right," Joyce chirped from the kitchen where she was preparing a sumptuous feast.

Alas, it wasn't destiny. It, or should I say he, was one Larry German calling in a considerable panic about that night's program at the Fennell Art Center and Theatre, aka: FAGAT.

"I thought everything was all set for tonight," Jimmy said. "That was certainly the impression I had this morning at the board meeting. In fact, I was planning to call you about my play in June because . . ."

"Laura Downs got a big catering job and can't emcee tonight," Larry said. "And nobody's cleaned up the place since you and Jeffrey left all that painting stuff everywhere, and nobody's gotten the flyers out, and the Merry Mood Makers are demanding $750 whether we fill the joint or not, and I'm not so sure we're gonna get anybody out because the weather's turned kind of crappy, and Dominick McGrath said he'd do all this marketing stuff, but I don't think he's done a thing because I sure haven't seen anything in the papers or heard anything on the radio. Have you?"

"No, but . . ."

"What are you doing right now?"

"Getting ready to eat dinner and then . . ."

"You've got to get over here and clean this place up. And you've got to be emcee. Only you can emcee the way you can emcee. I mean, you were so good at that Polish piano thing."

"He was from Lithuania, Larry."

"Yeah, one of them countries. I can never keep 'em straight. And what's the point? You just learn the name of one, and they go and change it on you. I was trying to help one of my kids with his geography homework the other night, and I tell you — nothing's the same as when we were kids. I remember the map we had in Mrs. Harrington's class. Big old thing with colors — red for the British Empire. God, half the world was red then. But not anymore. Poor Brits don't run anything anymore. Not even Hong Kong."

"They still govern Hong Kong, Larry, but they're giving it up in 1997."

"They are? Boy, that's the thing I like about you, Jack, you're so smart."

"Thanks, well, look, Joyce and I were kind of planning to just — well, you know."

"No time for nooky when the future of the Fennell is on the line, Jack."

"Larry, my name is Jimmy, and why don't you be emcee? You did a terrific job at the open house and . . ."

"I can't because the wife bought tickets to that concert out at the college."

"Ah, so . . ."

"It's all your shoulders, Jack. I mean, Jimmy."

"But what about Jeffrey Cantwell, or Dominick McGrath, or Harriett . . ."

"I've been on the phone all day, Jimmy. It's up to you. Bev's gonna be there to handle the tickets and all that, but it's up to you to get the place cleaned up and to emcee. Tell me you're not going to let us down. Please."

Jimmy sighed and didn't know what to say.

So Larry German said it for him: "Put on your Sunday-go-to-meetin' clothes and get over there as fast as you can. Bye. Click."

Jimmy stared at the phone until the obnoxious message came on about hanging up and dialing again.

So he did the modern equivalent of hanging up and dialed the number on the cheap flyer and got a long recorded message in a modulated man's voice about showtimes, ticket prices, coming attractions, and the general wonderfulness of the Performance Initiative Theatre, or PIT. While he was waiting for the beep, Jimmy scanned the flyer and saw that *Jack* was a two-act play about the life and times of America's 35th President, John F. Kennedy. There was even a quote from one of America's newspapers, the estimable KALAMAZOO GAZETTE, proclaiming that "Donald C. Adams as Kennedy is a pro through and through. His performance is memorable."

"Hot damn," Jimmy muttered at the beep. "Sign me up. Er, excuse me, my name is Jim Clarke and I'd like — uh, hold on a second . . ." he covered the mouthpiece and called, "Joyce, you want to go to a play in Kalamazoo tomorrow night at this PIT place? It's about Kennedy."

"You go."

"Are you sure?"

"Positive. Now keep it down over there — I'm trying to fix dinner."

"Right." Jimmy uncovered the mouthpiece and added: "Uh, just one ticket for tomorrow night's performance of *Jack*. One adult that is. I'm really looking forward to it because Kennedy was one of my heroes when I was a kid. I even built a model of PT-109. So, ah, oh yeah, I'm the playwright who . . ."

The tape ran out.

Jimmy shrugged. Probably an omen, he thought, but he was damned if he was going to tell Joyce. Not when she was all for him quitting theatre entirely and what — go out and get a job selling roofing products? Whole-term life insurance?

"So," Joyce said, looking up from the turkey carcass she was eviscerating, "you're going to that play about Kennedy in Kalamazoo tomorrow?"

"Yeah," Jimmy said, sauntering into the kitchen. "I figure I'd check it out. This is the theatre that Allan Hovington told me about a while back. Said they were really dedicated to producing work by regional playwrights, and, hey, I'm a regional playwright if ever there was one. Plus, they have lights and actors. I mean they're an operating theatre. No more having to produce and direct my own plays. No more jerks like George Streznik. No more Fennell."

"But what about tonight? I heard you promise Larry German that you'd basically go over there and do everything."

"Did I?"

"Sounded to me like you did."

"Yeah, I guess I did. But I'd rather stay here and have nooky with you." Jimmy nuzzled up to his wife from behind.

She pushed him away and said, "Jimmy, if you promised Larry you'd go over there and take care of tonight's concert, or whatever it is, then you'd better do it. Don't you think?"

"Yeah," Jimmy said, falling back against the counter. He sighed.

Joyce turned from her tortured turkey and said, "Are you all right?"

"Yeah, I'm fine."

"You don't look fine."

"I am, Joyce. It's just—well, you know."

"I know."

Now it was Joyce's turn to sigh. She turned back to her turkey and cried.

"What's wrong, Joyce?"

Joyce sobbed so hard her shoulders shook.

Jimmy rushed to her and folded her in a husbandly embrace, carefully offering a warm shoulder to cry on.

"I just wish we could have made it publishing our fiction," Joyce said. "I just wish the Dunery Press had been a commercial success."

"We tried our best, Joyce. God knows—we sure did that. I mean we even went to ABA in Las Vegas of all places and . . ."

"Enough!"

"You're right. It's too painful. And you're right—this theatre business is my way of deferring my grief over the press. I know it's insane. I know I should have been happy with *No Dice* and just left it at that."

Joyce nodded on Jimmy's shoulder as if to say, wasn't that enough suffering for one lifetime?

"All the crap I put up with trying to get that thing produced should have been enough suffering for one lifetime," Jimmy said, reading his wife's mind.

"Touché."

They kissed, and Jimmy wiped the tears from Joyce's cheeks with his sleeve. How romantic.

But it was.

Because these two lost and lonely artists had one another in the vast wilderness of the American mass-entertainment waste-dump. They were lucky to have found one another, and they knew it, which is why they clung all the more tenaciously to one another and worried when the other went off on some fame quest.

Joyce swallowed and said, "Why don't you go and get dressed and I'll finish getting dinner ready? Then you can eat and be on your way."

"Joyce?"

"What?"

"I don't suppose you'd like to . . ."

"Jimmy, that open house was my limit at the Fennell. Okay?"

"I hear you. But you can't blame me for trying."

"No, I sure can't."

Jimmy dressed; Joyce finished making dinner; they ate, and Jimmy dashed off to the Fennell Art Center and Theatre for what proved to be his final performance at FAGAT.

For starters, he got to clean up the absolute mess he and Jeffrey Cantwell had left, all the while wearing his Sunday-go-to-meeting clothes. Ever try to fold up paint-spattered plastic in your best duds?

Ain't easy, is it?

But Jimmy managed, and he also managed somehow to stash every last bit of paint stuff in the dank, dripping dressing room beneath the stage. The very same dressing room that the Melpomene Group was no doubt planning to use during its gala 12-week run of *A Midsummer Night's Dream* as part of Jeffrey Cantwell's dazzling "Midsummer at the Fennell" festival of fun, frolic, and froth.

Jimmy then took to his trusty broom with a vengeance and had the whole house swept by the time Big Bev Mantinkus rumbled in to sell tickets and complain about the weather. The latter, of course, was lousy because it was the cruelest month.

"God," Big Bev said, shedding her things in a dripping pile, "it's miserable out there! I hate this rain. All we ever get is rain. Rain, rain, rain, rain. God, it's never going to end. And if it doesn't end I just . . . " Big Bev paused for dramatic effect, and added, "I just don't know if I can go on."

Jimmy shrugged and said, "Say, I don't suppose you'd mind giving me a hand dusting down all these seats?"

Big Bev made a big face and had a big fret. "I can't do that. I have a bad back. All that bending would just kill my back. Do you have any idea what it's like raising a six-year-old boy?"

"Well, as a former six-year-old boy, I can . . ."

"Typical male chauvinist. You don't have a clue about what it's like to be a mother or a woman in this male-dominated patriarchy, do you?"

"Isn't that redundant, Bev?"

"What?"

"Male-dominated patriarchy. I mean . . ."

"Oh, go dust your seats. And sweep this place. God, look how filthy it is, and they'll all be here any minute, and if it's not clean and spotless this is going to be a total disaster, and if we don't have a community cultural center, I don't know how we're going to keep the arts alive, and this kind of thing is happening all across the country, because people just don't care any more, and if people just don't care any more, then how are we going to give our children an enriching and enlightening environment in which to grow and become whatever and whomever they want to be. Huh? Answer me that?"

"I don't have an answer, Bev, except that I already swept the place before you arrived."

"Well, sweep it again." Big Bev threw up her big hands and said, "Men! God, you're all so worthless. It's a wonder any of you get out of bed in the morning."

Jimmy was about to say something regretful but utterly therapeutic when a walking penis burst into the Fennell and demanded to speak to "whoever the hell's in charge around here."

Actually, he wasn't a walking penis, but with his utterly bald and waxed pate and light-brown turtleneck, the man looked like a walking penis. And he certainly acted like one.

"She's in charge," Jimmy said. "She's the secretary of the board." Big Bev sputtered but it did the poor fat girl no good.

The walking penis was all over her with bitter recriminations about the utter failure on the Fennell's part to publicize the appearance of Michigan's favorite big band, the Merry Mood Makers of Mattawan. The walking penis, whose name was Mac Douglas, was the band's road manager. More or less. He also sold a little real estate for his sister and hit the Indian casinos up north every chance he got. And he did a spot of bad acting himself. But why go into all that when this is just a throwaway character shamelessly introduced to move the plot right along to its inevitable conclusion? Which is coming soon.

Well, sort of soon.

But stay the course, and ye shall not thirst for enlightenment. Or words to that effect.

"Well," Mr. Mac "Penis Head" Douglas said to Big Bev, "since you're in charge, I want to tell you what a lousy job you people have done of publicizing this concert tonight. I haven't seen anything in the paper or heard anything on the radio. What are you people doing here — shouting out the front door for people to come on down and listen to the best big band in Michigan? Huh? Answer me that?"

Jimmy just shrugged and went to dust the seats.

When he finished, Big Bev was still trying to respond to a still fuming Mr. Mac "Penis Head" Douglas.

But no matter, because the first and only trickle of patrons was dripping into the Fennell Art Center and Theatre, aka: FAGAT.

Along with the 12 members of the Merry Mood Makers from Mattawan, Michigan. A snappier bunch you've never seen, believe me. Formed for the express purpose of preserving the marvelously mellow music of the 1930's and 1940's, the Merry Mood Makers were mostly declining World War II veterans, but their leader was a flinty young high school band director and music teacher who always made sure the band made money.

Which is why he had retained the services of Mr. Mac "Penis Head" Douglas, and why he was now buttonholing Big Bev and demanding: "We'd better get our $750. Do you hear me? The contract we signed with Laura Downs clearly stipulated that we would be paid $750 regardless of the turn-out." The band leader looked at the paltry turn-out and added, "Looks like you did a damn poor job of publicizing this. Especially after that Downs woman promised us a full house."

Big Bev sputtered, and Jimmy showed the Merry Mood Makers to the stage where they grumbled incessantly about the bad acoustics, the cold, the damp, and darn near everything they could think of. They were right to complain, of course, because the Fennell was a dank, dripping wreck of a place with inadequate lighting, wretched acoustics, and a stage on the verge of physical collapse.

But Jimmy didn't want any part of it.

He had heard enough "everything was better in the good old days" for one lifetime, and went off to make himself useful with his trusty broom.

After much fussing and fuming, the Merry Mood Makers signaled that they were ready to begin their concert for the 26 brave souls who had come out on a miserable April night and shelled out $10 to shiver and shake in the Fennell Art Center and Theatre, aka: FAGAT.

Mr. Mac "Penis Head" Douglas stomped over to Jimmy and said, "Get up there and introduce them. Your friend over there said you're the emcee, so get up there and be the emcee."

"Eat shit and die, dick head," Jimmy muttered.

"What'd you say?"

"I said eat sherry and pie with thick bread."

"No, you didn't."

"Yes, I did."

Mr. Mac "Penis Head" Douglas glowered at the upstart in the wardrobe by Monsieur Goodwill.

Jimmy gave his winningest smile back. He was already out of this dreadful theatre, but he figured he might as well make the most fun of his final moments. Jimmy paused for dramatic effect and said: "Anything special you want me to say about this stellar group?"

Mr. Mac "Penis Head" Douglas thrust a blue flyer into Jimmy's hand and snapped: "Just read this. That is, if you can read."

"I'll do my best, skipper."

Jimmy hopped up on the stage before the dick head could respond and said: "Good evening, ladies and gentlemen, and welcome to the Fennell Art Center and Theatre. Also known as FAGAT. Thank you for coming out on a truly wretched night, but as T.S. Elliot once wrote: 'April is the cruelest month.' Amen to that, Brother Elliot. Anyway, you didn't come out here tonight and shell out ten bucks to listen to me blither about T.S. Elliot.

"No, you came to put yourselves in a merry mood by journeying back to those golden good old days when everything was better. Even the sun shone brighter then, and kids sure minded their parents, and a nickel would buy you enough candy for a week. But enough of this nattering nostalgia, and on with the show."

Jimmy donned his red-rimmed reading glasses and unfolded the blue flyer. "Ladies and gentlemen, we are particularly proud to present Michigan's favorite big band, the Merry Mood Makers, who have come all the way from Mattawan to put you in the mood. The

Merry Mood Makers are a 12-member band with a violinist. They formed for the purpose of preserving the golden music of the '30's and '40's. The band members hail mainly from Mattawan, but some are from Kalamazoo, Paw Paw and points in-between. Two of the members arrange all the music. The band is directed by Mr. Gary Washburne, who also directs the marching band at Mattawan High School. Ladies and gentlemen, relax, and journey back with me to those golden days before I was born. By the way, dancing is optional but encouraged."

The 26 audience members, mostly old ducks with bad hearing, clapped feebly, and then Mr. Gary Washburne got up and led the Merry Mood Makers into a rousing rendition of Glenn Miller's immortal *In the Mood.*

Jimmy was in the mood for puking, because he had grown up listening to his father play that very song over and over and over and over again for his drunken pals in the living room of the big, brick house at 322 Forest Drive in Wynnwood, Pa.

Jimmy backed away into the darkness and was making for the exit when Big Bev barged into him.

"Come on," she said, "we've got to get out there and dance."

"What?!?"

"Jim, we've got to get out there and dance. If we don't get out there and dance, nobody else is going to get out there and dance, and then this is going to be a great, big failure, and the Fennell won't be here to be a beacon of enlightenment and entertainment for generations to come."

"You mean like your kids?"

Big Bev responded by shoving Jimmy toward the stage.

She was a big gal and got the jump on Jimmy, but the very sound of *In the Mood* was absolute anathema, so he resisted with all his might and finally got free of the fulsome female.

He was out the door and in his car and heading home before he blinked again.

"That's it," he said, gripping the steering wheel, "that's fucking it."

A deer dashed into his headlights, and he deftly avoided it.

Jimmy took a deep breath and remembered the last time that happened. He had turned around and gone back to the Fennell.

This time he continued homeward as an angel.

Chapter Twenty-Seven

Jimmy phoned Larry German first thing Sunday morning and said: "Larry, I'm afraid I have some bad news for you."

"You have some bad news for me?" Larry said, chewing on a biscuit. "Bev just called and said we lost a bundle last night. She had to pay the band $750 and we only took in $260 at the door which means we're in the hole. Big time. And she said you took off leaving her all alone. She was the only one there, Jack. I thought you were going to take care of things for us, Jack. What happened? Huh? How come you let us down, Jack?"

Jimmy exhaled and pressed his forehead. "Maybe my chakras are blocked," he thought aloud.

"What?"

"Nothing."

"You're talkin' to yourself again, aren't you, Jack?"

"Larry, my name is Jimmy. Jimmy Clarke. And the bad news I have is that I'm not going to do my play in June, and I'm resigning from the board."

"But you can't cancel your play and resign from the board. Actually you resigned from the board once already, but you came back, but anyway, we need your little play. It's going to be a big part of the 'Midnight Madness at the Fennell' or whatever Jeffrey's calling it. Besides, what will people think if we go around canceling stuff our first year in operation? The whole world's watching us, Jack—I mean, Jim."

"I'm sure they are, Larry, but I've got to cancel the play because one of my actors is turning out to be unreliable and you can't . . ."

"What's to acting? I could never figure out the big deal. I mean you just get up there and say something somebody else wrote. What's the big deal about that? Of course, I hate to get up in front of people. But once I get started, it's not too bad. You sort of forget all those people are out there. Or if you make them laugh or something, well, hey, it doesn't get better than that, does it, uh, Jim?"

"No, Larry, it sure doesn't but, look, I've really got to cancel this play, and if I wait any longer it'll only be worse, and this is the best time, because there's nothing worse than going through with rehearsals only to find that a third of your cast isn't off book, and isn't going to get off book, and . . ."

"What's all this talk about books? I thought you were doing a play?"

"Larry?"

"What?"

"I'm serious. I'm canceling the play, and I'm resigning from the board."

Larry finished chewing his biscuit and washed it down with a big gulp of whole milk. Then, while the whole glutinous mess was sliding down his throat he came up with a somber: "I'm really disappointed in you, Jim. Here, I thought you might be somebody who could really help get the Fennell off the ground, and now you're turning out to be just another quitter. I'm really disappointed, but you have to do your own thing, right?"

"Right."

Jimmy looked into the living room at Joyce who was loudly suggesting: "Tell that stupid hillbilly that you're cutting your losers and running with your winners."

Jimmy looked at the phone and pictured Larry on his end with a disapproving look on his face and milk on his chin.

"What was that?" Larry said, a disapproving look on his face and milk on his chin. "I thought I heard your wife say something in the background."

"Nothing, Larry. Look, I'm really sorry, but this is just something I have to do."

"Like I said, you do what you gotta do, but I sure know a lot of people who are going to feel let down, Jim. I know I am, and I know a whole lot of other people are, too. But if you've got something better to do, then, hey, who am I to stop you? Huh?"

"Right. Well, I'll be talking to you, Larry."

"Sure, my door's always open. I'm not a quitter. I'm not giving up just because the going got a little tough. But you do what you've got to do."

"Right."

They clicked off, and Jimmy sighed so big and so wide, the Dunery danced on the dunes.

"Jimmy," Joyce called the from the living room, "it's not the end of the world. If anything, it's a new beginning. Now you'll be in charge of your own destiny again. You won't be squandering all your time and energy on that stupid theatre."

"But, Joyce, how is it going to survive without me?"

"How did the sun come up this morning without you?"

"You really think I should quit all this theatre business all together, don't you?"

"No. You enjoy it. Do what you enjoy. Who knows, maybe this theatre in Kalamazoo might be what you're looking for." Joyce put her hand over her mouth and muttered, "But then maybe the Pope will join the Hare Krishna."

"What was that?"

"Nothing."

"I heard that."

"Just make your other calls so I can read in peace."

Jimmy called Justin Ward, Allan Q. Hovington, and George Streznik in quick succession.

Justin Ward could have cared less, or if he cared, he certainly didn't show it.

"No problem, man," he said, "I probably wasn't going to have time anyway what with all these things my mother's planning and our big trip and all."

Allan Q. Hovington was a bit more perturbed.

"You know," he said, "this is going to ruin your reputation in theatre."

"You think so?"

"Well, let's just say a lot of people are really going to be disappointed in you, Jim."

"Really?"

"Really. All I know is if I were you, I'd just fire that George character and take the part myself. You were perfect when you read it — much better than George. I don't know what your big problem is. You were a drama major in college. You've worked in Chicago theatre. What's the big deal?"

Jimmy sighed and almost signed on, but something made him say no. Something that knew a disaster when it saw one. Something that saw no audience, no lights, and a galloping case of stage fright to boot.

"There's no big deal, Allan. It's just that I've lost the touch. I've crossed over — I'm not an actor anymore; I'm a playwright."

"Athol Fugard acts in his own plays. Hell, he writes, directs, *and* acts in his own plays."

"Yeah, but I'm not Athol Fugard."

"No, you sure aren't. Well, you're letting a lot of people down, but it's your decision. I certainly don't understand it, but it's your decision."

"Yes, Allan, it's my decision. I'm really sorry."

"So am I. For you. You've just flushed any chance of being a successful playwright around here down the toilet."

"Right. Well, maybe we can get together sometime and . . ."

"I don't think so. Good-bye."

"Good-bye."

Jimmy thumbed the switchhook and then dialed George Streznik's number in Allegan.

He got Tracey, of course, and went through the usual schtick about bicycling in the driveway and finally got the little cupcake to go fetch her daddy.

Daddy was none too happy when he got the news that the play was off.

"Are you mental or something?" he said.

"I beg your pardon."

"Maybe you need psychiatric care. You ever consider that?"

"George, I'm not mental and I don't need psychiatric care. I just don't feel that we're going to have this play up and running by opening night."

"What are you talking about? We're doing fine. And you should see how things go at the Copper Works. Right down to the wire every time. Nobody seems to get their lines memorized until dress rehearsal, and half of them don't even have their lines by then, but it all comes together. It always does. And it will with this play. You'll see."

"No, George, I won't see, because I'm canceling it. I'm faxing a press release to that effect to the local papers after I get off the phone with you."

"You really are mental, aren't you? Just because I was a few
minutes late for one silly rehearsal you think things aren't going to
work out. Boy, do you ever have a thin skin. Maybe you should go
into something safe like working at the sewage treatment plant.
You'd always know what to expect every day—big piles of shit. Like
your play. Well, you can just go fuck yourself for all I'm concerned,
because as far as I'm concerned, you're finished as a playwright in
these parts. I'm spreading the word to everybody who's anybody in
theatre around here to avoid you and your plays like the plague.
Have a wretched life, asshole."

Jimmy got George's click in his ear and grimaced.

He gently cradled his phone and resolutely wrote the press
release informing the world that he was canceling his play at the
Fennell Art Center and Theatre, aka: FAGAT.

"Mind if I print?" he said, when he was finished keystroking his
opus into his computer.

Joyce marked her page, closed her book and went to her
husband's side. "This is awful for you, isn't it?"

Jimmy shrugged and wished he had been taught to cry when he
was a little boy.

Joyce put her arm around his shoulder and said, "It's too bad you
men aren't allowed to cry, because this would be a great time for a
good cry."

Jimmy nodded and tried to have a good cry, but the tears just
wouldn't come. It made him think of those times in navy boot camp
when he tried to squeeze out a bowel movement with some chief
petty officer screaming for his company to "fall out on the grinder."

"Grinder? What are you talking about, Jimmy?"

Jimmy blinked at his wife. "Did I say something?"

"Yes. You said something about falling out on the grinder. What
in God's name is a grinder?"

Jimmy laughed and hit the print command on his computer. His
two-line press release concerning the cancellation of *The Last
Haircut* pinned out of his Epson FX-185.

"Well, tell me. Don't just sit there laughing. Tell me what a
grinder is."

Jimmy tore the press release out of the printer and headed for
the fax machine in Joyce's writing booth.

"A grinder," he said, faxing, "is basically a parking lot with no cars in it. At least that's the way I remember it."

"What?"

"It was this big expanse of asphalt outside our barracks in boot camp at Great Lakes. After they'd awaken you for the day's activities with a melodious: 'Drop your cocks, and grab your socks, and hit the deck,' they'd have you fall out on the grinder for inspection. And then we'd all march off to the chow hall in a blizzard. Or some such thing."

"I still don't follow you."

"It's a guy thing. Of course, there probably are a hell of a lot of women who know what falling out on the grinder is all about because there are lots of women in the navy now. Or so I hear."

Jimmy watched the press release feed into the fax machine and bit his lip.

Joyce put her hand on his shoulder. "Maybe this theatre in Kalamazoo will be the one."

"I sure hope so. At least they have lights and actors who learn their parts and come to rehearsals. At least I hope they do. But then I'll find out tonight. Are you sure you don't want to come?"

Joyce was tempted, but then she said, "How about you scout it out, and if you like it, I'll come after you."

"Really?"

"Really. I've been kind of thinking of trying a play."

"You have?"

"Yeah. Jimmy, you must realize by now that I watch everything you do like a hawk. And if it looks like fun, then inevitably I jump in and join you."

"You mean you might take up running?"

"There are limits."

"Oh, but, Joyce, you'd be a natural. I've seen you run — you run like a gazelle."

"You mean a gazellia."

"Gazellia?"

"Gazellias are girl gazelles."

"Oh, right. Well, anyway, I long for the day when you join me out on the running trails."

"Well, long on, because I don't want to shred my knees. Every time I've ever tried to take up running, I've shredded my knees."

"That's because you've done too much too soon. You have to ease into it gradually. Almost all walking at first, and then you phase in the running until you're able to run for 45 minutes at a crack."

"I'll never be able to run for 45 minutes. Never."

Jimmy just looked at Joyce with those sparkling blue eyes of his.

"Jimmy!"

"What?"

"Don't you give me that look."

"What look?"

"The one you're giving me now. The same one you gave me when you told me I should write novels."

"Yeah, and look what happened when you finally saw the wisdom of my advice. Your fingers can't type fast enough to keep up with all the great novels that come out of you."

"They're really novellas. Or novelettes."

"Call 'em what you will, Joyce, but they're great. You're awesome, and you'll be an awesome runner when you finally wake up and realize how right I really am."

"I don't want to shred my knees. I'll stick to walking. It gives me all the exercise I need."

Jimmy just nodded. Then he went for a run just to show his wife how right he really was.

What he showed himself was that he needed to lose a good 20 to 30 pounds. His knees ached and his feet creaked from the extra tonnage he was carrying, and he vaguely remembered an orthopedic surgeon he had consulted in Chicago telling him that he shouldn't run unless he got his weight below 200.

"It can't be much above 200," Jimmy said to the trees. But then he couldn't remember the last time he had stepped on the scale because he had basically given up stepping on the scale for Lent, Advent, Epiphany, Septuagesima, Sexagesima, Easter, and Trinity. Not to mention the Purification, the Annunciation, and the Conversion of St. Paul.

"Maybe 205—210 tops," Jimmy said to a stout beech. "Anyway, stout is good—right? I mean you wouldn't have been standing there all these years if you weren't stout, and I'm a man of substance with a large frame and . . ."

Actually, Jimmy knew from a previous experience with Diet Center that he was not possessed of a large frame, but, in fact, was medium-framed and should weigh no more than 200. One doctor even had the temerity to suggest he shouldn't see the dark side of 190 again.

"But that was in an earlier life," Jimmy remarked to a maple. "I'm middle-aged now, and I'm entitled to a middle-age spread."

Still, there were those occasional chest pains in the middle of the night, and he didn't have to venture far to hear about contemporaries who were falling to cardiovascular disease and getting their 40-something chests cracked with alarming regularity.

Jimmy shrugged and told an oak that he had quit smoking and could lay off the designer beers, pretzels, pizza, and fudge-coated graham crackers any time he pleased.

"Any time," he vowed aloud. "You hear me — any time."

The trees waved their branches in silent assent, and Jimmy pushed himself an extra mile and paid for it by contracting a painful case of the dreaded "runner's knee," or chondromalacia. It sounded disastrous, but it essentially was an irritation of his left kneecap caused by, you guessed it — the pounding by all those extra pounds Jimmy was carrying on his medium frame.

He winced as the old familiar pain in his kneecap shot up his leg and had to hobble home muttering to himself about how maybe, just maybe, he'd cut back a tad on the designer beers and pizza.

"But the fudge-covered graham crackers stay, because I need the carbohydrates," he told a passing red squirrel.

The squirrel knew better than to listen to such rubbish.

And Jimmy knew better than to limp up to the Dunery, so he affected a brisk, manly stride and locked his lips into a healthful grin.

"How was your run?" Joyce asked as her man made his way through the door.

"Great. Just great."

Joyce watched Jimmy grimace as he bent to remove his shoes and said, "You shredded your knees, didn't you? I can tell."

"No. Just a little twinge of runner's knee, but it's nothing I can't deal with."

"Runner's knee. You mean chrondromalacia?"

"Yeah," Jimmy said, trying not to limp to the kitchen.

"I remember you had that so bad one time when we were in Chicago you had to go that fancy knee guy on Michigan Avenue and spend half your life in his designer waiting room, and then he told you you shouldn't run unless you were below 200 pounds. When was the last time you stepped on the scale, Jimmy?"

Jimmy shrugged and got one of his "ice cups" out of the freezer. He undressed, slung his wounded knee over the sink, peeled the paper cup away from the ice, and cold-massaged the affected area.

"You didn't answer my question, Jimmy. Are you going deaf too?"

"No, I heard you. It's just that — well, sure, I'm a little overweight."

"A little overweight?!?"

"All right — probably a lot, but . . ."

"How are you going to know if you don't step on the scale?"

"I'll step on the scale."

"When?"

"Soon."

"Like right now?"

"No, not like right now, but soon."

Joyce folded her arms and studied her stubborn husband. "You're going to leave me a widow — I just know it."

Jimmy stopped rubbing his sore knee with ice and looked at Joyce. He was in no position to refute her, because she was right. As always. Damn it.

"Don't swear at me."

"I didn't swear at you."

"Yes, you did."

"Joyce!!"

"Jimmy!!"

Joyce shook her head and retreated a step. "Well, you do whatever makes you happy, but I just wish you'd go see those people at Diet Center."

"Joyce, I'm not going to see those people at Diet Center because I don't need them. I can get this thing under control myself."

"How? By eating everything in sight just because you think you can go out and run it off? Well, you can't run it off if you can't run because you're too fat. You have to combine proper diet with regular exercise, Jimmy."

"You sound like some article in the READER'S DIGEST, Joyce."

"Well, I wish you'd read some of those articles in the READER'S DIGEST, Jimmy, because then you might get it through your thick head that you've got to be the proper weight if you want to live past 60."

"Joyce, I'm close to the proper weight."

"How do you know if you refuse to step on the scale?"

"Touché." Jimmy stopped ice-massaging his knee and hobbled directly to the bathroom scale and stepped up without flinching.

But he flinched when he saw that he had hit the big 245.

"My God," he gasped. "I'm big enough to be a linebacker in the NFL."

Jimmy looked at his man tits and manly paunch in the mirror and remembered seeing some chart somewhere that proclaimed that the so-called "beer belly" was the biggest killer of men in their 40s. Jimmy asked himself then and there if he was ready to die. To give up the sweet life with Joyce in the Dunery he had worked so hard to achieve.

"No way!"

"What was that?" Joyce said, running from the kitchen.

Jimmy stepped off the scale before she could see the incriminating evidence of his gluttony.

"What did you say? Come on, step back on the scale and let me see."

"You don't have to see, Joyce, because I'll tell you — I weigh 245 pounds."

"Time to call Diet Center."

"Time to call Diet Center."

Joyce sighed. "You mean that?"

"Yes, I mean that. I don't want you to be a young widow, Joyce."

"I'd be a middle-aged widow, but still . . ."

"But still is right. You're too young for widowhood, and you need somebody to keep an eye on you to keep you from being a total recluse and just burrowing in here with thick books with tiny print and never going out except for the occasional can of tuna fish. Provided, of course, it's on sale."

"Enough already. Take your shower. You'd better get going if you're going to get to that play on time."

"Aye aye, skipper."

Jimmy set out the bathmat, stepped into the tub, and closed the curtain.

"Jimmy?"

"What?"

"You're really going to call Diet Center?"

"First thing tomorrow morning, Joyce. I've had enough."

The resolutely irreligious Joyce nearly said a prayer of thanksgiving. Hell, she thought, why not say a prayer of thanksgiving, so she whispered: "Thank you, God. Thank you for sparing me from a long, lonely life with only thick books with tiny print for company. Amen."

"What'd you say, Joyce?"

"Nothing. Just take your shower, and I'll get dinner ready."

Jimmy took his shower, Joyce got dinner ready, and in no time flat the frustrated playwright was headed east on Michigan Highway 43 for the fame and glory he was sure he was going to find in the PIT.

Overhead, pigs flew and orioles oinked.

Chapter Twenty-Eight

A word or two about Michigan Highway 43, or simply M43, before before we descend into the PIT, aka: The Performance Initiative Theatre.

M43 begins near Lake Michigan in South Haven and runs mostly east through Kalamazoo and Lansing all the way to Detroit. A real Michigan highway if ever there was one.

Jimmy had once taken it all the way to Lansing and written eloquently of it in a piece titled "Dancing to Lansing" which was published in the estimable HAVENCREST HIGHLIGHTS. Back in another life when he was trying to be a journalist.

But now he was trying to actually make a living as a playwright in modern America, and he was bearing down on Bangor with one thought in mind: if these people at the PIT turn out to be flakes, then life as I know it is over.

A couple of good-young-boys glued their souped-up Dodge pick-up truck to Angel Car's tail.

Jimmy accelerated.

They accelerated, remaining glued to his bumper.

Jimmy looked in the rearview mirror and muttered: "Knuckle-dragging, scum-sucking hillbilly mother fuckers."

He wanted to whip his little car off the two-lane highway and have it out with the two underachievers then and there. But then he thought of their lives in comparison to his life.

They probably work construction for some abusive asshole who demands no less than 16-hour days in all kinds of weather with lots of heavy lifting and absolutely no health benefits. You get injured on the job — fuck you, scum bag, deal with it later. We got us a house to build for some rich Tunas from Chicago.

I on the other, Jimmy thought, work in climate-controlled comfort throughout the year — well, forget summer, but someday we're going to get air-conditioning "because I'm going to strangle that fucking Klaus Williams asshole and get a real heating and air-conditioning contractor to put in a real air-conditioning system that gives us real air-conditioning and . . ."

Jimmy realized he was ranting out loud and stopped.

He also stopped battling with the brain-dead hillbillies in the big American pick-up who were obviously picking on him because he was driving a little Jap car (even though it was made in nearby Ontario, Canada, which was still in North America last time he checked his atlas).

Jimmy took his foot off the accelerator and let Angel Car glide to a safe and sensible speed.

The idiot driving the pick-up reckoned the asshole in the little Jap car was going to turn or something, so he whipped around into oncoming traffic to pass. Never mind the oncoming traffic, never mind the solid double yellow lines indicating a no-passing zone. This was one young Michigan hillbilly in a hurry to go nowhere, and off he went in a blaze of American-made glory.

"With plenty of parts from Mexico and Malaysia," Jimmy said, waving the lads a hearty fare-thee-well.

Jimmy sighed and realized that there simply was no way of avoiding assholes. Even a Sunday drive was fraught with danger because other people were out and about.

If there were no other people, Jimmy decided, life would really be worth living.

Just me and Joyce and the Dunery and lots of thick books with tiny print.

Then a troubling thought: who would come and see my plays if it was just Joyce and I?

Hmm?

Answer me that one, boy wonder.

Jimmy wondered all the way through beautiful downtown Bangor and had decided by Glendale that maybe, just maybe, other people were permissible.

Certain other people, that is.

Preferably ones who would come and see his plays, laugh and cry and clap adoringly and then all disappear into caves or somewhere until the next dazzling premiere of a major work by the celebrated James Gordon Clarke III.

"Yeah, right," Jimmy said.

He flicked on the NPR affiliate out of Kalamazoo and listened to some professor at Western Michigan University gas on about the need for original "Midwest voices in literature."

Jimmy pounded the dashboard and said, "I'm an original Midwest voice in literature! Why don't you put me on the air, asshole?!?"

A woman in a van passed on the left and a little boy in the back seat stared in wide-eyed worry at the man talking to himself in the little Jap car.

Jimmy shut up and took some deep breaths.

Really deep.

Then he put the whole playwriting thing in perspective.

It all boils down to one thing, he thought — fame.

Fame.

Fucking fame.

If I could just learn to live without fame.

Yeah, and if pigs could fly and orioles could only oink.

Jimmy looked up and was sure he saw pigs flying and swore he heard orioles oinking.

"A sign from God," he gasped.

This means the PIT is it.

"The PIT is it."

Jimmy repeated that until it lost all meaning.

And then he settled back for what was really a beauty ride through the fruit basket of America. God's favorite corner of paradise on earth — western Michigan.

Jimmy soon found himself within the city limits of Kalamazoo and instinctively locked the doors. He remembered reading in the local papers about how the crack dealers had all been pushed west out of Detroit and had settled in Kalamazoo and Benton Harbor. Shoot-outs between rival dealers were common in both Michigan cities.

But still, Jimmy thought, descending into the Kalamazoo River valley past Kalamazoo College, this place does have its charms.

Seen from that vantage point, downtown Kalamazoo did indeed seem to be a place of enchantment. Well, at least a clean mid-sized American city with the usual line-up of bad architecture and failed attempts to lure the good burghers back into the center city from the outlying regional malls.

In Kalamazoo's case, the city parents had blocked off a key north/south thoroughfare and dubbed it the "Kalamazoo Mall." In reality, it was a open-air urinal for the "celery city's" growing population of bums and bumettes.

Excuse me, the homeless.

Oh, I'm so sorry for being politically incorrect in this time of enforced political correctness.   Mea culpa, mea culpa, mea maxima culpa. Amen.

Anyway, suffice it to say that downtown Kalamazoo was not a happening place, particularly on a Sunday evening in April in the year of Our Lord 1994.

But that didn't stop the city parents from putting parking meters everywhere, even on dimly lighted sidestreets in the vicinity of the Performance Initiative Theatre, or PIT.

Jimmy shrugged and shelled out four quarters.

"It's for a good cause," he told the meter. "Right?"

The meter remained mum.

But a bag lady appeared as if on cue and demanded "five bucks."

"Five bucks?" Jimmy said. "They only ask for a buck in Chicago."

"Yeah," she said, wiping snot off her nose with the back of her hand, "this is Ka'zoo, not Chicago. Now, you gonna give me five bucks for dinner, or am I gonna have to get rough?"

Jimmy stepped back and eyed the aging urchin. She was of stocky build, dressed in a tattered Robert Hall sweater, and in command of a commandeered shopping cart crammed full of found objects, including a baseball bat with a rubberized grip. The street woman wore a pair of worn-out batting gloves and looked like she was ready to step up to the plate.

"Five bucks, you say?"

"Five bucks. There's only one place I can get a decent meal around here, and nothin' short of five bucks is gonna do, and there ain't nobody else around this damn town because they're all out at the mall, and every time I take the bus out to the mall, them damn fascist security cops they got out there roust me out, and it don't do no good to tell 'em my constitutional rights, because nobody gives a flyin' fuck any more about the U.S. Constitution any more, because this country's been taken over by a bunch of soulless fucking suburbanites who only care about free parking at the mall and a good tee-time on the friggin' golf course on Saturday morning. If you catch my drift."

Jimmy caught her drift as a wasting whiff of unwashed armpits and crotch. It made him swoon.

"Hey, don't go faintin' on me, pal," the bag lady said. "Course, you go faintin' on me, I'll just clean out your pockets. Course, you drivin' a little wreck like that, I'm guessin' you ain't got too much in your pockets. In fact, I'd say you're not too far from the streets yourself."

"I beg your pardon."

The woman snorted derisively and said, "You're one of them theatre people, ain't you?"

Jimmy glanced across the street where a makeshift wooden sign pointed to the very portal of the PIT in an unpaved alley. Jimmy thought of George Orwell's brilliant book, DOWN AND OUT IN PARIS AND LONDON.

"What's that about down and out in Paris and London?"

"What?"

The homeless woman waved her hand in front of Jimmy's face. "I tell you—you theatre people—biggest bunch of fruitcakes I ever seen. I don't know why I even bother hangin' around here—never get no money from you people. And I certainly don't get no respect. And I coulda been one hell of a photographer—if that asshole hadn't stolen my negative." The woman gripped her bat and focused on infinity. "But don't get me started on that. Believe me, you don't want to get me started on that, but believe me, if I ever find that son-of-a-bitch, I'm gonna bust his fuckin' head like it was some rotten cantaloupe or something. You hear me?"

Jimmy nodded and handed the nice lady a faded five-dollar bill.

She sniffed it suspiciously, and when she was satisfied it was the real article she stuffed it deep down the front of her pants and pushed off into the twilight.

Jimmy watched her for a long moment and then followed the sign to the very portal of the PIT.

As mentioned earlier in this novel, the Performance Initiative Theatre really is a pit because it is located in the basement under a dry-cleaning establishment. Al's Dry Cleaning to be precise.

And Jimmy knew precisely because there was a sign to that effect in the window above the open door leading down a dimly lighted set of wooden stairs into the PIT.

As Jimmy began his descent into the PIT, he was overcome by the stench of dry-cleaning chemicals. He was audibly gagging by the time he stumbled into a desk at the bottom of the unsafe staircase.

A young woman's voice wafted out of the gloamin' and said, "You'll get used to the smell. Everybody does."

Jimmy squinted and just barely made out a walking stick-figure with an elongated mane of preternaturally red hair. The creature wore a wardrobe straight from Sears, complete with untucked flannel workshirt, work jeans, and steel-toed boots. She, if indeed she was a she, wore no make-up.

No wait — there was a swipe of lipstick. Kind of a burnt-orange residue actually.

But the creature more than compensated by sporting a great clanking clutter of jewelry, including dozens upon dozens of rings pierced through her ears, septum and nostrils.

Surely, Jimmy thought, she won't be happy until she goes completely native and gets her lower lip stretched like the Ubangis do in Africa.

"My father's from Africa," the she-creature said, bending her hand back until it touched her forearm. "South Africa actually. He was opposed to Apartheid before anybody was opposed to Apartheid. If it wasn't for him, Nelson Mandela would never have been released from prison, and Apartheid wouldn't have been ended, and all the wonderful and positive things that are finally happening in South Africa wouldn't be happening. It's because he wrote all these letters, see, and organized all these protests, see, and he was the one who got Western, and the state of Michigan, and all these other places to stop investing in South Africa when Apartheid was still in effect, and he's the chairperson of the Comparative Religions Department at the university, and he's like the most awesome intellect you'll ever meet."

"Yeah, I'm sure," Jimmy said, not sure he wanted to stay another nanosecond.

He peered into the gloom and saw only one other patron — a chubby young man trying to read a thick book with tiny print with the assistance of the theatre's "ghost light."

"So, do you like have a reservation? You'd better because we're expecting a totally full house tonight. I mean Donald is so incredibly brilliant as Jack, that people are going to come from all over the state to see him. The Democratic party is even talking about flying him to Washington for a benefit performance before the November elections, which wouldn't surprise me, because Donald is so totally brilliant, I'd have to say he's the most brilliant man I've ever met. Except for Daddy, of course. Nobody's as brilliant as my father, but Donald comes pretty close. And the really neat thing is they really, really like each other. My father and Donald, I mean. In fact, my parents are coming tonight. I thought you might even be them. But you're not them, are you?"

"No, I ah . . ."

"Bet you can't do this," the she-creature said, contorting herself into a pretzel.

"No, I ah . . ."

"Most men can't. Most women either. See, I'm double-jointed. Triple-jointed actually. I'm on like about 20 medications, but I only take half of them, because I don't think those doctors know what they're doing. I mean, I know as much as they do. Did you know I tested out of most of my required courses at Western? That's right, because I was so smart in high school, I like skipped a whole year. So I'm really a whole year ahead of my friends, except that since I started getting sick and all — actually I've been sick my whole life with a degenerative joint disorder — that's why I'm so limber and can twist myself like this — which I bet you can't do."

Jimmy was about to attempt an answer when a destitute band of Western Michigan University students clumped down the stairs and immediately engaged the enlarged she-creature in a desultory conversation about body piercing and other ailments of the modern age.

"Uh," Jimmy interrupted, "is there a bathroom or something? I've come a long way."

The she-creature aimed a triple-jointed limb at a curtained doorway, and Jimmy went hither.

When he parted the musty old black curtain, he entered the true nether land of America theatre, the veritable pit of the PIT.

Jimmy was feeling his way through the gaseous gloom when a great, fleshy-headed mutant appeared before him and said: "You must be that guy from South Haven — from the Fennell Theatre, right?"

Jimmy blinked and beheld a fat geek in a cheap suit. The hefty man was heavily made-up as if to play in a play, and had given great attention to his shock of reddish-brown hair. One could even say that he had attempted to comb and primp it after JFK's brushy fashion. A good effort, but it had failed utterly.

As did the thespian's attempt at mimicking Kennedy's accent as he added: "Ask not what the theatre can do for you, but ask what you can do for the theatre. And what you can do, my friend, is book *Jack* at the Fennell this summer. What do you say?" The man in the cheap suit slapped a clammy hand on Jimmy's shoulder and squeezed.

Jimmy felt as though he was in the grip of a known pedophile. A tenderfoot trapped in his tent by the great geek of a scoutmaster, come for his midnight goodies.

Good God!

"What was that?"

"I didn't say anything."

"Yes, you said something about God. Now, I know I'm considered the most daring actor — slash — director — slash — artistic director this side of the Hudson River, but I have never been called God. At least not to my face. You really know how to flatter a girl."

"Right. Uh, how did you know I'm from the Fennell?"

"Word gets around. So, can you book *Jack* there this summer, or can't you?"

Jimmy tried to moved away from the man's clammy vise grip, but could not.

"Actually," Jimmy said, struggling to be free, "I'm not really with the Fennell anymore. I resigned from the board. This morning in fact, and . . ."

"That doesn't mean you can't get *Jack* booked there this summer. Now I know you've got hundreds and hundreds — hell, probably thousands and thousands of rich Chicago people at your disposal over there, and those are just the kind of people who need to see *Jack* because it was Chicago, after all, that put Jack over the top in '60 against old Tricky Dick. And I know Jack always had a soft spot for Old Man Daley, and I bet you could get his son . . ."

"You mean Richard the Second?"

"Yeah, the current mayor of Chicago. I hear he's got a summer place in Michigan and . . ."

"Actually, it's down in Berrien County, practically on the state line."

"No problem. You could get him to come to the premiere of *Jack* at the Fennell, and then it would be off to Chicago. Hell, I bet you could book us at the Steppenwolf in no time, and then it's on to the Kennedy Center in Washington, and the Kennedy Library in Boston, and . . ."

"Why not the Abbey Theatre in Dublin?"

"You've got connections at the Abbey?"

"No, but I had the lead in *Playboy of the Western World* at the Stonebridge in Chicago and . . ."

"We're going to put you in charge of our marketing. You're the answer to our prayers. Now, if you'll excuse me, I've still got some lines to memorize."

"You're not off book?"

"I'm never off book until the lights go up." With that, the wise and wonderful Donald C. Adams, S.O.D. released his grip on the playwright's shoulder and disappeared into the dim recesses of the backstage area.

Jimmy continued on his journey to the men's room and found the urinal by following his nose. The thing reeked of stale urine and didn't flush properly. And there were no paper towels by the sink, and the water pressure was weak, and the mirror was badly smudged, and the only light came from a flickering little night light encased in a dusty old sea shell.

Jimmy nodded grimly and resolved to go straight home without stopping to see *Jack*.

Enough already.

But as he was walking to the exit he happened to glance down another dim corridor and saw a vision of feminine pulchritude in black silk. Black polyester actually, but the woman with the soulful eyes and great mane of thick black hair appeared to be wearing a black silk bra and panties.

She sat at a broken-down dressing table cursing herself in a cracked mirror.

"I'm so ugly," she hissed, "so stupid and ugly. God, I hate myself. I'm so ugly. So stupid and ugly. God, I hate myself."

Jimmy was instantly smitten and wanted to rush to her side and tell her she was the most wonderful woman he had seen since he first laid eyes on Joyce back in another life when Joyce's sister had just committed suicide in the family garage by burning herself to death.

But I'm a married man, Jimmy told himself. A happily married man.

Still . . .

The young woman turned and stared unabashedly at Jimmy.

Jimmy blinked, blushed, and backed away.

"I heard you talking to Donald," she said. "I hope you can get them to let us do *Jack* at your theatre because this is the most amazing play you're ever going to see, and Donald is so wonderful, you're not going to believe it. Of course, you're going to hate me because I'm so stupid and ugly."

"You're not stupid, and you're certainly not ugly," Jimmy said, trying not to stare at the ingenue's amazing breasts. Which were yearning to be free of the flimsy black brassiere and let their soft light shine forth and . . .

"What soft light?"

"Huh?"

"You were mumbling something about soft light shining forth."

"I was?"

"Yes, and you're staring at my boobs. God, aren't they disgusting? I'd like to just chop them off and be done with them. They're so disgusting and ugly. God!"

Jimmy took that as his cue to leave and turned right into a rail thin young man with the head and hair of young Caesar.

The gaunt young thespian wore a cheap suit and tons of make-up. He instantly enfolded Jimmy in a warm embrace, saying: "You must be that guy from the Fennell Theatre. God, we've all been dying to meet you. Welcome to the PIT. I'm Michael Mehlan, and that's Laura Langlade, and you probably already met Donald, because nobody comes to the PIT without meeting our fearless leader, but we'll all get together after the play and talk about how you're going to be our road manager this summer."

Jimmy backed out of the overly familiar embrace and nodded dully.

He thought fleetingly of leaving and never coming back, but he felt as though he had been caught in a sticky web of endless needs and neuroses. Strangely, it complemented his burning desire for fame.

The clincher came when the she-creature at the front desk said: "Donald gave me your play to read, and it was like really, really good, and I'm sure he'll make you a resident playwright if you stick around and like get *Jack* produced at that theatre of yours in South Haven, and you like get lots of rich Tunas to come and then get *Jack* produced at some of the big theatres in Chicago because that's what Donald really wants, and he's so brilliant as Jack, it's like he really is Jack. And that's not surprising, because he loved Jack more than anybody ever did. And after the play he'll tell you all about where he was when Jack was assassinated, and we'll go over to the Campus Club and get to know each other better, and you can be part of our growing family. Now where do you want to sit? I guess we're not going to have a full house after all, so you can kind of pick where you want to sit."

Jimmy surveyed the house and saw that that audience consisted entirely of the aforementioned chubby young man and the group of Western Michigan University students. The former had the center section all to himself, and the students had elected to sit in the left wing because they were no doubt left-wing drama majors.

The right wing of seats was entirely vacant, so Jimmy opted to sit there.

"That'll give the theatre a little balance if I sit there," he told the she-creature.

"Donald will like that," she said, proffering a ticket.

Jimmy proffered a ten dollar bill and said, "By the way, I'm Jim Clarke from . . ."

"I know who you are. We all know who you are. Word gets around in the theatre world."

"Right, so you must be — uh . . ."

"Lisa. Lisa Lambert. Donald's going to marry me and make me an honest woman."

Donald C. Adams, S.O.D. poked his great fleshy head out of the curtain and hissed: "Don't hold your breath, my dear."

He disappeared before lanky Lisa Lambert could reply.

Lisa swallowed her hurt and gave Jimmy his three dollars in change.

Jimmy tucked it in his pocket and just to be friendly said: "I thought your parents were coming. I'd love to talk to your father about South Africa."

A dark cloud passed across Lisa Lambert's sunny countenance. "Well, they said they were coming, but then something probably came up in the department or something. Something's always coming up in the department, and my father's getting ready for this really big international conference on comparative religions — it's going to be in Finland, and he's going to be the keynote speaker and all — anyway, I know they want to come and see the play. Because, I mean, it's all I've been talking about since I first came here with this friend of mine — well, she's not really my friend anymore after what she did that night we were at the Campus Club, and she about took her clothes off in front of Donald, because she was so totally infatuated with him, but it was me who saw what a real genius he really is, and, anyway, I like told my parents how wonderful Donald was as Jack, and when they decided to have this benefit performance to raise money for the resident company — and you wouldn't believe the resident company they have here because it's the most totally amazing group of talented actors and playwrights you're ever going to see anywhere in any time — well, my parents said, sure, they'd come and see Donald as Jack, and . . ."

"Five minutes to curtain," Donald C. Adams, S.O.D. called, poking his head through the curtain.

"I guess I'd better go find my seat," Jimmy said.

"Yeah," lanky Lisa Lambert said, "I guess you'd better. But we'll talk during the intermission, and then you'll go with us to the Campus Club after the play, because we always go to the Campus Club after the play, and Donald always gets a shot of single-malt scotch — neat, of course, because Donald believes that if you like put ice in single-malt scotch it's like polluting a pure mountain stream or something. And he gets a hot-fudge sundae. I mean the hot-fudge sundaes are to die for at the Campus Club, but I never get one because I'm watching my weight."

"Right. So what do you get at the Campus Club?"

"Oh, I just have some curly fries. And a Diet Coke. I like beer, but it's so fattening, so I gave it up, and you know, I don't really miss it, although what I do miss is acid. You ever do acid?"

Jimmy wondered if he could be busted for admitting to past trips and decided to go for it. "Yeah, I boarded a few astral planes in my day."

"God, isn't acid the greatest? My friend Gretchen, well, she's not my friend anymore since she hit on Donald after we first came to see *Jack* and went to the Campus Club afterwards — anyway, me and Gretchen used to trip all the time. One time we went out to Crossroads — that's this big mall out on South Westnedge . . ."

"I'm familiar with Crossroads."

"Yeah, who isn't? It's got to be the biggest mall in the country. One of them, anyway. So me and Gretchen each took a hit of this blotter acid she got, and then we went out to Crossroads, and it was the most amazing trip you can imagine. I mean the colors were so amazing, and we went into this one clothing store and just lost it when this saleslady came up to us and asked us what we wanted because she looked like a big green frog. God, it was hilarious."

"Yeah, I bet."

Lisa Lambert laughed herself into a silly pretzel and added, "Bet you can't do this."

Jimmy simply shook his head and took his seat.

The lights dimmed; the lights came up, and Donald C. Adams, S.O.D., Michael Mehlan, and the lovely Laura Langlade cranked out a two-act play about the life and times of John Fitzgerald "Jack" Kennedy that had Jimmy wishing he hadn't burned his model of PT-109.

It was that good.

Electrifying even, and when it was over, Jimmy made the big mistake of promising Donald C. Adams, S.O.D. that he would "get *Jack* produced at the Fennell if it's the last thing I ever do."

S.O.D., in case you forgot, stands for Society of Directors. Don't tell anybody, but anybody can join. All you have to do is send them ten bucks a year and you can belong. Your dog could belong if he sent them ten bucks.

"This calls for a celebration at the Campus Club," Donald C. Adams, S.O.D. said, clamping a clammy hand on Jimmy's shoulder. "You can buy me a shot of single-malt scotch, and we'll plan our marketing campaign."

Jimmy heard Joyce shout "run away, run away" from the Dunery, but he decided it was just the dry-cleaning chemicals seeping into his brain.

And so he sealed his fate by following the entourage to the celebrated Campus Club where Donald C. Adams, S.O.D. flamed up the first of thousands of generic cigarettes and graciously allowed the newcomer to ply him with single-malt scotch as he outlined his grand scheme for making them all rich and famous.

Chapter Twenty-Nine

Jimmy let himself into the darkened Dunery on creeping fog feet, shed his clothes in the living room, and tiptoed into the bedroom.

He slipped softly under the down comforter and listened to Joyce's gentle breathing.

She was fully committed to the act of sleeping, and he knew he shouldn't disturb her, but he couldn't resist.

So he laid a cold hand on her bare butt and kissed her shoulder.

Joyce awakened with a start, muttering: "Jimmy! You woke me up!! What time is it?!?"

"A little past midnight." Past 1:30 a.m. actually, but Jimmy didn't need to tell Joyce.

She sat up in bed, put her glasses on, and looked at the digital clock/radio on Jimmy's side of the bed. "Jimmy, it's past 1:30 in the morning!! I thought you were going to come home right after the play. Where have you been all night?!?" Joyce sniffed. "And you smell like a brewery." She sniffed again. "No, like you've been drinking hard stuff."

"Not hard stuff, Joyce, single-malt scotch, and I've been drinking it with a true artistic visionary who's going to make us rich and famous."

That got Joyce's attention, and she became fully awakened to the promise of wealth and fame, saying: "What are you talking about?"

"First of all, Joyce, I saw the most amazing play tonight — well, last night, since it's already Monday morning. Anyway, I didn't know what to expect, and, actually, I was kind of expecting to be disappointed, but I wasn't disappointed at all because this thing was really good. Amazingly good. The guy who had the lead — this Donald Adams character, was outstanding as Kennedy. He had a little trouble with the accent and some of his lines at first, but then this other guy in the cast kind of coached him along, and this woman — Laura Langlade — was just fabulous. God, that woman can act. And she had to play so many different parts, and shift gears so fast, and suggest changes in character with bare nuances in costume and props, and ..."

"Sounds like you have the hots for this broad."

"What?"

"You old fool—you're infatuated with some young cookie. Oh, God, I knew this would happen—I knew I'd be replaced by the new cookie."

"Joyce, what are you talking about?"

"I was watching this show on PBS while you were in Kalamazoo, and this expert said women my age produce old eggs. I've got old eggs, Jimmy. You don't love me any more because I'm all gray and wrinkled and just lay old eggs every month. And now you're ready to run off with some sultry young thing with big tits."

"How do you know she has big tits?"

"How do *you* know? Huh, answer me that, Mr. Mid-Life Crisis."

Jimmy sighed and settled himself for sleep.

"Jimmy, what are you doing?"

"What does it look like I'm doing, Joyce? I'm going to sleep. I want to get up and write tomorrow and then go to Diet Center."

"Don't try to change the subject on me."

"I'm not changing the subject, I'm just trying to go to sleep. And you should, too."

"I was asleep—sound asleep—until you went and put that ice hand on my butt."

"Sorry."

"You'd better be."

"I am."

Joyce relaxed slightly and removed her glasses. She settled back on her pillow and said, "So tell me all about this artistic visionary, and how he's going to make us rich and famous. I've always got time to hear how somebody's going to make us rich and famous."

"Can't it wait until morning?"

"No, you've got me completely waked up, and I'm not going to be able to sleep until you tell me all about what happened in Kalamazoo—besides discovering your new cookie with big tits."

"Actually, she hates her boobs and wants to cut them off."

"Now, how did you learn that?"

Jimmy walked Joyce through his entire introduction to the PIT. Then Joyce said: "God, they all sound like a bunch of psychos."

"Well, yeah, but . . ."

"But nothing, Jimmy. Maybe you should just write your ticket off as bad experience and go back to writing novels. I mean, you're a novelist first and foremost. Haven't you had enough bad theatre experience for one lifetime?"

"Yeah, but this Donald Adams guy had so many good ideas when we went to the Campus Club after the play, and he's really been around. I mean, he was practically raised on Broadway, and he has all kinds of theatre connections, and he wants us to write plays for him, and maybe even become part of his resident company, and they have a real theatre, Joyce. Lights and tickets and everything. And unbelievably talented actors. You wouldn't have believed how good that Michael and Laura were. When Michael did this one scene as old Joe Kennedy in a wheelchair after his stroke, it just tore your guts out. Unbelievable. And right there in Kalamazoo. It was like I had somehow been transported to some really gutsy little Off-Broadway theatre in New York or something. It was that incredible."

"Tell me about how he's going to make us rich and famous. I want to hear all about that."

"Well, he wants me to get *Jack* — that's the play I saw — produced at the Fennell."

"But you can't do that. You quit the Fennell."

"Well, Larry said to stay in touch, and I figure Jeffrey Cantwell's 'Midsummer at the Fennell' is going to be a monumental flop, because the stupid rich boy can't even get out of bed and chew gum at the same time, so anyway, I'll ride in like the savior of the race or whatever and get *Jack* produced at the Fennell this summer, and everybody will just go crazy over it, and there will be some high-powered theatre people in the audience. Hell, all we have to do is get Wendy Filbaitus to see it, and she'll be on the phone in a nanosecond to all her Chicago theatre contacts, and *Jack* will be up for an extended run at the Steppenwolf, or Goodman, or . . ."

"Jimmy!"

"What?"

"You're getting all excited about somebody else's play. What did this guy say about your play? The one you sent him."

"Well, actually he didn't get around to reading it, but he gave it to his girlfriend, well, she thinks she's his girlfriend, but he hardly even notices she's breathing, but, anyway, she really liked it."

"Well, good for her. But what good does that do you if he won't even read your play or listen to his girlfriend who did and who obviously is some kind of human doormat?"

Jimmy was silenced by the weight of Joyce's truth.

"Jimmy! Are you asleep already?"

"No, I was just thinking."

"About what? You were so excited just a second ago. Now it's like I just let the air out of your tires."

"Well, you were right, Joyce. She is a doormat. Lisa. Lisa Lambert. God, you should see her. She looks like a gigantic walking stick, only skinnier. And she's got so many earrings through her ears and nose she looks like some tribal princess from the African bush. And, oh, does she think she's hot shit. Well, she thinks her daddy is hot shit because he's chairman of some department at Western and is from South Africa. Of course, never mind that he and his wife were supposed to come and see the play, but just blew it off without notice . . ."

"What about how this guy is going to make us rich and famous? Let's get back to that part."

"Right. Well, I told you. I'm going to be his marketing director and do this big campaign for *Jack* and get it into all these big Chicago and New York theatres and . . ."

"Is he going to pay you to be his marketing director?"

"No, but he did sort of mention a percentage of the box."

"What percentage?"

"Well, he didn't really say because . . ."

"He didn't really say. I know. Jimmy, stick to writing novels and go to Diet Center."

That made so much sense, Jimmy decided to follow it.

But he also quietly resolved to follow the wise and wonderful Donald C. Adams, S.O.D. over the nearest cliff.

He instantly fell into a deep, peaceful sleep with thoughts of theatrical fame and fortune frolicking in his head and was impervious to all of Joyce's attempts to stop his snoring.

On the morrow, Jimmy awakened refreshed, renewed, ready to write, lose weight, feel great, and become the agent for the PIT's greatness.

Joyce, on the other hand, was slow to awaken because she had slept fitfully and had been plagued by nightmares about strange men chasing her through darkened, bombed-out cities.

Jimmy gave her a huge hug in the kitchen and said: "You just need to go to a play at the PIT, Joyce. When you see how incredible these people are, you'll be as excited as I am. I promise."

Joyce sighed and looked at her perpetually hopeful husband.

"What's that supposed to mean, Joyce?"

"It just means I wish I could share your enthusiasm, but I can't."

Jimmy rubbed his wife's back and asked, "Why not?"

"Because I've given up hope."

"What?!?"

"I've given up hope, Jimmy. It's that simple."

"But, Joyce, you can't give up hope. You have to have hope."

"Why?"

"Because—well, because it fuels your life force." Yeah, Jimmy thought, that sounds pretty heavy.

"What was that last bit?"

"Nothing. Joyce, don't talk like this, okay?"

"Why not? What's the point of hoping for things that are never going to happen? All we ever get in the mail are bills, and we're all going to die in the end and be dead forever—so what's the point of hoping for anything good to happen when nothing good ever happens?"

"But Joyce, we have the Dunery. We have each other. We have our health—well, you have yours, and I really am going to go to Diet Center this morning."

A spark of hope flashed in Joyce's combustion chamber, and she went to fast idle. "Really?"

"Really."

"And you're really going to do whatever they tell you to do? Even if it means giving up designer beer and single-malt scotch?"

"Even if it means giving up designer beer and single-malt scotch. Now, ye of no hope, get thee to thy writing booth and write some more of your brilliant books. Your devoted readers await."

"What devoted readers? I don't have any devoted readers."

Jimmy went and got a scrapbook, flipped it open and read: "'Dear Joyce Clarke, I really enjoy your writing! I am a published short-story writer and constant reader. I love your fast-paced style and real, yet unique characters. I can't wait to get another one of your books, because I know it means I will be laughing as I read.' Signed Flora Allison of New York, New York. Now get in there and write, Joyce, or Flora Allison of New York, New York is going to have a complete mental collapse."

Joyce cracked a slight smile and said, "Read that again."

Jimmy gladly reread the fan letter from Flora Allison of New York, New York. "Now do you have hope, Joyce?"

"Come here, you."

Jimmy went to his wife and got a great, big, slurpy kiss for his efforts.

"What was that for?" he said.

"For being you. And for being us. And for being kooks in the woods who don't march to anybody's drum but our own. Now get to your writing booth and hit those keys."

Jimmy looked at his wife and saw sparks of hope flash in her eyes. The sparks leapt through the void and inflamed him.

Thus afire, they went to their respective writing booths and hit the keys.

In Joyce's case, it was to begin a short novel based on the exploits of her psychotic client, Jerry Mappers.

"Oh, this is going to be good," Joyce cackled. "I'm going to have her go on one of those pathetic all-women cruises in the Caribbean, and put the moves on the captain but get rejected, and then . . ."

"Keep it down over there, Joyce. I'm trying to write."

Joyce poked her head around the partitioning wall and said, "Sorry." But she lingered and added, "What are you going to write — another play?"

Jimmy sighed at the thought. Then Joyce's earlier suggestion crept into his psyche, and he smiled so big and so wide the Dunery danced again on the dunes.

"Jimmy, why are you grinning like that?"

"Because, Joyce, I'm going to do what you suggested and go back to writing novels. In fact, I'm going to start one this morning — a roman a clef about a novelist who thinks he's going to become a playwright and actually goes out and writes a play and gets it produced. Actually, he ends up having to direct, produce and . . ."

"Don't tell me — tell your computer."

"Right."

And write they both did.

Happily and for a long stretch.

And then Jimmy phoned the nice lady at Diet Center in South Haven, made an appointment for 11, and appeared right on time.

The nice lady at Diet Center took Jimmy's photograph with a Polaroid camera, explaining: "This will be your 'before' picture. In less than six months, I'm going to take your 'after' picture, and you're not going to believe it's the same person. Now step in here, and we'll have the moment of truth on the scale."

Normally, this was when newcomers balked and/or bolted, but Jimmy went willingly to the snazzy medical scale with sliding counterweights, kicked off his shoes and stepped right up.

He felt the earth move as he did so and laughed.

"I guess that's a sign from God that I need to lose weight," he said.

"No," the nice lady from Diet Center said, "the earth *did* move. Like a — I don't know . . ." The woman went to the window and looked out. "Everything seems to be okay, but — I don't know . . ."

"Yeah, it felt kind of weird. You don't suppose there was an earthquake or something? They were talking about that fault near St. Louis going a while back. It's supposed to be really big when it goes — last time, I think it was in the early 1800s — it altered the course of the Mississippi River it was so strong. And all the trees in Michigan were toppled."

"Well, let's pray it's nothing like that," the Diet Center lady said, putting her hand to her heart.

They waited expectantly, and when all was still, the Diet Center counselor duly recorded Jimmy's 245 pounds and extra wide measurements in a computer file she created just for Jimmy. The computer crunched the big numbers and dutifully recommended a sensible diet and exercise plan that Jimmy promised to begin immediately.

And he did.

And, just as the nice lady at Diet Center, promised, he presented himself in six months' time for an "after" picture and scarcely recognized the lean and mean running machine in the photograph.

But the narrator gets ahead of himself. Just a bit, mind you.

You're no doubt wondering what became of Jimmy's brilliant career as a playwright. Fame and fortune in the PIT with the wise and wonderful Donald C. Adams, S.O.D. And all that.

Well, when Jimmy returned to the Dunery with his starter kit from Diet Center and two bags of fruits and vegetables from the supermarket, he asked Joyce if she had felt any rumblings earlier.

"What," she said, "you think that when you stepped on the scale at Diet Center, the whole earth moved?"

"Well, it did feel like the earth moved when I stepped up on the scale, but . . ."

"What time was that, exactly?"

"Well, I got there right at 11, so it couldn't have been much past the hour. Why? Did you feel something?"

"Yeah, I did as a matter of fact. Like a heavy truck coming down the road or somebody unloading a dumpster like that time the Craigs had all that work done. I even looked out the window, but I didn't see anything, so I just figured it was my imagination. But still, it did feel a little strange."

"Didn't you turn on the TV, Joyce, and see if maybe Palisades blew up or something?"

"Palisades didn't blow up, Jimmy!! God, you have a lurid imagination. If you thought something happened, why didn't you listen to the radio on your way home? You always have the radio on when you're in the car."

"I know, but I wanted to listen to this motivational tape the lady at Diet Center gave me. Besides, I figured it was just something falling off a truck, but if you felt it too, then it must have been something big. I'm going to check and see. Just to be sure."

"And I'm going to make lunch, and don't worry, I'll gladly follow your Diet Center menu to the letter."

While Joyce happily unloaded Jimmy's sacks of "rabbit food," Jimmy went to the Zenith portable he kept by his reading chair and channel-surfed.

Nothing but fat women telling talk-show hosts about how rats were coming up out of their toilets and nibbling randily at their glistening nether regions. That and the usual desultory soaps, some weather hysteria, home shopping hucksters, and . . .

"Holy shit!!"

"What?"

"Joyce, you gotta come here and look at this!!"

"What? What is it?"

"Come here and see this, Joyce!!"

Joyce went to the living room, gazed at the tiny TV screen, and gasped at the live, overhead image of overwhelming death and destruction in, as the caption informed viewers, Kalamazoo, Michigan.

"Ladies and gentlemen," the shaken announcer said, "we are looking at a live picture of downtown Kalamazoo, Michigan, and I must say I haven't seen anything like this since I covered the Gulf War from a hotel in Baghdad. As you can see from this aerial view, a four-square block area has been totally devastated by what, from all indications, was a severe blast in the center of the downtown business district. We are literally looking into a huge, smoking pit, ladies and gentlemen, and while officials at the scene are not yet prepared to estimate the number of fatalities, it is clear from this picture that the death toll could number in the hundreds or even more than . . ."

"Jimmy, isn't that . . ."

"The PIT, Joyce. Or where it used to be because I think the PIT is in a . . ."

"Pit! Oh, my God, that's horrible. I hope nobody was in the theatre."

But, as they later learned, they were all in the theatre for a special meeting of the resident company to discuss the brilliant marketing campaign Donald C. Adams, S.O.D. was cooking up for *Jack*. The one that that "guy from South Haven" was going to do for free, of course, and the one that was going to make them all rich and famous. Especially Donald C. Adams, S.O.D.

Excuse me — the late and totally toasted Donald C. Adams, S.O.D.

The blast, which was eventually linked to an unfortunate convergence of a ruptured gas main, leaking dry-cleaning chemicals, and a cigarette carelessly discarded by a homeless woman pushing a commandeered shopping cart, began in the basement under Al's Dry Cleaning.

In the PIT as it were.

And watching the scene of utter destruction, Jimmy felt all aflutter in the pit of his stomach. Not a bad feeling, mind you, because there on the screen was said homeless woman shamelessly cadging five bucks from a rescue worker.

Jimmy grinned and said, "Atta girl," and felt all together liberated and holistically whole. "Truly, a sign from God," he muttered.

"What'd you say, Jimmy?"

Jimmy turned off the TV, got up, hugged his wife, and said, "I said it's a sign from God, Joyce. The fact that that crazy bag lady survived the blast is a sign from God that we should just settle back and revel in writing novels that nobody reads. We should devote the rest of our lives to being seedy and in love."

And, you know, they did just that. And they lived and wrote happily ever after in air-conditioned comfort because they fired Klaus Williams and got a real heating and air-conditioning contractor to install a real heating and air-conditioning system.

The End

P.S. Oh, by the way, Jeffrey Cantwell never got his "Midsummer at the Fennell" off Mommy's kitchen table. Turned out the pampered rich boy truly could not get out of bed and chew gum at the same time — surprise, surprise! As for the Fennell Art Center and Theatre, aka: FAGAT, it's yours for a very large (yet undisclosed) sum of money and would be perfect as an archery range and/or antique mall. For more information, kindly contact Larry German in care of his sister who said he was last seen heading out west to "get his head on straight."

Casey's Basement

"Studs was a small, broad-shouldered lad. His face was wide and planed; his hair was a light brown. His long nose was too large for his other features; almost a sheeny's nose. His lips were thick and wide, and they did not seem at home on his otherwise frank and boyish face. He was always twisting them into his familiar tough-guy sneers. He had blue eyes; his mother rightly called them baby-blue eyes."

—James T. Farrell, STUDS LONIGAN

Chapter One

"Betcha can't throw a rock this far."

I measured the distance to Kevin Charles Ignatius "Casey" O'Neal and his older brother Donald and shook my head.

"What's the matter, you a chicken?" Casey called from his end of the alley.

Later, he'd sign his name K.C. O'Neal, but on that last day of school in June 1957 we first-graders at the Alice L. Harwood Elementary School on the far southwest side of Chicago knew him as Casey. In fact, I'll always think of him as Casey. His house, which faced Indian Trail Avenue, backed on the alley which intersected Dray Street where my house was. My name, by the way, is John Yardley Junior, but everybody called me Jackie in those days. Well, most everybody.

Now back to the alley.

"No," I hollered, "I'm not a chicken. I just don't want to hurt you is all."

"You're a chicken, Yardley, and I'm gonna tell everybody in the neighborhood that you couldn't throw a rock halfway down the alley," Casey taunted. He was a little piece of leather, but he was well put together with his broad shoulders, a shock of sandy hair, baby-blue eyes, and fair Irish features.

I, on the other hand, was a chunky kid with a crew-cut who hated to look at himself in the mirror.

"I could throw a rock over your head if I wanted, but I just don't want to."

"Chicken."

"Am not."

"Are too."

"All right, Casey," I said, picking up a rock. "I'll throw this right over your head, you stupid Catholic."

"Go ahead, you stupid Public."

By local reasoning, the world was divided between Catholics and Publics. Catholics went to Catholic schools and churches, so Publics naturally went to Public schools and churches. You might call yourself an Episcopalian as I did, or a Presbyterian, Lutheran,

Methodist, or Baptist, but to Catholics like Casey O'Neal, you were just a dumb Public.

And never mind that Casey and his older brother Donald had just completed kindergarten and first grade at a public school. Lots of Catholic parents sent their kids to public school for the first year or two to save on tuition. Besides, Casey and Donald went to catechism every Wednesday at Saint Bartholomew's.

Donald O'Neal stepped between us and said, "You know what Mother said about throwing rocks, Kevin. Come on, she's expecting us."

Today, we'd say that Donald O'Neal was developmentally disabled, but then we figured he just wasn't right in the head. Otherwise, why would they have kept him back a year so he and his younger brother ended up in the same grade. It wasn't that we made fun of Donald or anything; he was just so literal and unvarnished and such a total tattletale that we hated to have him around. But we had no choice, as you will see.

"Why don't you run home and have some milk and cookies?" Casey said to his brother.

"Mother told me to stay with you," Donald said.

"Then you'd better get out of the way, because that stupid Public's gonna try to hit me with a rock. Which he'll never do in a million years. Will ya, Yardley?"

"Casey, I could hit your house if I wanted."

"Then why don't ya?"

"All right," I said, winding up, "I will. Better look out."

"For what?"

"For this rock, because here she comes."

I thought all the way through my wind-up about how my mother had given my beloved dog, Billy, away because my father had had an operation on his throat. I was so mad when I released that rock, I really believed I could hit Casey's house with it. I know I wanted to hit something or someone with that rock.

I gasped in amazement at my own strength as the rock left my right hand and arced over the alley.

"Casey," I hollered, "it's gonna hit you! Scram!!"

Donald saw that I was right, and tried to pull his little brother out of harm's way, but Casey defiantly stood his ground and laughed at me.

"It's not gonna hit me, you dumb . . ."

The rock cracked Casey over his right eye, and the bleeding was profuse and instantaneous. Casey clutched his head and screamed: "You tried to kill me, you dumb Public!"

Donald whooped at the cascade of crimson on his brother's face, grabbed Casey's arm, and tore off toward home yelling, "Mother, John Yardley Junior's just tried to kill Kevin with a rock! Mother, John Yardley Junior's just tried to kill Kevin with a rock! Mother, John Yardley Junior's just tried to kill Kevin with a rock! Mother."

I watched them disappear up the alley and tried to undo the awful moment. I couldn't, so I went to the rock and picked it up. There was a bright splash of Casey's blood on its smooth surface. I flung the rock in some bushes behind Old Man Schermer's house and ran after the O'Neal brothers yelling how sorry I was.

I followed the trail of Casey's blood to his back fence and froze.

Having heard Donald's whooping, Mrs. O'Neal was just opening the back door and having her first look at her wounded baby. Casey would always be her baby, no matter how big and bad he got.

"Mother, John Yardley Junior's just tried to kill Kevin with a rock!" Donald said.

Casey moaned, and his mother keened: "You're bleeding like a stuck pig! Who did you say did this, Donald?"

Sensing I must have followed, Donald O'Neal pointed at the back fence.

Mary Theresa Cavanaugh O'Neal speared her emerald-green eyes into my heart.

"Don't let me ever catch you anywhere near my baby again!" she screamed like a banshee. "Do you hear me, you little devil?"

I nodded furiously and tried to speak but couldn't.

Mrs. O'Neal told Donald to open the door and frantically but gingerly helped her stricken baby into the house. Donald followed them, slammed the door, and they were gone.

I stood frozen at the gate for an eternal minute and then dragged myself home.

My mother, Doris Yardley, had her bridge club over so I really couldn't talk to her. Not that I ever could really talk to her, but it was totally out of the question when the bridge club was over.

So, as per standing orders, I gaily greeted each of the "guesties" in turn, calling most of them Aunt-this or Aunt-that even though they weren't blood aunts. They were the wives of the men at my father's good, big insurance company in the Loop, and the company was being very good to my father after his bout with cancer of the larynx, so I knew without thinking to call these over-perfumed and girdled women Aunt Lu and Aunt Max and Aunt Shirley and Aunt So-and-So. And to let them kiss me on the cheek, and in Aunt Lu's case, fondle me all she wanted.

Aunt Lu's husband, after all, was my father's boss, and he had let my father return to work after his operation. Sometimes I even stayed overnight at Aunt Lu's, and once she had given me a bath and tried to rub my "dingle dangle" off. When I told her it hurt, she laughed and said she'd never hurt "Mr. Dingle Dangle" again. She even made me stand up so she could kiss it. I didn't know what to do or think, except to obey because she was an adult, and adults were always to be obeyed.

Sure enough, when I greeted her that June day in my living room, she got her hand on Mr. Dingle Dangle and gave him a good squeeze. "Your Aunt Lu loves you, sweetie," she whispered as she planted her moist lips on my cheek.

I looked up at her and wondered if she'd still love me if I brained one of her kids with a rock.

Probably not.

I sighed, and though I was starving, I passed right by the bowl of salted nuts next to the card table without even dreaming of taking one because the standing rule at our house, which was known throughout the neighborhood as "Yardley's Bar & Grill," was FAMILY HOLD BACK. Or FHB for short. Meaning that if you got caught with your hot little hand in the bowl of salted nuts, you'd get it slapped off. And having recently recovered from two broken wrists, I didn't want anyone slapping my hands again.

So I politely excused myself and went straight to the second-floor bedroom I shared with my little brother, Timmy. Still too young for school, he was quietly playing with this stuffed rag of a thing he called "Mr. Monkey." I wanted to pull its head off and punch him one just for good measure, but I knew I was in enough trouble, so I just left him alone and lay down on my bed and waited for Mrs. O'Neal to call my mother.

I didn't have to wait long.

Phones were a lot louder in those days, and I about blasted to the ceiling on the first ring. I knew it was Mrs. O'Neal. I just knew.

I looked at Timmy and said, "I've got to hide. You've got to help me. You're real good at hiding. Where should I hide?"

Timmy sensed trouble of somebody else's making and compressed himself around Mr. Monkey.

I grabbed his shoulder and said, "Timmy! Didn't you hear me? I've got to hide from Mom because she's gonna kill me after she talks to Mrs. O'Neal."

Timmy lurched out of my grasp and hollered, "Leave me alone, Jackie!! You leave me and Mr. Monkey alone!!"

"Okay, okay," I said, trying to whisper. "I'm not trying to hurt you, Timmy. I just want you to show me a good hiding place, because you know all the good hiding places."

"No," Timmy said, thrusting out his little chin. "I'm not gonna help you hide, and I hope Mom gives you a really, really big spanking. And I'm gonna tell her you tried to hurt Mr. Monkey again."

He ran toward the door, and when I moved to intercept him he screamed like a banshee.

Damn banshees.

"Shut up, Timmy."

"Mom, Jackie's trying to hurt Mr. Monkey!"

"Timmy!"

"Mom!!!"

I let the little squealer run off to his mommy and tried to squirm under my bed. But as I said, I was a chunky kid and I wouldn't quite fit. I sucked in my belly and pushed at the frame, but there was just no way I was going to get all the way under.

And I could hear Mom down there in the living room telling her "guesties" to "play the next hand without me because I've got a little matter to discuss with Jackie."

Then as I fought with the bed frame, I heard her intercept Timmy on the stairs.

"Mom," Timmy said, "Jackie tried to hurt Mr. Monkey again. You told me to tell you if he ever tried to hurt Mr. Monkey again, and he just tried to hurt him again."

"You little tattletale," I hissed, frantically fighting to get under the bed.

"Well, that's not all that little monster's done. Why don't you and Mr. Monkey go and play in the backyard while I have a little talk with your brother."

"But I don't want to go past all those ladies."

"All right. Wait here. I'll be right back."

"Oh God," I prayed, "please protect me. I'm just a little kid, and I really need your . . ."

"Jackie!"

"What, Mom?"

"You're too fat to fit under the bed. Now come out from under there this instant."

"No!"

Mom closed the bedroom door, scrunched down as far as her Playtex Maidenform girdle would allow and grabbed my nearest wrist.

I howled.

She grunted and pulled with all her might.

"Mom, you're hurting me!"

"I'll break your arm if you don't come out from under there this instant."

I knew she meant it because when I broke both wrists after falling off a stool in the kitchen while trying to get pretzels for Dad, she said she hoped I broke my arm. And though I begged her to take me to the hospital, she waited a good 24 hours before she got around to it, and then she was mad because the doctor had had the nerve to lecture her right there in the emergency room in front of all those other mothers about her failings as a mother.

"Okay, I'm coming out, but let go of my wrist. You're gonna break it again."

"I didn't break your wrists; you did."

Mom gave me a big yank, and I tumbled out. She kicked me in the ribs with the pointed toe of her high-heel shoe and hauled me to my feet by my wrist.

"I just got a call from Mrs. O'Neal who said you practically killed her son Kevin with a rock. Their family doctor is there now, and he's going to have to have stitches." Mom yanked me by the wrist. "Do you hear me — stitches?"

"Yes, ma'am."

"I told her I was mortified and that naturally we would pay all the doctor's bills, and she sounded like she was satisfied with that, but she said she never wants you near her son again." Mom yanked me by the wrist. "You hear me?"

"Yes, ma'am."

Mom pursed her lips and bore her eyes into my brain. "I don't know where you went wrong. Maybe it's all the radiation in the atmosphere from those A-bombs they're always testing. That must be it. Because you certainly didn't inherit this kind of behavior from my side of the family. And certainly not your father's. Your father's people go all the way back to the Revolution. You're a direct descendant of John Adams and John Quincy Adams. You certainly wouldn't have seen them hitting their friends in the heads with rocks."

Mom slapped me a backhand shot to the cheek and yanked my wrist again.

"Now, I want you to write a letter of apology to Kevin O'Neal. This instant. Do you understand?"

"Yes, ma'am, but . . ."

"Don't but me, young man." Mom slapped me another backhand. "Do I make myself clear?"

"Yes, ma'am."

Mom slapped one more time for good measure and flung me on my bed. "Now do as I say and write that letter, and I don't want to hear another peep out of you for the rest of the day. You're confined to your room until further notice. And when your father comes home, we'll decide what the rest of your punishment is going to be. Is that clear?"

"Yes, ma'am."

"Now get off your bed and write that letter."

"Yes, ma'am."

Mom shoved me to the desk I shared with Timmy, and I got a pen and a sheet of stationery my grandmother had given me for Christmas and wrote:

"Dear Casey,

"I am sorry I hit you with a rock. I did not mean to hit you with a rock. I still want to be your freind. If you want to be my freind.

"Your freind,

Jackie Yardley."

Mom tore the letter out of my hand and read it, moving her lips as she did so. "Don't you learn anything at school? You misspelled 'friend' three times. Oh, what am I going to do with you?"

I shrugged hopelessly and thought of her usual rejoinder about giving me "to the next passing Indian." Casey and I had looked at pictures of teepees in a book his father had in the basement and had decided the Plains Indians knew how to live. No school, horses to ride, buffalo to hunt, and all the battles you ever wanted.

Mom grabbed me by the back of the neck and said: "I'm speaking to you, young man."

"Yes, ma'am."

"Well, what am I supposed to do with a little monster like you? You know that janitor in South Shore used to call you the 'goddamned kid' when you rode around the building on your tricycle knocking old ladies over."

"Yes, ma'am."

"Don't 'yes, ma'am' me like a parrot. Answer my question."

I stared out the window at the remnants of an oak forest behind our house and said, "Give me to the next passing Indian?"

Mom snorted and released my neck. "Believe me, if some redskin walked down Dray Street right now, I'd give you to him in a second. Not Timmy, mind you. Timmy's a perfect little boy. So quiet and well-behaved. Not like you. The 'goddamned kid'—that's what the janitor in South Shore called you. And he was right. You used to lock yourself in the bathroom, and he had to come and take the door off the hinges. You were such a little monster. But not your brother. Timmy's so quiet and well-behaved. I almost wish—well, never mind. Now rewrite that letter and spell 'friend' right this time."

"But how . . ."

"Here, you little moron." Mom bent down and scrawled the correct spelling on my letter. "Now write another letter and take it over to Kevin O'Neal."

"But I thought I was never supposed to see Casey again. I thought Mrs. . . ."

"His name is Kevin, not Casey, and, of course, you're not supposed to see him again, but I don't want that shanty-Irish bitch running around the neighborhood telling everyone that I raised you without manners. After you rewrite the letter with proper spelling, I want you to march over there and give the letter to that little Catholic brat. And I want that shanty-Irish bitch to know that the Yardleys know how to handle themselves in all situations. Do I make myself clear, young man?"

I gulped and looked up at my mother. She was cocking for another backhand slap, so I said: "Yes, ma'am."

She smiled icily and hurried back down to her guesties.

I thought more about going off with the next passing Indian and remembered that one book Casey's father had in the basement about a white boy who had been raised by the Sioux and could out-shoot, out-swim, out-run, out-hunt, out-ride, and out-fight any ten white soldiers.

I wanted to be that boy.

So bad.

So bad.

So bad I cried.

Then I got hold of myself and rewrote the letter with Mom's illegible scrawl as my guide to the correct spelling of "friend."

When I was done, I folded the letter, put it in my shirt pocket and headed downstairs. Timmy had settled in the middle of the stairwell with Mr. Monkey so I had to pick my way around him without touching a hair on his beloved little hide.

He stuck out his tongue at me as I passed, but I didn't retaliate. What was the use with Mom just around the corner?

I simply sighed and continued on down the stairs.

Mom was carrying on like the Queen of the May when I got to the living room, so I waited until they finished their hand or whatever they do in bridge. (To this day, I steadfastly refuse to learn the stupid game.)

Mom trumped or triumphed or whatever the hell they do in bridge, gloated at the losing guesties and glanced at me.

"Did you do as I said?" she said, smiling tightly.

"Yes, ma'am."

"Let me see."

I handed Mom the letter, and she proofed it in a twinkling. "Good. Now go and do as I told you, and then come straight home and go to your room. Then you can wait until your father comes home. He'll decide what to do with you."

"Yes, ma'am."

Aunt Lu grabbed me as I passed her table and said, "How about another kiss for your Aunt Lu?"

"Go ahead, Jackie," Mom said, anxious to accommodate the boss's wife.

I sighed and let Aunt Lu slurp my cheek and fondle Mr. Dingle Dangle. What choice did I have?

Then I continued on through the living room, dining room, kitchen and out the side door. It would have been easier to exit the front door from the living room, but when guesties were present the family had to use the servants' entrance. Excuse me, the side door.

When I got outside I wished I still had my dog Billy to go with me. But Mom had given my beloved Billy away after Dad's operation because she said Dad couldn't cope with having a big, dumb springer spaniel around the house. Never mind that I had met a kid whose father had actually gone out and bought him a puppy after the father had had the same exact operation.

Never mind a whole bunch of things.

Okay?

Okay, let's go on with the story.

I made myself think that Billy was probably better off with his new owner, some man Mom said was training him to pluck dead birds out of wet, swampy places. I knew Billy was a hunting dog, and I figured I had no right to raise him in a dry, old, city neighborhood with nothing but squirrels to chase, but I missed him so. I missed that liver-eyed dog like a torn-out lung or a sawed-off leg.

I still miss him.

But I knew then as I know now that there was no bringing Billy back, so I put on a happy mask and headed east on Dray Street for Casey's house.

Two doors down the block, old Man Holmstrom was out rubbing some kind of crud into the whitewalls of his new Cadillac. He glared at me as I passed and said: "You kids should play in your own neighborhood."

"But this is my neighborhood," I said.

"The hell it is. And I ever catch you kids playing around my new car, I'll see that they throw you in the Audey Home for life."

The Audey Home is what everybody called the Cook County Juvenile Detention Home. Don't ask me why everybody called it the Audey Home, because fortunately I was never sent there. But to this day the mere mention of those two words — Audey Home — arrests my heart.

"Yes, sir," I said to mean old Mr. Holmstrom.

"Now get the hell out of here."

"Yes, sir."

I trotted to the alley and hung a right.

I saw Casey's back fence and stopped trotting.

What if Mrs. O'Neal's planning to tar and feather me if I ever show my face at her door again?

I knew all about tar and feathering from a book Casey's father had in the basement.

Nah, she wouldn't do that.

She's a nice mom.

Well, sort of.

Well, sort of not really.

I took a deep breath and asked God what to do. Just like they taught me in Sunday School. Along with the story about that Christian boy my same age who had to chose between being thrown to the lions and renouncing Christ and living a comfortable pagan life. The story said he chose the lions without hesitation, and God kept him from feeling any pain.

But God wasn't relieving my pain as I stood there fretting, and He was not speaking to me in any language I recognized. However, I did find my feet moving me toward Casey's back gate. And then my hands were undoing the latch, and my feet were taking me right up to the back porch where my right hand reached right up and knocked.

The inside glass door was open so I could hear and see in through the screen door.

Casey was there at the kitchen table with some old man in a brown suit hovering over his head.

A doctor.

Had to be a doctor.

And Mrs. O'Neal was hovering behind the doctor holding herself like she was going to come apart if she didn't hold herself. Donald was handing the doctor things as he asked for them.

Obviously nobody heard me, so I knocked again.

Mrs. O'Neal looked at me with a start.

She screamed: "Get out of here, you little devil! And don't you ever come back!"

I took the letter out of my pocket and said, "My mom told me to give this to Casey."

"His name is Kevin, and he never wants to see you again. Now go, you little heathen!"

"Mom!"

It was Casey, and he wanted me to stay.

So did the doctor whose name turned out to be William A. Corcoran, M.D. A retired pediatrician from South Shore, he still called on the children of favored families like the O'Neals.

"All right," Mrs. O'Neal said with a nod to Dr. Corcoran. "But make it quick. Dr. Corcoran has other calls to make today, don't you, Doctor?"

"My only other appointment is with the first tee at South Shore Country Club," Dr. Corcoran said, winking at me. His voice was a buzz saw with honey on it, but it sure was music to my ears that day.

"Well, don't just stand there, John Yardley. Come in and give your letter to Kevin. And then go back where you belong," Mrs. O'Neal said.

She was a pretty woman with blonde hair, blue-green eyes and a Donna Reed dress. She had a regal bearing about her which came from being president of the Saint Bartholomew Rosary Altar Society. Although they actually lived in Saint Margaret of Scotland parish, the O'Neal's attended Mass at Saint Bartholomew Catholic

Church because that was the parish for lace-curtain Irish. Saint Margaret's was for the shanty-Irish and mixed breeds who lived on the eastern edge of our white enclave.

My hand gripped the door, but I couldn't pull it open.

"That's John Yardley Junior," Donald O'Neal explained to the doctor. "He's the one who tried to kill Kevin with the rock."

"I'm sure he didn't mean to kill Kevin," Dr. Corcoran said. "Come in, son. Nobody's going to hurt you."

I advanced into the O'Neal kitchen and swallowed.

Although he had this great big bandage on his head, Casey didn't look so bad for a boy who had been hit in the hit with a rock. He smiled at me.

I smiled at him and handed him in the letter.

"Let me see that," Mrs. O'Neal said, tearing it out of his hands.

I noticed that Mrs. O'Neal didn't move her lips as she read like Mom. She smiled ever so slightly and said, "That's a very nice letter. Now you can go."

"Can't I see it, Mom?" Casey said.

Mrs. O'Neal folded the letter and handed it to me.

I took it and handed it to Casey.

Mrs. O'Neal reached for the letter, but Dr. Corcoran shook his finger at her, and she restrained herself.

Casey read the letter real fast because he was the best reader in our class and grinned. "Course you're still my friend. You'll always be my friend. You weren't trying to kill me. You were just stronger than I thought. I never should have dared you to throw that rock."

"That's true, Mother," Donald said. "Kevin did dare John Yardley Junior to the throw the rock. His exact words were: 'Betcha can't throw a rock this far.' And John Yardley Junior did throw a rock that far, and it hit Kevin right in the head, and that's just what happened."

"Well, there's no serious damage done," Dr. Corcoran proclaimed. "Just a few stitches, and I doubt he'll have a scar when I take them out. Maybe a little one, but it'll be something to show the young ladies when he gets older."

"My baby is never going to get older," Mrs. O'Neal said, pursing her lips.

"Mom, I'm seven years old already, and . . ."

"Well, that's as old as I'm going to let you get. And that's my final word on the subject. And as for you, Mr. Yardley, you've done what your mother told you to do, and now you can see yourself out. Dr. Corcoran still has lots of work to do on my baby."

"I'm nearly done, Mrs. O'Neal. Let the boy stay. It'll be good for them both."

"Yeah, Mom," Casey said, "let Jackie stay. Pretty please."

Mrs. O'Neal looked into my dark little Public soul and saw something sparkle because she said, "All right. John Yardley can stay for 10 minutes, but I want to you to play in the basement."

Not just any basement, mind you.

Casey's Basement.

Chapter Two

The one inside stairway to the basement started right there in the kitchen.

Casey grabbed my hand when Dr. Corcoran had finished with his head and said: "Come on, Jackie, I want to show you somethin'."

Casey tore down the rubber-coated wooden stairs, and I scrambled after him.

"Don't run, Kevin," Mrs. O'Neal called after us. "You've just had a severe head injury. And no rough-housing down there. Do you hear me?"

Casey stopped at the landing and said, "Yes, ma'am."

Then he winked at me, and we jumped the last flight to the concrete basement floor.

A heady mixture of mildew, paint thinner, drying clothes and grass clippings hit me in nostrils. I looked into the vast, gloomy gray rectangle that was Casey's basement and became fully alive.

For this was our world.

A world where Mr. O'Neal tread only twice a year — once in the spring to exchange the storms for the screens and once in the fall for the reverse. Sure, Mrs. O'Neal had her laundry room in the basement, but she never came down when we were playing in the basement. Actually, we weren't allowed to play in the basement when she was doing her laundry because she feared we would tear it all down or something. And she only did her laundry once a week on Monday mornings, so we always made other plans on Monday mornings.

But the best thing was that because of the mildew and mold and creeping crude down in Casey's basement, Donald couldn't stay down there for more than five minutes. Made him cough and sneeze.

So when Casey and I went to play in the basement, Donald would go and practice on the piano in the living room. I never even saw Casey's living room until I was 16, but Casey said it was right over the storeroom where his father's wooden ship models were, and I took his word for it.

Casey's two oldest siblings, Russell, 16, and Laura, 12, had long ago forsaken the basement for their rooms on the second floor of the O'Neal stretch bungalow.

That's why we called it Casey's basement, because it was his entire floor.

Granted it wasn't much of a floor — square foot after square foot of bucking and heaving poured concrete. It was painted battleship gray with genuine U.S. Navy paint Casey's retired Navy Captain of a father had procured for that purpose.

Casey's basement was frightfully cold in the winter except in the middle room by the smelly, blue-flame-shooting gas heater.

But in summer it was the coolest part of the O'Neal house, even if it did smell like rotting old Indian bones.

Which is precisely what Casey wanted to show me that fateful day I beaned him with a rock.

"Come on," he said, leading me forward to the storage room under the right front corner of the house.

He pulled the chain on the hanging light bulb and said, "I found this really neat book about the Iroquois. It tells all about how they'd capture Jesuit priests and then do this really neat torture stuff to them. Usually it would take all night and even longer to kill the priest, and he was never supposed to make a peep, because he was becoming a Catholic martyr, and Catholic martyrs never cried, even while they were sticking red-hot pokers in their eyes. Come on, Jackie, you'll love it. And it's got really cool pictures."

Boy, did it have really cool pictures.

Like the one of the Iroquois placing a collar of red-hot hatchets on the neck of Father Jean de Brebeuf, founder of the Huron mission. There was another picture of the Iroquois "baptizing" de Brebeuf and his associate Lalemant with boiling water.

"Cool," Casey said.

"Yeah," I said.

"And it says the guy with the red-hot hatchets on his neck didn't make a peep until he died. I guess the other guy yelled and screamed sometimes, but they tortured him a lot longer. Think you'd scream if somebody put red-hot hatchets on your neck?"

I remembered how I had hollered when I fell and broke both my wrists and shook my head.

"I could take it," Casey said. "It's because I'm Catholic. God gives Catholics extra strength for stuff like this. That's what Sister teaches us in Catechism. Like this guy in the picture – when they Indians put those red-hot hatchets on his neck, he didn't feel a thing."

"You think so? His face looks kind of – well, he doesn't look real happy."

"That's because this isn't a photograph. If it was a photograph of the way he really looked at the time, he'd look really happy because he knew he was becoming a Catholic martyr. You Publics don't have martyrs so you don't know what it's like, but believe me – he didn't feel a thing."

"Okay. Casey?"

"What?"

"You feel all right?"

"Sure, Jackie. I'm fine. No big deal. You just hit me in the head with rock is all. It's not like you put red-hot hatchets around my neck or poured boiling water on my head."

"Yeah."

Casey flipped the page. "Look at this – they're cutting his lip off and sticking a red-hot poker down his throat. Neat!"

"Yeah!"

Casey flipped us all the way through the exposition of atrocities visited on the Jesuit missionaries, and then he found a book about Ancient Greece.

"You know the story of the 300 Spartans?"

"Sort of."

"Boy, you Publics don't know anything. Here, I'll show you."

Casey transported me back to 486 B.C. and was positioning me with the 300 Spartans and 700 Thespians in the pass of Thermopylae against Xerxes's 180,000 Persians when Mrs. O'Neal came down to the first landing and called, "Okay, John Yardley. It's time for you to go home. And, Kevin, it's time for you to come upstairs and rest. You've had a terrible shock."

"Okay, Mom." Casey shrugged. "Guess you've got to go."

"Yeah," I said, looking at my friend. "Casey, I'm really sorry I hit you with that rock. I really didn't mean . . ."

"You didn't mean to hit me, and my head doesn't even hurt. I was just scared because of all the blood. That's why I ran home like that. But now it's like it never even happened. Except the stitches sting a little bit, and he gave me this shot so I wouldn't get . . ."

"He gave you a shot?"

"Yeah."

"In the butt?"

"Yeah."

"Those are the worst."

"You're tellin' me. I could take the red-hot hatchets or all those Persian guys shootin' arrows at me, but give me a shot in the butt and I'd tell 'em where the secret A-bomb base is in a second."

"Me too."

We looked at one another and laughed.

Then Casey punched me on the bicep. I counter-punched him, and he pulled the light chain.

"Kevin!" Mrs. O'Neal called. "Didn't you hear me?"

"Coming, Mom."

Casey punched me in the dark. "It was like this for the slaves in the Underground Railroad. That old house on Morgan Street was on the Underground Railroad. My dad says the old lady who lives there will show kids where they hid the slaves if you ask real nice. Wanna go sometime?"

"Yeah! I'd like that."

"Me too. Come on, Jackie, we'd better go, or my mom's gonna kill me."

Casey led me to the door to the backyard.

I turned at the door and said, "Casey?"

"What?"

"You sure we're still friends?"

He punched me again. "Of course I'm sure. Now go on home, and you can come over tomorrow. We've got the whole summer in front of us—we've got to start making plans. There's all these books in here, and we haven't even started on my dad's wooden ships from the Navy. You like the Civil War?"

"I think so."

"Well, my dad's got this really neat book with all these pictures about it. Did you know in the Battle of the Wilderness there was this big fire and all the wounded guys got burned up alive?"

"Neat."

"Yeah. And there was this prison camp in Georgia called Andersonville where the Yankee prisoners were so starved they had to go looking through their own turds for food."

"Really?"

"Yeah, it's all there in my dad's book."

"Your dad's sure got a lot of neat books."

"Yeah. It's 'cause he was in the Navy and all that stuff. And from college and all."

"My dad was in college and the Navy and all, but he doesn't have all the neat books your dad has."

Casey shrugged. "My dad's a Catholic, and your dad's a Public. That's why."

"Yeah, that's probably . . ."

"Kevin!" Mrs. O'Neal called.

"Coming, Mom." Casey opened the door and whispered, "Come by tomorrow, and we'll look at that Civil War book. Okay?"

"Okay. If I can."

"Why couldn't you?"

I shrugged. "My mom said my dad's going to decide what my punishment's going to be when he gets home, and sometimes when he gets home — ah, you don't want to hear it."

"Kevin! Do you hear me?"

"Coming, Mom." Casey whispered to me, "Well, if they hold you prisoner, I'll come by and help you escape. How's that?"

"Neat."

We punched one another again for good measure, and I skeedaddled home.

Mom was in the kitchen washing the bridge club dishes and draining the unfinished sherry out of her fancy crystal glasses.

She turned on me when I came in and demanded: "Where the hell have you been all afternoon?!?"

"It wasn't all afternoon, and I was at Casey's giving him the letter you told me to . . ."

Slap!

Right in the little kisser with the back of Mom's hand.

I fell back against the stove and covered my face.

"His name is Kevin, and I told you to give him the letter and come straight home. But did you listen to me? No, you deliberately disobeyed me and stayed over there half the afternoon." Mom tore my hand away from my face and added: "Are you listening to me?"

"Yes, ma'am, but I . . ."

"Don't but me, young man." She slapped me another backhand and asked if I had shown my letter to Mrs. O'Neal.

"Yes, ma'am."

"Well?"

"Well what?"

Mom yanked my wrist and said, "Well, what did she say?"

"She said it was a nice letter."

Mom flung me against the stove. "That's good. The shanty-Irish bitch. You wouldn't see that little runt of hers running over here to apologize if he hit you in the head with a rock, would you?"

"I don't know. Casey, I mean, Kevin would . . ."

"Oh shut up and go to your room. I've had enough of your lip for one day. Your father can decide what to do with you when he comes home from work."

I swallowed the blood from Mom's slaps and slunk toward the dining room.

Mom turned to her dishes and drained another glass of sherry. Then she lighted a Kent cigarette and sucked the smoke deep into her lungs. She had told Dad after his operation she was going to quit when she was good and ready, and she pretty much had, but she smoked whenever I was a trial to her. And it was sure obvious that I was being a trial to her that afternoon.

Poor Mom.

Poor, poor Mom.

I stopped at the edge of the dining room and watched Mom smoke. I prayed to God to make her stop because I sure didn't want two parents with holes in their throats. Excuse me, stomas. They're called stomas. The holes in the throats of laryngectomees like my dad.

John Yardley Senior.

I gulped.

He'd be home before long and I hadn't picked up the front yard or brought up the mixes from the basement for "grown-up time."

"Mom?"

Mom turned on me with a jolt. "Are you still here? I thought I told you to go to your room."

"I-I-I will, but maybe I should pick up the front yard first. Before Dad comes home. And bring up the mixes for the guesties."

"He's not having guesties tonight. I've had a long day at the bridge table, and the last thing I need is guesties. Especially that dreadful creature from across the street and that big lunk of a Lithuanian from next door. If Pearl Carroll wants to carry on an affair with Big Mike Jozaitus, she can go rent a motel room like all the other tramps. She's not going to use my living room for her seductions. Do you hear me?"

"Yes, ma'am."

"Good. Now do as you're told and go to your room."

"But what about the front yard? If I don't pick up the front yard, Dad's gonna be real . . ."

"Oh, let your father pick up the front yard for a change. He's probably been having one of his long, liquid lunches this afternoon, so he'll be pickled when he gets home from work. And in a foul mood."

Mom exhaled and glared at her cigarette. "See what you've made me do, Jackie? You've made me so upset with all your hooliganism that I've gone and had a cigarette after I promised your father I'd quit."

"I'm sorry, Mom."

"Well, you'd better be, you goddamned kid." Mom smiled wistfully and added: "You know, That's just what that janitor in South Shore called you — 'the goddamned kid.' You were the unholy terror of the whole apartment building. You were such a little devil the old ladies would call me to see if you were taking a nap before they'd leave their apartments. They called you the 'little monster,' but the janitor called you the goddamned kid. He used to have to come and take the door off the hinges because you'd lock yourself in the bathroom and hide behind the toilet. I can still hear him with that German accent of his calling you the goddamn kid."

So could I, and the memory of that evil man made my knees
buckle. I wanted desperately to ask Mom what I could do to redeem
myself in her eyes and stop being the goddamn kid, but I could not
speak.

Mom smelled my terror and laughed. "That's more like it. This
is the way you should behave all the time. Now go to your room and
don't come down until I tell you to."

"Yes, ma'am."

I went straight to the room I shared with Timmy and found him
sitting on his bed engrossed in conversation with Mr. Monkey. He
hugged his monkey at the sight of me and said he'd tell Mom if I
even blinked at him twice.

The little shit.

"I'm not going to touch you or Mr. Monkey," I said.

"Well, you'd better not, or I'll tell Mom."

"Since you like Mom so much, why don't you go down and play
with her?"

"This is my room too. And I was here first."

"Well, I was here before you were even born, Timmy."

"No, you weren't, Jackie. We lived in South Shore when I was
born. You weren't here when I was born, because we lived in South
Shore when I was born. I remember."

"Good for you."

I went to the desk we were supposed to share and found Timmy's
Crayolas and coloring books covering my things.

"Timmy!"

"What?"

"I told you not to leave your stuff out like this. When you're done
coloring, put your Crayolas and books in your drawer where they
belong. Don't leave them out like this. This is my desk too and you
left your junk all over my things."

"It's my desk as much as yours, Jackie. Besides, I'm not done
coloring."

"Yes, you are. You're playing with that stupid monkey."

"He's not stupid."

"Is too."

"Is not."

"Is too."

Timmy screamed: "IS NOT!!!"

I defecated my heart and waited in terror for Mom to come charging up from the kitchen.

"She's really gonna get you this time," Timmy said, gloating.

"Shhh," I said, listening intently.

All quiet on the kitchen front.

"She's coming. Don't you worry."

I shook my head. "I don't think she heard you, Timmy."

"Well, I'll scream even louder this time."

"No," I said, rushing to his side.

"Don't touch me!"

"All right," I said, backing away. "But don't scream again. Okay?"

Timmy hugged his monkey and glowered at me. "I hate you, Jackie. I wish Mom *would* give you to the next passing Indian. I wish she had given you away with your dumb dog."

I wanted to kill the little fucker on the spot, but I knew I was trapped. Trapped with an alcoholic and his enabling wife and the eternal guesties and a snitch of a brother. So I held my breath for five seconds, exhaled and smiled so big and so wide at Timmy he giggled.

"What's so funny?"

"You. You look like that clown Uncle Kenny painted for us."

I looked at the oil Mom's brother Kenny painted for us and smiled. I liked Uncle Kenny even though I had only seen him twice in my whole life. He lived by himself in Philadelphia, and Dad was always saying how "crazy" he was, but he sure painted a wonderful clown picture for Timmy and me, and he sure signed it: "To my two nice boys, Love, Uncle Kenny."

"Thanks," I said.

Timmy stared at me. "Why are you thanking me? It's a really dumb picture."

"No it's not. I think it's the best clown picture I've ever seen."

"There's one in my coloring book that's better."

"Hah."

"Hah yourself, Jackie."

I sighed. "Well, since you hate Uncle Kenny's picture so much, I'll take it when we get older and leave home."

"And I'm going to take the desk," Timmy retorted.

"Oh no you won't."

Oh yes he did, but that's another story.

In this story, Timmy and I soon tired of fighting and had retreated to our respective corners when Mom called up the stairwell: "Jackie, your father's going to be home any minute. You'd better pick up the front yard, or you'll be in even more trouble than you're in already."

I looked up from the picture I was drawing of Indians putting red-hot hatchets around this Catholic guy's neck and shook my head at the inconsistent logic of adults. Hadn't Mom told me in the kitchen not to worry about the front lawn? Hadn't she said that it was time Dad picked up the sticks and leaves that fell from our oak trees himself?

"Jackie!"

"Yes, ma'am."

"Did you hear what I said, or are you going deaf on me?"

"I heard you, Mom, but . . ."

"Don't but me, young man. Get out there and pick up the front lawn. And bring up the mixes from the basement."

"But . . ."

"Jackie!"

"Yes, ma'am." I turned to Timmy and whispered, "Why don't you help me? If you help me, I'll show you how to draw without a coloring book."

"I don't want to draw without a coloring book. Besides, she told you to do it, not me. Mom says I'm not old enough to have to do chores. Just you, Jackie."

The kid had a point.

The kid always had a point.

"Come on, Timmy."

"You go on, Jackie. Mom said I don't have to help you, and I'm not gonna."

I sighed. "Okay. But I'll remember this."

"Good. So will I."

"Jackie! Are you deaf, or are you . . ."

"Coming, Mom."

I raced down to her, and she slapped me one on the cheek.

"When I call, you come. Do you understand?"

"Yes, ma'am."

"Now get cracking. Your father's going to be home any minute."

I cracked straight down to the basement and, though it pained and strained my still-healing wrists, brought up four quarts of Canada Dry "mixes" in a single trip. And these were heavy glass bottles with metal caps that dug into my hands as I carried them.

Mom was waiting in the kitchen and inspected my load.

"Get two more bottles of tonic. It's summer — they'll all be drinking gin and tonics tonight. Don't you know anything?"

"Sorry."

I raced back down to the basement and dutifully fetched two bottles of tonic.

Then I dashed out the side door to the front yard and picked up every last leaf and twig. I was bending over for the last one when I glanced west down Dray Street and saw Dad lumbering around the corner from Forest Avenue. He walked to and from the Rock Island commuter station at 107th Street every day, and although it was barely half-a-mile, he likened it to the Bataan Death March.

Poor Dad.

Poor, poor Dad.

I could tell from two blocks away that he was in one of his "moods," so I policed the yard one more time and slunk back into the house via the side door. I went to the living room and took my usual vigil at the edge of the picture window. Mom appeared and surveyed the yard.

She said "good" and went to the kitchen to fill Dad's ice bucket and arrange his bottles.

Timmy remained upstairs with Mr. Monkey.

I felt Dad before I saw him. He was a big, menacing Republican in a gray, summer-weight wool suit with a hole in his throat. Excuse me, stoma. His thick waves of black hair and broad Saxon face reminded people of the English actor, Jack Hawkins.

That evening he wore a menacing scowl which meant he'd done just as Mom had said and gone out for a long, liquid lunch to either Binyon's, the Berghoff, or Miller's. Or probably, as Dad said, a triple-header, with turtle soup and pot roast and martinis and stingers at Binyon's, a few glasses of famous Berghoff beer at the

Berghoff's stand-up men's bar, and then a long afternoon at Miller's with Mr. Gin and his Tonics and Lime. Dad said nobody knew how to make better gin and tonics than his good pal Andy the bartender at Miller's on Adams.

Nobody that is but Dad. AKA: John Yardley Senior.

I cowered as he halted in front of our house and inspected the yard. At first he seemed pleased with my work, but then a June wind rustled through the pin oak at the point of our front yard, showering the old man with leaves and twigs.

Dad cursed, kicked the tree and snatched a handful of debris.

If he's mad now, I thought, wait'll Mom tells him what I did to Casey. He'll kill me for sure. Dear God protect me!

I thought of hiding in the basement, but I'd have to run Mom's gauntlet in the kitchen to get there. No use in going upstairs: Dad'd just kick the door down like the time he thought I had taken his leather Navy flight jacket. Never mind that Mom's weekly maid, Daisy, had put it in the wrong closet. I still got kicked in the ribs and cursed to hell.

So that day I just stood my ground and waited for the big guy to burst through the front door. If I knew then what I know now, I would have given the bastard the finger, but I was just a cowering little kid who loved his daddy.

So I gulped and said, "I'm sorry" as soon as he appeared.

He scowled at me, threw the tree debris at my feet, and grabbed his voice box, or electro-larynx, out of his pocket.

Yes, the battery-powered electro-larynx is a miracle product that has given voice to millions of silenced citizens, but I still cower every time I hear a person speak with one.

"Goddamn kid!" Dad buzzed. "I thought I told you to pick up the front yard before I get home."

"Yes, Dad."

"Then why the hell was the yard full of branches?"

'The wind, Dad. The wind knocked . . ."

"Like hell it did." He grabbed me by the shirt and shook me. "Your mother works and slaves for you kids all day—the least you can do is pick up the front yard for her. Now get out there and do it right this time."

He dropped me like a rotten fish and was stomping off to his "bar" in the corner of the kitchen when Mom appeared and said, "Did you tell your father what you did to Kevin O'Neal today?"

Thanks Mom.

Thanks a whole fucking bundle.

Dad about-faced and said, "Well?!? I've had a long, hard day so spit it out."

I spat it out, and Dad shrugged.

"Don't you have anything to say, John?" Mom said.

"I told you, Doris, I had a long, hard day at the office. This is grown-up time — do you think I care what this stupid kid does when I'm not home? As long as he didn't kill the little mick and they're not going to sue us, I don't give a damn. Just tell the little brat to get out there and pick up the yard right. That's all I ask. Now get the hell out of my way so I can get a drink."

Mom moved her lips in protest but wisely got out of Dad's way. He was not adverse to kicking her in the shins when she got in his way. I know because I saw him do it many times until I was big enough to stop him.

Mom came over and grabbed me by the ear and said, "Well even if he doesn't care, I do, and you're not to play outside for an entire week."

"But, Mom, summer vacation just started and . . ."

SLAP!!

"But, Mom . . ."

SLAP!!

"Don't but me, young man. You can just sit up there in your room and think about what you did to that poor boy. Even if he is Catholic."

"Yes, ma'am."

"That's better. Now get out there and pick up the yard the way your father wants. I'm going to finish dinner if I can get in my kitchen. Just for once I'd like to have a real family dinner."

"Yes, ma'am."

"Just go."

"Yes, ma'am."

I scrambled out the front door and was just finishing up in the front yard when Dad appeared, gin and tonic in hand, at the picture window. He took a long, satisfied sip and went to the phonograph where I could see him unsheathe the old Glen Miller album.

Then he returned and hoisted his glass. It was the signal for the other drunks on the block that "Yardley's Bar & Grill" was officially open for the night.

Margaret "Pearl" Carroll was the first to answer the call. She lived directly across the street in a rambling old frame house and dressed like the madam of a declining whorehouse.

Dad pounded on the picture window and gestured angrily toward "Aunt" Pearl. That meant I was supposed to go over and help the buxom lush across the street. Not because Dray Street was so congested at that time of night, but because the old girl favored heels halfway up the Himalayas.

"Hi, sweetie," she said, teetering at the curb with her empty cocktail glass. "Did you come to get your Aunt Pearl?"

No relation, but we were one big, happy family in the old neighborhood.

"Yes, Aunt Pearl."

"How about a kiss for your Aunt Pearl?"

Watching those glistening, red lips descend on my face, I knew how John the Baptist felt as the sword came slashing down on his neck. We had studied all about John the Baptist in Sunday School. I closed my eyes and puckered my little lips.

SMACK!!

Her high-octane breath and man-killer perfume intoxicated me as she kissed me fully on the lips. Then she patted me on the rump and took my hand.

"Okay, sweetie," she said, hiking up her gold-on-silver house dress, "the queen is ready to cross the Thames."

And what a queen. Even at seven, I sensed her raw sexuality. So did every man in the neighborhood, especially "Big Mike" Jozaitus, the towering Lithuanian cop who lived next door to us. Didn't matter that Pearl and Big Mike were both married with kids, they liked to meet at Yardley's Bar & Grill and head out from there for a night of true debauchery.

Pearl's crossing of the "Thames" was always Big Mike's signal to head over with his half-gallon of bourbon, so I got my two cents in fast. Pearl was the only adult who ever listened to me.

When we reached my side of the street I said: "I hit my best friend Casey O'Neal in the head with a rock today on the way home from school. In the alley by Mr. Shermer's. It was an accident, and Casey's not mad at me or anything, but Mom thinks I tried to kill him, and she won't let me go out for a week even though it's the very, very beginning of summer vacation. It was an accident, Aunt Pearl. Honest Injun."

"I believe you, sweetie."

"Casey was standing way aways from me in the alley, and he dared me to throw a rock as far as him, and I did."

Aunt Pearl bent down and squeezed my bicep. "I always knew you were going to be a star baseball pitcher. I've told your father that at least ten thousand times."

"You told Dad that?"

"Oh yes." Aunt Pearl smiled. "So you just turned out to be stronger than your friend thought. If you ask me, the whole thing was his fault because he underestimated your strength."

"What?"

"He should have known better than to dare a big, strong boy like you to throw a rock that far. And he certainly should have had the good sense to get out of the way."

"Yeah," I said, digesting Aunt Pearl Pearl's wisdom. "Aunt Pearl?"

"What, sweetie?"

"Do you think you could maybe talk to Mom and . . ."

"Consider it done, sweetie. Now, if you'll be kind enough to escort your old Aunt Pearl up the steps, I'll have a long talk with your mother and get you out of the dog house."

"Really?"

"Really."

I looked up at her and said, "Aunt Pearl, you're not old. You'll never be old. And you'll always be a beautiful lady."

That made perfect sense to Aunt Pearl, and she gave me another wet kiss as I escorted her up the front steps to Yardley's Bar & Grill.

Chapter Three

Aunt Pearl never did get around to talking to Mom that night.

How could she when she was in the living room having a high old time with Dad and Big Mike Jozaitus and the rest of the guesties, and Mom was in the kitchen trying to feed Timmy and me in the breakfast nook?

All Mom said was: "Just for once I'd like to have a normal family dinner without all these guesties."

And all Aunt Pearl said was: "Sweetie, you'd better bring up some more tonic, because more guesties are arriving."

I went to bed listening to Glen Miller music and drunken laughter and awoke to Dad putzing around in the bathroom and Mom telling me that the punishment was still on — I had to stay in my room for a week.

Despite the fact that it was just the most beautiful June day a let-out-of-school kid could dream up. Not too hot, no humidity, and a delicious wind from the northeast with great gobs of white clouds. It was a day for playing army in the backyard, or bike riding over to the park, or putting pennies on the Rock Island tracks, or eight million other things.

It was not a day for sitting in my room watching Timmy talk to Mr. Monkey.

But Mom was adamant.

Absolutely.

"As soon as I get your father off to work, you can come down and have breakfast, do your chores, and then it's back up to your room. Do I make myself clear, young man?"

"Yes, ma'am."

"And don't wake your brother. He's littler than you and needs his rest."

"Yes, ma'am."

Mom breezed off to get Dad's juice, coffee and toast, and I lay in bed listening to the old man force his bowels to move. I swore then and there that I'd eat whatever it took to have good healthy bowel movements, because I sure didn't want to go through what Dad suffered every morning.

When he was finally out of the bathroom, I slipped in there and did a fast poop and wash. Mom had put Timmy and me in the tub the night before, so I just ran a wash rag over my face and slunk back to my room.

I got out my clothes and waited for Dad to lumber downstairs.

After an eternity squared, he did. I could hear him downstairs buzzing at Mom about something, probably telling her to tell me to do a better job of picking up the front yard.

And then he was off to his good, big insurance company in the Loop. And surely another triple-header, and then another evening at Yardley's Bar & Grill.

But we were free of him for the next nine hours, and, oh, what a feeling.

What glory!

What ecstasy!!

I threw on some red shorts, a t-shirt, the brand-new short-sleeve shirt Mom had bought me, white socks and my trusty pair of Keds and descended.

"Did you wake up your brother?" Mom asked when I walked into the kitchen.

"No."

"I thought I told you to wake up your brother."

"Mom, you told me not to . . ."

SLAP!!

"Go wake up your brother, you little brat!"

"Yes, ma'am."

"And be gentle. He's just a little boy."

"Yes, ma'am."

I went back upstairs, lifted Timmy's covers and tickled his feet.

Timmy giggled in his sleep.

I tickled some more.

Timmy's eyes fluttered.

I continued tickling.

Timmy awakened, looked at me, and screamed: "Mom, Jackie's tryin' to hurt me!!!"

Mom was up the stairs in a flash and laying the back of her hand against my cheek.

"I thought I told you to be gentle with your little brother."

"Yes, ma'am. But I was . . ."

"Don't you but me."

"But . . ."

SLAP!!

"Now apologize to your little brother."

"Yes, ma'am." I turned to Timmy and said, "I'm sorry, Timmy."

Timmy gave me a withering look and opened his arms so Mom could give him a big kiss and hug.

I wanted to go in the bathroom and puke, but I knew that would send Mom over the edge, so I just stood there like a little angel.

A little fallen angel that is.

Anyway, Mom sent me downstairs to feed myself while she tended to her tender Timmy, and I was just finishing my second bowl of Frosted Flakes when Casey appeared at the side door and hollered: "Yo, Jack-ee!!"

I choked on my Frosted Flakes.

"Yo, Jack-ee!!"

I held my breath and willed Casey to go away.

"Yo, Jack-ee!!"

I slunk to the side door and whispered, "Hi, Casey."

Casey grinned and said in a normal voice, "Come on, Jackie, I got a whole bunch of pennies — let's go over to the Rock Island tracks. Then we can go to Ridge Park and Reed's Toy Store and get some more soldiers and go play in my basement. What do you say?"

I put my finger to my lips and looked up.

Nothing.

"What's the matter?" Casey whispered.

"My mom."

"What's the matter with your mom?"

"She says I can't go out for a week because I hit you with a rock."

Casey banged his stitches with the back of his hand and laughed. "Is that all?"

"Well . . ."

"Let me talk to her, Jackie."

"Casey, I don't know if that's such a good idea. She's awful mad this morning, and . . ."

"Outta my way," Casey said, pulling open the door and pushing past me.

He walked right into the living room and waited for Mom to come down with Timmy.

"Good morning, Mrs. Yardley," he said, angelically.

Mom was moved.

I was awe-struck. Casey was worth watching.

"Good morning, Kevin," Mom said, clutching Timmy. "How is your head?"

"Just fine, Mrs. Yardley. Just a few stitches is all, but it feels like it never even happened, and it really wasn't Jackie's fault. Honest."

Mom pursed her lips and looked at me.

I shrugged.

Casey said: "I bet Jackie that he couldn't throw a rock as far as me, and I just didn't think he was as strong as he is, so it's really my fault, and I forgive him, and my mom says it's okay for him to come over and for me to play with him, and it's the first day of summer vacation, and I thought we'd maybe go for a bike ride or something and then play at my house."

Timmy nodded at the notion of having Mom all to himself, and Mom seemed swayed by Casey's sweet reason.

What a little brown nose, I thought. Even then I knew Casey was destined to go into public relations.

"Please, Mrs. Yardley," Casey said. "Jackie's my best friend in the whole world, and I sure don't think he should have to suffer because of something that was my fault."

"You say your mother will let you play with Jackie?"

"Oh yes, Mrs. Yardley. She said you can call her if you want."

"Well, I have been meaning to invite your mother to join my bridge group, so I suppose I will call her. Is she home right now?"

"Yes, ma'am."

I looked at Casey, and he batted his blue eyes at me.

"Very well, I'm going to phone your mother, Kevin, and see what she has to say about all this. Jackie, get your brother a bowl of cereal. Do you hear me?"

"Yes, ma'am."

Casey and I took Timmy to the breakfast nook and got him cereal while Mom called Mrs. O'Neal from the phone in the kitchen. She put on her best bridge club voice and chatted for quite some time about the rock-throwing incident.

I judged from her expression that Mrs. O'Neal was telling her just what she wanted to hear: namely, that the O'Neals weren't going to sue us, charge us for Casey's stitches, or spread awful things about us around the neighborhood.

Mom was so impressed with what Mrs. O'Neal had to say that she finally made herself say: "Say, Mrs. O'Neal . . . all right, Mary Theresa, I was thinking—we can always use another player in our bridge club, and I was wondering if you'd care to join us. We're meeting next week at Lu Hinchcliff's, and I'd be happy to drive you. I think you'd really like the group." (Even though this is 1957, and they're all Protestants, and you're Catholic. And we've never had a Catholic in our bridge club. Never.)

Way to go, Mom, I thought. You might slap me silly, but you're doing the right thing by inviting Casey's mom to join your bridge club. Of course, you're really just following my example, and Dad's been friends with Big Mike Jozaitus since we moved here, and Big Mike's as Catholic as they come, at least his wife is, but this is really something for you to invite a Catholic to your bridge club.

Way to go, Mom!

Mom gasped when Mrs. O'Neal accepted her offer but quickly recovered with a valiant "that's wonderful, Mrs. O'Neal, I mean Mary Theresa. I'll plan on picking you up next Monday morning at 10:30 . . . Yes, I'm glad we've had this conversation too . . . Yes, I will . . . That would be lovely . . . Yes, I'll talk to John about it . . . Of course . . . You too. Bye bye."

Mom cradled the phone and came over to Casey. "You have a lovely mother, Kevin." (For a shanty-Irish Catholic.)

"Thank you, Mrs. Yardley," Casey said, unctuous as ever.

"I'm sorry I didn't invite her to join my bridge club sooner." Mom licked her upper lip and muttered, "I'm sure she'll be just fine. The others will accept her as the lovely lady she is. What difference does it make that she's a . . . well, Jackie, you can go play with Kevin if you're finished eating."

"I'm finished, Mom. But what about my chores?"

"Chores?"

"You know—taking out the trash and picking up the front yard."

"I'll take out the trash, and you can pick up the front yard before your father comes home."

I blinked up at Mom and thought, gee, Casey's mom must be even better with the blarney than Casey.

"Really?"

"Yes. Now go. I've got lots to do today, and I don't need you getting under foot."

The prison gates opened wide, and Casey and I tumbled gleefully into the driveway.

"That was great, Casey," I whispered.

He shrugged modestly. "You just have to know what to say to grown-ups is all. Now get your bike, and let's ride."

I got my red Schwinn Hornet out of the garage, and Casey and I tore over to the Rock Island Railroad's "South Suburban" commuter line and looked south along the tracks toward Blue Island.

"One comin'?" Casey said, reaching in his pocket.

"Yeah. Looks like he's at 115th Street."

"Good. That'll give me plenty of time to put all these pennies on the tracks."

"All of 'em? But won't that derail the train?"

"No way. Not if I spread 'em out on both rails. Just watch the train, okay?"

"Okay."

I watched the end-of-rush-hour commuter train grow ever closer as it made its scheduled stops at 111th and 107th streets.

"Casey, it's leaving 107th Street. Time to get away from the tracks."

Casey glanced at the approaching train and shrugged. "Nah, there's still plenty of time."

"Are you nuts? He's comin'!! Come on, Casey, I don't like this."

"Well, how about this then?" Casey got on his knees and put his head on the rail with his face turned away from the approaching train.

The engineer in the Electro-Motive E8 hit the air horn, and I hollered, "Casey, he's comin'!! Get off the tracks!!"

Casey looked up at me and laughed. "I can feel the train through the rail. Put your head down here and feel the train, Jackie. It's really neat."

I looked at the big, bulb-nosed diesel locomotive bearing down on Casey and pleaded: "Please, Casey. He's gonna hit you if you don't get off the tracks."

"Don't worry, Jackie, I can feel just when it's time to scram." And he did.

Don't ask me how, but the little son-of-a-bitch picked his head off the track and scrammed at exactly the right moment. Would have made a great scene in a movie, because it would have left audiences wondering for weeks how Hollywood pulled off such a stunt without killing anyone.

It left me weak in the knees and short of breath, and it made the poor engineer madder than hell.

He leaned out of the cab as he surged past and yelled: "Goddamn kids! I'm gonna report you to the police."

"Go ahead," Casey said, flinging a rock at the train. "You big jerk!"

The passengers in the heavyweight green coaches looked at us with alarm as Casey's rock caromed off the side of the second car.

"Casey!"

"What?"

"What's wrong with you?"

Casey pointed at his stitches and said, "You. You hit me in the head with a rock. I was fine until you hit me in the head with a rock yesterday. I never would have done something like this if you hadn't hit me in the head with a rock. I was looking in one of my dad's books, and it said people go nuts when they get blows to their heads."

"How do you know it said that? We're only in first grade; we can't read that much."

"We're in second grade now, Jackie, and I can read ten times more than you. It's 'cause I practice all the time on my dad's books. There's one I want to show you later. It's really neat. All about this German doctor during the war who conducted these experiments on people in concentration camps. You'll really like it. And don't worry, it's got plenty of pictures for dumb Publics like you who can't read much."

"You want a fat lip?"

"You already hit me in the head with a rock and messed up my brain, Jackie. What else do you got to do to me? Huh?"

"Casey, I'm sorry I hit you in the head with a rock. I really am. I didn't . . ."

"I know, Jackie. I'm just teasin' you is all. Let's go to Reed's Toy Store and see if she's got any new stuff."

We got on our bikes and headed north on Harding Street toward the most wonderful toy store in the whole world.

As we rode, Casey said, "Hey, did I tell you — some of the older kids at Saint Bartholomew's are planning to derail a Rock Island train on Halloween. They're gonna build this big bonfire on the tracks, and then when the train derails, they're gonna throw firecrackers at the passengers. That'll really be neat, don't you think?"

"What if my dad's on the train? He rides on the Rock Island every day."

"He wasn't on this train just now, was he?"

"No, he takes an earlier train."

"Right. So he'll be on a earlier train. I'll make sure. And my dad too. Or I'll make him drive to work that day. Don't worry — nobody we know's gonna get hurt. Even if they do, it's Halloween, and you've got to do neat stuff like that on Halloween. Besides, that's how the Indians used to stop trains in the Old West. I read about it in one of my Dad's books. And then they'd scalp everybody. And like when they ambushed wagon trains, they'd tie guys to the wagon wheel and set the wagon on fire and the guy would burn alive with his wagon. It was in my Dad's book. I'll show you later."

"Neat."

"Race you to 103rd Street!"

"You're on."

I let Casey beat me to 103rd Street, but I beat him clean off his Schwinn to 99th Street.

Reed's Toy Store was right there at the corner of 99th and Harding by the Rock Island tracks, so we set our kick-stands and tore inside.

Old Mrs. Reed was there with a toothy smile and a ready cash register. She liked kids who had money to buy toys, and Casey always had money to buy toys.

In case you're wondering, the place had a creaky wooden floor and airplane models hanging from the pressed-tin ceiling. There were five big glass cases full of toys of every kind, and shelves and shelves and shelves of more toys than a boy could ever want.

Yes, it was decidedly a boy's toy store.

Hey, this was 1957.

There was a place on Western Avenue where girls could go and buy dolls, and Mrs. Reed did have a small doll section, but she knew boys like Casey were funding her one-way ticket to Florida.

One other thing: if there was a Mr. Reed, we never saw him, and Mrs. Reed never mentioned him. And if she had any kids of her own, she must have put them in a dungeon somewhere and thrown away the key because we sure never spotted them anywhere.

"What's new, Mrs. Reed?" Casey said, spinning his head.

"Do you like Ancient Rome, Kevin?"

Casey looked at me and grinned triumphantly. "Oh yes, Mrs. Reed. Me and my friend Jackie here love Ancient Rome. Don't we, Jackie?"

"Yes, ma'am."

"Well," Mrs. Reed said, reaching into a glass case, "I've just gotten these cards in. You get five to a pack, plus a flat piece of bubble gum, and they're going to issue a new set every month. Here, since you're such a good customer, Kevin, I'll let you have a look."

Casey thanked Mrs. Reed profusely in his best kiss-up-to-the-grown-ups voice, and carefully opened the pack. He cracked an enormous grin as he examined the top card.

"Look, Jackie, it's a naval battle from the First Punic War."

"Huh?"

"Don't you know anything? The Romans versus the guys from Carthage. In North Africa. It's all in one of my dad's books in my basement. I'll show you sometime. But my dad's book doesn't have neat pictures like this of guys getting spears stuck through them. And look how this one Roman ship is ramming this Carthage guy ship, and all these guys are getting cut in half by the ram. Did you ever seen anything so neat in your whole life?"

I looked at the lurid card and agreed with Casey.

Casey looked up at Mrs. Reed and said, "How much?"

"A nickel."

"I'll take 'em," Casey said, reaching in his pocket. "And one for my friend Jackie."

"Casey, you don't have to . . ."

"No, I want to."

He plunked a shiny new dime on the counter, and Mrs. Reed handed him two fresh packs of "Ancient Rome Cards." Complete with stale bubble gum and all the gore a couple of sick little seven year olds could ever want.

Rather than open the cards right away, we rode two blocks north over to Ridge Park and found a quiet bench away from the big kids and opened our cards.

Were they ever neat or what?

The second card showed Claudius Marcellus slaying a Gallic chief in single combat during the battle of Clastidium.

"See," Casey said pointing, "that Gallic guy was bigger, but the Roman got him with his battle sword. There was nothing better than the Roman battle sword. They made 'em real strong so they wouldn't break, and they were short for close-in fighting. Isn't it neat the way the Roman's sword is sticking through the Gallic guy's neck?"

"Do you think it really happened like that?" I asked, touching my neck. "The sword's practically coming out of the hairy guy's mouth."

"They wouldn't put it on these cards unless it happened exactly that way. The guys who do these cards are professors of history and stuff. They really research these things. They don't want kids to get the wrong idea about Ancient Rome." Casey flipped to the third card and said, "Get a load of this one."

I flipped to my third card and beheld Hannibal destroying Saguntum in 219 B.C. The card was alive with bright orange flames and glistening red blood.

"Neat."

"Yeah. Now look at this one."

The fourth card showed Hannibal leading his soldiers and elephants through the Alps.

"There's no blood," I said, disappointed.

"You can't have blood on everyone, but isn't it neat how Hannibal tricked the Romans and went through the Alps? They didn't think he would since he had elephants and stuff, but he did, and here it is right here on this card. Proof."

"Yeah."

The fifth and final card of the month depicted Hannibal's victory over the Romans at the Ticinus in 218 B.C. To show what a crushing defeat it was for the Romans, the illustrator drew a Carthaginian battle elephant crushing a legionnaire's head.

"Neat!!" Casey and I chorused.

We agreed that we would have to collect the whole series.

"But you're gonna have to buy your own pack next time, Jackie. I'm not made out of money."

I was too ashamed to talk.

Casey punched my arm. "What's the matter?"

"Nothing."

"Well then you don't have nothing to be sad about." Casey crammed the bubble gum in his mouth, stuffed the cards in his shirt pocket and hopped on his bike. "Come on, I'll race you back to my house."

Casey tore off before I could cram my bubble gum, stash my cards in my shirt pocket, and mount up.

"Wait up!" I hollered.

"Last one there's a dead Roman soldier," he called over his shoulder.

I pedaled furiously but couldn't catch up until Casey stopped by some big kids who were hanging around a bench by the entrance to the park. He pointed at me, said something to them and raced homeward.

I gulped and followed.

What choice did I have?

The only alternative was turning around and leaving through the parking lot at the north end of the park, but then I'd never have a chance of beating Casey to his house.

A big kid with a "flattop" haircut and a white t-shirt with rolled-up sleeves hopped off the bench as I approached and blocked the path. He sucked his cigarette, squared his hips and said, "I hear you think the Pope's a sissy. That true, punk?"

I slowed my bike and looked ahead at Casey who had stopped to watch. I waved my arm for Casey to come back and help me, and Casey waved his arm for me to come and catch him.

"I'm talkin' to you, punk," the big kid said, grabbing for my handlebar.

Without thinking, I kicked him in the balls and veered off the path into the unmown grass.

The big kid hollered something terrible, and he and his friends took after me.

I pedaled my little Public ass off and got that big old bike of mine haulin' fast across the grass.

"Come on, Jackie," Casey yelled, "you can beat 'em. They can't run far with all those cigarettes they smoke."

I felt the big kids gaining on my backside and veered back onto the path. With rubber on the asphalt, I had them, but one of the big kids grabbed my shirt as I accelerated away.

Although it was a brand new shirt, I rode for dear life.

The big kid cursed and held on, and my shirt and its cargo of Ancient Rome cards ripped right off my back.

I knew Mom was going to kill me, but I kept right on riding in my t-shirt.

"Good goin', Jackie," Casey said as I pulled abreast of him. Come on, let's get outta here, they're still comin'."

We rode as fast as our little legs could pedal and didn't look back until 103rd Street.

"They still followin' us?" I said, panting.

"Nah, we ditched 'em."

We slackened, and I demanded to know why Casey had done such a dumb thing.

Casey pointed at his stitches and said, "You hit me in the head with a rock yesterday, Jackie. Don't you remember?"

"Yeah," I said, guiltily, "but what does that have to do with it?"

"It has everything to do with it. I told you — my dad has this book in the basement that shows how crazy you are after you've had a head injury. Some guys even go out and murder people and do stuff to girls."

"Do stuff to girls? What stuff?"

"You're too little to know."

"So are you."
"Am not."
"Am too."
We reached 103rd Street, and I dutifully stopped at the sign.
Casey kept right on going and was nearly hit by a big green-and-yellow Chicago Transit Authority bus.
"God-damn kid," the driver yelled, shaking his fist out the window.
Casey stopped on the other side of 103rd Street and laughed.
I watched him and wondered if I had made a serious mistake in choosing him as a friend.
Nah.
Casey was never dull, and his story about being crazy because of my rock to his head was just bunk, because he had been crazy since the day I first met him. And I knew he'd be crazy 'til the day I last set eyes on him.
And that was just fine.
Because I was more than a little crazy myself.
Sure it was the fabulous '50s, and we were living in an upper-middle-class white neighborhood in America's second city during a time of unbridled prosperity and record housing starts, but both sides in the Cold War were doing lots of above-ground nuclear testing in those days, and there was even a free x-ray machine at the shoe store so kids could laugh at all the funny bones in their feet, and there was the small matter of our respective parents.
Small matter.
Very small.
"Come on, Jackie," Casey yelled across the busy commercial street. "I'm not gonna wait all day for you. Pretend this is the Po River, and you're Hannibal with your elephants, and I'm the Romans, and I'm tellin' you you're nothin' but a lily-livered chicken from Africa. A real Sambo."
"But what about my shirt and my Ancient Rome cards?" I called.
"Forget your shirt and your Ancient Rome cards. Unless you want to go back there and get stomped to death."
"But my mom's gonna . . ."
"I'll talk to your mom. Now come on, or I'm gonna ditch you."

No kid in the old neighborhood ever wanted to be ditched, so I looked both ways, held my breath and dashed across 103rd Street.

Somebody honked at me, and when I looked back, I saw it was Aunt Lu Hinchcliff in her shiny new '56 Chevy. They were going to get a '57 just as soon as the new ones came out in September.

Although I didn't normally repeat the bad words I heard every night at Yardley's Bar & Grill, I said, "Oh, shit!"

Chapter Four

"Who's that?" Casey said.

"That's my Aunt Lu. She's not my real aunt, but I call her Aunt Lu because my mom and dad told me to. Her husband is my dad's boss."

"Well," Casey said pointing back at 103rd Street, "whoever she is, she sure is yelling at you."

I followed his finger to Aunt Lu's shiny '56 Chevy and saw that she had pulled over to the curb and was indeed yelling at me.

I had good hearing then and could get every word: "I'm going to tell your mother, Jackie. Now you go straight home, and don't let me ever catch you riding across a busy street like that again. Do you hear me?"

I nodded.

Aunt Lu shook her fist at me and popped her car back into gear and lurched west on 103rd Street.

I muttered, "Oh, shit."

Casey laughed and punched me on the arm. "You said a bad word, you dumb Public. Boy, if my parents heard me say a word like that, they'd make me go straight to confession. And the priest would probably have me say 10 'Our Fathers' and 20 'Hail Marys.' But you bein' a Public an' all, you don't have to go to confession when you say a bad word. You're lucky. Of course, bein' a Public means you can't go to Heaven 'cause only Catholics can go to Heaven 'cause that's what Sister teaches us at Catechism every Wednesday."

"But what if I'm really good?" I said.

"If you were really, really good, and you hadn't hit me in the head with a rock, then maybe if me and a whole bunch of Catholics really prayed for you, then maybe you could go to Purgatory and we could throw crab apples and acorns and stuff down at you from Heaven."

"What's Purgatory?"

"You never heard of Purgatory?"

"No."

Casey laughed. "Man, you Publics don't know nothin'. Purgatory's for good people who aren't Catholic and for Catholics who weren't good people. Catholics can go from Purgatory to

Heaven after they've worked off their sins, but Publics can never leave Purgatory. But mainly it's just Catholics in Purgatory because most Publics go straight to Hell when they die."

I felt the hot winds of Hell on my neck and said, "You think I'll go straight to Hell when I die?"

Casey shrugged. "Nah. I'll put in a good word for you at my next confession. I'll get you into Purgatory. You'll see."

"But what's Purgatory like? Is it as nice as Heaven?"

"I already told you it's below Heaven, didn't I?"

"No."

"Jackie, I told you we'd throw crab apples, and acorns and stuff *down* at you. Down at you, Jackie. That means that Heaven's above Purgatory. Get it?"

"Yeah, I get it, but I still don't know what Purgatory's like. Is it as bad as Hell?"

"Nah. But it's not as nice as Heaven either. It's like Rainbow Beach after summer."

"Kind of yucky?"

"Yeah, kind of yucky. Still nice and all, but you can't go swimming, and there's nobody selling Dreamsicles or anything. But they got bathrooms and stuff, and you'd probably be able to get books if you wanted. But not like the ones I'll have up in Heaven."

I frowned.

"What's the matter?" Casey said.

"I was thinking—maybe I should become a Catholic like you so we could keep on playing in Heaven after we die."

"If you want. I know I would if I were you, but your parents probably won't let you."

"Casey," I proclaimed, "if I became a Catholic, I could go to Saint Bartholomew's with you in September. We'd be in the same class and still see each other all the time. We could ride our bikes to school together."

"Kids at Saint Bartholomew's don't ride their bikes to school."

"Oh. Well, we could walk together."

"Maybe. Come on, let's go to my house. I want to show you that book about the German doctor and these neat experiments he did on people in concentration camps."

We headed south on Forest Avenue and Casey explained how the evil Nazi doctor had brothers and sisters torture one another.

"See," Casey said, "he'd put them in these different rooms with a pane of glass in between, and then he'd hook them up with wires and turn on the juice. And one of them could stop his own electricity by pushing a button and giving it to his brother or sister. What would you have done, Jackie, if it was you and Timmy in there?"

"I would have pushed the button as hard as I could and killed his guts out."

Casey laughed.

"What's so funny?"

"You. You just think of yourself. That's the difference between Publics and Catholics. Publics just think of themselves, but we Catholics think of others. If it was me in there, and Donald on the other side, I would give myself all the juice so Donald wouldn't have to suffer."

"Really?"

"Really."

And Donald O'Neal himself really appeared at that moment on his green Schwinn to tell Casey that he had to get right home.

"This instant."

"Why?" Casey said.

"Because Mother sent me to find you. You were supposed to wait for me this morning, but you left before I finished my piano lesson and before Mother could tell you that the Sisters of Mercy are coming over for tea today. And she wants you home right away, Kevin, so you'd better do as she says, because if you don't I'll tell her, and you'll be in big trouble."

Ah, Donald O'Neal, the mobile wet blanket of life.

"The Sisters of Mercy are coming? Today?" Casey said.

"That's right," Donald O'Neal said. "The Sisters of Mercy are coming over for tea this very day, and Mother wants you home right away, Kevin. So you'd better do as she says, because if you don't I'll tell her, and you'll be in big trouble. Big trouble."

"I heard you the first time, Donald. Jeez, you don't have to repeat everything ten hundred million times. I'm not deaf, you know."

"I'm just telling you what Mother told me to tell you," Donald said, his eyes wide as saucers.

Donald's eyes always got wide as saucers when he was on a mission from Mother. Especially one that involved the sacred Sisters of Mercy.

Casey looked at me and shrugged. "I guess we won't be able to play the rest of the day. I'll call on you tomorrow. Okay?"

"But I thought you were gonna talk to my mom about my shirt."

"I'd like to, Jackie, but I've gotta get home quick, or my mom's gonna skin me alive. She gets real weird when the Sisters come over. We all have to be on our best behavior, and she'll want me to take a bath and all before they come, and, hey—I'd better give you my Ancient Rome cards to hang on to because if Mom catches me with these when the Sisters of Mercy are coming over she'll cook me in oil. Alive."

"Like they did to that guy in that book in your basement?"

"Yeah." Casey handed me his Ancient Rome cards. "Here, keep 'em for me until tomorrow. You can look at 'em all you want, but don't slobber on 'em or bend 'em or anything."

"I won't!"

"Better not, or I'll pull your fingernails out with pliers."

"You do, and I'll put red-hot hatchets around your neck."

"And I'll baptize you with boiling water."

"And I'll kill your guts out with electricity."

"And I'll pour molten lava down your throat."

"Kevin," Donald interrupted, "you'd better come home with me right this instant, or Mother's going to be very mad. She told me to come and get you home before the Sisters of Mercy come for tea, and you know how . . ."

"All right, Donald, I heard you the first time. Well, Jackie, I gotta scram. See you tomorrow, huh?"

"But can't you just stop in and tell my mom what happened with my shirt? She'll listen to you."

"She'll listen to you too," Casey called over his shoulder as he rode off. "You'll be all right. Don't worry."

I watched Casey pedal away with his stupid brother and shuddered.

What was I going to tell Mom?

What was Mom going to do to me now?

Maybe *she'd* pull my fingernails out with pliers.

Why not?

I deserved it, didn't I?

Let some big kid rip the new shirt she had just bought me for the summer clean off my back.

But it *wasn't* my fault.

No.

It was Casey's fault.

He started it.

He told that big kid that I had called the Pope a sissy.

And I never called the Pope a sissy.

Never ever.

And I never ever would.

Even if I didn't believe in the Pope like Casey and the other Catholics did.

But that didn't mean I thought he was a sissy.

I thought of turning around and running away from home on my bike. I knew if I rode west far enough on 107th Street and then on 111th Street I'd get to the Palos Division of the Cook County Forest Preserve and maybe I could hide in this nature center called the Little Red School House.

That's where Aunt Pearl took me and Timmy sometimes on Friday afternoons when she wasn't drunk. She was really a neat lady when she wasn't drunk and knew all the different birds just by sight and sound. The only ones I knew for sure were cardinals and blue jays, but Aunt Pearl could tell a chickadee from a titmouse just like that.

The Little Red School House.

I sighed.

It closed at dark, and the rangers would find me I if tried to hide behind the raccoon cage or something. And what was I going to eat? There was no food there or anything. At least not for kids.

Sure, they had stuff for the raccoon and skunk and opossum and fox and other animals they kept on display, but there was no food for us kids. You had to bring your own lunch to the Little Red School House, and there sure weren't any restaurants anywhere nearby.

If we ever went to eat something with Aunt Pearl after the Little Red School House it was to this place way far away in Palos where she could get a "drinky pinky" and we'd eat bar nuts and weird kinds of sausage and eggs out of big brown jars.

I sighed again and wondered if I could just live in the woods.

No way.

Too many bugs.

Not that I didn't have a kid's curiosity about bugs, but I sure didn't want them crawling all over me all night.

And what was I going to sleep in — a tepee?

I didn't know how to make a tepee.

And I sure didn't want to have to poop in those smelly awful outhouses for the rest of my life, and that well water they had by the Little Red School House tasted like rotten eggs, and what was I going to wear in the winter when it got really cold? A whole host of other problems crowded my little head as I stood there on Forest Avenue watching my best friend in the whole world ride off with his brother to have tea with the Sisters of Mercy.

I exhaled a great breath of resignation and went my weary way home and found Mom on the kitchen phone with Aunt Lu.

Boy, that Aunt Lu worked fast.

And so did Mom.

"Well, speak of the devil," she said to Aunt Lu as I walked in. "The little monster just appeared. Thanks for calling me and telling me, Lu . . . Oh, yes, I'll see that he's properly punished . . . No, I can promise you it'll never happen again. Never . . . Thanks again for calling me, Lu . . . Right . . . See you next week at bridge club . . . Bye bye."

Mom cradled the phone and clutched my throat.

"That was your Aunt Lu, and she just called from a gas station to tell me that she saw you ride across 103rd Street without looking either way. What do you have to say for yourself, you goddamn kid?"

"I uh . . ."

SLAP!

"I asked you a question."

"I uh . . ."

SLAP!

Mom threw me against the stove and studied me. "Where's your new shirt?"

I cowered into the corner and stammered: "A big kid at Ridge Park tore it off me."

Mom grabbed my arm and swatted my butt off with her hand, and when her hand hurt too much she made me get her big wooden spoon and take my pants down. Then she paddled my butt until I could feel blood running down my legs.

Dear old Mom.

She sure wasn't one for sparing the rod and spoiling the child. Even if she did have to substitute an old wooden spoon for the rod.

"Look at you," Mom said, panting, "you're bleeding all over the floor. Pull up your pants and go to your room! This instant!! Do you hear me?"

"Yes, ma'am."

I gingerly hoisted my underpants and pants over my blistered bottom, and Casey's and my Ancient Rome cards fell to the floor.

"What are those?!?" Mom demanded.

"Nothing."

"Don't tell me nothing, young man. Give me those!"

I picked up the cards and handed them to Mom.

She leafed through them, made an ugly face and then tore our beautiful Ancient Rome cards to shreds before I could stop her.

"Mom, half of those are Casey's cards! I'm supposed to . . ."

SLAP!

"Mom, I'm . . ."

SLAP!

Mom threw the shreds of the Ancient Rome cards into the trash and slapped me another one for good measure. Then she said: "If you ever bring filth like that in this house again, I'll break you arm. Do you hear me?"

"Yes, ma'am. But those were Casey's cards."

"You mean Kevin."

"Yes, but . . ."

"Don't but me. If they're his cards, then why doesn't he have them?"

I exhaled. She had me there. She always had me there.

"Answer me."

"Because, well, because he said he'd get in trouble with his mom if he brought them home. They're having the Sisters of Mercy over for tea and . . ."

"Oh we mustn't offend the Sisters of Mercy, must we? Who does that shanty-Irish bitch think she's fooling?"

"But I thought you invited Casey's mom, I mean Mrs. O'Neal to your bridge club next week."

"Well, I'll just have to uninvite her won't I."

"But, Mom, you invited her."

Mom found a cigarette and fired up. "See what you've made me do, you little brat. You've made me smoke again. How am I ever going to quit with you getting in trouble every time I turn around. It's only the first day of summer vacation, and you've already lost that beautiful new shirt I bought you and brought home a pack of filthy cards that even that shanty-Irish bitch won't allow in her house. And not to mention nearly killing your little Catholic friend yesterday with a rock. I'm going to be a nervous wreck by the end of the summer. I swear I will."

I looked up at the cloud of smoke billowing from Mom's face and wanted to say just the right thing to make her happy, but I didn't have a clue as to what that right thing was.

"Should I go to my room now?"

"Yes. No. I don't want you bothering your brother. You can go to the basement. You always liked to go down there when you had that stupid dog of yours. Now you can go down there all by yourself where you won't be able to hurt anyone else."

"But what if I have to pee?"

"You can just hold it until I tell you to come up. Now get the hell down there."

"But, Mom . . ."

SLAP!

"Yes, ma'am."

I tumbled down to our dank old basement and half-expected my silly dog Billy to be so happy to see me he'd pee all over my leg. Then I'd hug him and let him lick my face, and we'd talk for hours.

But Mom had given Billy away.

Not to the next passing Indian.

No.

In Mom's exact words: "The vet sold Billy while we were in Florida. To a man who's going to raise him to hunt ducks."

We went to Florida after the operation on Dad's throat. And the man who was going to raise my beautiful Billy to hunt ducks never called or wrote or sent a picture or anything.

Never ever.

I went to the corner by the furnace where I used to sit with Billy and made my beloved springer spaniel appear out of thin air.

"Billy," I said, "how you been, boy?"

The phantom dog licked my face and peed on my leg.

I laughed, but not too loud, because I sure didn't want to ruin Mom's day anymore than I already had.

Then I had my pretend dog fetch an imaginary ball, and then we wrestled, and then we took a nap all curled up together on the cold concrete floor.

When I awakened, there was no Billy. Just a faint, fading scent of him.

I sighed and tried to make him appear, but I just couldn't.

All I could do was cry.

But I had to do even that quietly lest I disturb Mom.

And when I had to pee, I just held it for two hours until she called me upstairs for lunch.

Bet you never saw somebody pee like I did that day.

Mom sure never did, because she opened the door while I was piddling in the downstairs toilet and said: "You sound like a Goddamn race horse in there. Now hurry up, your lunch is getting cold."

Good old Mom.

Chapter Five

Mom made me stay in the basement all the rest of that day which was okay because I got to play all I wanted with my pretend dog Billy.

She let me up in time to pick up the front yard for Dad, and, of course, a few twigs and branches fell between the time I fled into the house and he rumbled into sight. He yelled at me and then went to make himself a drink and stand in the picture window. Aunt Pearl took that as her signal to "cross the Thames" and the whole sorry Yardley Bar & Grill schtick reran for another summer night.

As usual, Mom complained bitterly but did nothing to throw the guesties out. She fed Timmy and me in the breakfast nook, smoked a cigarette on the sly and made herself a big scotch and soda and drank it down in three gulps.

Like it was pop or something.

And believe me, it wasn't pop.

Oh yes, I knew.

I knew from the age of three when Dad first made me drink scotch. He told me I'd be drinking it for the rest of my life, and I'd better get used to the taste of it, so he and his drinking buddies poured me a shot of Black & White and forced it down my little throat.

They laughed and laughed when I coughed and coughed.

Hah hah.

Dad was such a comic in the good old days.

But I digress, when I should progress.

Mom took Timmy upstairs for his bath after supper, and Dad made me hang around the living room and serve the guesties. Although I was only seven, I could put any downtown bartender to shame. Even Aunt Pearl said I made the driest martini she had ever tasted.

Quite a compliment.

But that night the guesties were drinking gin and tonics because it was summer, and that's what the discerning drinker drank in summer. With a fresh wedge of lime in each drink. Which meant I had to fish out the old wedges and put in new ones every time I

"freshened up" a drink. Plus, rinse the glass, put in new ice cubes
and basically start from scratch every damn time.

I also had to work the mountainous basement stairs taking down
empty bottles of tonic and bringing up full ones and bags of ice.

Dad, of course, had no praise for my efforts.

Only curses.

And he didn't ask one question about my day.

I didn't have a day as far as he was concerned.

To him, it would have been like asking the lawnmower what it
had done while he was at work all day. Slaving his life away playing
triple-headers at Binyon's, the Berghoff and Miller's.

Poor old Dad.

But I sure loved him in spite of it all, and I desperately wanted
his approval. Which is why I huffed up and down the basement
stairs and smiled so big and so wide at the guesties and made sure
the nut bowl was always brimming and never even thought for a
micro-second of having one for myself.

It was when I was refilling the nut bowl for the umpteenth time
that night that the idea hit me.

The solution.

The way to Dad's heart.

A means of winning his love, affection and approval for all times.

Simple: the licorice stick.

The what?

You know, the clarinet.

As in the instrument played by "The King of Swing" himself, Mr.
Benny Goodman.

Then playing on Dad's phonograph.

"That little Jew sure could play one hell of a licorice stick," Big
Mike Jozaitus said, dancing with Aunt Pearl.

"Sure as hell could," Dad said, tapping his feet. "I'd give anything
to go back and hear those great bands. Now that was music."

"What do you mean *could*, boys?" Pearl said. "Benny Goodman's
still going strong."

"Yeah," Dad said, "but it's not like it used to be. Nothing's like
the way it was. God, nothing good's happened since 1945."

Well, for one thing, I thought, I was born in 1950.

But other than that . . .

Then it hit me.

Yes, I thought. All I have to do is learn to play the clarinet like Benny Goodman, the King of Swing, and Dad would love me for a million years.

He wouldn't want to go back before 1945 anymore.

He'd be happy right in the here-and-now listening to his very own son playing the licorice stick as good as Benny Goodman and then some. And he'd be so proud, and he'd love me, and we'd all be happy and maybe even go on picnics together or something.

I don't know.

But I do know that the idea consumed me that night in the living room, and as soon as Dad relieved me from bartending duty, I tore upstairs and tugged at Mom's dress.

She was bent over the bathtub scrubbing Timmy and was none to pleased to have me at her side.

"What do *you* want?!?"

"Mom, do you think I could get a licorice stick?"

"A what?"

"A clarinet. Like Benny Goodman plays."

"A clarinet?!? Are you out of your mind?!? What makes you think you could ever play a clarinet?"

I shrugged and bit my lip.

"I asked you a question, young man."

"I can learn. There's a man over on 103rd Street who gives lessons, and there's going to be a band at school in the fall. I was thinking maybe I could get a clarinet and take lessons and join the band and . . ."

"I think it was you who got hit in the head with that rock. Not that little Catholic brat."

I exhaled.

Mom scrubbed Timmy for a while and then some idea hit her so hard she about levitated. "So you want a clarinet, do you?"

"Yes, ma'am."

"You know you'd have to practice every day. You can't get good at an instrument unless you practice every day."

"Yes, ma'am. I'll practice every day. I promise."

Mom smiled so hard it made me sick to my stomach. I sensed that she didn't have my best interests at heart, but I was blinded by my desire to win Dad's approval, so I held my breath.

"Hand me Timmy's towel," Mom said.

I handed Mom Timmy's towel and watched her tenderly dry my little brother.

When she was done, she helped Timmy into his pajamas and sent him off to our room to await his bedtime story. Mom shook out Timmy's towel, draped it over the towel rack and considered me. "It's funny you want to play the clarinet because Peggy Herrod's boy Johnny used to play one. She was talking about it last time we had bridge club at her house. In fact, she asked if anyone wanted to buy it. I, of course, didn't say anything, because I could never imagine you doing anything musical. You couldn't carry a tune in a bucket if your life depended on it. But if you promise to practice every day, and work really hard at it, well, then I just might consider buying Johnny Herrod's clarinet for you. Of course, you'll have to do extra chores to pay for it."

Holy, holy, holy, Lord God of hosts, Heaven and earth are full of thy glory; Glory be to thee, O Lord Most High!!!

"Yes, ma'am."

Mom tousled my head and laughed.

I looked up at her in wonderment.

She looked down at me in contempt and told me to brush my teeth and wash my face while she read Timmy his bedtime story. She had decided I was too old for bedtime stories and asked too many questions, so Timmy had her all to himself at that point.

Just as well.

Thanks to Casey's basement, I had plenty of my own bedtime stories to chew on.

That night I serenaded the 300 Spartans at Thermopylae, and, boy, did they ever stomp their feet and clap their hands as I tootled away on my licorice stick. And old Benny Goodman was there somewhere just turning bright green from jealousy because he knew he'd never play that good in a million years.

And the next day, the 300 Spartans reversed history and beat those dumb old Persians because I had played so good for them on my licorice stick.

It was indeed a sweet dream, and when I awakened the next morning to Dad's labored bowel sounds, I thanked the good, big God above for giving me the clarinet idea because I knew it was going to solve all my problems.

I just knew.

But I wasn't so sure a short time later as I was feeding myself a bowl of Frosted Flakes and Casey appeared at the side door and hollered: "Yo, Jack-ee!!"

I hunkered down and pretended I didn't hear Casey.

He banged on the door and yelled: "Yo, Jack-ee!!"

I heard Mom coming downstairs.

"Yo, Jack-ee!!"

I took a deep breath and forced myself to become invisible. It didn't happen.

But Casey's voice was visible as he hollered: "Yo, Jack-ee!! Come on out and play!!"

I spooned some more Frosted Flakes into my mouth and chewed slowly with my mouth closed. Then I got up and went to the door.

"Hey, Jackie," Casey said, grinning. "Come on, we gots lot to do today. The colored are having a big picnic over at Dan Ryan Woods, and I figured you and me could hide in the bushes and shoot 'em with my slingshot. What do you think?"

"I think you'll have to find somebody else to make trouble with today, Mr. O'Neal." It was Mom and she had appeared phantasmagorically at my shoulder.

"Hi, Mrs. Yardley," Casey said, smiling brightly at my mother. "I was just telling Jackie here how we should go over to the park and play on . . ."

"I heard what you just told Jackie. I'm not deaf, Kevin. Now, as I said, you'll have to find somebody else to lead into temptation, because Jackie is not to leave the house today. Not after the report I received yesterday about his behavior with you."

"He didn't do anything wrong, Mrs. Yardley. Honest."

"That's not the way my friend saw it, and she's an adult, and I'll always take an adult's word over a child's. Now run along, Kevin, because Jackie has lots of chores to do."

"But, Mrs. Yardley, it wasn't . . ."

"Shoo. Surely there must be some Sisters of Something-or-Other coming over to your house today. You mustn't keep them waiting."

"No, Mrs. Yardley. That was yesterday. The Sisters of Mercy came yesterday."

"Well then you should go over to your basilica and polish the candles or whatever good little Catholic boys do. Oh yes, and please tell your mother that we've canceled our bridge club next week, and I just don't know when we're going to reschedule. But I'll surely call her. Now get along, Kevin, and leave Jackie to his chores."

Mom silenced Casey's protests by closing the inner door in his face.

"Mom," I said, "Casey's my best friend and . . ."

SLAP!

"But, Mom, Casey didn't do anything, and . . ."

SLAP!!

I put my hand to my swelling mouth and swallowed blood.

Mom told me to go finish my breakfast and not bother my brother.

I did as I was told.

As if I had any choice.

Then, after I helped her with the dishes, she had me take out the trash.

Then she ordered me to sweep the basement.

Then the driveway.

Next the patio in the backyard.

And then she ordered me to go to my room and stay there until lunch-time.

"And after lunch, maybe, just maybe, we'll go over to Peggy Herrod's and look at Johnny's clarinet. Assuming you've behaved yourself."

"Yes, ma'am."

Oh joy of joys!!

Thrill of thrills!!!

I was going to be the new King of Swing. Take a back-seat, old Mr. Benny Goodman, I thought heading for my room, because Jackie Yardley is gonna make you so jealous. So jealous because nobody's ever gonna play the old licorice stick like me.

And, boy, is Dad ever gonna love me now.

And never ever talk about how nothing good happened after 1945. Not ever.

And instead of putting on old Benny Goodman records, Dad and Aunt Pearl and Big Mike and all the other guesties would just sit back and listen to me play my clarinet.

I was even thinking maybe I'd somehow get a tuxedo and slick my hair back. Even though I had a crewcut.

Small problem, but it could all be worked out in time.

And in time I was going to be all Dad ever talked about. He'd come home from work and actually ask me how *my* day had been. And he'd listen and really want to know, and we'd go on a picnic or something, and somehow it would all be wonderful.

I think.

I don't know.

All I know is I went to my room that morning, closed the door and sat at my desk drawing pictures of brave Spartans fighting off thousands of Persians. The Persians fired so many arrows at my Spartan heroes, that they had to fight in the dark. But that was all right, because they were brave beyond belief.

Just like me.

And when arrows came flying at them, they didn't flinch.

Just as I didn't flinch when a stone hit the screened window in front of my face.

Must be a squirrel with a good arm, I thought, continuing to draw.

Another stone hit the screen, and I knew it hadn't been thrown by a squirrel with a good arm, because squirrels didn't have arms. They had legs.

I looked out the window, and there was Casey on our garage roof loading up his slingshot for another blast at my screen.

How he ever got up on our garage I'll never know, because our garage was the tallest in the neighborhood, and there were no footholds anywhere near it.

Casey fired his third rock with all his might and nearly put a hole in my screen.

I dashed out on the deck that adjoined our bedroom room and whispered frantically, "Casey, what are you doing?!?"

"I've come to liberate you, Jackie."

"What?"

"Liberate. It means to free somebody. Like how we liberated France."

"Oh."

"Come on and jump over to the garage, and we'll scram out of here on our bikes."

I looked at the five-foot gap that separated the deck from the garage roof and shook my head.

"What's the matter—you chicken?"

I shrugged.

"You think the 300 Spartans wouldn't have jumped in a second? You think that priest with the red-hot hatchets around his neck wouldn't have jumped in a second?"

"Casey, you heard what my mom said. I've got to stay in my room," I whispered.

"Why?" Casey said in a normal voice. "It's the most beautiful day ever, and this is the beginning of summer vacation. It's against the law for kids to stay in their rooms at the beginning of summer vacation when it's not even raining or nothing. Come on, jump. I'll catch ya."

I considered the gap and shuddered. God, how my wrists had hurt when I had broken them falling from a stool. Imagine how they'd hurt after a fall from the second floor.

"Casey, I don't think this is such a good idea."

"All right, I'll jump over to you. Just watch."

I watched in amazement as Casey backed up to the peak, ran down the valley and vaulted the gap in a single bound. He caught the railing that rimmed our deck and scrambled over.

"Nothing to it," he said, dusting himself off. "Now we'll go the other way. Just do what I do."

I grabbed him and shook my head.

"What's the matter with you, Jackie? You're turning into a real scaredy pants."

"My mom's downstairs. If she knows you're here, she'll kill me. And if she catches me trying to jump on the garage roof she'll really kill me. Honest injun."

Casey looked into my eyes and smiled. "Your mom is kind of mean. Let's just play in your room."

"All right. But we've got to be real quiet, because if she catches you here, she'll slap my head off." I touched my swollen mouth and added, "And I sure wouldn't want that."

"No, she could end up knocking all your teeth down your throat and you wouldn't be able to eat candy bars and stuff. Plus, I heard my parents talking about this kid from some other parish who ran into a tree with his sled and got all his teeth knocked down his throat and his teeth ripped a hole in his throat or something, and he bled to death before they could do anything to save him. Can you imagine?"

"Yeah," I whispered. "Come on, let's go inside before Mom hears us."

We went into my room and since we had to be quiet, Casey suggested we hide under the beds and pretend that we were runaway slaves hiding in an attic on the "Underground Railroad."

"Your mom can be the evil slave-catcher," Casey whispered. "I read all about it in this book my father has in the basement. The slaves would get all the way to a northern state and be almost to Canada and freedom, and these slave-catcher guys from the South would find them and take them back to Virginia or wherever and the master would whip the skin off their backs. Can you imagine having the skin whipped off your back?"

"Yeah."

"There were even pictures in my father's book of slave's backs after they got whipped with these special whips the slave owners had. They used the hardest leather they could find, and they'd put little bits of metal and stuff in the ends of the whip so it would really tear the skin right off, and the slaves would just have to take it. But there was this one slave, Nat Turner, who did try to liberate the slaves—but they shot him real good, and nothing else happened until the Civil War. You know about the Civil War?"

"A little bit. My mom says her grandfather was a doctor in the Union Army or something."

"Yeah. Did you know what he had to do?"

"No."

"Well, see, my father's got this book all about doctors in the Civil War—I'll show you next time you come over to my basement—and, anyway, when a guy got shot in the leg or arm, they couldn't just take the bullet out like they do now."

"Why not?"

"'Cause, Jackie, they had rifled barrels."

"What?"

"Don't you know nothin'?"

"I know lots of stuff."

"Yeah, then how come I got better grades than you?"

I shrugged. Casey had me there. He always had me there.

"So you don't know about rifled barrels, do you?"

"No."

"Okay. I'm gonna tell you all about . . ."

"Wait, I think I hear my mother."

We stilled ourselves and listened.

"She's just walking around down there," Casey said at last.

"Yeah. Go ahead and tell me about — you know."

"Rifled barrels?"

"Yeah."

Casey proceeded to tell me all about how the Civil War was an example of when the technology of taking life far exceeded that of saving it.

"So," he said, "when one of these rifled minie balls hit you in the wrist, all the bones in your arm would shatter. Like this." He grabbed my recovered wrist and squeezed hard.

I moaned.

"Hurts, doesn't it?"

"Yes. Let go!"

Casey let go, but he said, "Now you know what those guys in the Civil War felt like. Only they hurt ten thousand zillion times more than you just did. I just grabbed your dumb old wrist that used to be broken, but they got hit with rifled minie balls. And that was only the beginning."

"It was?"

"Yeah. Because then they had to take the guy all the way back to a field hospital. On a stretcher usually. And then the doctors . . ."

"Like my mother's grandfather."

"You mean your great-grandfather."

"Yeah."

"Boy, I have to tell you everything, don't I?"

"Not everything. So tell me what happened when they brought the guy back to the field hospital."

Casey said: "Well, then a guy like your great-grandfather would just hack the wounded guy's arm off with a big old saw."

"Wouldn't they give the guy some — you know?"

"Anesthetic?"

"Yeah."

"They used chloroform in those days, but they'd run out right away, so they'd either give the wounded guy some whiskey to drink, or they'd give him a minie ball to bite on. That's where that saying 'bite the bullet' comes from."

"Oh. Boy, Casey, you really know a lot of neat stuff."

"It's because of all my father's books in the basement. I'll show you as soon as your dumb old mother lets you out of prison."

"She's not dumb, and she's not old."

"Is too."

"Is not."

"Is too."

"Is ..."

"Jackie!"

It was Mom, and she was coming up the stairs.

"It's your mom," Casey hissed. "She's coming!!"

"I know," I said.

"What'll we do?"

"You stay right here and be real quiet, and I'll take care of her." And I did.

When Mom came into my room without knocking, I was seated at the desk I shared with Timmy drawing a happy summer scene of two boys playing on the beach.

Mom glanced at my picture and said, "Well, one thing's certain, you'll never be an artist like your Uncle Kenny. Of course, your Uncle Kenny went crazy when he was 12 and had to have to electroshock, but don't get me started on *him* this early in the day. Anyway, I just got off the phone with Peggy Herrod — God, that woman can talk — and she said we could go over this afternoon and look at Johnny's clarinet. Assuming you still want to play."

"Yes, ma'am."

"You promise to practice every day?"

"Yes, ma'am."

"All right. Then we'll go after lunch. And lunch is served promptly at noon. Is that clear?"

"Yes, ma'am."

Mom went to the door, turned and said: "Did you hear something on the garage earlier?"

"I think it was a squirrel. They jump on the garage sometimes from the oak tree."

Mom nodded thoughtfully and said, "That's what I thought. Well, maybe we will have to get Big Mike to shoot them with his service revolver."

It was true.

Big Mike Jozaitus had boasted many times at Yardley's Bar & Grill that he was going to "blast every last one of them little fuckers out of the trees."

He just hadn't gotten around to it yet.

"Now don't forget," Mom said, "lunch is served promptly at noon. I'm not running a restaurant here."

"Yes, ma'am."

Mom charged off downstairs to call another one of her 10,000 closest friends, and I whispered for Casey to come out from under the bed.

Casey came out and said in a normal voice: "Is that true about that Big Mike guy blasting the squirrels with his service revolver?"

I shushed him and nodded.

"Boy," he said, "I sure wanna be around for that. That guy you have next door is crazy, but I'll bet he'll hit 'em on the first shot. You have to be a good shot to be a Chicago policeman. That's what my big brother says, because he knows some older kids who went to the police academy, and it was really hard, and you had to be a really good shot, because when you're on duty, somebody's gonna just jump out of nowhere and try to kill you, and unless you're a really, really good shot, you're gonna be dead. And since your neighbor's not dead, he must be a really good shot."

"Yeah. Plus, he knows all these holds that he's always putting on me."

"That's because he has to wrestle criminals and stuff to the ground."

"Yeah. He says it's what they do to the shines on the West Side. Casey?"

"What?"

"How they call 'em shines?"

"Because a lot of 'em shine shoes for a living. It's in one of my father's books in my basement. It says Italians used to shine shoes for a living, but now the colored do it, and that's why they call them shines."

"Do you think they like to be called shines?"

"No. But I don't think they have any choice. Not unless another Nat Turner guy comes along. But then look what they did to him—shot him all full of holes. But someday, all the colored are going to rise up and kill all the white people in this country for what we did to them. And when they do, I'm gonna be on their side."

"But you're white."

"So?"

"So, you can't be on the coloreds' side if you're white."

"Why not?"

"Because they'd see that you're not one of them and kill you, too."

"No. They'd know I'm really colored inside. They'd see in a second."

"No, they wouldn't."

"Yes, they would. And you know what?"

"What?"

"When the colored have their big uprising, and I join them and get a big Browning Automatic Rifle—they call 'em BARs in the army—I'd come and kill your guts out first."

"What?!?"

"Yeah."

"Why? I'm your best friend."

"Yeah, but who was it who hit me in the head with a rock the other day?"

"Casey, I thought you said . . ."

"I know what I said," Casey said, punching my arm. "And I meant it too. It was an accident. You didn't mean to hit me in the head with a rock. But you did hit me in the head with a rock, Jackie. Accident or not. And a lot of times when guys get hit in the head with rocks they go crazy and kill their best friends."

"Really?"

"Yeah. It's in one of my father's books in the my basement. I'll show you next time you come over."

"But I don't know when I'll be able to come over again. My mom's actin' real . . ."

"She'll get over it. Moms always do. Just give her a little time. She just hates Catholics is all. Like all Publics. She's just jealous because she's not going to go to Heaven like my mom."

"Really?"

"Yeah. Hey, let's look at our Ancient Rome cards. Where'd you hide 'em?" Casey went right to the desk and opened drawers. "Come on, tell me."

"Uh, Casey?"

"What?"

"Uh, my mom found 'em."

"So?"

"Well, she tore 'em all up. Mine *and* yours."

"What?!?"

"You heard me."

Casey turned on me and said, "No I didn't. No, I didn't hear anything. And I won't hear anything until I see *my* Ancient Rome cards. The ones I bought with my money. For me and for you, you dumb Public."

I gulped.

Then Mom called from downstairs that it was time for lunch.

"You'd better go," I said to Casey.

He grabbed me by the shirt and put his smelly face right in mine. "You'd better get me another pack of Ancient Rome cards by this time tomorrow, Jackie, or I'm gonna take that Nazi dagger my father has in the basement and come over here tomorrow night and kill your guts out while you're sleeping. You won't even know what happened until it's too late, and then you'll get up, and all your guts'll spill right out on the floor. And you'll die a slow, painful death, and, boy, will you ever be sorry you let your mom tear up my Ancient Rome cards."

"Let go of my shirt, Casey."

"Not until you promise to get me some new Ancient Rome cards by tomorrow."

"But, I can't . . ."

"You want your guts cut out?"

"No."

"Then do it." Casey pushed me back across my bed and slipped away.

Shortly thereafter, I was sitting down for lunch with Timmy in the breakfast nook when Mom said, "Did you hear that?"

"What?"

She looked out the window. "Something just jumped on the garage roof."

"Must be those squirrels again."

"No, it sounded too big to be a squirrel."

"Then it must have been a cat. I think the Ryans have a cat. I've seen it around the backyards."

Mom stopped looking and nodded. "Then it must have been a cat. Now hurry up and eat your lunch. I don't want to keep Peggy Herrod waiting."

"Yes, ma'am."

God forbid that Peggy Herrod should ever be kept waiting.

Chapter Six

Don't worry.

We didn't keep Peggy Herrod waiting.

We got to her house at 9840 S. Forest Avenue just when Mom said we would – at 1:30 on the dot.

Good old Mom wouldn't think twice about waiting a whole day to take me to the hospital after I broke my wrists, but she'd never keep one of her bridge club friends waiting a nano-second. Especially one whose husband was a good, big client of Dad's insurance company.

No, ma'am.

The Herrods had a little girl who was Timmy's age, so the two of them went off and played somewhere, and Mom and "Aunt Peggy" – she wasn't my real aunt but I was supposed to call her that because we were one big happy family in the old neighborhood especially if you did business with Dad's insurance company – retired to the kitchen where they drank endless cups of coffee and devoured this enormous coffee cake.

I was told to stay out of trouble until they were ready to talk clarinet, so I read LIFE MAGAZINE in the living room. Well, I mostly looked at the pictures of President Eisenhower and stuff, but I could understand some of the words.

Honestly.

I finished LIFE MAGAZINE and went to the kitchen to see if it was time to look at the clarinet.

Not quite.

"And so," Mom was saying to Aunt Peggy Herrod, "I told that bitch just what she could do with her fancy mink stole and pearls, and – what do you want?!?"

"Mom, when are we gonna look at the clarinet?"

"We'll look at the clarinet when your Aunt Peggy and I are done visiting. Now go back in the living room and be quiet."

"Mom?"

"What?!?"

"Nothing."

I was going to ask her if I could go to Reed's Toy Store since it was right around the corner, but I knew she'd never let me do that in a million years. Especially when she'd read my mind and know that I just wanted to go there so I could replace Casey's Ancient Rome cards to keep from getting my guts killed out in the middle of the night with the Nazi dagger Casey's father had in his basement. Of course, there was the small problem of not having any money to pay for the cards, but maybe Mrs. Reed would . . .

"What are you mumbling about?"

"Nothing."

"Well, if you have nothing to say, then go and amuse yourself somewhere else. We'll call you when we're ready to look at Johnny's clarinet. Is that clear?"

"Yes, ma'am."

I slunk back to the living room and thumbed through an illustrated encyclopedia for a while. Then my courage bubbled up my throat, and I tiptoed out the Herrod's front door. When I was free of their house, I raced south on Forest Avenue toward Reed's Toy Store. I had no idea how I was going to pay for Casey's new Ancient Rome cards, but I knew I would think of a way, because there was no way Casey wasn't going to kill my guts out if I didn't replace his cards.

Casey was just that way.

Believe me.

"Back already?" old Mrs. Reed said with a toothy smile and ready cash register as I entered her store.

"Yes, ma'am," I said, rubbing my hands on my pants.

"Where's your little friend?"

"He's at home — I think. Uh, Mrs. Reed?"

"What?"

I looked around and continued rubbing my hands on my pants.

"Cat got your tongue, child? Speak!"

I looked up at Mrs. Reed and prayed for somebody else to come into the store.

Somebody else came into the store, and she got busy with him.

I exhaled and watched her take the other kid back where the really neat models were. A kid with money to burn, obviously.

I prayed to God to put a nickel in my pocket so I could buy Casey's Ancient Rome cards and not get my guts killed out with a Nazi dagger, but God was busy that afternoon.

Still, I dug deep into my pockets and came up with nothing.

Then I spotted a pack of Ancient Rome cards on the counter. Mrs. Reed must have shown them to a kid and forgotten to put them back in the case.

And she sure was busy with that kid back by the models, and maybe she'd never know they were gone, and all I had to do was grab them and run.

Which I did.

But I wasn't halfway through the door when old Mrs. Reed grabbed me by the scruff of the neck and hauled me back into her store.

"You little thief," she said, seizing my hand. "Give me those cards!"

"I was just going to look at them. I wasn't going to . . ."

"You were going to steal them, you little thief," Mrs. Reed said. She grabbed the cards out of my hand and hauled me back behind the counter into a little room with a telephone. "What's your name? I know your friend calls you Jackie, but I don't know your last name."

"Yardley. My name is John Yardley Junior.

"Well, John Yardley Junior, your name is mud to me. Now you stand right there while I call your mother. What's your telephone number?"

"Uh, my mother's not home right now."

"Don't give me that, you little monster," Mrs. Reed said, glowering down at me.

"Honestly. She's at Aunt Peggy's around the corner."

"Well, what's your aunt's number?"

"She's not my real aunt, she's . . ."

"Shut up, boy, and tell me her number."

"I don't know her number."

Mrs. Reed made a scary face and looked like she really wanted to slap me one.

I cowered.

Mrs. Reed took a deep breath and said, "Well, what's her last name? I'll have to look it up in the phone book."

"Her name is Herrod."

"How do you spell that?"

"I don't know."

Mrs. Reed got out the big, thick Chicago phone book and leafed through the gossamer pages. "Oh, what good are you? If you were my child, I'd boil you in oil. I swear I would. But thank heavens you're not my child. Thank heavens." Mrs. Reed found the right page and ran her finger down the names. "What street do they live on?"

"Forest Avenue."

"Ah, here they are. Now you just stand there while I call your mother."

"Yes, ma'am."

As Mrs. Reed telephoned Aunt Peggy's house, I glanced out into the store and saw that the kid by the models was up to something. He had slipped the kit for the *U.S.S. Missouri* under his arm and was tiptoeing toward the door. The little jerk was going to steal it clean away, and Mrs. Reed didn't even see what was going on.

That was because she was so busy demanding that Aunt Peggy put Mom on the phone "right away because I've caught her little monster trying to steal from my store."

I gulped and wanted to tell Mrs. Reed that the other kid was about to steal the *Big Mo*, but I was too scared to speak. I could already see Mom's hand slashing down at my face.

Mrs. Reed glared at me while she waited for Mom to come to Aunt Peggy's phone, and then when Mom was on the line, she said: "Mrs. Yardley, this is Mrs. Reed at Reed's Toy Store, and I'm afraid to have to report that I've caught your son red-handed trying to steal a pack of cards from my store . . Yes . . . Of course . . . Fine . . . Good-bye."

Mrs. Reed cradled her old black telephone and folded her arms over her bosom. "Your mother is coming right over, and judging from her tone of voice, I'd say you're not going to be able to sit down for at least a week."

"Mrs. Reed?"

"What?!?"

I looked out at the store and saw that the other kid had gotten clean away with America's pride and joy. I gulped.

"What, boy?"

"Nothing."

"Don't nothing me, you little thief. What did you want to tell me?"

I shrugged and murmured, "I forgot."

I wasn't about to tell that old witch that some kid with money had stolen her most expensive model kit. No way.

"Well, I'm sure you'll remember as soon as your mother gets here. And judging from her tone, that shouldn't be but a few minutes. All I know is if you were my child, I'd boil you in oil. Do you hear me – boil you in oil."

I nodded, imagining full well what it would be like to be boiled in oil. Hey, I had read all about it in Casey's basement. Well, Casey had read me all about it in his basement, but I sure knew that it wasn't a fun way to die. And I sure knew old Mrs. Reed was no different than those evil Romans who had done that to the early Christian martyrs.

No different at all.

Evil was evil was evil throughout the ages.

And I knew in my heart at the tender age of seven that evil *did* exist in the world. And no sex had a monopoly on it.

No, ma'am.

Mrs. Reed gave me another scary look and told me to stay right where I was while she went out and took care of the kid with money before Mom arrived.

I nodded, and old Mrs. Reed tottered out into her store.

It wasn't long before she was tottering back in a full state of rage and panic.

"That little thief stole the *U.S.S. Missouri*," she cackled, "and you were his accomplice. Weren't you?"

I shook my head desperately, but Mrs. Reed slapped me one anyway.

Sure, I was somebody else's kid, but what the heck.

And, boy, did she ever slap hard for such an old lady.

"Just wait until your mother gets here, you little savage."

And no sooner had Mrs. Reed said that than dear old Mom was blasting through the front door and grabbing me by the wrist and hauling me off the floor and swatting my bottom with a wooden spoon she had borrowed from Aunt Peggy for the occasion.

"That's it," Mrs. Reed whispered approvingly, "spare the rod, and spoil the child."

When Mom was done making sure I wouldn't be able to sit for at least two weeks, she turned to Mrs. Reed and humbly apologized for my grievous sin.

"He's hyperactive," Mom explained. "He's been this way since he was three. He was such a beautiful little baby, but ever since he was three, he's been hyperactive. He tried to kill his brother when he was born, you know. Tried to choke him to death with a rattle, and once he pushed his baby buggy out in the street in front of a car. That was when we lived in South Shore. But he hasn't gotten any better since we've moved here."

Mrs. Reed nodded and clucked.

Mom dug in her purse and said, "How much do I owe you?"

Mrs. Reed said: "Nothing for the cards, because I managed to stop him from stealing those, but I'm afraid he helped another child steal my most expensive model."

"Is that true?" Mom said, turning on me.

"No. I don't even know the kid who . . ."

SLAP!!

"Mom, I . . ."

SLAP!!

"How much was the model?" Mom asked Mrs. Reed.

Old Mrs. Reed knew in a twinkling that it was $8.45, and, boy, was Mom sore when she had to shell out that kind of money to pay for one of my misdeeds.

Mom reddened and said, "I'm afraid I don't have that much cash with me. Will you take a check?"

"If it's a check on a local bank."

"Of course it's a check on a local bank!"

Oh boy, I thought, am I ever gonna get it when we get home. If we ever get home. Maybe Mom'll just drive around 'til she finds the next passing Indian and give me to him. And then they'll put red-hot hatchets around my neck, and . . .

"Quit mumbling," Mom said, rummaging in her purse for her checkbook. "Children are to be seen and not heard. Is that clear?"

"Yes, ma'am."

I willed myself into a state of total silence and watched Mom write a check for $8.45 to Reed Toy Store, tear it out, and slap it on the counter.

"There," Mom said. "now we're even, Mrs. Reed. Again, I'm terribly sorry that Jackie's stolen from your store. And believe me, I will see that it never happens again because I'll never let him come back here."

Mrs. Reed was about to agree, but then she realized what I really represented — a faithful little customer for at least six more years. Plus, she knew I was the kind of kid who was going to get a paper route in a few years and spend all of his pay envelope on her worthless toys.

"Well, Mrs. Yardley, I'm sure that as soon as you're finished punishing him, he'll realize the error of his ways. Then he can come back, as long as he agrees to behave and not steal anything ever again."

Mom grabbed me by the ear and said, "Did you hear that, Jackie?"

"Yes, ma'am."

"Then say something."

"Ow, you're hurting my ear!"

SLAP!!

"I'm sorry, Mrs. Reed. I'll never steal anything from you again. Ever never. Honest injun."

Mrs. Reed smiled thinly.

Why not?

The old girl had just gotten Mom to pay for the *Big Mo,* and she knew I'd never think twice about stealing another thing from her precious store.

So why not smile and pat me on the head and say, "Apology accepted. But just remember what they do to thieves in Moslem countries."

"They cut their hands off," I said in a rush. "My friend Casey has a book about it in his basement."

Mom yanked my ear and cuffed me one. "It's Kevin, and he's not your friend anymore. Is that clear?"

"But, Mom . . ."

"Is that clear?" Mom said, pulling harder on my ear.

"Yes, ma'am."

"Good, now let's leave Mrs. Reed to run her store, and we'll go back to your Aunt Peggy's where you can apologize to her for running off like this."

"Yes, ma'am."

And so we went back to Aunt Peggy's where I apologized profusely for my egregious folly.

Aunt Peggy, God bless her soul, took it all in stride because her Johnny had once been arrested for breaking all the windows in his school, and then she and Mom took Timmy and Aunt Peggy's little girl out in the backyard and had them run around naked in a wading pool while Aunt Peggy filmed them with her Super-8 movie camera.

I just stood there and watched because I sure couldn't sit there and watch with my butt still burning. Not to mention my ear and face.

I was one beat-up little kid, and I decided then and there that the only way to survive my childhood was to crawl deep inside some secret cave of my own making anytime a grown-up growled. I'd be safe and warm in there, and nobody would ever know where I was or what I was doing. And I wouldn't get slapped again, or beaten with a wooden spoon or have my ear pulled off.

Of course, there was the small problem of the Nazi dagger.

Wasn't that why I got into all this trouble in the first place?

To get Casey another pack of Ancient Rome cards so he wouldn't kill my guts out with the Nazi dagger his father had in the basement?

Yes.

Of course.

And what good was my stupid, imaginary cave going to do that night when Casey came and killed my guts out with the Nazi dagger?

He had already shown that he could climb my garage, and even Timmy could push in the door to the deck—I know because I had locked him out there once. So what was to keep Casey from killing my guts out that night after he found out that I had failed utterly to replace his precious Ancient Rome cards?

And after he had been such a true and trusted friend by buying me my very own pack.

Indeed.

I gulped and watched Timmy and Aunt Peggy's daughter act like dumb little kids for the camera.

Boy, I thought, are you two ever going to be embarrassed when you have to look at this movie when you're older.

But then I realized they didn't know any better, and they were distracting Mom from hitting me, so they were serving a useful purpose.

And so it went for another half hour or so, and then Aunt Peggy finally got around to showing me the clarinet her son Johnny didn't want anymore because basically he had become a juvenile delinquent and didn't want to do anything useful with his life.

Like play the licorice stick better than old Benny Goodman.

The King of Swing.

It was all taken apart and stored in a musty old case lined with what must have been velvet at one time.

Aunt Peggy had no idea how to put the thing together, and neither did Mom.

I took a stab at it, and after a lot of grunting and groaning, finally formed my first clarinet.

"Now play something, Mr. Smarty-Pants," Mom said.

I put the clarinet to my mouth and blew into it.

Nothing.

I blew harder.

Still nothing.

"You little idiot," Mom said, just trying to help. "You expect me to buy you this clarinet, and you can't even play it."

"Well," Aunt Peggy said, also just trying to help, "I do remember that Johnny had quite a time learning to play at first. Apparently there's a certain way you have to form your mouth. You can't just blow into it like it was a trumpet."

I nodded thoughtfully and pictured the cover of Dad's Benny Goodman album. The King of Swing himself appeared in my mind and told me just how it should be done.

I pursed my lips and tried again.

HONK!!!

Mom and Aunt Peggy lost it completely.

Funniest damn thing they ever did hear.

Even Timmy and Aunt Peggy's little girl came running to join the fun.

I turned bright red and inspected Johnny Herrod's clarinet.

"No wonder," I said, pointing, "this thing's cracked."

Mom grabbed the clarinet out of my hands and said, "What thing?"

I pointed again. "That thing."

Aunt Peggy looked and said, "Oh, that."

"What is that?" Mom said, staring.

"That's the reed. Johnny always chewed on them which is why they always cracked. His music teacher always told him not to chew on his reeds, but he didn't listen to him."

"Well, how much are these reeds?"

"They were about 50 cents a piece last time we bought them."

Mom made a face at me and said, "Well, you'd better not chew your reeds, young man. Do you hear me?"

"Yes, ma'am."

"Because I'm not going to spend 50 cents every time you chew your reeds. Do you hear me?"

"Yes, ma'am."

"I'm going to expect you to get a lot of use out of one reed. Do you hear me?"

"Yes, ma'am."

"Especially after I had to spend $8.45 to pay for your little plot at the toy store. Who was that kid, anyway?"

"Mom, I don't . . ."

SLAP!!

"A kid from Saint Bartholomew's I think."

"That's better. Well, it figures he would have been a Catholic. You can't trust those mackerel snappers as far as you can spit."

Aunt Peggy nodded, and she and Mom were off on another one of their conversational loops.

I retreated with the clarinet to the living room and arranged my hands and fingers on it just the way I pictured Benny Goodman doing it on Dad's album.

Then without making a sound, I made that old licorice stick sing the saddest song you ever did hear.

Chapter Seven

That night when the guesties were in full sway, Mom came to me and said, "Get your clarinet."

"What?"

"You heard me—get your clarinet. I want you to play for the guesties."

"But, Mom, I haven't even . . ."

SLAP!!

"Yes, ma'am."

I went and got my clarinet, and Mom strode purposefully into the living room and switched off the phonograph.

You could have heard an ant fart.

When Dad recovered, he put his electro-larynx, or voice box, to his neck and said, "What are you doing, Doris?!?" He smiled at the guesties, because he always smiled at the guesties, but he stared daggers right into Mom's heart. "The guesties and I were listening to Benny Goodman, Doris, and . . ."

"Well," Mom said, standing her ground, "it's time you all listened to your son play the clarinet."

"What?!?"

Mom turned so all the guesties could hear her and said, "I bought Jackie a clarinet today, and he'd like to play it for you. Jackie, play your clarinet for the guesties."

I put Johnny Herrod's licorice stick to my lips and asked God to make me play like Benny Goodman, the King of Swing.

HONK!!

"Sounds like somebody just stuck a pig with a rusty knife," Big Mike Jozaitus joked.

"Try again, sweetie," Aunt Pearl said, swishing her gin and tonic.

I tried again and produced an even more ear-splitting HONK!!

Big Mike reached in his pocket and said, "Okay, kid, we get the point—you're raisin' money for lessons. How much do you want?" He waved a ten spot in my face.

Dad simultaneously smiled at his big lunk of a friend and glared at Mom and me.

Aunt Pearl winked at Big Mike and said: "You know, I think I've got to run out and get some eggs and milk. Mike, I don't suppose you'd care to give me a ride over to Western Avenue?"

Big Mike caught her drift and they were gone in a snap.

Dad struggled valiantly to retain the other guesties, but face it, sports fans, there just was no party without Bike Mike and Aunt Pearl.

Within five minutes the only ones left at Yardley's Bar & Grill were the Yardleys.

After sending off the last guestie with the warmest possible "good-night," Dad stomped into the kitchen and said, "God-damn it, Doris, what the hell kind of lousy trick was that?!?"

Mom shrugged, and I cowered.

Dad put down his voice box and grabbed Mom's shoulders. "I'm talking to you," he mouthed.

"You know I can't understand you when you don't use your voice box."

Dad kicked Mom in the left shin.

Mom moaned.

Dad kicked Mom in the right shin.

I crawled into the back of my imaginary cave.

Dad looked at me and mouthed, "You didn't see anything."

I shuddered.

Mom moaned.

Dad kicked Mom in the left shin.

Mom groaned.

Dad kicked Mom in the right shin.

I crawled out of my cave and advanced on Dad, determined to put red-hot hatchets around the bastard's neck and kill his guts out with Casey's Nazi dagger.

Dad flung Mom against the counter and turned on me. "Come on you little son of a bitch," he mouthed. "You think you're tough?"

Mom pushed away from the counter and said, "Leave him alone, John Yardley! Do you hear me?"

Dad turned to Mom.

Mom said, "If you so much as touch him, I'll take him and his brother and never come back. Do you hear me?"

It was Mom's secret weapon, and it always worked.

Dad blinked and picked up his voice box.

Mom glowered at him.

I held my breath.

Dad heaved his shoulders and said, "It was the booze talking, Doris. You know it was the booze talking. Not me."

It was Mom's turn to blink.

"I work and slave all day in that hot, stuffy office and have to ride that old rattletrap of a train, so I'm entitled to a few drinks with my friends when I get home. And I don't have to remind you that I went through hell with this goddamned operation, and if you think it's easy having to talk with one of these stupid things all day, you've got another thing coming. Let me tell you."

I cleared my throat.

Mom and Dad looked at me.

"Uh," I said, "could I go out and play?"

Dad shrugged. He didn't care if I went over to the lake and swam to Michigan.

Mom didn't either, but just to show Dad that she was the one true parent in the house, she said: "All right. But just be back before the street lights come on. And put your clarinet away."

"Yes, ma'am."

I stashed my clarinet and was out of that hell-hole in a flash.

Being June, the sun acted like it never wanted to set, so I knew there was lots of time before the street lights came on.

But what to do?

Where to go?

Casey's basement, of course.

Like there was some other choice.

I hopped on my bike and headed over to Casey's back door and was soon hollering: "Yo, Cas-ee!!"

Mrs. O'Neal came to the screen door directly and made a great show of wiping her hands on her apron. Like she just loved washing dishes and hated to be interrupted.

"Yes?" she said, staring down at me.

"Mrs. O'Neal, can Casey come out and play?"

"His name is Kevin."

"Yes, ma'am. Well, can Kevin come out and play?"

"Kevin is already out playing—with his brother Donald. Now I suggest you run along home before your mother misses you."

"But . . ."

"Vamoose."

"Yes, ma'am."

I dragged myself back to my bike and pedaled up the alley to Dray Street.

Just as I got there a strange little truck fluttered past, leaving a great billowing cloud in its wake.

I stared in wonder.

Then I heard laughter in the cloud.

Casey's laughter.

"Casey," I called.

"Come on, Jackie," Casey hollered from the mist. "This is the neatest thing ever!!"

"But, Casey . . ."

"Come on, Jackie. You'll love it!!"

I rode into the mist and barely made out Casey, his brother Donald, and a whole bunch of other kids bellowing along on their bikes.

"What is this?"

"It's DDT," Casey said. "They're spraying it to kill the mosquitoes."

"But isn't it bad for you?"

"No. My father's got a book about it in the basement. They used it during the war around soldiers, and nobody got hurt. Don't worry, Jackie. Just have fun."

"Okay."

We tore along in the cloud and soon we were pretending that we were PT boats in the South Pacific attacking a Jap convoy.

"This is just the way it was, too," Casey said. "After they'd launch their torpedoes, the lead boat would lay down a smoke screen and they'd retreat into it so the Japs couldn't see them. Senator Kennedy from Massachusetts was on a PT boat. He's gonna be the next president in 1960. That's what my father says."

"My dad says Nixon'll be president after Eisenhower. He says only the Republicans can run the country."

"Your dad's a dope."

"Your father's an idiot."

"Your dad's got a hole in his throat and has to talk like a robot."

"Your father's fatter than a big old pig."

"Your dad just drinks all the time."

"Your father just reads all the time."

Donald O'Neal zoomed in close to my bike and hollered, "Don't you ever say bad things about our father, John Yardley Junior. Don't you ever."

Casey laughed and said, "Better listen to him, Jackie, or he'll get you. Won't you, Donald?"

"I just don't think John Yardley Junior should speak about our father like that, Kevin," Donald said.

"You better apologize to Donald, Jackie."

"You better apologize to me, Casey."

"You started it, Yardley."

"No, you started it, O'Neal. You called my dad a dope."

"Well, he is. He's not only a Public, but he's a Republican. My father says those are the dumbest things anybody can be."

"Well, you're the dumbest thing. You big fatso. And you know what?"

"What?"

"I didn't get you another pack of Ancient Rome cards. There! What do you think of that?"

Casey swooped close, cuffed me on the head, and said, "Got you first!"

I kicked him in the butt and said, "Got you last!"

"Bet you can't ride behind the sprayer."

"Bet I can too."

I rode right behind the sprayer for a while, then Casey took a turn. Then some other kid.

"Let's pretend we're B-17s on a mission over Germany," Casey said. "We're up in the pea soup, and the krauts are blasting away at us with their ak-aks, and suddenly your port wing is blasted off."

"What?"

Casey kicked me off-balance for emphasis, and I crashed to the ground.

I wasn't hurt, but I was so surprised I couldn't pick myself up fast enough to rejoin the fools' parade.

Casey called back from the DDT cloud: "See you later, Public, when I come to kill your guts out with my father's Nazi dagger."

I stood and wondered why.

Why was Casey so mean?

Why did Dad kick Mom in the shins?

Why did Mom want me to play my clarinet for the guesties when I hadn't even had my first lesson yet?

Why hadn't God listened to my prayer and let me play like Benny Goodman, the King of Swing? Just once.

Why didn't Dad love me?

Why didn't Mom?

Why did Mom have to give my dog Billy away?

Why didn't Mom believe me when I said I had nothing to do with that other kid stealing the *Big Mo* from Reed's Toy Store?

Why hadn't I been able to get away with stealing another pack of Ancient Rome cards for Casey?

Why was I always getting caught when kids like Casey were always getting away with murder?

And why was I going to die that night when it was really Mom's fault that Casey didn't have any Ancient Rome cards?

And why didn't Casey just take them home himself yesterday?

Why had he made me take them for him?

Why was he so afraid of his mother? And those Sisters of Mercy?

Why were there Sisters of Mercy anyway?

And why had God let there be Catholics and Publics?

Why, why, why, why, why, why, why, why?????

No answers were forthcoming, so I sadly turned and rode home.

When I came in the side door, I heard Mom on the phone to one of her 10,000 closest friends saying: "No, I haven't told him yet . . . No, there's never a good time . . . Yes, you're right . . . I know . . . Of course . . . Well, I thought after the operation—you know . . . It is funny isn't it? . . . The boys? . . . Yes, I'll have to tell them too . . . Timmy'll be fine, but Jackie's so unstable, you never know what he's going to do . . . Yes, I'll let you know . . . Of course . . . Right . . . I love you too . . . Sure . . . Nightie night."

Mom cradled the phone and stared out the window.

I crept into the kitchen on clumsy cat feet and cleared my throat. That only made me cough out a cloud of mosquito mist.

Mom rumbled out of her reverie and regarded me with scorn. "Where have you been?!?" she said. "You smell like a refinery."

I gulped and admitted I had been "riding behind this really neat truck spraying all this stuff to kill the mosquitoes."

SLAP!!

"That's poison, you little idiot! Don't you know any better?!?"

"But, Mom, I . . ."

SLAP!!

"Whatever possessed you to ride your bike behind a truck like that?"

"Casey was doing it."

"You mean Kevin, don't you?"

"Yes, ma'am, I mean Kevin."

"Well, I suppose if Kevin O'Neal jumped off the Empire State Building, you'd be right behind him, wouldn't you?"

I reflected for a moment and said, "If we were both wearing parachutes."

Mom went to slap me again and stopped. She was tired, and slapping sapped too much of her precious energy. So she merely shook her head and muttered, "I really am going to give you to the next passing Indian. I swear. Now go upstairs and take a bath. And you'd better scrub yourself within an inch of your life, because I'm not going to have you smelling up your clean sheets. Do you hear me?"

"Yes, ma'am."

"Then why are you standing there? When I tell you to do something, I expect you to do it, not just stand there with your mouth open collecting flies."

"Yes, ma'am."

"Go take your bath, and don't bother your brother. If I hear a peep out of your brother, you're going to pay for it. Do I make myself clear?"

"Yes, ma'am."

"Good. Now vamoose."

I wanted to ask Mom what she had been talking about on the phone, but I could see that her patience with me was all used up. So

I went upstairs, undressed, filled the tub and scrubbed my skin off. I wanted to settle back and enjoy the hot water, but I could hear Dad rumbling around in the big bedroom he shared with Mom.

He'd want to come in the bathroom any second and do whatever he did after a hard night at Yardley's Bar & Grill.

So I pulled the plug on my pleasure, dried off, put on my pajamas and went to bed.

Timmy was already in his bed talking softly to Mr. Monkey.

"Is Mom going to read me a bedtime story, Jackie?"

"I don't think so, Timmy. She seemed kind of mad or something."

"Aw. She always reads me a bedtime story."

"I know, but she's had a hard day."

"Why?"

"Because I was bad."

"Why were you bad?"

"I don't know. Go to sleep, Timmy."

"No. You can't make me go to sleep."

"All right. Don't go to sleep. Stay up all night and talk to Mr. Monkey. I don't care. But talk softly because I want to go to sleep."

We heard Dad lumber past our door into the bathroom. Timmy and I held our breaths until he slammed the door and turned on the faucet.

"Jackie?"

"What?"

"Do you think Mom's going to have a new baby?"

"What?"

"I think Mom's going to have a new baby."

I thought of what Mom had been saying on the phone to her friend about "telling the boys." Telling the boys what? Telling us that she was going to have a new baby? Maybe, but how would Timmy know?

"How do you know, Timmy?"

"I don't know, but I know."

Typical five-year-old, I thought.

"Do you think it'll be a boy or a girl, Jackie?"

"Timmy, I don't even know Mom's having a baby. Did she tell you she's having a baby?"

"No."

"Then how do you know she's having a baby?"

"I just know."

"Okay, you just know. Good for you. Now go to sleep."

"Jackie?"

"What?"

"Do you think it's going to be a boy or a girl?"

"I don't even know if Mom's going to have a baby. Although I did hear her talking kind of funny on the phone when I came in. Like she has some big secret she hasn't told us – not even Dad."

"Not even Dad?"

"Nope."

We listened to Dad rooting around in the bathroom.

Then Timmy whispered, "Do you think Dad'll be mean to the new baby?"

"Yeah. Probably. Now go to sleep."

"I can't go to sleep."

"Why not?"

"Because Mom didn't read me a bedtime story."

"Well, she's not going to read you a bedtime story tonight, Timmy, so you'd better go to sleep without one."

"Jackie?"

"What?"

"Will you read me a bedtime story?"

"I can't read all those big words."

"Well, can you make one up?"

I sighed and thought of the day that had just passed. "All right. I'll make one up. You ready?"

Timmy snuggled deeper into his bed and said, "Uh huh."

"Okay. Well, there was this sailor, see, and actually he was an officer, and he had this PT boat, and there was this big Jap convoy, and . . ."

"I don't like that story! That's not like the stories Mom reads to me. The stories Mom reads to me have animals and stuff. Nice stories. Not like your story, Jackie. Tell me a nice story, or I'll tell Mom."

I sighed.

God, there was just no winning with this family, and now it looked like Mom had another one on the way. Just what I needed.

"All right, Timmy, I'll tell you a nice story. With animals and stuff."

"What kind of animals?"

I looked out the window. "Squirrels."

"Squirrels?"

"Yeah, squirrels."

"I like squirrels."

"So do I. And here's the story: See there was this squirrel named Scamp who lived in this big oak tree behind this house where this mean old policeman lived and . . ."

"Like Big Mike?"

"Like Big Mike, but even meaner."

"Nobody's meaner than Big Mike. I don't like Big Mike."

"Neither do I. Anyway, Scamp lived up in this big oak tree with his squirrel family behind the mean old policeman's house, and one day . . ."

"Where the hell have you been, you cheating bastard?!?"

It was Marge Jozaitus, Big Mike's feisty second-generation Irish-American wife, and she had caught her husband tiptoeing in the back door after his Western Avenue assignation with Aunt Pearl.

Timmy and I could hear every word because our bedroom windows were right above all the important rooms in the Jozaitus bungalow. Like the back porch where Marge was about to mangle Big Mike.

"Do you mind if I finish the story later, Timmy?" I whispered.

Timmy nodded. Nothing was better than a Jozaitus battle, especially when you caught it right at the beginning.

Marge Jozaitus said, "Answer me, you big Lugan."

"Who the hell do you think you're talking to, you shanty-Irish bitch," Big Mike countered.

But Marge had all the good marbles that night, and she was right back with: "You've been out catting around with that whore from across the street again, haven't you? I can smell her cheap perfume all over you, you big stupid slob. What, she give you a quickie behind Ken's on Western Avenue? I wouldn't put it past her."

"Marge, you're all wet. Pearl and I didn't do a goddamn thing. All I did was drive her over to the the Stop-and-Shop so she could get some milk and eggs. That's the honest-to-God truth. So help me God."

"You're going to need God's help after I get through with you," Marge yelled.

There followed a series of dull thuds as though she was hitting him with a rolling pin.

"What's she doing?" Timmy whispered.

"I think she's beating him with her rolling pin," I whispered.

"Will Big Mike kick her in the legs like Dad kicks Mom?"

"How do you know Dad kicks Mom?"

"I know a lot of things, Jackie. Just as much as you, and even more. I knew Mom's going to have a baby before you. And I know it's going to be a girl."

"How do you know it's going to be a girl?"

There was a loud crash and a dull roar before Timmy could answer.

I went to the window and peeked.

"What's happening?" Timmy said, cowering under his covers.

"Mrs. Jozaitus is throwing beer bottles at Big Mike."

"I hope she kills him," Timmy said.

"Me too," another voice said.

I spun around and there was Casey standing in our bedroom with his father's Nazi dagger at the ready.

Chapter Eight

"How'd you get in here, Casey?"

Casey advanced with the dagger aimed at my guts. "How do you think?"

"I think you climbed the garage and jumped over to the deck while the Jozaituses were fighting and then pushed in the door, because it never really locks, and because even Timmy can push it in. That's what I think, and I think you'd better go home before I call my Mom."

"Why don't you call your Dad — he's right next door in the bathroom."

"How do you know?"

"'Cause I'm a good spy, you dumb Public. Now hold still and take it like a man. Like the Japs do when they commit sepiku."

"What's that?" Timmy said.

Casey turned slightly to my little brother and grinned. "It's when they cut their own guts out with these really sharp Jap knives. My father's got a book all about it in our basement."

"Why would they do that?"

"He always ask this many questions?" Casey asked me.

I shrugged and said, "Casey, put down the dagger before you hurt somebody."

"I'm not gonna hurt anybody, Jackie. I'm just gonna kill your stupid guts out with this Nazi dagger for not getting me another pack of Ancient Rome cards."

"Are you really going to kill my brother?"

Casey smiled at Timmy. "Yeah. Any reason I shouldn't?"

"No. I want you to kill him. He's mean to me."

"Timmy, how can you . . ."

Casey cut me off by poking the dagger at my belly button. "One good slice, Jackie, and your guts'll spill out all over the floor. You have any idea how long your guts are?"

I shook my head.

"Really, really long. My father's got a book all about it in the basement. And he's got this other book about how the Indians would do that to settlers — cut out part of their guts, and then tie it to a tree and make them run around the tree so their guts were all wrapped around the tree. Isn't that neat?"

I laughed nervously.

Timmy said, "Go on and kill him, Kevin. I won't tell Mom."

"Call me 'Casey', kid."

"Really?"

"Really." Casey turned on me and said, "All right, you stupid Public, prepare to die and go straight to Hell where you're gonna burn for all eternity."

"But I thought you said I was going to go to — you know."

"Purgatory?"

"Yeah."

"I changed my mind. You're not good enough for Purgatory. Purgatory's for good people who aren't Catholic and Catholics who aren't good people, and since you didn't get me another pack of Ancient Rome cards, you're neither. And you never will be. Now be prepared to die like the true heathen you are."

I was preparing to die like the true heathen Casey said I was when Marge Jozaitus threw a beer bottle through a window in their back porch.

"Now you've done it," Big Mike bellowed. "You stupid shanty-Irish bitch."

Casey couldn't help but glance down at the Jozaitus porch, and I couldn't help but grab the Nazi dagger out of his hand.

"Gimme that!"

"No."

"Gimme it, Yardley, or I'll . . ."

"Or you'll what, O'Neal?" I said, brandishing the dagger at Casey's guts.

God, the power.

God, the control.

Casey blinked and gulped.

Timmy cheered.

"I thought you were on my side, kid," Casey hissed.

"I am," Timmy said.

"Then why are you cheering, you little dope?"

"Don't call my brother a dope."

Casey backed toward the deck door and said, "You know, I never should have come over here tonight. I never should have come over here again after you hit me with that rock. You know your brother tried to kill me the other day with this huge, gimongous rock. He was only standing about three feet away which is why he was able to hit me with it."

That lie made me so mad I wanted to kill Casey's guts out right then and there and drag his limp and lifeless body back to Casey's basement and arrange it so everybody would think Casey did that thing to himself he said the Japs did, and everyone would think Casey had killed himself, and nobody would ever suspect me, and hadn't Casey once told me himself that if you committed suicide you'd never go to Heaven because that was the one sin that God could never forgive you of because it was so final and . . .

"You're talkin' to yourself, Jackie," Casey coolly observed. "That means your brain's goin'."

I blinked and realized I would just have to live with Casey. And Timmy, and Mom and Dad and the new baby which was going to be a girl since Timmy said it was going to be a girl and who could ever dispute a little know-it-all like Timmy.

I sighed and handed Casey his Nazi dagger, handle first.

"Here," I said, "go ahead and kill my guts out. I'm ready to die." And I was.

Casey grinned maniacally and said, "Lift up your shirt."

"What?"

"You heard me — lift up your shirt."

"Why?"

"Because I want to see what I'm cutting. I don't want to make any mistakes."

"Are you really going to cut his guts out, Casey?" Timmy asked, sitting up in bed.

"Yeah. Now be quiet. Your dad's right next door."

"He won't hear anything," Timmy said. "He never hears anything after grown-up time. Does he, Jackie?"

"No." I gulped and lifted up my shirt. "Okay, I'm ready."

"You want to say a prayer or something before I kill you? Not that it's going to do you any good or anything, but I'll let you if you want."

I shrugged. "What's the point? You said I won't even go to Purgatory."

"Well, maybe you would if you said a prayer right now."

"What kind of prayer?"

"The 'Our Father' always works."

"All right. But you mean the 'Lord's Prayer' don't you?"

"No, I mean the 'Our Father.' It's called the 'Our Father' because Catholics call it the 'Our Father' so it's the 'Our Father' because there's only one true church, and that's the Catholic Church and that's just what Sister says at catechism. Now say it, you dumb Public, while you've still got breath to say it." Casey jabbed me in the belly button for emphasis.

"Ow, that hurts."

"And it's gonna hurt a lot more when I stab it in to the hilt. Now say an 'Our Father' and let's get it over with. I've got to be home before it gets real dark."

I gulped and bowed my head. "Okay, here goes: 'Our Father, who art in heaven, hallowed be thy Name. Thy kingdom come. They will be done, on earth as it is in heaven. Give us this day our daily bread. And forgive us our trespasses, as we forgive those who trespass against us . . . '"

Casey said "Amen" and prepared to stab me.

"I'm not done yet."

"Yes, you are. That's the end of the prayer."

"No it's not. There's still 'And lead us not into temptation, but deliver us from evil.' And then 'Amen.'"

"No, the priest says that. Not the people. Boy, no wonder you Publics don't go to Heaven. God doesn't want stupid people in Heaven, and He'd sure have a whole bunch of 'em if He let you in. Now the prayer's finished, and so are you, Yardley. You ready?"

I clenched my fists, shut my mouth, closed my eyes, nodded and waited for the flames of Hell to begin their eternal licking.

But all I heard was the clock ticking.

I peeled an eye at Casey and said, "What are you doing?"

"Listening," he said, distractedly.

"Listening for what? I don't hear anything."

"That's just it," he said, lowering the Nazi dagger, "notice how quiet it's gotten next door?"

"Yeah," I said, back away from the Nazi dagger. "It sure has."

"You think she killed him?"

"Maybe *he* killed her."

"Who cares?" Timmy said. "Come on, Casey, and kill Jackie. You said you were going to. Now kill him so I can have this room all to myself."

Casey put his finger to his lips and listened.

So did Timmy and I.

It wasn't long before we heard the distinctive sound of rounds being loaded into a rifle.

Chapter Nine

Casey lowered the Nazi dagger altogether and peered out the window.

"What's happening?" Timmy said.

I went to another window and shuddered at what I saw.

"What's happening?" Timmy repeated.

"Big Mike's loading his rifle," I whispered.

"Why?"

Casey put his finger to his lips.

"Is he going to shoot us?"

"Quiet, Timmy," I hissed.

Timmy came to the window, and we watched as Big Mike finished loading his deer rifle and took a sweeping aim at the tops of the oak trees rimming his yard.

Marge Jozaitus yelled at him from the porch to cut it out, but Big Mike ignored her.

"Is he gonna shoot her?" Timmy asked.

"Nah," Casey whispered. "I think he's goin' for squirrels. Yep, he's definitely goin' for . . ."

CRACK!!

"Did he get one?"

Casey and I shook our heads at Timmy.

CRACK!!

"Did he get one that time?"

"Just a branch," Casey whispered. "But a big branch. Jeez, that thing's really . . ."

CRACK!!

"What? What happened?"

I told Timmy to "be quiet," and he wanted to know why.

"Because he might shoot at us, that's why."

"Yeah, kid, shut up."

"Don't tell my brother to shut up."

Casey waved the Nazi dagger in my face. "I'll tell whoever I want to shut up because I've got the Nazi dagger. Now both of you stupid Publics shut up and let me watch . . ."

CRACK!!

". . . him blast that squirrel out of the tree. Man oh man, he almost got one that time! I'm goin' out to look." And with that Casey was leaping off through the twilight's last gleaming to our garage roof.

His timing couldn't have been better, because seconds later Mom barged into our room without knocking.

"What are you boys doing?!?" she said, rushing to Timmy.

"Watching Big Mike shoot squirrels," I explained.

Mom grabbed Timmy and hauled him away from the window. "You get away from that window too, Jackie."

"But, Mom, he's not shooting at us. He's shooting at squirrels."

"I don't care if he's trying to shoot the man on the moon. Get away from that window this instant, do you hear me?"

I nodded and backed away from the window.

"That crazy lugan," Mom said, stroking Timmy. "I was going to call the police, but how can you call the police when the police are the ones committing crimes?"

"Mom, he's not committing a crime. All he's doing is blasting squirrels out of the trees like he said he was going to do."

"He's crazy, and you're crazy for standing there watching him. What if he turned his gun this way?"

"It's a rifle not a gun, and he's aiming at the trees behind his house."

"Fine. Contradict me. You always do. In fact, you can go out on the deck and watch if you want. I don't care what you do, Jackie, just so long as you don't drag your brother into it."

"Can I go outside and watch?"

"Go outside, go to the moon—I really don't care. Just leave your brother out of it. You hear me?"

"Yes, ma'am."

I dressed back into my day clothes and tore downstairs before she could change her mind. Then I crept out into the backyard where I found Casey crouching behind a blue spruce.

"We're on recon," he whispered when I joined him, "and he's this big, fat kraut sniper, and we've got to take him with this dagger. You cover me while I go after him."

"Casey, are you crazy?!?"

"Quiet, Jackie, he'll hear us."

"He won't hear us," I whispered. "He's drunk. He never hears anything when he's drunk."

"Good, 'cause I'm gonna sneak up on him and cut his head off with this dagger."

"Casey!"

"What?"

"You're crazy!"

"I'm crazy because you hit me in the head with that rock, you stupid Public. Now cover me while I sneak up on him."

"Cover you with what? He's got a rifle, and I don't even have a slingshot."

"Use your imagination. Now cover me!"

I imagined myself into a big old battle tank as Casey crawled off into the gloamin' with his Nazi dagger and blood lust.

All was quiet for the longest time, then there was another angry CRACK!! from Big Mike's rifle and a horrible howl.

I didn't know what to do.

I was so scared.

So scared I wet my pants.

Casey was hit!

Casey was bleeding!!

That was him out there in the dark bleeding from a horrible gaping wound from Big Mike's deer rifle, and all I was doing was crouching by the blue spruce wetting my pants because I was such a chicken.

Well, I decided, that's my best friend in the whole wide world out there dying, and I'm not going to let him die alone.

I forced myself to my feet, ran to the fence and tumbled over.

"Casey," I called, "how bad are you hurt?"

Nothing.

Then more howling.

Then Big Mike shining a flashlight in my face and yelling, "What the hell are you doing in *my* yard, you little punk?!?"

"I ah . . ."

"I thought I told you goddamn kids to stay the hell out of this yard."

"Yes, sir, but . . ."

"You want me to put one of those holds on you we use on the niggers on the West Side? Huh?"

I backed toward the fence and shook my head.

"Then get the hell back on your side of the fence where you belong."

"Yes, sir, but . . ."

"You got shit in your ears, you little bastard—I gave you a direct order, now move!! Pronto!!"

"But you hit my friend Casey with your rifle. He's over here somewhere. That's what's making that awful howling noise."

Big Mike shined his flashlight over toward the back of his yard and there lay Miss Paschley's beloved toy poodle, Jacques. The poor creature had taken a bullet through the hind quarters and was howling and bleeding its little life out.

Big Mike shrugged and said, "Could have sworn it was a rabbit. Oh well. Stupid mutt shouldn't have been runnin' loose like that. Serves it right."

I gulped and said, "But that's Miss Paschley's poodle, Jacques."

"He's dead meat now, son. Come on, and you can watch me put it out of its misery just like we had to do to them Jap sons-of-bitches on Iwo. Little yellow pricks wouldn't surrender even after you took a flame thrower to 'em, so the only live ones we ever saw were more dead than alive, and we sure as hell weren't gonna do anything to patch 'em up after what they'd done to us, so we'd just put a .45 in their skull and send them to that big rice bowl in the sky. Now quit your snivelin' and be a man and watch me put this mutt out of its misery."

I watched as Bike Mike bolted another round, took careful aim at Jacques's little poodle brain, and blew the animal to kingdom come. It was messy, bloody and just plain awful.

I wanted to vomit but couldn't.

"There," Big Mike said, "that'll keep that stupid mutt from wandering around other people's yards. Last thing I need when I'm cuttin' the grass is a big pile of poodle shit to step in. You hear me, son?"

I looked up at Big Mike and knew there would be a nuclear holocaust in my lifetime. With people like him wearing uniforms, there was no other possibility.

"Yes, sir. Uh, Mr. Jozaitus?"

"What?"

I looked around wondering what had become of Casey. There was no sight or sound of him.

"What?"

"Uh, nothing. Uh, well, actually, are you going to tell Miss Paschley about her dog? I mean since you — well, you know."

Big Mike kicked at the dead dog with his shiny police shoe and grunted. "Screw that prune-faced bitch. I'm gonna throw her mutt in the trash can where it belongs."

Just then Marge Jozaitus called from the back porch: "What the hell's going on back there?!?"

I was afraid Big Mike was going to turn his rifle on his wife, but all he did was mutter, "Nothin', Marge. Go to bed."

"How can I go to bed when you're blasting away out there like the war was still on. And what was that dreadful howling?"

"Nothin', Marge," Big Mike meekly repeated. "Go to bed."

I looked up and saw that the ex-Marine was afraid of his wife. And he had to outweigh her by at least 150 pounds. Or more.

But then Marge Jozaitus, despite her married name, was all Back-of-the-Yards Irish, and they didn't come feistier than that. She worked for the phone company in some bad neighborhood closer to the Loop, and she didn't take bunk from anybody. Especially her big lunk of a lugan husband.

But then why did she marry him in the first place?

Nobody ever said, but even I figured it was because he was such a smooth talker, and because, well, whatever he did with Aunt Pearl behind Ken's on Western Avenue and other places sure made her awfully happy, and at one time he must have done that for Marge. Probably when she was younger and liked that kind of thing. Whatever that thing was.

But I had a pretty good idea.

It wasn't like it wasn't happening all around me all the time. See.

Anyway, I digress when I should progress.

Sorry.

Marge Jozaitus repeated: "I will not go to bed until you tell me what that dreadful howling was. What did you hit with that stupid gun of yours?"

"It's a rifle not a gun, and I didn't hit nothin' with it. Just a rabbit. Now go to bed."

"Rabbits don't howl like that—what did you hit? It sounded like a dog."

"Just a stray. I'll take care of it, Marge. Now be quiet—you're gonna wake up the neighbors."

I almost laughed.

Almost.

But not quite, because you never laughed at Big Mike. Only with him. If you wanted to live to see 10. And I sure did.

"All right," Marge said, "I'll be quiet and go to bed. But you're not crawling in bed with me tonight. Do you hear me?"

Big Mike nodded sadly like somebody had stolen his puppy.

I couldn't believe it.

He sighed and said softly, "I've got a little proposition for you son."

"A what?"

"A deal."

"A deal? What kind of deal?"

Big Mike fished in his pocket and hooked a fresh bill. "You put that mutt in my wheelbarrow and haul it over to that Paschley broad and tell her there was an accident or something, and I'll give you this ten spot. What do you say?"

"A ten spot?"

"Yeah, ain't you never seen a ten spot before?"

"You mean ten dollars?"

"What the hell else would I mean? Course I mean ten bucks. Like I was gonna pay you earlier if you'd stop playin' that damn clarinet. But first you got to earn it."

First I thought of Big Mike's kids Chuck and Carol. It was their yard, and he was their father, so why couldn't they take Jacques to Miss Paschley? They were both older and bigger than me, but they were probably hiding in their closets like they usually did when their father came home drunk.

Then I thought of how far ten dollars would get me at Reed's Toy Store—beyond the *Big Mo* and then some. Wow!!

"What'd you say, son?"

"Uh, how about if you give me the money before I take Jacques over to Miss Paschley? In case she gets mad or something and I have to run away."

"That dried-up bitch ain't gonna get mad at you, son. You're not the one who killed her dog. You're just the messenger. Nobody ever kills the messenger. Now we got a deal, or we got a deal?"

I scanned the descended darkness and wondered what had become of Casey. Where was he when I needed him?

"What are you mumbling about, son?"

"Nothing, Mr. Jozaitus."

"Hey, how many times I got to tell you—name's Big Mike. Okay?"

"Yes, sir. I mean Big Mike. But I really think you should give me the money first. Just in case."

Big Mike sighed and said, "You're worse than them niggers on the West Side. You know that?"

"Yes, sir. I mean Big Mike."

Big Mike handed me the ten spot and went to get his wheelbarrow and a shovel. He used the latter to lift poor dead Jacques into the wheelbarrow and sent me on my woeful errand with a reminder to return the wheelbarrow and shovel to his garage.

"Yes, sir," I said, starting down his driveway.

"Don't screw up, son," he said.

"No, sir. I mean Big Mike."

"Because it ain't like I don't know where you live or nothin'."

He laughed softly to himself, and that was the last I saw of him that night.

* * *

Miss Ruth Paschley lived across the street with her aged mother in a two-story frame house with a big yard full of poodle poop. I know because she had paid me once to run her ancient lawnmower through the tall grass. She had promised that she had thoroughly "policed" the yard, but I still managed to hit one of Jacques's fresh turds head on, and the lawnmower splattered it all over me.

Yuck!

Still, I was awfully sorry for Jacques, and I could barely look at his bloody remains as we passed under the street light.

"He didn't mean to kill you, boy," I said softly. "He thought you were a rabbit. Honest. Although he was shooting at squirrels, but since he couldn't hit any, I guess he must have figured it'd be easier to hit rabbits, and you just happened to be where he thought the rabbits were, and you got hit, and now you're dead, and I'm awful sorry, Jacques. And if I could bring you back to life, I sure would, but I can't because I'm just a little kid who lost his own dog."

I was wiping tears off my face by the time I got to Miss Paschley's front door.

I was just going to push the buzzer and run away, but my feet froze to her porch. Even though it was still in the 70s out.

The porch light came on, and Miss Paschley opened the inner door.

She smiled at me and said, "Why, Jackie Yardley, what a pleasant surprise. But isn't it past your bedtime?"

I nodded and stuffed my hands in my pockets.

Miss Paschley was a prim and proper type whose face reminded me of those red-hot hatchets in that book in Casey's basement. She taught seventh grade at Alice L. Harwood Elementary School and made her students collect 21 different kinds of leaves every fall and press them between wax paper. Any kid could find 10 different kinds of leaves in our neighborhood, but the hard part was finding those last 11.

Miss Paschley was 42 and had never married.

Although I'd heard Aunt Pearl saying one time that Miss Paschley had been "quite the runabout in her prime."

Needless to say, Miss Paschley was not a regular at Yardley's Bar & Grill. In fact, Miss Ruth Paschley had never been to Yardley's Bar & Grill.

Never ever.

Miss Paschley studied me and said, "You've been crying. What's the matter?"

"It's uh, well, I, uh, your, uh . . ."

"Come on, Jackie, you can tell me." Miss Paschley bent down and saw that I had wet my shorts. She didn't say anything with her mouth, but she did with her eyes. "Please tell me."

I took a deep breath and pointed at the wheelbarrow at the base of her porch. "It's your dog, Miss Paschley. Jacques. Big Mike, I mean Mr. Jozaitus shot him and . . ."

"Shot Jacques?!?"

"Yes, but he thought . . ."

"Shot my Jacques?!?"

"Yes, but . . ."

Miss Paschley pushed past me and tumbled down to her dead dog. In no time flat she was letting out a howl more horrible than the one Jacques had emitted.

"That bastard!" Miss Paschley hissed when she could finally talk. "I'm going to call the police and have them arrest that maniac."

"But, Miss Paschley, he is the police."

She looked up at me and just moved her lips for the longest time. Then she shuddered and collapsed.

I ran down to her and picked her up as best I could. "Are you all right?"

Her eyelids fluttered, and her eyeballs rolled around for a while and then she got right back in the game and said in the coldest voice I ever heard: "Someday, I'm going to get that bastard. You hear me, Jackie Yardley? Someday that big monster is going to regret the day he was born."

I nodded solemnly and said in a small voice, "Uhm, you want me to help you — you know . . . "

"Bury Jacques?"

"Well, yeah."

Miss Paschley shook her head violently. "No, it's way past your bedtime. You should go home. I'll take care of Jacques. You leave him to me, you hear?"

"Yes, ma'am. Uhm, Miss Paschley?"

"What?"

"I, uh, better take the wheelbarrow and shovel back to Mr. Jozaitus because . . ."

"You leave the wheelbarrow and shovel to me, you hear?"

"Yes, ma'am."

"Now vamoose."

"Yes, ma'am."

I vamoosed into the night and was crossing under the street light in front of my house when I heard a sharp hissing.

I looked around but saw nothing.

More hissing.

Still nothing.

So I called, "Who's there?"

"It's me—Casey."

"Casey! Where are you?"

"Over here—by the bushes. Be quiet, you idiot."

I tiptoed over to the bushes at the end of our driveway and squinted hard enough to make out Casey's silhouette. I reached out to touch him and felt something wet and sticky.

"Casey, what's that on your face?"

"Nothing, Jackie. Just some blood. Come on, let's go over to my house. I want to show you something."

"Some blood?!?"

I dragged Casey under the streetlight and saw that his face and t-shirt were covered with blood.

"Casey, you've got blood all over . . ."

"It's nothin', Jackie. Come on, let's go over to my house. I want to show you something."

"But you've got blood all over you. Did you get hit?"

Casey shushed me and simply dragged me off to his house.

When we got to his back fence, he said: "We're gonna have to sneak in through a basement window because my mom thinks I've been home all this time. Okay?"

"Okay, but what about all that blood? What happened?"

Casey sighed and promised he'd tell me just as soon as we were safely arrived in his basement.

"Now follow me," he whispered, "and don't make any noise, or I'll cut your guts out with this Nazi dagger. You understand?"

Only too well.

Chapter Ten

Casey led me through the dark to the northeast corner of his basement and bent down.

"I always leave this window unlatched," he whispered.

He pushed it open and slipped into the darkness.

"Come on," he called.

"Turn on a light."

"Not 'til you get in here and we recon the perimeter."

I shuddered at the thought of descending into darkness and shuddered again at the thought of what Mom was going to say to me when I finally got home. I had never been out this late after dark in my whole entire life, and I knew Mom was just going to kill me when I got home.

If I ever got home.

And it was beginning to feel like I was never going to get home.

I wondered if I really did want to go home.

Home.

What a strange sounding word, I thought.

Home.

"What are you doin' up there, Yardley?"

"Huh?"

"Come on—get your butt down here. Before my dad hears you and calls the police."

I laughed.

"What's so funny?"

"You said the police."

"Yeah?"

"Well, the police are—you know."

"No, I don't know."

"Well, Big Mike's the police, and he just shot Miss Paschley's poodle, Jacques. And probably nothing's ever going to happen to him because he's the police."

"So?"

"So, it just doesn't seem right. You know?"

"All I know is my dad's gonna hear you if you don't get down here right now."

"All right. But could you turn on the light, Casey? I can't see where I'm jumpin'."

"Chicken."

"Am not."

"Am too."

I took a deep breath and said, "Okay, here I come, but you'd better catch me."

"Sure."

Casey sure didn't catch me; his battleship gray basement floor did.

"Hey," I said, clutching my banged knee, "I thought you were gonna catch me. You jerk."

"You're the jerk. Now be quiet, we've got to recon the perimeter."

"Okay."

Casey pulled me through the absolute darkness to a door. He popped it open, and a dim light illuminated his bloody face. He looked scarier than any monster I had ever seen.

"Somebody's by the washing machine," he whispered. "Come on, let's go and scout it out."

Casey clamped the Nazi dagger between his teeth, got on his hands and knees and crawled toward the washing machine.

What choice did I have but to follow him?

We passed undetected through a door, under the ping-pong table, and right up to the slatted wooden wall separating the play room from Mrs. O'Neal's washing room.

And speaking of Mrs. O'Neal there she stool under a naked 30-watt bulb with her 12-year-old daughter, Laura. Laura was weeping inconsolably, and Mrs. O'Neal was patting her shoulder and muttering: "There, there, dear, it happens to all girls when they get to be your age."

Casey and I looked at one another in wonder and strained our ears.

"Oh, Mother," Laura O'Neal said between sobs, "I've ruined a perfectly good pair of underpants. It looks like I was bleeding to death."

"Laura, you've just had your first monthly visitor — that's all. It's perfectly natural."

"Then why didn't you tell me, Mother? Why didn't you tell me this was going to happen? Oh, it's so awful. So embarrassing. And I was wearing white shorts when it happened, and they're absolutely ruined. Ruined, Mother!"

Mrs. O'Neal kept on patting Laura like she was a dog or something and sighed. Then she said: "I honestly didn't think you were ready, Dear. I didn't get my first monthly visitor until I was — well, I think I was nearly 14. And your Aunt Noreen didn't get hers until she was practically 15, and I'm not actually sure about my own mother, because it was just something you didn't discuss with her, but . . ."

"Mother, I thought I was going to die!" Laura sobbed.

"Oh hush. You silly! You weren't going to die. You just had your monthly visitor is all. Every girl has her first monthly visitor. It's nothing to be ashamed of, although I do want you to pray to the Blessed Virgin tonight to cleanse your thoughts, words and deeds from this day forward."

"Why?"

"Because — well, because you ask too many questions. You silly. I've got a little book I want you to read. It's all about how women's bodies work. Here."

Casey and I watched as Mrs. O'Neal handed her daughter a book with a bright cover.

"I'm gonna get that," Casey whispered. "Just you wait — we're gonna have a real good look at that book."

I shushed him, and we watched as his beautiful sister with the nut-brown hair thumbed through the book her mother had given her.

"Oh, Mother," Laura sobbed, "these pictures are awful. There's blood everywhere. If this is what being a woman's all about, I want to be a boy. Right now!"

"Oh, hush. You don't want to be a boy. Boys are filthy little things. Disgusting. And they only want one thing. That's all they ever think about, and it's certainly all they ever want. They're worse than dogs."

"What thing, Mother?"

"Never mind. You're too young to know."

"But you said I'm a woman now. You said . . ."

"Never mind what I said." Mrs. O'Neal sighed and patted her only daughter. "All I meant to say was you have the body of a woman now. But not the brains and emotions to go with it. That's why you have to pray to the Blessed Virgin every day for guidance. Only the Blessed Virgin can protect you from evil boys. Do you understand?"

Laura O'Neal wiped her almond eyes and and shook her head.

Mrs. O'Neal patted her some more and said, "There, there. Now you go up and take a nice bath and read that book, and I'll come up after I've finished washing your things and tell you how to wear a sanitary pad and belt."

"A what?!?"

"It's all in the book, dear. But don't worry, I'll show you. Millions of women wear them every month. Now it's your turn—that's all. You'll get used to it. You'll see. Now scoot."

Laura shuffled upstairs and Mrs. O'Neal busied herself at the washing machine. Then she turned and called, "Kevin, are you playing in the basement?"

Casey and I crab-raced away from his mother to the front of the basement, and Casey took the Nazi dagger out of his mouth and called back, "Yeah, Mom, I'm up here playing with Dad's ships."

"Then why don't you have a light on?"

"I'm playin' night patrol."

"Well turn a light on, or you'll be blind as a bat. And come to bed in ten minutes. It's getting late."

"But it's summer vacation, Mom."

"Don't but me, young man."

"Yes, ma'am."

I chuckled softly.

"What are you laughin' at?" Casey whispered.

"Nothin'."

"Kevin!" Mrs. O'Neal called.

"Yes, ma'am."

"I told you to turn a light on, now do it!"

"Yes, ma'am."

Casey prodded me behind a box with the Nazi dagger and pulled on an overhead light.

"Now be up in ten minutes. You understand?"

"Yes, ma'am."

We held our breaths as Mrs. O'Neal activated her washing machine and trundled upstairs.

"That was close," I said, coming out of hiding.

Casey brandished the Nazi dagger at me and said, "Stay there, Public, you're my prisoner."

"Casey!"

"Do what I say or I'll still kill your guts out."

I exhaled and changed the subject: "What's wrong with your sister?"

Casey lowered the Nazi dagger and said, "I'm not sure, but I'm gonna get that book Mom gave her, and we'll find out. It's something to do with hemorrhages or something."

"Hemorrhages?"

"Yeah, girls hemorrhage a whole lot when they get to my sister's age. Hemorrhage means uncontrollable bleeding. It was in one of my father's books."

"Yuck."

"Yeah, that's what I say."

I looked at Casey's bloody face and said, "Casey?"

"What?"

"Speaking of bleeding, what happened to you?"

"You mean all this blood?"

"Yeah. Did Big Mike hit you with a bullet?"

"Nah, but he almost did. I dug this tunnel under his fence with my Nazi dagger, and I was sneakin' up on him in the dark when that dumb poodle came over and sniffed me. I was just reachin' out to knock the stupid mutt away when—BLAM!!—Big Mike blasted it!! You wouldn't have believed all the blood that came squirtin' out. All over me. It was so neat!"

"Neat?"

"Yeah, just like combat." Casey dabbed at the blood caking his face. "How much more realistic can you get than this. And you know what was really neat?"

"No."

"I could almost see the bullet go through that dog. It was like in slow motion or something. Must be the way guys in combat see it. Don't you think?"

I shrugged and said, "Don't you think you should wash your face? And your shirt. I mean, if you mother sees you like that, she'll . . ."

"I'll wash my face and shirt before I go to bed. Don't worry, Jackie." Casey set down the Nazi dagger and added, "Now come on, I want to show you something."

"What?"

"Just shut up and follow me."

I shut up and followed Casey into the storeroom where we had made our daring entry into the basement and where his father kept the storm windows and wooden ship models.

Casey turned on the light and opened one of the gray wooden boxes that had "Top Secret — Official U.S. Navy Property" stamped on it.

"I ever shown you these?" he asked.

"No. You said they were top secret."

"Well, my father says it's okay to show you now that the war's been over for a while. Besides, the Navy's got all these new ships and stuff. Pretty soon they'll even have atomic subs that can go all the way around the world submerged. Without ever once having to come up for air. My father says it's just a matter of time before . . ."

Casey waved the Nazi dagger in my face. "You breathe a word of that to anyone, you stupid little Public, and I'll kill your guts out with this Nazi dagger. You hear me?"

I nodded solemnly and said, "You know, my father was in the Navy too."

"Yeah, but he wasn't in the Pentagon like my father, and he was only a crummy Lieutenant not a full Captain like my father."

"My dad made Lieutenant Commander."

"Yeah, but I remember you saying that he just made that at the very, very end of the war. Right before he was discharged."

"Yeah, but . . ."

"But nothing. My father went to the Naval Academy, and he made full Captain right in the middle of the war, and he served in a top-secret part of the Pentagon during the war, and he still can't talk about most of the stuff he did because it was so top secret. Which means if you tell anybody — even your dumb brother — about what we did here tonight, I'll be forced by special Naval Intelligence orders to sneak into your bedroom and kill your guts out. And don't think I can't do it, because I sure did it tonight – didn't I?"

I looked at my maniacal little friend and wondered if it wouldn't be better to spend time with imaginary playmates. I did have an overactive imagination after all, and . . .

"Quit talkin' to yourself, you dumb Public and answer my question."

"Yeah, Casey, you sure did sneak into my bedroom tonight. And I sure thought it was you Big Mike hit with his rifle when poor old Jacques let out that howl. I never heard anything like that, have you?"

"Millions of time. Okay, enough of this blabbin' – let's go to war."

"Huh."

Casey withdrew a flat-bottomed scale wooden model of the *U.S.S. Suwannee* and said, "You know anything about the Battle of Leyte Gulf?"

He had me there, so I simply shrugged.

Casey laughed triumphantly and said, "Man, they don't teach you Publics nothin.'"

"Casey, you were just in Public school too."

"Yeah, but I'm goin' to a real school in the fall, and I already know ten jillion times as much as you just from goin' to catechism every Wednesday afternoon."

"Right. So tell me about the Battle of Leyte Gulf."

Casey held up the model of the *Suwannee* and explained, "My father used model ships like this in this big, top-secret war room in the Pentagon to follow all the big battles in the Pacific, so he knew before anybody just what happened. Especially at the Battle of Leyte Gulf. And you know what happened to this ship?"

"No."

"You even know what kind of ship this is?"

Casey set it down on a table so I could see it in realistic profile.

I shrugged and ventured, "It's an aircraft carrier."

"Escort carrier actually, you dumb Public, but I'll give you credit for a right answer. Now you pretend like you're part of the arresting gear crew on the flight deck and you're getting ready to recover your Avenger bombers that are coming back from blasting Jap positions on Leyte."

"What's arresting gear?"

"Don't you know anything?"

"Well, sure but . . ."

"Good thing you've got me for a friend, Yardley, because it looks like I'm gonna have to explain everything to you your whole life." Casey pointed at the model and said, "You *do* see the flight deck, don't you?"

"Yeah."

"Which end do the planes land on?"

I pointed to the aft end.

"Very good. Now, do you really think an Avenger bomber is just going to come to a complete stop after flying along at 200 miles per hour?"

"No."

"Then *how* is it going to stop?"

I pointed at the raised lines across the aft end of the model's flight deck and said, "Those things."

"Good. There's hope for you yet, Yardley. Those things are called arresting cables, and on the tail of each plane is this thing called an arresting hook, or a tailhook, because it drops down just before landing and it catches the arresting cable when the pilot brings it in for a landing. See, he's got to come in full throttle in case he scrubs his landing, so those cables have to really be strong, but sometimes something would go wrong and a cable would snap and guys like you on the arresting gear crew would get cut in half and stuff by the broken cable. There'd be blood and guts all over the flight deck, and the other planes would skid on it and then there'd be even more blood and guts."

"Yuck."

"Nah, I think it's neat. Anyway, I want you to pretend like its October 26, 1944, and you're helping land Avenger bombers on the flight deck. Okay?"

"Okay."

I scrunched down to eye level with the *Suwannee* and easily slipped back in time and place to that fateful fall day in the Philippine Archipelago. The deck heaved gently and an incoming Avenger droned in the near distance. I and my crew were preparing to recover the bomber when Casey clopped me in the back of the head.

"What are you doing?!?"

"Kamikaze," Casey said, continuing his attack on my person. "The *Suwannee* was the first American ship to get attacked by a Kamikaze."

I shielded my head from Casey and said, "Stop hitting me."

"No, you're on the flight deck, and the Kamikaze crashed right into it while the crews were all up there recovering bombers. The whole flight deck and bridge went up in flames and you were one of the guys who got burned to a crisp."

Casey came up with a lighted match and tossed it at me.

I flailed it away from my head, stomped it out on the floor and hollered, "What are you doing?!?"

"Tryin' to be realistic, Yardley. Now hold still and let me light your hair on fire. You ever smell burned hair?"

"Casey!"

Casey calmly lighted another match and tossed it at my head.

I batted it away and ran for the window.

"Where're you goin'?"

"Home. I don't like your games, Casey."

I jumped up and batted the window open. I jumped again and caught the sill with my left forearm. I was shinnying up when Casey came over and pulled me down to the floor by my legs.

We tussled and spat and kicked and punched and gouged and probably would have killed one another if Donald O'Neal hadn't barged in on us and said: "Kevin, Mother wants you to come upstairs to bed this very instant."

"Beat it, Donald," Casey said, trying to choke me.

"I will not beat it, Kevin," Donald said. "And I'm going to tell Mother that you have John Yardley Junior down here when you're not supposed to have anyone down here at night."

"Get him off me, Donald," I gasped.

Donald O'Neal just stood there in his summer pajamas and slippers.

Casey knocked my head against the cement floor, and I kidney-punched him.

Casey groaned and rolled off me.

I groaned and stumbled back toward the window. This time, I got a chair, put it under the window, and used it to effect my escape.

"Wait," Casey called.

I turned and stuck my head back into the basement. "Wait for what, you little jerk."

Casey got up panting and grunted, "Tomorrow."

"What about tomorrow?"

"I saw Big Mike give you that ten spot."

"How could you?"

"Because I'm the best spy in the whole world, that's how. And I saw him give you that ten spot for taking that stupid dog over to Old Lady Paschley. And I saw you put it in your pocket, Yardley."

"What if I did, Casey? I earned it, because I took Jacques over to Miss Paschley, and I sure didn't see you do anything. I didn't even see you, and I called your name and came over to help you, and you didn't come out of hiding until it was all over."

Donald followed all this with the mechanical interest of a tape recorder and said, "I'm telling Mother, Kevin. And I'm telling her that you've got blood all over your face and shirt. And I'm telling her that you let John Yardley Junior in the basement without her permission, and I'm telling her . . ."

"Shut up, Donald."

"I'm telling Mother you told me to shut up, Kevin."

"Casey, I'm goin'. I'm not gonna sit here and listen to you two argue. I'm gonna get killed when I get home. I've never been out this late before."

"Wait."

"Wait for what."

Casey turned to his brother and hissed, "Go upstairs, Donald. Now!"

"No, Kevin. Not until you come up with me. Mother told me to come and get you, and I'm not going upstairs unless you come with me. Is that clear?"

"Okay, Donald. Just a minute — all right?"

"No. Mother told me to come and get you this instant, Kevin, and I'm going to do just what she told me."

Casey sighed and said, "All right." He turned back to me and whispered, "We'll recon at your house tomorrow at 0800. You'd better be ready, because I've got a really neat plan for that ten spot."

"Casey . . ."

"Just be ready, Yardley, because I've still got the Nazi dagger, and I'll still cut your guts out with it if you're not ready. You hear?"

All I heard was Mom slapping my ears for staying out so late.

"You hear, Yardley?"

"I hear you, Casey."

"Good. I'll be at your door at 0800. You'd better be ready for a really big adventure. And have that ten spot with you. You hear?"

"Casey, it's my money. I earned it. I . . ."

"No, you owe me for my Ancient Rome cards that you let your mother tear up to shreds. Just be ready is all."

I nodded and escaped into the night.

I tried the side door when I got home.

Naturally, it was locked.

Of course.

And I sure didn't have a key because who in his right mind would entrust a willful little seven-year-old with the key to something as big and important as Yardley's Bar & Grill?

I went to the front door and tried it.

Naturally, it was locked.

Of course.

I rubbed my hands on my short and panted. Then I prayed to the Lord God Almighty up in His big wide Heaven to help me.

"Just help me get in my house without getting killed, God," I whispered, "and I'll do anything you want. Honestly. Anything. Even hang around with Donald O'Neal if that's what you want. I mean really, really want. And I'll also be good to Timmy. I promise. Cross my heart and hope to die. Amen."

"Who's that down there?"

It was Mom and she was at the screen above me.

"It's me, Mom," I called softly.

"Do you know what time it is, young man?"

"Yes, ma'am."

"Your father and brother are asleep, and I was just about to go to bed. Where have you been all night?"

"You said I could go out and watch Mr. Jozaitus shoot squirrels, and . . ."

"That was hours ago. Where have you been since?"

"Casey's basement."

"You mean that little Catholic brat?"

"Yes, ma'am."

"I thought I told you I don't want you playing with him."

"But he's my best friend in the whole world."

"If Adolf Hitler was still alive, he'd probably be your best friend in the whole world. And Tojo and Mussolini." Mom sighed and said, "All I know, is you certainly didn't inherit my genes. Because if you had, you'd be like your brother Timmy."

"Mom, can you let me in?"

"Why?"

"'Cause I want to go to bed."

"Why don't you sleep out there? Or go sleep in your best friend's basement if you like it so much over there. Why don't you do that?"

"'Cause it's dark out here. And there's bugs."

"Bugs? What about that spray truck you rode behind? I wouldn't think a mosquito would land on you for at least ten years with all the chemicals you've got on you."

"Well, some are, and — please, Mom!"

Mom sighed and moved away from the screen.

Then nothing.

Then sounds of her waking Dad.

Then nothing.

Then Dad at the door in a pajama top and no bottom. He didn't have his voicebox, so he couldn't say much beyond and burped, "Get in here."

I looked at his big, hairy dingle dangle in wonder and got in there.

Dad closed the door behind me and I raced upstairs. I thought for sure Mom would intercept me at my door, but she didn't.

She didn't do anything but mutter from her room, "You can go and live in that O'Neal kid's basement for all I'm concerned. I've got another one on the way, and I'm sure this one's going to be a girl. Finally."

Yeah, finally.

Chapter Eleven

As soon as Mom got Dad off to work the next morning, she called Timmy and me down for breakfast.

It was 0715.

Casey would be by at 0800.

I knew all about keeping 24-hour military time at the tender age of seven thanks to Casey.

I knew a lot of things at the age of seven thanks to Casey.

Like my newly acquired knowledge of hemorraghing girls compliments of Casey and his sister and mother. Not to mention the *Suwannee* having been the first American ship to be attacked by a Kamikaze during World War II.

Yeah, by 1957 we were definitely calling it World War II because we were expecting World War III any day.

At least Casey and I were.

Casey was looking forward to it because he said he had stored enough secret stuff in his basement to survive after the Russians blasted all the steel mills in nearby Gary, Indiana with their A-bombs.

"H-bombs," Casey would correct me. "Don't you know anything, Yardley? The Russkies have the hydrogen bomb."

"Yeah," I'd counter, "but so do we."

"Lot of good that's gonna do when the Russkies drop their H-bombs on the southern end of Lake Michigan and create this huge steam cloud that's gonna boil everybody to death but me 'cause I'll be hiding in my basement with all my secret stuff."

Casey, of course, would never show me his secret stuff, and he said if I happened to be playing in his basement with him when the Russian attack came, he'd throw me out and watch me "get boiled up with all the rest."

What a pal.

And he was just the pal I was anticipating with fluttering bowels as I made my way down for breakfast that fateful morning in June, 1957.

"Where's your brother?" Mom said as I took my seat in the breakfast nook.

"He's coming."

"You didn't do anything to him, did you?"

"No, ma'am."

She looked sternly at me and then went to scramble the eggs.

I poured orange juice for Timmy and me and made the toast.

Timmy appeared with Mr. Monkey, rubbed his eyes and sat where I had been sitting.

"That's my chair," I hissed.

"I want to sit here."

"But you always sit over there."

"Well, I want to sit here today."

I tugged at Timmy, and he hollered until I let him go.

Mom dashed over and slapped my little face before I knew what hit me.

"Mom, Timmy's sitting in my chair! He's . . ."

SLAP!!

Then: "You leave your little brother alone. Do you hear me, young man?"

"Yes, ma'am."

Timmy smiled triumphantly and said, "This is my chair from now on."

I nodded woodenly and sat in what had been Timmy's chair.

Then Mom served us our breakfast and said, "I have an announcement to make. I told your father before he went to work, and now it's time to tell you boys."

Timmy forked scrambled eggs into his mouth and said, "I already know, Mom — you're gonna have a baby. And it's gonna be a girl."

Mom dropped her spatula.

She picked it up and said, "How did you know?!?"

Timmy shrugged and chewed. Then he said, "I just knew."

"But how do you know it's going to be a girl?"

"'Cause you want a girl so bad, it's got to be a girl. And I prayed that it would be a girl, so it's going to be a girl."

Mom looked adoringly at Timmy.

I cleared my throat.

Mom looked hatefuly at me and said, "Yes?"

"When is the baby going to come, Mom?"

"She — or he — is due in February. If all goes well that is, and I'm sure it will."

I looked up at Mom and forced a smile. "This is good news — right, Mom?"

A dark expression crossed Mom's face, then she too forced a smile and said, "Eat your breakfast."

I wanted to ask her how Dad had reacted to the news, but I figured her dark expression was my answer. So I just ate my eggs and toast in silence until 0800 when my clockwork friend Casey called: "Yo, Jack-ee!!"

"What's *he* doing here?!?" Mom barked.

"He's my best friend in the whole world," I whispered. "I told him he could come by at 8 o'clock."

"I suppose you think you're going to run off and play with that little Catholic brat all day, don't you?"

I shrugged and looked at the remains of my eggs.

Casey called again: "Yo, Jack-ee!!"

Mom exhaled and shrugged. "All right. Go off and play with your 'best friend in the whole world.' I was planning on giving you to the next passing Indian today anyway, so you might as well run off to the ends of the earth with that little troublemaker. I've got bridge club today anyway, and I'll take Timmy, so just plan on being home for dinner. If that's not too much trouble, your Lordship."

I gulped, took my plate to the sink and began washing it.

"What are you doing?"

"Washing my dishes like I always do."

"Just go."

I looked up at Mom and prayed that she'd change her mind and start loving me. I was her first-born after all. Didn't that count for something?

Apparently not, because she just stared Nazi daggers down at me.

I gulped and said, "Maybe I should take a key."

"You're too young to have a key. Just be home for dinner. That's all I ask. And don't get arrested and disgrace the family name. You understand?"

"Yes, ma'am. But . . ."

"Don't but me. Just vamoose."

Popular word in 1957—vamoose.

Casey was launching into another "Yo, Jack-ee!!" when I tumbled down the steps and burst through the screen door.

"I can stay out 'til dinner time," I blurted.

Casey smiled at me and said, "Get your bike."

I got my bike and said, "Where to?"

"You got that ten spot Big Mike gave you last night?"

I nodded.

Casey's smile widened. "Good. Now just follow me."

I followed Casey out of my driveway, and we nearly collided with a big green truck with a bunch of shovels and stuff on the back.

The truck lurched to a halt, and a man leaned out of the window and said, "You kids know where a Ruth Pooschie lives?"

"There's a Miss Ruth Paschley over there," I said, pointing.

The man squinted at a piece of paper and said, "Never can read the damn secretary's writing. Yeah, Paschley. That's it. That's her house?"

"Yes, sir."

"Thanks, kid."

The man drove his big green truck over to Miss Paschley's house and parked in the driveway.

I followed him with my eyes and saw that Big Mike's shovel and wheelbarrow were just where I had left them the night before. And so was poor dead Jacques.

Yuck!

"Come on, Yardley, we got to be somewhere in five minutes."

"Huh?"

"Let's go!"

"But don't you want to see what's going on at Miss Paschley's?"

"We can see it when we get back. Now peel rubber or we'll miss our train."

"Our train?!?"

"You heard me—now come on."

I peeled after Casey up Dray Street. He didn't even slow down at the corner and almost got hit by a northbound car on Forest Avenue.

I sighed and realized Casey had more lives than 9,000 cats.

Casey flew all the way to Harding Street, hung a hard left without signaling, blazed south to 107th Street, barely paused at the stop sign and tore west toward the Rock Island tracks.

The Rock Island tracks!

Was he crazy?

We were seven year-old kids, and seven-year-old kids sure didn't ride Rock Island trains in 1957 unless they were with their parents.

And that was usually only at Christmas time when we got taken downtown to have breakfast under the tree in the Walnut Room in Marshall Field's.

But Casey was heading right for the rickety old station just south of 107th Street.

I tore after him and caught him as he was taking his bike around back.

"We'll ditch our bikes back here. Nobody'll even know they're here," he said.

"You sure? If anything happens to my bike, my parents'll kill me."

"Nothing's going to happen to your bike. Now just leave it here with mine, and we'll camouflage them with branches and stuff."

Casey tore branches off a sapling and did a halfway decent job of disguising our bikes.

Then he led me into the station and whispered, "Let me do all the talking."

I nodded bravely, but I was sure we were going to get caught and sent straight to the Audey Home for the rest of our natural lives.

Casey was finally going to get us in really big, big trouble, and there was nothing I could do about it because he had me in some kind of spell. Like he had poured Jello around me during the night, and all I could do was wobble after him.

Like some dummy.

But I wasn't a dummy.

I was just a lonely, abused little kid looking for a friend.

And Casey was as far as I could see at the moment.

And at that precise moment he stepped boldly up to the ticket window and declared: "I'd like to two children's round-trip tickets to LaSalle Street Station."

The woman in the ticket office bent down so she could see us through the grate. "Where's your mother, little boy? We don't allow little children to travel alone."

A northbound train growled into earshot.

Casey fished a note out of his pocket, handed it to the woman and waited.

The woman unfolded the note, read it with intense concentration, smiled, handed the note back to Casey and said, "That'll be $4 for you and your cousin, Kevin."

Casey put the note back in his pocket and nudged me.

I didn't budge.

"Give her the money, Cousin John," Casey hissed, smiling all the while at the ticket woman.

"Oh," I said, coming out of my trance. I dug the ten spot out of my pocket and handed it to the woman.

She stamped four tickets, got six dollar bills out of a drawer and handed it all to me. "Now don't lose your return tickets, boys."

"No, ma'am," I said, looking at the tickets like they were Spanish dubloons.

Casey grabbed the tickets and money out of my hand and said, "Come on, the train's coming."

I ran after him out to the platform and watched in awe as an Alco RS3 braked its consist of four 2500-series open-window coaches to a halt outside the station.

This was an end of the rush-hour train, so there were just a few men in suits waiting to board.

They were too busy reading their newspapers to even notice us, and once Casey showed the conductor our tickets, he let us spring right up the steps at the end of the first coach.

Casey led me to a forward-facing rattan seat on the starboard side and deftly slid two of our tickets into the clip on the back of the front seat.

Then, of course, he sat closest to the window.

"Hey, I get to sit by the window."

"No. It was *your* mom who tore up my Ancient Rome cards, so I get to sit by the window. And it was you who let her tear them up. You dumb Public."

I was too excited about being on a train to fight back. So I settled down and said, "You can sit by the window going downtown, and I'll sit by it coming back. How's that?"

"I'll think about it."

The train lurched forward, and we were really on our way downtown with no parents.

Just Casey and me.

On the Rock Island.

Neat!!!

"Casey?"

"What?"

"What'd that letter say that you showed that lady?"

"Nothin' much."

"Nothin' much? Then how come that lady let us ride the train? She never would have let us ride the train if you hadn't shown her that note, and there must have been something really, really . . ."

"Shhh, here comes the conductor."

The conductor came and punched our tickets.

Then he looked at us and said, "Aren't you boys a little young to be traveling all the way downtown by yourselves?"

Casey handed him the note, and the conductor read it with a serious expression. He nodded officiously and handed the note back to Casey.

"Well, I hope your cousin enjoys our fair city. And go straight to your father's office when you get downtown. I'm not saying it's not safe downtown, but you never know what kind of character you're going to meet, especially on Van Buren Street. It's not like the old days. No sir."

The conductor went off to punch other tickets and to board passengers at the next stop, 103rd Street.

I looked at Casey and said, "Let me see the note."

"Why? You can hardly read."

"I can too read. Now let me see the note. And give me my money back."

"Shhh," Casey said looking around, "people are gonna hear you, Cousin John."

"I'm not your cousin, and nobody calls me John," I hissed. "Now let me see the note, or I'll scream real loud, and they'll throw us off the train."

Casey sighed and handed me the note.

I unfolded it and saw that it was neatly typed on his mother's personal stationary. It read:

"To Whom it May Concern:

This note will introduce my beloved son, Kevin Charles O'Neal and his dear cousin John Patrick O'Neal who is visiting from Philadelphia. I hereby give permission for these two wonderful boys to ride your lovely railroad downtown so the boys might tour my husband's office and have lunch with him.

I regret that I am unable to travel with the boys, but I must tend to my daughter who has taken ill.

Sincerely,

Mary Theresa Cavanaugh O'Neal"

It was signed in green ink and sure looked like a note from a real adult.

I looked at Casey in awe.

"Did you get your mom to do this?"

Casey snatched the note out of my hand and smirked. "Are you kidding? She thinks I'm going over to Beverly Park to watch Little League. If she knew I was doing this, she'd boil me in oil and then kill my guts out."

"Then where'd the note come from?"

"From me, you idiot. Where else?"

"But it's typed."

"So?"

"So, you don't know how to type."

"How do you know? You ever see me type?"

"No, but . . ."

"But then you don't know, Yardley. Do you?"

"Okay, so you typed it. I'll believe that because I know you said your brother Russell has a typewriter and maybe you snuck into his room and took forever to type it and had to look up all those big words in the dictionary, but what about the signature? That sure looks like your mom's handwriting."

"My father has a book in the basement all about forging signatures. So I forged her signature. It was so easy, I laughed."

I didn't know what to say except to ask for my money.

Casey smirked.

"Come on, Casey, give me my money."

"No. If it wasn't for me, we wouldn't be on this train right now, and if it wasn't for me, you wouldn't know half the things you do, so you'd better let me keep the money. Besides, it's mine."

"No it's not. I earned that money for taking Jacques over to Miss Paschley."

"No, I earned it for digging through the enemy perimeter with my Nazi dagger."

I sighed and looked out the window. We were already past 103rd Street and bending around the curve to the station at 99th Street.

"All right, you can keep the money, Casey. I was gonna split it with you anyway because you're my best friend in the whole world."

Casey responded with a wry look, and we sat in silence all the way to the junction with the Rock Island mainline at Vincennes Avenue.

Our train had to wait for an outbound *Rocket* to clear the junction.

"Neat," I said, watching the long-distance streamliner streak by our window. "I wish we were on that train and we were going to California to be prospectors for gold."

"That's stupid," Casey said.

"Why?"

"Because there's no more gold in California. They tapped it out more than a hundred years ago. Back in 1849. That's why they call people in San Francisco '49ers, because their ancestors all went out there in 1849 to strike it rich panning for gold. But so many of 'em came, they tapped out all the gold real fast. It'd be a waste of time to go out there now because there's hardly any more gold—I know because my father has a book all about it my basement."

Casey's basement, the ultimate source of all knowledge.

However arcane.

Of course.

I shrugged wistfully and said, "Hey, want to know something?"

"You got a green booger hanging from your nose?"

"Do I?" I said, fingering my nose.

"No, but I made you stick your finger in your nose."

Casey laughed.

I blushed and said, "I was gonna tell you that my mom's gonna have a baby."

"Today?"

"Not today—February."

"That's nice."

"Aren't you excited?"

"Are you?"

I looked out the window and we advanced up the main and slowed for the Gresham stop. We had climbed above street level and could see the tops of houses and church steeples in the distance. Neat.

"Well," Casey repeated, "are you excited that your mom's having another baby? You sure don't sound excited."

"I guess I am."

"Jackie, you either *are* excited, or you're *not* excited. Now which is it?"

I made myself look at Casey and say, "I'm not excited."

Casey actually sensed my distress and patted my shoulder. "I wouldn't be happy if my mom was going to have another baby. Not that she's going to or anything, because she can't because—well, I'm not supposed to say—but I know I sure wouldn't like it if she went off to the hospital and brought home some little baby that I had to take care of."

"Yeah."

"But then babies come from God—that's what Sister teaches us at catechism—even Public babies, so it's a sin if you don't welcome every baby that God brings into the world, so you'd better welcome this baby, Jackie, or you'll be put in the lowest level of Hell for all of eternity."

"Yeah."

The train took on a gaggle of passengers at Gresham and headed north for stops at Hamilton and Englewood.

A hot summer wind whipped railroad dust through the window and a woman across the aisle complained to the conductor that she had snagged her hosiery on the rattan seat.

But Casey and I didn't care.

Casey and I were heading for that great big wonderland called downtown, and we'd be free to do whatever we liked and go wherever we wanted.

Which prompted me to ask: "Casey, what are we gonna do when we get downtown?"

His only answer was an enigmatic smile.

Chapter Twelve

Before we arrived at LaSalle Street Station in the shadow of the Board of Trade Building, we saw the Pennsylvania Railroad's celebrated *Broadway Limited* at Englewood Station.

Then we saw them backing Santa Fe's *Super Chief* into Dearborn Station, and we didn't have to crane our necks too far to see plenty of B&O and C&O action over at Central Station.

It was like riding in some rich kid's gigantic train set.

Only better.

Because when we pulled into LaSalle Street Station, we were greeted by the New York Central's freshly arrived *Twentieth Century Limited* from New York.

Now there was a train!!

"Maybe we should go to New York?" I said to Casey as we headed for the head end of our Harriman coach. "I heard that the *Twentieth Century's* the best train ever built, and it goes so fast you barely have time to sleep and eat before you get to New York."

"Quit dreamin' and follow me, Cousin John. We got lots of ground to cover."

"Quit callin' me 'Cousin John.' I'm not you're cousin, and I don't like to be called John."

"Sure thing, Cousin John. Now come on."

"Where are we goin'?"

"Quit whinin' and follow me, you sissy."

I ran after Casey as he ran toward the station and complained, "I'm not a sissy. I'm the one who paid for this, Casey. If it wasn't for me, we wouldn't be here right now. If I hadn't taken Jacques' body over to Miss Paschley last night, I wouldn't have gotten a ten spot from Big Mike, and . . ."

"Shut up."

"You shut up."

Casey stopped and yanked my wrist.

It hurt like hell and I howled.

Casey gloated.

"What'd you do that for?"

"'Cause there's a policeman up there. Now behave, or he'll throw us both in the Audey Home. You hear?"

I looked at the policeman who was looking at a pretty young woman and said, "He's not even looking at us."

"He will if you don't stop acting like a dumb little kid."

"Well, what about you?"

"What about me?"

"You're a dumb little kid, too."

"Am not."

"Am too."

"All right — if I'm so dumb, how come we're standing in LaSalle Street Station with six big bucks to spend and return tickets to 107th Street and no adults to tell us what to do and the whole day to do whatever we want downtown. Huh? Tell me that, you dumb Public."

"Casey, I'm not a dumb Public, and it was my money that paid for this trip. While you were off hiding in the bushes somewhere I was the one who had to take poor dead Jacques over to Miss Paschley's."

"Are you boys lost?"

We looked up, and there was the policeman who had been looking at the pretty woman.

"No, sir," Casey said, automatically shifting to charm-the-authority-figure mode. "I was just explaining to my Cousin John here, who's visiting from Philadelphia, that this is where they made that movie about that guy from New York who's being chased by these spies or something, and he gets off the train here, and they're waiting for him at the station, and . . ."

"Right, kid," the policeman said, smiling. "Great picture. Grant Sherman and what's her name end up on Mount Rushmore climbing up Washington's nose or something. And that great scene where he's standing out in a field somewhere and this plane tries to kill him. Yeah, that was a terrific movie. Saw it two times, in fact. So, ah, where you kids going?"

Casey had his note in the lawman's hands in a twinkling.

The policeman read it carefully, nodded officiously, and handed it back to Casey. "Where's your father's office, Kevin?"

"Two-oh-eight South LaSalle."

I looked at Casey in surprise and wanted to say that was where my father worked, but there was no stopping him now.

The policeman smiled and pointed to an escalator. "You just take that down to Van Buren, cross Van Buren — you can take a short cut through the Board of Trade if you want — and that'll put you at the foot of LaSalle at Jackson. Then it's just a hop, skip and a jump from there, kid, and you're home free at your old man's office."

The policeman handed Casey his note, and Casey thanked him profusely.

When we were safely descending the escalator, I said, "Why'd you say your father works at 208 South LaSalle? That's where my father works. And we'd better not go anywhere near there, because if we do, he'll probably see me, and if he sees me downtown, he'll kill me."

"You're the biggest chicken I ever met."

"Am not."

"Am too."

"All right — if I'm a chicken and you're not, Casey, then why don't we walk by *your* father's office and see what happens?"

"We can't."

"Why not?"

"Because he works down on Pershing Road. That's a million miles from here."

"Oh. But your note said that we were going to visit your father's office, so I thought your father worked downtown."

"Well, you thought wrong, you dumb Public. Now come on, we gots lots of walking to do to get where we're going."

Casey hit the bottom of the escalator and took off at a trot. He was halfway through the Board of Trade's art deco lobby before I caught him.

"Where are we going?"

"Just follow me."

I followed Casey up LaSalle Street and darned if he didn't head right through a revolving door into the lobby of the big granite building at 208 South.

I looked up and thought of my father up there somewhere doing whatever it was he was supposed to do all day as the office manager of the Combined Midwest Insurance Company. He had been out on "the street" selling policies before his operation, and had had his best year ever in 1956, but since he now had to talk with his voice box, his boss, Tom Hinchcliff, thought it was best for Dad just to be around the office managing things.

Tom Hinchcliff, by the way, was "Aunt Lu's" husband, and I was supposed to call him "Uncle Tom" even though he wasn't my real uncle or anything.

And I was glad he wasn't my real uncle because he was, well, not exactly mean, but not really nice either. Like he didn't really care if you lived or died or something. All I know is I didn't like to be around when "Uncle Tom" Hinchcliff was around.

Like the time I was over at their house and this squirrel got in their basement somehow, and I thought he would just trap it in a garbage can or something, but instead he went down there with this big shovel and beat it to death and brought it out to the yard still dripping blood from its mouth and told us kids: "This is what you've got to do when you catch a pest in your house."

It wasn't a pest.

It was Scamp the Squirrel.

Poor Scamp.

Somebody like Uncle Tom Hinchcliff was always beating him to death with a shovel, or Big Mike Jozaitus was trying to blast his guts out with a high-powered rifle.

It wasn't safe to be Scamp the Squirrel in our neighborhood.

No way.

I sighed and peered through the revolving door at Casey.

He waved me in.

I looked around for signs of Dad or Uncle Tom.

Nothing.

I advanced cautiously to the revolving door and was pushing at it when some adult from the other side whooshed into it and blasted me into the building so fast I didn't know if I still had socks on.

"Come on, you scaredy-cat," Casey said, grabbing my wrist.

"Let go — that hurts."

"Not until you tell me where your father works."

"What?"

"You heard me. What floor does he work on?" Casey said, twisting my wrist.

I hollered, and he let me go.

"You idiot," he said, looking around, "you're gonna get us in trouble. Now tell me what floor he works on."

"Why?"

"Because."

"Casey, if he catches me downtown like this, he's gonna kill me. I'm not supposed to go beyond Ridge Park, and you know it."

"So he's never gonna know because we're invisible."

"What?!?"

"You heard me. Now what floor does he work on?"

I exhaled and had to think for a minute. We only came down to Dad's office the day before Christmas after our big breakfast under the tree in the Walnut Room at Marshall Field's, and Mom always picked up Timmy and let him push the button for Dad's floor, so I didn't really remember what floor Dad was on.

"What'd you say, Jackie?"

"Nothing."

"Then why were you just moving your lips? You goin' crazy on me or something? Because if you are, I sure don't want you hangin' around with me downtown."

"No, I'm not goin' crazy, Casey, I'm just trying to remember what floor my dad works on. That's all."

"You don't know what floor your father works on? Jeez, I've never heard of anything so stupid in my whole, entire life."

"I've only been here a couple of times, Casey, and that was on Christmas Eve."

"So?"

"So, I don't remember what floor he works on. But I think it's the tenth floor. Yeah, I'm pretty sure it's the tenth floor because . . ."

"You boys lost or something?"

It was an older man in a dark blue uniform and he was looming over us like Almighty God.

I elbowed Casey and whispered, "I thought you said we were invisible."

Casey ignored me and raised his reverential face to the adult face. "No, sir, we're not lost, because my mom sent us on ahead — she's back a block with my little brother — but she wants us to go on up to my dad's office anyway — she'll be along in a minute — he works for a big insurance company, but I don't really remember which floor it's on, because the last time I was here was at Christmas, but . . ."

"You'd have to mean the Combined Midwest Insurance Company on ten," the man said. We looked vaguely like all the kids who visited their dads' offices on Christmas Eve and occasionally during summer vacation, and we were certainly the right color, well-dressed, washed and fed, so why not?

"That's it," Casey said. "This is my Cousin John. He's visiting from Philadelphia. They don't have big buildings like this in Philadephia, so my dad thought he should come downtown today and see his office."

The man nodded and smiled.

Casey nodded and smiled. Then he added, "What elevator should we take, sir?"

The man pointed, and Casey thanked him graciously.

Then he pulled me over to the elevator, pushed the button and yanked me aboard when one appeared. These were modern elevators that you could operate yourself, so we were all alone when the door closed.

Casey hopped up and pushed "10" and smiled wickedly at me.

I shuddered.

Casey laughed and said, "You're the biggest scaredy-cat I've ever met in my whole, entire life, Yardley."

"Casey, if my father catches us, he's gonna throw me out the window. And he'll tell your dad. Don't think he won't even if he never talks to your dad or anything, because he will, and your dad'll kill your guts out too, and then we'll both be in trouble for the whole summer, and . . ."

"Shut up!"

"You shut up!"

"We'd better both shut up 'cause here comes your father's floor. Now remember — we're both invisible."

"Casey, what are you gonna do?"

"Nothin', Yardley. Just follow me and you'll live to tell about it."

The elevator glided to a smooth stop at 10, and the doors slid open.

Casey popped out onto the marble floor and surveyed the scene.

"This way," he whispered.

I remained planted inside the elevator with my thumb plastered on the "Open Door" button.

"Come on, you little chicken."

"Casey!!"

Casey grabbed my wrist and hauled me out of the elevator.

I dared not holler, and he did not let me go until we were right outside Dad's office.

The bottom part of the door was wood, and the top was made of a kind of glass that you can't really see through. At least not all the way, but we could hear voices — women's voices — and see their silhouettes.

Yes, silhouettes was part of our vocabularies at the tender age of seven because we had spent a lot of time in Casey's basement identifying silhouettes of World War II fighters and bombers in one of his father's books.

Although I couldn't really read them, I knew the words painted on the window part of the door were: Combined Midwest Insurance Company.

And although I couldn't see or hear him, I knew Dad was in there somewhere doing whatever an office manager did.

"Okay," I whispered, "we did it. Now let's get out of here."

Casey ignored me and bent down and peered through the keyhole.

"I can look up this lady's dress," he announced. "Come on, Jackie, getta a look at this. You can almost see her girdle and everything."

"Casey!!"

Casey ignored me and kept on looking.

I was so scared and worried, I thought I was going to poop in my pants.

Right there in front of Dad's office.

Jeez!

Was Casey nuts or what?

All he ever wanted to do was get us in trouble, and all I ever wanted to do was go somewhere quiet and read a book or something, but for some reason that I still don't understand, I found him absolutely irresistible. Couldn't stop following him — even when he did totally dumb things like spy on Dad's office, and . . .

Then there was Dad's voice box droning away in there.

Casey jumped for joy and announced, "I see your old man, Yardley! He's talkin' to one of those ladies. Darn. She moved. Now I can't see up her dress anymore."

I almost fainted from panic. Then I got my wits back and pulled Casey away from the door.

"Come on," I said, "this is enough. Let's get out of here. Now!"

"Sure, scaredy-cat," Casey said, grinning.

He pounded on the door to Dad's office, let out a whoop and took off down the hall toward a door marked: Stairway.

I froze.

I thought I was going to die.

I thought my heart was going to explode.

I thought I was going to wet my pants.

I thought my hair was on fire.

Then I stopped thinking and ran for my life.

Casey got to the door first, of course, and he tried to close it on me.

But I was so charged with adrenaline that I could have lifted the entire building off its base at that point.

I tumbled past Casey and collapsed on the landing.

Casey ignored me and peered out the door.

He watched for a long while, and then closed the door.

"Don't worry, scaredy-cat, nothing happened. Just one of those ladies came out and looked around — that was all."

I picked myself up and failed to talk.

"Jeez, Yardley, you act like we were in a real battle or something when all I did was just knock on your old man's office door. He didn't see us. He was too busy talking with that stupid thing of his. Boy, does that sound funny through a door. Of course, it sounds funny anyway. I wonder if those ladies laugh when he talks to them. I know I would."

I slugged Casey.

Casey slugged me back.

We rolled into a regular old fight and would have easily killed one another's guts out if we hadn't heard someone opening the stairway door.

We disentangled ourselves and bounded down those ten flights of stairs so fast, old Isaac Newton would have had to discover a fourth law of motion if he had seen us.

When we got to the lobby, the older man in the blue uniform was at his stand talking into a telephone.

"Yes," he said, "I'll be up right away, Mr. Yardley — Yes, Mr. Yardley, I did direct two boys up to your office, but — No, Mr. Yardley, they didn't . . ."

"Come on, Jackie, this is our big chance."

Casey tore past the man in the uniform, but I hestitated.

The man saw Casey and hollered for him to stop.

Casey kept right on running through the revolving door.

The man put down his phone and turned. He saw me.

I froze.

Then I ran for my life.

He almost got me, but I ditched him just in time.

Then I was out on the sidewalk watching Casey laugh until he cried.

When he finally stopped, he grabbed my wrist and pulled me ever northward on LaSalle for our next big adventure.

Chapter Thirteen

Casey took me straight away to a candy store at Monroe and LaSalle and spent one of our remaining six dollars on assorted candies.

"It's for my mother," Casey explained brightly to the woman behind the counter. "We're all visiting my father's office today since it's summer vacation, and since my Cousin John is here from Philadelphia. And my father sent us out to get some candy for my mother since she's got a sweet tooth anyway, and because she's going to have another baby, and all she ever wants to do now is eat candy, and . . ."

"That's nice, dear," the woman behind the counter said, gladly taking our money.

Casey dug his hand into the bag when we got outside and crammed half of the candy into his mouth.

"Casey!!"

"What?" he mumbled between chews.

"Leave some for me."

"You don't need any candy."

"What?"

"You're a tub of lard. The last thing you need is candy."

"Yeah, but you bought that with my money."

"*My* money, Yardley. *Your* mother tore up *my* Ancient Rome cards, and you never bought me another pack, so this is *my* money to spend any way I want. Now come on—I'll race you to the next corner."

Just to show Casey I wasn't a tub of lard, I beat him to the next corner.

But he had a ready explanation for that: "You won because you cheated, Yardley."

"How'd I cheat?"

"You tried to trip me."

"Did not."

"Did too."

"Did not."

"Did too. And besides, I'm carryin' the candy bag."

"Then give it to me."

"No. Not until I've eaten all the ones I want."

"Casey!"

"What, Yardley?"

"Give me some candy!"

"No, you little jerk. Now let's go before that light changes and a million cars run us over."

"But it's gonna change any second—"

It changed, and Casey said: "So? You scared to run through cars?"

"Yes."

But Casey wasn't, and he dashed across Washington Street through a phalanx of speeding Yellow and Checker cabs.

I merely marveled at him from the south side of the street.

When he somehow safely reached the other side, Casey waved good-bye to me and trotted north.

Asshole.

I waited for the light to change and followed.

But there was no sign of him.

Not at Randolph, and not at Lake Street under the elevated tracks.

I even looked behind some pylons but didn't find him.

I looked around in a total panic.

Casey had the tickets.

Casey had the money.

Casey even had the candy.

Asshole.

What was I going to do?

A seven-year-old kid all alone by himself in downtown Chicago on a weekday with a million men in suits streaming around me.

And cabs and buses and clattering trains overhead, and it was all too much.

Way too much.

But I kept going.

North.

True north.

Without a compass no less, but I knew I had to go north.

I crossed wild Wacker Drive with the light and started across the bascule bridge that carried LaSalle Street over the main channel of the Chicago River.

A tugboat pushed a barge full of sand or something underneath me and a southbound bus made the whole bridge shake.

I wondered if I should attempt a crossing.

What if the bridge broke and I fell in that awful water down there? You couldn't see the bottom or anything, and if you got anywhere near the back of that churning tugboat you'd be all ground up like hamburger at the butcher's shop on 103rd Street that Mom went to.

I paused for a breath and a look around.

No sign of Casey, but the fresh breath made me feel better, and I resumed my northward journey.

I was halfway across the bridge when someone seized me from behind and tried to fling me over the rail into the river.

I hollered and fought and hollered and fought.

But my attacker had me by surprise and got me halfway over the rail before he stopped.

Then he laughed.

It was Casey, of course.

Who else?

"Casey!!"

"What?"

"Let me go!!"

"Why? You can swim. You're a good swimmer, and there's a ladder down there where you can climb out. Come on, Yardley, take a little swim in the river." He nudged me further over the rail.

I kicked at him and hollered, but that only encouraged him to hoist me more.

Passersby laughed at us.

Hey, we were just a couple of clowning little kids.

And wasn't that what kids were for — clowning?

General amusement of adults.

Adults.

Fucking asshole adults!!

Seeing that no one was going to help me, and that Casey was determined to throw me in the river, I became a hydrogen bomb and blasted him with everything I had.

EVERYTHING!!

And it worked.

Finally.

Casey fell to the sidewalk moaning and groaning from my multitude of kicks and punches, and I took off north at a full gallop.

I didn't know where I was going exactly, but I did know I was headed north.

And that was all that mattered.

I was headed north but not to the North Pole and some Santa's Cottage like they had at Marshall Field's at Christmas.

No way.

I was through with Santa Claus and the Easter Bunny and the Tooth Fairy.

And I was through with Casey.

Through with Mom, Dad, and Timmy, too.

Done with Dray Street, Big Mike, Aunt Pearl, old Mrs. Reed and her stupid toy store, "Uncle Tom" and "Aunt Lu" Hinchcliff, the goddamn guesties, Benny Goodman and his licorice stick, my clarinet and any hope of ever playing it, Catholics and Publics.

Forever.

Casey yelled for me to stop, but I didn't stop.

I just kept on running north along LaSalle Street.

Casey picked himself up and ran after me.

But he couldn't catch me.

Not quite, because I was riding the Furies.

"Jackie!!" he hollered. "Wait up!!"

I didn't even look back.

No way.

Because I was on my way.

I ran all the way to Chicago Avenue without stopping or looking back.

I don't know how I didn't get run over at the cross streets because I didn't even look twice for lights or traffic.

It was all a blur.

Honking horns and hollering adults and Casey yelling and yelling for me to stop, but damn him, I wouldn't stop.

I couldn't stop.

Not even when I got all the way to Division Street. And that was a long, long way from where we had started.

God!

I had never been so far away from home on my own.

Never!

But, you know, it felt good.

Oh so good!

I glanced back and saw Casey was still doggedly pursuing me.

But not gaining ground.

Losing ground actually. But keeping me in sight.

"Hey, slow up, Apache Runner," he yelled.

I stopped and hollered, "What'd you call me?"

"Apache Runner."

"Why?"

"Because the Apaches could run all day and never get tired. Even the Seventh Cavalry couldn't catch 'em. My father has a book all about it in the basement."

Of course.

Casey's fucking basement.

But no more Casey's fucking basement.

And no more fucking Casey.

I waved good-bye to Casey and resumed running.

I turned right at North Avenue and crossed Clark Street into Lincoln Park.

I knew all about Lincoln Park because Mom had taken me there many times when we lived in South Shore.

Before Timmy.

When Mom was more or less nice to me.

But that was ancient history.

And now I was only interested in the future.

A safe and secure future.

So I found a path and followed it as it tunneled under LaSalle Drive and passed under the statue of General U.S. Grant astride his horse.

I didn't even look up at the man who had given Lincoln Vicksburg as a 4th of July present way back in 1863, because I knew all about him from Casey's basement.

Of course.

I kept on running into the Lincoln Park Zoo and didn't stop until I got to the lion house.

My lungs burned like flaming bushes in my chest, and there was a pain in my side I had never known before.

I went to the first bench and collapsed.

"Casey'll never find me here," I muttered. "He's a million-zillion miles behind, and he'll never find me here."

But damn it — he did.

In less than five minutes Casey was clattering into the lion house and hollering, "Give up, Apache Runner! This is the Seventh Cavalry, and we've got you surrounded. Surrender like a man, or be shot like a dog."

I looked around in desperation.

Casey had me for sure.

He'd make me go home with him, and Dad would know that it was Casey and I who were banging on his office door, and Mom would be furious and slap both my ears off, and . . .

"Follow me."

I turned, and there was a kid my own age gesturing at me.

I looked back at Casey and saw that he was wearing that maniacal grin of his. The one he always wore before he wrestled me down and gave me a pink belly.

Pink belly?

Oh, that's when you hold a kid down, pull up his shirt and poke his belly with a stiff finger until it turns really pink. Really, really pink.

Does it hurt?

Does surgery without anesthesia hurt?

Of course, and, yes, there's a book all about it in Casey's basement. About this Nazi doctor called the "Angel of Death" who would operate on Jews without anesthetizing them. It's Casey's favorite book.

Naturally.

Casey edged toward me and said, "Surrender like a man, Apache Runner, or die like a dog."

The kid who had appeared from nowhere grabbed my arm and we took off running. He led me down a winding staircase, and we found ourselves in the long, dank men's room where a whole bunch of smelly old men were peeing and pooping their guts out.

It was awful.

But this strange kid didn't seem to mind and he took me all the way back to the last stall.

What a dumb kid.

Casey was coming and there was no escape.

I was so scared, I couldn't breathe.

But the boy in the zoo calmly took a key out of his pocket, opened a green metal door on the wall behind the toilet and motioned me through the door.

I entered into a dark, wet place, and the boy in the zoo followed.

He secured the door, and put his finger to my lips.

Then we sat in silence and listened as Casey arrived on the scene and clumped around calling me every dirty name he could think of.

Plus: "I know you're around here somewhere, you stupid Public, now come on out, before I call the police and they throw you in the Audey Home for your whole entire life. Come on, Yardley. Quit playing games and come out and face me like a man. I'll kill your guts out if you don't come out right now."

I started to respond, but the boy in the zoo shushed me. Then he took me gently by the hand and led me deeper into the dark.

I didn't want to follow, but there was something about his touch that made me deny my instincts.

I sensed this boy could be trusted.

I sensed this boy could be my friend.

I even sensed that I might finally have found my first really, really good friend since Mom gave away my dog Billy who I named for my very best friend in the whole world, Billy Mills. The latter was my best friend when we lived in South Shore, and though Mom kept promising that she'd take me back to see him sometime, she had never quite found the time to take me.

I guess Mom didn't really like Billy Mills' mom, so what was the point?

Right?

I mean why drive all that way just so a stupid seven-year-old can see his best friend in the whole world?

Right?

Right.

I don't know, but I did know at that moment under the lion house in the Lincoln Park Zoo that I was home safe with somebody who would really be my friend.

I could just tell by the way he was holding my wrist.

Gently.

Not grabbing it and squeezing it like Casey always did, knowing that I had broken both my wrists and hoping like hell to inflict real pain on me.

This strange boy in the zoo didn't even know me from boo, so how could he know I had broken both my wrists, yet he just seemed to know from the start that I didn't like anybody squeezing my wrists real hard.

But those thoughts didn't stop me from whispering: "Who are you, and where are you taking me?"

"Just keep your head down, and you'll see."

I liked his voice right away and quietly let him lead me through the dark.

I soon saw light at the end of the tunnel and sensed something really good was about to happen.

Really, really, really good.

And, boy, was I ever right!!

Chapter Fourteen

The light grew ever brighter and suddenly we were right between a lion and a tiger.

Well, we were actually in this crawl space or something between a lion and a tiger, but the lion and the tiger were real all right, and they sure could see through this metal grate that was all that protected us from those giant teeth and claws.

Was I ever afraid.

But the boy in the zoo sure wasn't.

"That's Billy," he whispered, "and the tiger's Tommy. I named the lion for my best friend in the whole world, Billy Mills, and I named the tiger for me because I always wanted to be a tiger."

I was dumbstruck.

When I could speak, I said, "You have a friend named Billy Mills?"

"Yeah. So?"

"So, does he live in South Shore?"

"Yeah and so did I before I moved here. But Billy's mom brings him here all the time, so we still see each other a lot. She won't go in the snake house because she's afraid of snakes, so I just meet Billy in there, and we have a great time. Sometimes I even take him in back to pet some of the snakes. You won't believe how friendly some of them are. But why do you ask if he lives in South Shore? Do you know Billy Mills?"

"Yeah. He was my best friend in the whole world before we moved away from South Shore."

"Did he live on 72nd Street near the Grand Haven?"

"Yeah. Right across the street. In a house by a church 'cause his dad's the minister there or something."

"That's the same Billy Mills. And you were his friend?"

"Yeah," I said, "his best friend in the whole world. Before we moved away from South Shore. But I haven't seen him for a really, really long time because my mom won't take me back to see him, so I guess we're not best friends any more."

"Sure you are. You are if you say you are. And you can see him all you want if you stay here with me. If you want to stay here with me, Apache Runner."

I looked at the boy in the zoo and then at Billy the Lion and Tommy the Tiger. All three of them looked at me with kind interest.

Then I said: "My real name's John Yardley Junior. But you can call me Jackie."

"Okay. So you want to stay here with me, Jackie?"

"Well, I don't know. I've got to go home with my friend Casey because my mom'll kill my guts out if I don't go home. See, we snuck downtown on the Rock Island because I got this money from our neighbor, Big Mike — he's a policeman and he shot our other neighbor's dog last night, and he made me take it to her because he was a big chicken — and, anyway, Casey had this idea how we could spend my money by coming downtown on the Rock Island. But then he did this really dumb thing by going up to my dad's office at 208 South LaSalle Street and pounding on the door and . . ."

"Shhh, there he is now."

We peered out through the lion cage at Casey who was practically crying.

"Yardley," he yelled, "where are you? Come on, Jackie, where'd you go? Come on! Quit playin' games and come out. I'll give you some of the money. And there's even one piece of candy left that I'll split with you."

"Is he really your friend?" the boy in the zoo whispered.

I shrugged and whispered, "I don't know. He's, well, he's all I've got."

The boy in the zoo put his hand on my shoulder and whispered, "Not any more. You've got me now, Jackie, and my name's Tommy Kruger, and I ran away from home in 1954 to come and live here, and you can live here with me if you want because there's no better place to live, and you're absolutely safe because Billy and Tommy won't let anything happen to you. And there's plenty of free food to eat, and that bathroom downstairs to use, and sometimes at night I even go for a swim in the lake. You can too if you want."

"But don't you need adults?"

"For what?"

"To watch you while you swim."

"We don't need adults for anything. Have adults ever done you any good?"

"Well, uh, I wouldn't say . . ."

"You mean no, don't you, Jackie?"

"Yeah, I guess I do, Tommy."

"Of course you do. Now you want to get that little creep?"

"What do you mean?"

Tommy Kruger reached into a crevice and produced the best slingshot I'd ever seen. Better than anything even old Mrs. Reed sold at her toy store. That is, before all the parents got mad and made her stop selling slingshots.

Like they would probably make her stop selling Ancient Rome Cards. Mom was already mad, wasn't she, and all she'd have to do was talk to some other moms, and pretty soon old Mrs. Reed would have one less item to sell.

"Where'd you get such a neat slingshot?"

"Out of a rich kid's back pocket. While he wasn't looking. People bring everything you could ever want to the zoo. Everything. Warm clothes for winter, towels and swimsuits for the beach in summer, all kinds of food — you name it. All you have to do is go get it. It's so easy, you won't believe it. Now you want to get that creep out there, or don't you? If I was you, I'd give him a really good one."

I looked at Casey out there looking for me and then at Tommy Kruger. I could really see him now and saw that he was wearing really nice clothes. Brand new. But he didn't have a crewcut like all the other kids in the world — his hair was really kind of long for those days. But cut like a real barber had done it. And he did smell a little bit. Like maybe he hadn't had a bath in a while. Which wasn't such a bad thing.

I mean, I wouldn't have minded not having a bath every day. Or even every other day. Maybe just a swim in the lake once in a while.

And come to think of it, that's what Tommy Kruger smelled like. The lake.

"Give me the slingshot."

Tommy Kruger handed me the slingshot.

"You got any good marbles?"

"The best." He withdrew a big blue breaker out of his pocket and handed it to me. "This'll really knock his head off."

I fitted the marble into the pouch, gripped the handle with my left hand and drew back the sling with my right. I sighted right in on the back of Casey's head and for a long moment wanted to kill him deader than any picture in his stupid basement.

But then I realized I had done all I ever wanted to do to Casey when I hit him in the head with the rock on the last day of school. Just a couple of days ago.

Was that right?

Seemed liked forever.

Or least a lifetime.

"Go on," Tommy Kruger whispered, "blast him one."

I exhaled and lowered the slingshot.

I couldn't hurt Casey.

I wouldn't hurt Casey.

I shouldn't hurt Casey.

"What's the matter?"

I shrugged.

"You chicken?"

"No, I'm not chicken. I just . . ."

"Well, then let me. I'll blast him a good one."

"No. I'll do it."

I raised the slingshot, drew back the sling, sighted and let the big blue marble fly.

It hit its intended target right where I intended – in the meatiest part of the buttocks.

But not Casey's buttocks.

No.

No, I aimed at and hit a big fat policeman in the butt. He was bending over to tie his shoe, and I blasted him right in the butt because he reminded so much of Big Mike Jozaitus I had absolutely no trouble at all giving him a good one.

And boy did he ever let out a shout.

Billy the Lion and Tommy the Tiger roared, and so did all the other big cats in their respective cages.

Tommy Kruger and I even allowed ourselves to laugh out loud.

Nobody was going to hear us now. Not with all those big cats roaring away like that, and that stupid cop bellowing from having a big blue marble smacked into his fat butt from out of nowhere.

He turned to see who had perpetrated such a dastardly deed, and there stood Casey.

And before Casey could utter a word of explanation, there went Casey hanging by the ear from the enraged policeman's meaty paw.

"Good one," Tommy said.

"Thanks," I said.

We watched the cop haul the squealing Casey off to the Audey Home or wherever, and then Tommy took me on a grand tour of my new home.

Epilogue

In case you wanted to know, they never found Tommy and me.
Not that they didn't look real hard.

They tore through the zoo the next couple of days, and there
were stories in all the papers, and even a picture of Casey pointing at
the lion house.

The story said they didn't take Casey to the Audey Home like I
hoped. They only took him to a police station where they
questioned him and called his parents.

And then he told one of his famous stories, and the newspaper
printed every last word of it like it was true. All about how Red
spies had kidnaped me and Casey from our neighborhood and
dragged us downtown and were going to take us out to the lake to
meet this disguised Russian boat that was going to take us to
Moscow where we were going to be brainwashed and trained to be
double-agents and then sent back to Chicago where we'd sabotage
the World Series if and when the Cubs or White Sox ever got in the
World Series and destroy the morale of America's second city.

Or words to that effect.

All I know is the White Sox ruined the World Series all by
themselves in 1959 without any help from me or Casey. (I know
because Tommy and I snuck into Comiskey Park through a secret
passageway and had the best seats in the whole ballpark, but that's
another day's story.)

Another thing I know is I've never believed anything I've read in
the newspapers ever since they printed Casey's lies. (Except the
funnies.)

The newspaper also had a picture of Mom crying big crocodile
tears. Timmy was standing beside her, and, boy, was he ever smiling.

I couldn't blame him. He and Mr. Monkey would have our room
all to themselves.

And hadn't Mom said a million times on Sundays when she made
pancakes for us after church "that you always spoil the first batch."

And: "The second batch is always the best one."

Being the second batch, Timmy liked that a lot.

Good for Timmy.

Have a good life, Timmy. You and your new sister.

Just make sure Dad has plenty of tonic and soda and ginger ale for his "guesties."

And in the same paper there was the police commissioner saying that it was the worst crime since some "thrill murder" back in the 1920s, and foul play was suspected, and the usual suspects were rounded up and beaten silly by big burly cops like Big Mike, but nobody knew where we were, because we were hiding under the zoo in all these wonderful secret passageways that only Tommy Kruger knew existed.

And there was plenty to eat, and plenty to wear, and Tommy introduced me to all the animals, even the scariest-looking snakes that turned out to be quite friendly as long as you didn't make any sudden movements.

And, boy, was I ever happy the next time Billy Mills came to visit, and he said: "Of course, we're still best friends in the whole world, Jackie, because we both have the best friend in the whole world—Tommy Kruger."

The incomparable Tommy Kruger.

But Billy Mills was too happy at home with his mom and dad to come and live with us in the zoo.

Which was okay.

Tommy and I could accept that.

Accept that God gave some kids like Billy Mills loving parents and a quiet home in which to grow up into normal, well-adjusted adults who go out and work for corporate America, and pay their taxes on time, and generally uphold the GNP.

Fine.

So be it.

But we also accepted the fact that our parents were anything but loving and our homes anything but quiet. And we could not go back.

Would not go back.

Should not go back.

And did not go back.

Ever never.

Nor did we ever get jobs for corporate America, pay our taxes on time, or generally uphold the GNP. (But that's a story for another day, isn't it?)

One more thing.

An item in the papers the day after my "abduction by evil Red spies."

It was actually a picture.

Of a tombstone on the lawn in front of somebody's house.

Miss Paschley's to be exact.

And on the marble tombstone were these words:

Here lies my beloved Jacques.

Shot and killed by Michael Jozaitus,

Chicago Police Department,

June 26, 1957.

RIP, mon cheri.

There was a slab of concrete over Jacques' grave, and set in that concrete were Big Mike's shovel and wheelbarrow. For all the world to see.

What a great story!!

The End